Isaac Asimov's
I, Robot:
to obey

Also by Mickey Zucker Reichert

I, Robot: To Protect

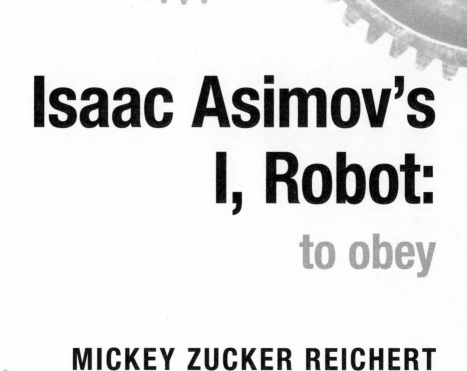

Isaac Asimov's
I, Robot:
to obey

MICKEY ZUCKER REICHERT

A ROC BOOK

ROC
Published by the Penguin Group
Penguin Group (USA), 375 Hudson Street,
New York, New York 10014, USA

USA | Canada | UK | Ireland | Australia | New Zealand | India | South Africa | China

Penguin Books Ltd., Registered Offices: 80 Strand, London WC2R 0RL, England
For more information about the Penguin Group visit penguin.com.

First published by Roc, an imprint of New American Library,
a division of Penguin Group (USA)

First Printing, September 2013

 REGISTERED TRADEMARK—MARCA REGISTRADA

LIBRARY OF CONGRESS CATALOGING-IN-PUBLICATION DATA:

Reichert, Mickey Zucker.
  Isaac Asimov's I, Robot: to obey/Mickey Zucker Reichert.
    p. cm
  ISBN 978-0-451-46482-8
  I. Title.
  PS3568.E476334I73 2013
  813'.54—dc23   2013005138

Printed in the United States of America
10 9 8 7 6 5 4 3 2 1

Set in Mentor STD
Designed by Alissa Amell

To Martin H. Greenberg,
who personified kindness and fairness in life, in business, in friendships.
Like a meteor, a brilliant inspiration who carved a path across the sky
to illuminate so many others, his own life far too fleeting.
We miss you, Marty.

Acknowledgments

I owe a mountain of thanks to Pat Rogers, Chief Warrant Officer 3, U.S. Marine Corps (retired), Sergeant NYPD (retired), who put up with a daily barrage of outlandish questions. Without his encouragement and assistance, this would be a far less accurate novel.

Also thanks to Attila Torkos, for assistance with the Asimovian timeline and necessary adjustments, for his tireless dedication to the works of Isaac Asimov, and for keeping me on my toes. To Susan Allison, for professionalism, excellence, and knowing when to push. To Sheila Gilbert, the very definition of editing excellence, for superhuman patience and a kindness that rivals Marty's.

To Mark Moore (always), who helps in so many ways every single day.

And, of course, to Isaac, Janet, and Robyn Asimov.

Anti-intellectualism has been a constant thread winding through our political and cultural life, nurtured by the false notion that democracy means that "my ignorance is just as good as your knowledge."

—Isaac Asimov

Isaac Asimov's
I, Robot:
to obey

Chapter 1

June 27, 2036

B rilliant summer sunshine struck glimmers from the window rims and ledges of Manhattan Hasbro Hospital and lit up the bobbing signs of the usual horde of protestors. Susan Calvin walked stoically along the sidewalk with the other workers, visitors, and outpatients. A year of psychiatry residency had practically immunized her from their shouts, demands, and taunts; they had become background noise no more noticeable than the antiseptic odors of the corridors or the rumble of cafeteria chatter at all hours of the day. Except today. For reasons she could not wholly explain, Susan not only noticed the weaving, screaming protestors, but suffered a jab of annoyance at their presence. They defined chaos—their intentions myriad, their dress and demeanors spanning the gamut from timid insistence to scarlet-faced rage, their signs clashing not only visually but causally. One condemned euthanasia, while another demanded that tax dollars go to "real cases, not lost causes." In the back, a sign read: PROCREATIVE BENEFICENCE BENEFITS CHILDREN while another, deeper in the crowd, touted, DESIGNER BABIES ARE A SIN.

The last filled Susan with an eerie sense of déjà vu. Her thoughts straggled back to the first day of her internship, when the protesters had surprised her and intimidated many of the first-year residents. A young man carrying a sign with those words had tripped into her path,

1

and she had shared a short and direct argument with him. Less than an hour later, the administrators had informed all of the brand-new doctors that speaking with protestors was strictly forbidden. Many of them had violent intentions and agendas, seeking any reason to spark a fight that might draw the attention of media to their cause.

Susan quickened her pace, stepping through the mechanical doors that shooshed behind her, then opened again almost immediately for other entrants. Air-conditioning blasted into her face, a welcome relief from the sweltering crowd. The sights and smells of the hospital had become all too familiar in the past year. She rarely noticed them. Yet this sunny Friday, she did. The well-known odors of cleaners, sanitizers, and topical medications blended into a weird cacophony she could not ignore. The rows of connected seats drew her attention, and the banks of computer monitors flashed conspicuously around the periphery. She noticed the glass cases on the walls that held the quilts of a local artist, crafts on sale as a fund-raiser for the current crop of pediatric patients, and the usual display of Hasbro toys as they had evolved through the decades.

Susan found herself having to consider her steps as she walked the long-known route to the psychiatry residents' locker room. The journey past cafeterias and lawyers, ethicists and faculty doctors' offices, even the rarely changing artwork covering every wall, seemed strange. It reminded her of her first day at Manhattan Hasbro, when she tingled with the excitement of a grand new adventure. Fresh out of medical school, she had not known what to expect, only that she intended to give her all to excellence and take advantage of every opportunity to become the best psychiatrist she possibly could be.

Almost exactly a year had passed since that awesome and daunting day in 2035 when she had begun her career as a first-year resident, an R-1, at one of the largest and most progressive hospitals in the country. She had been a different person then, she realized, full of optimism and hope, worried the challenge might crush her or, worse, she would prove inadequate as a doctor, that some mistake she made would result in the death or suffering of an innocent patient.

Now that seemed like such a guileless and foolish concern. In the past year, she had seen her fill of death and madness, of inexplicable emotions and tragedy. She no longer believed in poetic justice or happy endings. Life was a quiet crapshoot that sometimes bucked the odds, for good or ill, indiscriminately. Insanity, disease, misfortune came to the righteous and the sinners, the generous and the selfish, the good and the evil without distinction. Calamity followed no rules of fairness or justice.

Susan stepped into the room, joining her fellow psychiatry R-1s. Their conversations flowed through and around her, unheard. She barely noticed the furnishings: the lockers built into all but one wall and personally decorated with names, comics, articles, and small toys; the cubbies affixed to the remaining wall; the tables and chairs that now held most of her peers; and a self-standing whiteboard with writing on it. Susan could scarcely summon the curiosity to look over its written contents, though it would determine her fate over the next year.

The R-1 year had kept the thirty of them in rotating groups of three to six, supervised by at least one R-2, an R-3, and a faculty attending physician. Teamed with various peers, they spent two months each on the three inpatient units: the Pediatrics Inpatient Psychiatry Unit (PIPU), the Adult Psychiatry Unit (APU), and the Provisional Care Psychiatry Unit (PCPU). The first two catered to patients with long-term needs, while the third, affectionately called Limbo, was where patients were kept until the decision was made to place them in institutional care or onto one of the other units. The R-1s had also performed two months of outpatient psychiatry, a month on the Behavioral Neurology Unit (BNU), a month of clinical neurology, a month of general internal medicine, and a month on the Psychiatry Consultative Service.

According to the whiteboard, as well as to the tips given from next year's R-3s, the R-2 year consisted of a month as middle supervisor on each of the three inpatient units; two months of intensive outpatient experience, one at Manhattan Hasbro and the other at any one of several private clinics; a month on night rotation, serving the hospital from midnight to noon; two months in the emergency room; one month in a public dementia facility; one month in a public facility catering to developmental and intellectual disabilities; one month in an addiction facility; and the last month an open elective.

Most of her peers' discussions centered on the best order of performing those rotations. The coveted position was the night rotation, and whoever served it at the time earned the nickname "the Mole." Though it was initially intimidating to find oneself the go-to psychiatrist for all nighttime problems and emergencies, it involved none of the boring routine and all of the most exciting moments of medicine. It was said that once an R-2 survived that most intense of the rotations, he gained a confidence and competence that made him a better and more self-assured doctor. The moment the Mole successfully finished his month, and they all did, his life changed forever. He gained the respect of the nurses, his peers, the R-3s, and the faculty. Whether this came from the observer or from a radiation of personal conviction was unclear. Most of the R-2s tried to get past the Mole phase as quickly as possible. It lightened the burden of every other rotation.

Those not quite ready for the responsibility of Mole preferred to start with the open elective or the outside private outpatient clinic rotation. Those served as nice summer segues from the rigors of the R-1 year to the more responsible inpatient positions of the R-2. Some of the private clinics paid the residents cash under the table to encourage residents to choose them. The more patients the private practitioner saw, the more prestigious his clinic and the more money he made. The residents passed the information along to their younger peers, and the most

popular outpatient sites either paid the most or had easygoing attendings and better hours.

Over the past two weeks, as she completed her second rotation on
the Pediatrics Inpatient Psychiatry Unit with four of her peers, Susan,
along with the others, had fantasized about her ideal rotation order.
Not that anyone was likely to get what he wanted, at least not exactly.
The names got plucked out of a box in random order. Each picked a
first-month rotation, except for the last person drawn, who got to choose
his first two rotations. Then the choices went backward, so the first
resident was last to choose his second rotation, but first, again, to choose
the third.

Now, Susan found, the excitement that had once suffused her had
disappeared. She felt empty, dull, apathetic, and cold. While the others
chatted with those they had befriended on earlier rotations, she stood
alone, staring with unseeing eyes at a random locker. She had nothing
to say to anyone, and she hoped no one would bother her.

Then, suddenly, a hand snaked over hers. Warm air entered her left
ear, accompanied by words she had learned to hate. "I know how you
feel, Calvin. And I share the emotion."

Susan tensed, seized with the urge to deck the person who had
dared to shatter her comfortable, self-inflicted silence. No one could
possibly understand how she felt at that moment. Even she had no clue
how to describe her current emotional state or even why it had
descended so fully upon her at this time. She twisted her head toward
the jerk, intending to give him a piece of her mind, only to find herself
staring directly into the face of Kendall Stevens.

Her fellow R-1 gave her a look so uncharacteristic of his joking self
that it stole her breath and left her incapable of scolding. His dark eyes
held a melancholy so deep, it might actually have exceeded her own.
His broad lips were pursed, his jaw set, and his cheeks sagged. His
ginger hair hung limply. Even the friendly splash of freckles across his

face looked dim and lifeless. Instead, she squeezed his hand back tightly, realizing what she should have known all along.

This day reminded her of her first day at Manhattan Hasbro Hospital as a bewildered medical-school graduate about to embark on a journey of infinite possibilities. It was also the day she had met her soul mate, Remington Hawthorn, a first-year neurosurgery resident. An image of him filled her memory, perfect in every detail: the mop of tousled dark blond curls; eyes like emeralds beneath prominent brows; the straight, generous nose; chiseled cheekbones; and fine lips. She had always felt safe in his strong arms, and he always seemed to know the right thing to say. Confident and capable, he had fully captured her heart and, nearly, finally, her virginity.

Then Susan's thoughts breeched the walls she had spent nearly a year building. Another image came to her mind's eye, one she wished she could forget. She saw a mall guard lying still on the floor, another staggering to his feet, and her last image of Remington. Still dressed in his working polo and khakis, he was wrapped around a small, struggling figure whose hand was firmly planted on the detonator of a bomb. Then white light slammed through Susan's memory, pain seemed to enwrap every part, and the odor of gasoline filled her nose so completely it seemed more a taste than a smell. The agony of that had haunted her longer than anything, the taste rising to her mouth in weaker moments, driving her to vomit.

Susan shook the thought from her mind for at least the thousandth time. It had not bothered her in more than two months, yet it rushed back with the same raw intensity, not the least diminished by time or effort. Remington Hawthorn was a hero. His self-sacrifice had saved Susan, one of the security guards, and possibly several patrons of the mall as well. Susan loved him with every rational part of her being. But she had irrational parts, too, and, rarely, they won out. At those times, she hated him for surrendering his life, for taking away the most wonderful thing that had ever happened to her, for leaving her to suffer the guilt of surviving the catastrophe he had not. The pain cut too deep for anyone to bear.

Only Kendall could truly understand what she had suffered. Standing atop the mall roof with a pistol, he had had the opportunity to shoot the bomber before she even entered the mall. Instead his finger had frozen on the trigger. Only since the incident had Susan done enough research to know that even trained army snipers would have had difficulty successfully carrying off such a shot. A man who had taken a vow to do no harm, trained only to heal and help the sick and injured, who had never fired a gun, had had little to no chance of striking a four-year-old target intent on murder. Likely, Remington had positioned Kendall there solely to keep him out of harm's way.

But Kendall did not see it like that. The fellow psychiatry R-1 blamed himself for the death of Susan's greatest love, felt responsible for destroying the lives of friends, despite Susan's attempts to soothe him. She had liked Kendall before the incident. She appreciated his quick wit, his intelligence, and his ability to find humor in almost any situation. After the explosion, when she had physically recovered, she shared a camaraderie with him that only those who have faced death together can. Unfortunately, their grueling schedules and the need to spread the R-1s around in different groupings had made it difficult for them to spend much time together since the tragedy.

Dr. Mirschaum, a squat woman with thinning blond hair, a prodigious nose, and a small café au lait spot on her left cheek, entered the room. An associate professor who specialized in clinical research on selective serotonin reuptake inhibitors, Dr. Mirschaum had served as Susan's attending during one of her adult-inpatient rotations. She had a solid, conservative style that got the job done but frequently clashed with Susan's more aggressive approach to medicine. Despite that, they had gotten along well, learned to respect one another, and discharged an unusually large number of patients.

The R-1s fell silent as Dr. Mirschaum walked to the table with her current psychiatry fellow in tow. A compact man who clearly worked out at the gym, he carried one of the older portable computers, larger than a palm-pross but smaller than the antiquated laptops. He also held a cardboard box. Kendall released Susan's hand.

The fellow placed the computer in the middle of the table, facing one lockered wall. He set the box beside it. Some of the R-1s toward the back adjusted the Vox on their wrists to the screen so they would not have to crowd around the portable.

Susan had a clear view of the screen and remained in position without bothering to set her Vox. It currently displayed a grid with the residents' names along the left side, at the moment in alphabetical order, and the year's rotations, beginning on July 1, across the top. All around her, residents fidgeted, but their conversations dropped to whispers, then disappeared.

The fellow faded back to allow the R-1s better access to the portable. Dr. Mirschaum stood directly beside the table and cleared her throat. "As you all know why you're here and how this works, I don't see any need for preamble." She stuffed an arm into the box, swished bits of paper about with her fingers, then pulled out her hand.

The room went utterly silent, waiting.

Susan found her mind roaming to odd considerations. It amused her they still drew names out of a box when a simple random-generator program could do the job much faster and just as fairly. Yet, she realized, there was some comfort in watching each and every name get drawn from the box exactly one time. There could be no question about errors or fairness.

Dr. Mirschaum called out the first name, then the second, and

Susan watched her peers claim the prime rotations. There was a strategy to the process, though it varied somewhat by the individual, particularly for the initial round. Everyone had to do a month on the same inpatient units, but the Adult and Limbo units used two R-2s, while the Pediatrics Unit had only one. A resident who chose one of the double-staffed units first had to worry about who might partner up with him or her.

Five R-2s would work together on Hasbro's Outpatient Psychiatry Unit, which could mitigate any personal issues. While only four R-2s had open electives at the same time, they each had to choose a different one of eight possibilities. If a resident's first choice disappeared quickly in any given round, he still had an excellent chance of getting it in a later one. It helped that not everyone wanted to do the same elective, because the outpatient electives required the most cautious strategies. Five residents worked them a month, in exactly five different locations. Some paid, while most did not. Others had better schedules or staffing, for various reasons. The patient population also varied, with some having personality disorders and simple neuroses, while others seemed plagued with psychotics. As their rotations were already psychosis heavy because of the inpatient work, the neuroses clinics tended to go fast, especially if they paid.

The Mole and the Emergency Room rotations allowed only one resident at a time, while the developmental-disabilities clinic and the addictions clinic took three. The Dementia Unit, a particularly dreary place, especially for a summer rotation, was staffed by two R-2s.

The next several picks went by without Susan's name. On the tenth pick, Dr. Mirschaum called Kendall Stevens. Susan surveyed the board, smiling for him. The best slots were already filled: the top three outpatient clinics, the Mole, both ER positions, two open electives, and one of the Adult Inpatient Unit spaces. It still left Kendall with some great first-rotation options. He could pick a different elective if others had not already taken the one he wanted. He could select any of the three inpatient units, the PIPU alone, the first open Limbo space, or the second man on adult psychiatry. Several of her peers fidgeted or bit their lips, hoping but doubting their choices would remain by the time their names were drawn.

Kendall hesitated, then finally spoke, "I'll take Dementia."

It was the last thing anyone expected him to say, including Susan. Even Dr. Mirschaum paused to squint at him through narrowed, dark eyes. "Are you certain, Dr. Stevens?"

Kendall must have nodded, because Dr. Mirschaum pressed the appropriate button on the remote, and Kendall's name filled the first blank beside the Dementia rotation. Susan turned to whisper a "Why?" only to find Kendall no longer at her side. She considered texting him, but supposed she would find it futile. He had a reason for his sudden disappearance as well as for his decision, and he clearly wanted Susan to figure it out on her own.

But Susan was in no mood for puzzles. She scowled in silence, watching as the next few names got called and the second Adult Psychiatry Inpatient slot, the first Limbo slot, two electives, and all five of the Hasbro Outpatient slots filled. Without intention, she found herself gradually working out the reasons for Kendall's odd selection; even her subconscious found it impossible to resist a riddle. She tried to discern what the Dementia rotation afforded that others did not. The unpopularity of it had to serve a function other than shock value; his choice clearly had some positive purpose. It had two other features that might come into play: it took the resident away from Manhattan Hasbro and it featured exactly two slots per month. There were a total of two R-2s on call on any given day. The Mole handled in-house call five nights per week, while the two on ER rotations took the other two nights. The R-2s on the inpatient units rotated through call with the R-1s to serve only their own units. The ten R-2s on outpatient services took no call at all, those with open electives took call with their chosen services, and the eight assigned to the public facilities, including the Dementia Unit, shared backup call, which consisted of being available to assist the in-house R-2s if they became overwhelmed. This rarely happened, but it did require the backup to remain available.

It all came together swiftly. Kendall clearly wanted a rotation requiring two R-2s working together. That he did not wish to work alone seemed obvious, and he could just as easily have chosen Development and Intellectual Disabilities or Addiction, equally unpopular but with three slots apiece. He had deliberately taken the one with only two openings. He wanted to work with someone and only that person, and Susan knew exactly whom he intended to join him on the rotation. The only question remaining was why he wanted her.

The answer came chillingly fast and, with it, the explanation for her own intolerable mood. Now it seemed so obvious, she wondered how she could have missed it. She had met Remington almost exactly one year ago to the day, had started their whirlwind courtship within a week, and had lost him less than halfway through her first rotation. As the anniversary approached, all the pain and anguish, all the anger and frustration she had finally managed to control, would come roaring back with a vengeance. She could think of nothing she would prefer more than a rotation as far away from Manhattan Hasbro's Pediatric Inpatient Psychiatry Unit as possible, with the only other person who truly understood her ordeal. Kendall probably needed her as much as she needed him.

Then, finally, Dr. Mirschaum announced: "Susan Calvin."

Susan studied the board, despite her firm decision. The choices had narrowed considerably. There was still an opening on the Provisional Care Psychiatry Unit (Limbo), two at Hasbro Outpatient, two on the least-popular outpatient electives, one elective, two spaces on each of the other public facilities, and the remaining opening on Dementia.

Though she had not paid close attention, Susan could easily pick out the eight residents still waiting for their names to be called. They fixed their gazes on her and some displayed nervous habits, such as chewing at the side of a fingernail, fidgeting, or biting a lower lip. She did not leave them in suspense long. "Dementia," she said confidently, pointing at the screen.

Several of the others loosed pent-up breaths as Susan backed away from the list to let those others study their remaining options. She suddenly found Kendall Stevens back at her side. "I was starting to worry your name wasn't in the box. You have a knack for being first when last is better, and last when first is better."

Susan forced a grin and noticed her hands were shaking, which irritated her. She did not usually demonstrate such obvious signs of weakness. Now that she understood her mood, she dreaded revisiting the agony of last July. If she had to do so, however, she was glad to have Kendall at her side, her father at home, and N8-C at Manhattan Hasbro. The positronic robot affectionately called Nate had helped her through the worst of times. "Thanks."

"Thanks?" Kendall's dark eyes slitted. "Thanks for what?"

Susan responded before he could deny his kind gesture and turn the whole thing into a joke. "Thanks for sacrificing your first rotation to be with me."

Kendall snorted and rolled his eyes. "Yeah, that's right. I sacrificed a chance to suffer torment alone to work with a brilliant and beautiful woman. I should qualify for sainthood."

They both knew there was more to it than that. With her waveless mouse-brown hair and curveless body, she barely qualified as pretty, and that solely on the basis of youth. She could never be troubled to learn how to use makeup, and most of her fellow residents considered her a cocky know-it-all who deliberately showed them up at the most inopportune times. Kendall appreciated rather than resented her diagnostic acumen, and he had pointed out that, unlike most of their fellows, his self-esteem stemmed more from clowning than competence.

"Well, thanks for understanding me better than I do." Susan wondered if Kendall realized just how good a psychiatrist he was. He seemed able to read her like a book. "Thanks, also, for the undeserved compliments."

"Yup, that's me," Kendall quipped. "Tossing around undeserved compliments like popcorn." He waved a hand. "You never know when those nice things will just come flying out of my mouth unbidden." He gave her a sterner look. "I need you this month as much as you need me. You would have done the same."

Except she would not have. Or, at least, she did not know for certain she would. Steeped in her own miserable apathy, Susan probably would have taken whatever rotation she had planned during her more lucid moments, assuming this was not the time for deep consideration. Even now, though, she was dimly wise enough to realize saying so would not help cement Kendall's trust. She could not deny that she truly appreciated what he had done, and she wished she could be sure she would have done the same if her name had come up first.

Chapter 2

Winter Wine Dementia Facility had a distinctive odor Susan finally decided represented a unique combination of body odor, urine, disinfectants, and 2-nonenal, the musty omega-7 fatty acid degradation product known in slang as "old person's smell." The front entrance brought Susan and Kendall into a clean waiting area with neat rows of chairs on a deep blue carpet, off-white walls, and an enormous desk surrounded by windows. Hallways branched off on either side of the desk, where a middle-aged woman dressed in white scrubs leaned over a pile of papers. She looked up as the residents entered, then smiled. "You must be the new doctors."

"We must be," Kendall said, striding forward with his right hand extended. "Kendall Stevens and Susan Calvin reporting for duty." He jabbed his left thumb over his shoulder. "That one's Susan."

Susan let the door snap closed behind her.

Still grinning, the woman took Kendall's hand. "Well, I certainly hope so, Dr. Stevens."

Susan stepped forward. "Just call me Susan, please. If you say Dr. Calvin, I'll be looking over my shoulder for my father."

The woman dropped Kendall's hand to take Susan's and give it a brief shake. "Ah, so you followed in his medical footsteps."

"Only if you consider robotics medical." Susan reclaimed her hand. "He has a PhD in engineering."

"Ah," the woman said. "That kind of doctor." There was a hint of condescension in her tone, which bothered Susan. She never understood why people gave less credence to university doctorates than medical-school graduates.

Kendall must have noted it, also, and came to the subtle defense of PhD's everywhere. "I'm sure Dr. Calvin could diagnose what ails you, too. If, for example, you were an exponential assembly unit having difficulty with your kinematic influence coefficients."

Silence followed the remark, during which the woman studied Kendall as if trying to determine whether he had insulted her. Apparently deciding he had not, she smiled again. "I'm Hazel Atkinson. I'm a CNA. Most medical receptionists are these days, so we can pull double duty."

Susan nodded. It made sense for medical centers of all types to hire certified nursing assistants as receptionists so the front-desk personnel had at least a minimal understanding of medical terminology and could help in a crisis. "Nice to meet you, Ms. Atkinson."

"Hazel," she corrected, to Susan's relief. It would seem entirely weird for the CNA to address the doctor by her first name while the doctor used the receptionist's title. "Let me show you around."

Susan appreciated that. She still suffered from suffocating ennui, and the July 1 date only made it seem worse. The sooner they jumped into medical work, even of a depressing nature, the better.

Hazel pointed to the hallway to the right of her station. "That's the entrance to the foyer, where we take the families through to see their loved ones."

Susan caught a glimpse of the same fresh blue carpeting and clean walls as in the entry room before being herded down the left hallway. Her soles clicked against worn tile flooring, and the walls, though the same color, looked infinitely drabber. Though well scrubbed, they had clearly not been painted for years. The odor Susan had parsed earlier grew stronger and more unpleasant as they wandered farther into the bowels of Winter Wine Dementia Facility, and the hallway opened into a small charting area filled with palm-prosses and larger computers. Currently, only a pair of white-scrub-clad nurses occupied the area, chatting softly with one another. As Hazel approached, they both rose.

Hazel made the introductions: "Doctors Susan Calvin and Kendall Stevens, this is Gray Halbrin." The larger of the two men bowed and raised his head. He had dark curls, brown eyes, and a short goatee. The other nurse was a shorter blond with a broad baby face and brilliant blue eyes. "And this"—Hazel indicated the blond—"is Milan Penderghast." Heads bobbed all around, and Hazel pushed open a heavy door to lead the young doctors deeper into the facility.

As the door closed behind them, Susan noticed a bright red sign on it reading CAUTION: DO NOT ENTER.

Noticing the direction of Susan's gaze, Hazel explained. "That's not for you. It's to keep the patients from wandering outside."

"Does it work?" Kendall asked.

"Quite well." Hazel walked through a short empty space, more air lock than hallway. "Most of our patients can't manipulate the heavy metal doors. If they do, we nearly always catch them in this area." She gestured to the hallway, then pulled open the far door to reveal another hallway, this one broken by several doors. Again, Susan noticed a sign on the door they had come through, this time stating STAFF ONLY.

Several of the new doors also sported signs. Three had only numbers, one was labeled STAFF & VISITORS' RESTROOM, and another WAITING AREA. Three others had no signs. Susan noted all the numbered doors had keyholes and sturdy twist knobs, which would make them more difficult to open. The others had handles easily depressed, even with full arms.

Hazel opened the door marked 3 and leaned against it to hold it open for the doctors. "Might as well start with the end-stagers."

A blast of the smell Susan associated with the dementia facility assaulted them, partially covered by a rosy scent clearly intended to help mask the odor. They entered an enormous room filled with rows of hospital beds, the walls lined with chairs. Thick privacy curtains surrounded each bed, most of them fully open to reveal patients dressed mainly in pajamas and nightgowns. Most stared blankly at the ceiling or walls, their jaws working soundlessly. Others wandered aimlessly around the room or sat in one of the chairs. Susan saw feet beneath the few drawn curtains; staff working on patients in delicate stages of dress, or family members visiting. No sound emerged from these areas. Apparently, the fabric fully muffled conversation, keeping visits and medical interventions private.

Walking, sitting, or lying, the patients all wore the same blank stare, their faces wrinkled with age and confusion, their expressions neutral, their eyes dead. No real life looked out from them. They were automatons, emotionally empty, breathing from habit, without intention of any kind. Most had withered to pale, skeletal figures, as if they planned to gradually disappear, leaving no trace of body or soul. Their skin and lips gleamed with emollients intended to prevent cracking and sores. A sense of horror stole over Susan, and she found it difficult to breathe.

Multiple doors led off of this unit; several were labeled as toilets, a couple as bathing areas, and a few others bore no labels at all. Hazel opened and walked through one of these, and Susan followed gratefully. She could scarcely believe she was going to have to spend an entire month catering to patients who no longer had the capacity to care about anything, hopeless cases she had no means to help, people who remembered nothing and could not even recognize their own faces in a mirror.

The psychiatry residents found themselves in another staffing room, this one with desks built into the wall, topped with cupboards, covered with palm-prosses and even a couple of old-fashioned desktop computers too heavy to move. A platter of chocolate chip cookies sat amid a clutter of paper and pens.

Hazel took a seat and flicked on a light attached to the underside of the cupboards. She snatched up a cookie and gestured for Susan and Kendall to do the same. "Winter Wine has three units," she explained. "And you just saw the worst of them. It's officially named the End-Stage Dementia Unit, or ESDU, but most of us just call it, DUm." She pronounced it like "doom." "If we discuss the possibility of moving there, and the patient responds in any way, they're not ready for it." She took a bite of her cookie.

Kendall took a cookie, but Susan found herself wholly without appetite. She had known patients with any type of progressive dementia eventually died from it, but she had never considered the detailed reality of those last few months or years. It seemed like nothing less than profound, unremitting misery. The lucky ones had weak hearts, so they could slip away to true oblivion rather than drag on in a state of living death. "They're . . . zombies," she observed.

"Except with less purpose," Kendall pointed out. "Zombies, at least, have a goal."

Susan could not imagine what he meant. She hoped he wasn't working up to a tasteless joke. Though his way of dealing with stress, it seemed grotesquely out of place in this environment. She gave him a pointed stare.

"What?" Kendall surely understood Susan's consternation but played ignorant. "I just meant to eat human brains."

His explanation did not help the situation.

Hazel easily joined the morbid conversation. "Zombies are ambulatory. Most of our end-stage patients aren't. They have no real consciousness, no self-awareness. And, for many of them, that's a strange sort of blessing."

Now both R-2s stared at the receptionist.

Hazel shrugged and took another bite of cookie. "It's the mid-stagers I feel sorry for, the ones on Unit 2. They still have bits and pieces of memory, individual pieces of a puzzle that no longer fits together. The world comes in and out of focus, but it's a life without sense or logic. The struggle to remember the missing portions, to fill in the gaps, to come to grips with enough detail to make sense of the situation causes them to lash out in ways that suggest they're in a constant state of agony. It's only after those last bits of memory are extinguished that they finally find a weird bit of peace in a dementia-induced oblivion."

Susan turned Kendall another look. This one, she hoped, conveyed anger and betrayal. She could have spent this painful month of renewal in a cushy outpatient clinic. Instead, in the depths of her own depression, she had to deal with the most hopeless creatures in existence. She wondered if she could ever crawl out of the deep black hole that circumstances and a poorly chosen rotation had created.

"Cheery," Kendall said, popping his own cookie in his mouth and chewing thoughtfully. "These are delicious. I don't suppose the patients made them."

Hazel finished her own cookie and dusted the crumbs from her scrubs. "A family member brought them. Sweet, but totally impractical. Most of the end-stagers have forgotten how to swallow properly, and we'd have a run on aspiration pneumonia. We give the family the option of taking the cookies home or leaving them for the staff. Most choose to leave them. One of the few perks of working here."

Susan brought an image of the unit to her mind's eye. She supposed families could find a reasonable degree of privacy behind the sound-dampening curtains. "Do many people come and visit their relatives at . . . this stage?"

Hazel leaned back in her chair. "It varies a lot. Some people come every day, some never, and you see everything in between. It's not always the ones you expect, either. The relatives who kept them home the longest are often the ones who disappear completely when they reach this stage."

Susan found herself wondering how she would handle a similar situation if her father ever developed Alzheimer's, then blocked her own considerations before they came to full fruition. Now did not feel like the time to grapple with additional weighty thoughts, no matter how appropriate to the situation. Not only would it borrow trouble at a time when she owned enough, but it was also rarely ever a good idea to judge the motives of patients and families, at least until she managed to get inside their heads. Once she had formed her own ideas of how she would handle a given situation, she could not help comparing it to others'.

Having finished her own cookie, Hazel looked expectantly at Kendall. Noting he had swallowed the last bite of his own, she gestured back toward the door. "Ready to move on to Unit 2?"

Susan doubted she would ever be fully prepared. However, she had never run from a challenge and did not intend to do so now. "Ready," she said.

"Can't wait," Kendall added with a smile.

Susan rolled her eyes, but also forced a grin. She knew he was acting as much to keep her spirits up as his own. When they got off work that evening, they both knew she fully intended to kill him.

But by the time the day ended, Susan found herself with a pounding headache and a mood that would not make her polite company for any other human being, including her fellow resident. Worried that she might say something so heinous she permanently drove away the one person who could commiserate with her most times, she begged off the glide-bus ride that would take them closest to their respective homes. Instead, she went to the one place she thought she would want to avoid but that drew her inexorably: Manhattan Hasbro Hospital.

Susan arrived at 6:00 p.m., as most of the physicians left for the night and the on-call residents took over. She had come only to finish up a few charts from her last rotation, which she could do anywhere. However, she found herself heading straight for the little first-floor charting room, tucked between an insulated staircase and the central processing area for information storage, where she most often found Nate, the hospital's resident robot.

Susan had gotten to know Nate in this room on her first night of call on her first rotation: the Pediatrics Inpatient Psychiatry Unit. As anyone would, she had mistaken him for a tall young man. He had not only set her straight, but had also told her more than she knew herself about her father and the company for which he worked: U.S. Robots and Mechanical Men, Inc. It was Nate who had led to her discovery that her father was not the simple bookkeeper he had claimed to be, but actually played an important role at USR.

Though well hidden and seldom visited by anyone but Nate, the area was known to a handful of staff and occasionally used as a quiet place for charting or private conversation. In fact, Susan's senior resident on her first rotation, Stony Lipschitz, had mentioned it as his favorite on-call hideaway during the basement PIPU rotations. Last year's R-3s had left for fellowships or to join private practices, except for Stony, who had decided to stay on as chief resident. As he now had a private office on the third floor, Susan doubted she would run into him here. Most of the other residents had not yet discovered it, considered it too far from their current assignments, or had found other places to disappear to between routine assignments and emergencies.

There was another reason, Susan knew, that might keep staff from this particular charting room—the very one that kept her returning to it. Nate and her father had both described the Frankenstein Complex, a surprisingly common fear of mechanical men, particularly android types, based on a concern promulgated and intensified by books and movies through the ages. An alarmingly large number of people worried about robots harming or replacing human beings. To Susan and her father, this fear seemed wholly irrational, although she could understand the logical basis for it. Nate was physically and intellectually superior to nearly all humans, in Susan's experience, and the average person would find himself outmatched in a contest of strength, intelligence, speed, or stamina. She wondered if those same people also feared or despised human beings who were more competent than themselves. That would certainly explain some of the reactions she had experienced in her own life.

Reaching the charting room, Susan turned the knob and quietly pushed open the door. The room looked the same as it usually did, covered in modular shelving bulging with labeled opaque plastic boxes and a weird array of textbooks. To the right, the cozy nook with its odd assortment of couches and chairs beckoned, especially when she saw Nate sitting in a plush chair and leaning over a palm-pross on the central table. As she entered, he looked up. A smile spread across his features, as natural as any human expression. "Dr. Susan Calvin, what an unexpected pleasure. I heard you were on an outside rotation. Didn't expect to see you for at least a month." His hands moved from the keyboard to his sides.

"I couldn't stay away from you, could I, N8-C?" Susan used his model number to remind him she preferred just plain Susan as much as he did Nate. "I'd suffer Nate withdrawal."

Nate chuckled. "Well, I guess I thought you could go longer than a day without my handsome face." He sobered suddenly. "What's wrong, Susan?"

Susan flung herself down on a couch, her head resting against the armrest nearest Nate's chair. "Wrong? What could possibly be wrong?" She knew better than to try to fool him. He recognized and expressed emotion better than many humans she knew. "It's almost exactly a year since the best man in the world was killed in an explosion that left me critically injured. I'm a twenty-seven-year-old virgin. And, for the next month, I'm stuck in a freaking . . . garden."

Nate narrowed his eyes. Since he had a perfect memory, it was rare someone used a term he did not know. "You're stuck in a garden?"

Susan rolled her eyes toward him and explained the slang. "Treating a unit of vegetables. A garden."

"Ah." Nate figured out the rest based on previous conversations. "You're working in the public dementia facility." His brow furrowed. "Isn't it a wee bit unkind to refer to your patients as edibles?"

Not feeling in a particularly benevolent mood, Susan shrugged her shoulders nearly up to her ears. "Most medical slang has a nasty edge. That's why we don't share it with the patients."

Nate made a thoughtful noise. "You've changed, Susan."

Susan rolled her head toward Nate. "Of course I've changed. Everything we do, everything that happens in our lives changes us." Susan considered her own words. "That's why people who survive the same tragedy feel so drawn to one another and so isolated from everyone else. It's probably the root cause of post-traumatic stress disorder, at least in layman's terms."

Nate made a thoughtful noise, the type of instinctive sound Susan expected only from a human. She had always found it difficult to think of Nate as anything other than a man. It surprised her more when he acted like a robot than when he did something characteristically human.

Susan tried to reassure him. "But I don't think I've changed in any unexpected or unreasonable way. I mean, I never did have a lot of tolerance for prolonging undignified and hopeless life, even without clear suffering." She remembered her pediatrics rotation in medical school. A child born anencephalic, missing most of its brain and skull, came onto the service because the parents insisted on aggressive resuscitation. It survived two weeks with nothing above its enormous blue eyes, a single fused nostril, and a relatively normal mouth.

Nate apparently caught the unspoken leap. "You're not talking about your dementia patients. They had a conscious existence, at least at one time."

Susan rewarded Nate with the truth. "You're right. I'm thinking about rare and fatal birth defects, situations I saw in medical school that I guess the Dementia Unit reminds me of. There were parents who insisted on throwing away other people's time and money to avoid making the difficult but necessary decision to let nature take its course and put the child out of its misery. When did we decide, as a species, that allowing people to die of lethal defects was 'playing God,' but jamming tubes and needles into soulless bodies was 'natural'?" Susan rolled her eyes, head shaking. "When that's clearly ass-backward."

Nate sat back, crossing his legs. "I'd like to get back to your garden, Susan. Here we're talking about once-normal people, with full lives and loved ones who've known their history, all their strengths and foibles. It's not the same thing."

Nate was right, of course, but it did not really matter. "Different, yes. Better, no." Susan sat up. "It's impossible not to think about what I would do in the same situation." She drew a deep breath and let it out slowly before revealing thoughts she could not share with anyone else. "For the past year, I desperately wished Remy had survived the explosion. If he had sustained brain damage, I would have been with him every step of the way, would have helped him recover every bit of ability he possibly could. But . . ." She met Nate's eyes, trying to read them to decide whether she should finish.

Susan found encouragement there, the same she might have found in Kendall's, had she given him the opportunity. "If he . . . wound up like those patients, incapable of any worthwhile thought process"–she steeled herself and continued–"I hope I would have the strength and fortitude to kill him."

"Kill him?" Nate's brows flung upward. "Isn't that a bit . . . active? I mean, withdrawing nutrition or fluids is one thing. Killing is . . . murder."

Susan should have expected that reaction. It was the embodiment of the USR-patented First Law of Robotics: *A robot may not injure a human being, or, through inaction, allow a human being to come to harm.* Her father had made one thing abundantly clear: even the most rudimentary positronic brain could not exist without all three Laws present and intact. "A young, strong man like Remy"–she appreciated that she could now speak his name without tearing up–"could live for decades in a vegetative state. He would not have wanted that, and neither would I if it happened to me."

Nate played devil's advocate. "But how can you possibly know that other people and their loved ones feel the same way? From my research, the suicide rate for people with mental retardation is no higher than the general population. If you don't understand the concept of normal, who's to say you're not content, that life's not worth living? Admittedly, this is anecdotal evidence, but the patients with congenital intellectual disabilities I've met have always seemed quite happy."

"Someone never read *Flowers for Algernon.*" Susan sighed and sank back into the couch. Nate raised an eyebrow in query, and suddenly she had an insight about positronic robots. Despite their amazing ability to retain every piece of information presented to them, they were wholly ignorant of anything else. Most of what Nate knew, he had gleaned from this room: the textbooks, the charts, his chats with visitors like her. There had never been any reason for anyone to give him a novel or take him to a movie.

She explained, "*Flowers for Algernon* was a story, and then a movie, about an experimental treatment that triples intelligence. It's first performed on a mouse—that's Algernon—then on an intellectually disabled human, Charlie. The reader gets to see the transformation and the problems it creates for Charlie. He's at the peak at of his intelligence when he discovers a mistake in the experiment which invariably leads to Algernon's intellectual deterioration and death. Once blissful in his ignorance, Charlie now knows the world of genius, where he no longer belongs, and it drives him into desperation and madness."

Nate nodded thoughtfully. "So, you're saying people with congenital mental retardation—"

Susan winced at the use of the term. Though medically technically correct, "mental retardation" wasn't a phrase most people were comfortable using.

"—are usually happy because they don't realize or understand they're"—apparently noticing her discomfort, Nate softened his approach—"less than perfect."

"Exactly."

"But people with dementia are aware they've lost something precious and vitally important."

Susan elaborated, "Even remembering bits and pieces of it, which they can't quite fit together as a whole anymore. It's torture of the worst kind. They're miserable, degraded, humiliated. Given the opportunity, I know I'd want to die as swiftly and painlessly as possible."

She added without thinking, "Wouldn't you?"

Nate laughed. "Susan, it doesn't apply to me. I'm just random human stem cells coaxed into a dermal and muscular system grown over a skeleton of porous silicon. If something happened to my body, USR could just make me another one."

Susan did not agree. "You've just described your shell, not you. Nate is the positronic brain inside the skull portion of that framework, the network of neuron equivalents connecting thought to action." Susan did not know the specifics of building a positronic robot, but she knew enough to realize Nate had made her point for her. "People aren't that much different. Despite all the mushy poetry about what's in our hearts, it's only our brains that matter. You can remove the heart from our bodies and transplant one from an accident victim or even an animal, and we're still the same person, for all intents and purposes. But if you remove the brain, assuming you could effectively transplant another, we become someone else entirely. The humanity, the intellect, the essence of everything we are is entirely in that one convoluted, double-fist-sized structure hidden in our craniums. Damage that one organ and we are—"

"Different?" Nate tried.

"Nothing," Susan insisted.

Nate sat back, stroking his hairless chin like a stereotypical psychiatrist. For the first time ever, Susan wondered whether he had to shave. She could not think of a reason, other than to enable him to pass for human, to create such a feature. On the other hand, he did have real and growing hair on his head from the human dermal tissue comprising his scalp, so he probably had the same issues as any normal human male. "So, when someone survives a brain injury—say, an accident or a stroke or the removal of a tumor—we should kill him?"

Susan snorted vigorously, blowing out her lips in a gentle raspberry of derision. "Please, Nate. Surely you're above those kinds of extremes. Naturally, we have to stay within the boundaries of logical sense. I'm tired of the 'where do we draw the line' offense. We draw lines every day of our lives."

Nate quirked an eyebrow, an all-too-human gesture to encourage her to speak her mind. Susan again found it difficult to believe he was a robot. Invented by the president and founder of U.S. Robots, Lawrence Robertson, the positronic brain was a miracle of science and technology. "Okay, let's talk about the abortion argument. A lot of people on the antiabortion side won't listen to anything, on the pretext we can't be drawing lines. Yet they do draw the line, some would say randomly, at conception. Whereas, the abortion crowd draws the line, equally randomly, at viability outside the womb."

Nate frowned, brows drawing downward again. "I'm not sure I would call either of those lines random."

Susan clarified her thought. "I don't mean random in a logical sense. I mean random in an intellectual sense. The nice thing about both lines is they're solidly concrete, though wholly incompatible. But difficult individual decisions shouldn't be made with a single brushstroke."

"As opposed to laws," Nate pointed out. "Which have to be."

Susan nodded. "Which is why medicine should be bounded, not governed, by law. We need to stop legislating personal details without understanding the situation or the wishes of those involved."

Nate studied Susan for several moments. "So, you're promoting . . . anarchy?"

Susan slid back down on the couch, with her head propped against the armrest. "Certainly not. I'm a huge fan of lawful civilization. We need laws, and probably even leaders, to protect us from our own power, greed, stupidity, madness, immorality, and blind self-interest. Most things in life easily confine themselves to basic ethics and logical guidelines: Don't murder other people, except in self-defense. Don't take things that don't belong to you. Don't sell things to people that are addictive and deadly. Don't do things that might incite masses to riot."

Nate followed Susan's tack this time. "But you have difficulty with laws when they're applied to medical practice."

"Not on principle, no." Susan sighed deeply. "I have trouble when otherwise well-meaning laws cause terrible suffering in the name of preventing suffering. Medicine is not mathematics. Every individual case differs, and one scenario does not fit all. In fact, you can rarely find a scenario that fits two or three. That's why we need the best and brightest to become doctors, why the years of study are so very long and arduous, why we still take the ancient Hippocratic oath."

Now Nate's head bobbed in clear understanding. "So medical legislation should be confined to the obvious extremes. For everything else, the doctor and patient need to decide the best course of action based on the patient's or family's wishes and the doctor's expertise."

"Correct. And if those clash, we could have boards of ethics consisting of medical and moral experts rather than the great unwashed."

"Meaning, I assume, regular people."

Susan accepted his gentle rebuke. "And elected officials. Anyone who doesn't have the specialized education and wisdom born of experience to fully understand the specific situation."

"Closed sessions?" Nate suggested.

Susan paused, wondering if he was trying to steer her into a trap. "Not necessarily. That could be at the discretion of the board, which would be no different, really, than the way we run courts now. What is decided is decided, and the only way to overturn it is to appeal to a higher court. That court then has the right to accept or deny the case. Ultimately, a decision is made and set in stone."

"So, we would have an ethics board of appeal and, ultimately, a national supreme board."

Susan challenged. "Why not?"

Nate hesitated, then smiled. "I can't think of a single reason. It would cut down on the protestors at hospitals as well."

Susan nodded enthusiastically. She had grown weary of the shouting and sign waving that always heralded her entrance into Manhattan Hasbro Hospital. "Then we should encourage, but not mandate, everyone to sign a living will that specifies under what circumstances they would want treatment, the level of that treatment, and when to surrender or even euthanize."

Nate's eyes widened. "You mean, contemplate every possible sce-nario?"

"Impossible." Susan squeezed her left hand between her cheek and the armrest. "And unnecessary. Broad categories would do the trick: per-manent physical dependence, permanent mental dependence, untreat-able madness without intervening sanity. Obviously, if the patient is able to express his wishes, we should try to honor them, within reason."

"What about the argument that a deeply depressed person might choose euthanasia when simple antidepressant therapy might do?"

Susan met his gaze. "A competent doctor would never let that happen."

"With emphasis on the word 'competent.'"

Susan sighed at Nate's undeniable point. *She* would never allow that to happen. In a perfect world all doctors would be infallible geniuses, or at least the closest humanity had to offer. Unfortunately, bad doctors existed. In fact, she felt certain she had met one earlier that day: Dr. Mitchell Reefes, the head of Winter Wine Dementia Facility. He had regaled Susan and Kendall with a twenty-minute lecture on his expec-tations, particularly in regard to punctuality and thoroughness, after which he left for a three-hour lunch. During his absence, the nurses explained, choosing their words carefully, that Dr. Reefes was essen-tially lazy and almost fully reliant on protocols he had created to cover almost any situation, so the nurses did not need to call or question him. He generally allowed the rotating R-2s free rein, as long as they did not cost money or burden him.

Still deliberately taking the other point of view, Nate asked, "What if a family chose euthanasia to get a difficult or rich family member out of the picture?"

Susan did not see it as much of an issue. "Again, that's where the competent doctor comes in. It's not like wealthy Aunt Beryl would go in for a routine visit and a family member would have the opportunity to choose to end her life. But if Aunt Beryl is in a permanent vegetative state, the family shouldn't have to disclaim their inheritance or prolong her suffering just to prove money is not their primary motive."

Nate opened his mouth, but Susan forestalled him with a wave. "I'm not saying it's a perfect system. Everything's fallible, but you don't hear many people arguing we should discard life-saving antibiotics because a few people might have an unexpected allergy, or dismantling the legal system because an occasional innocent person gets punished. Humans do make mistakes. We can minimize them, but we can't make the world, or any system in it, perfect. Just because one person in a billion might awaken from a coma doesn't mean we should keep every coma- tose person alive indefinitely. Just because one criminal works hard at rehabilitation doesn't mean we should throw open every jail cell. My system might not be flawless, but it's a damn sight better than what we have now."

Nate brought their conversation definitively back to the original subject. "Meaning patient gardens."

Susan nodded. "Wards of patients sobbing in desperate misery, clinging to their last incomplete memories, bits and pieces of un- matched pictures that can never interlace. Wards of patients utterly devoid of intellectual functioning or spontaneous actions, wandering around like so much animate meat."

"Now you're mixing metaphors," Nate pointed out. "They can either be vegetables or meats, not both."

The ludicrousness of Nate's comment did not escape Susan, and it reached to the true root of her concern. Tears sprang to her eyes, wholly unbidden and equally unexpected. "Nate, what's wrong with me?"

The spectacular leap somehow did not seem to bother Nate, though he did appear a bit confused. "You mean medically?"

"Psychologically," she clarified.

"You're in a much better position to evaluate that than I am."

Susan was not so sure. Nate had read all the medical textbooks in this room, had absorbed the material in the charts and articles presented to him for review, and even had access to the global web. He retained everything, and his positronic brain gave him the ability to incorporate the material into understanding and action, so much so that he even appeared to have human emotions. For him, such simple things were not instinct but learned over a course of time interacting with, studying, and reading about humanity.

Susan got control of herself. "A year ago, I came to Manhattan Hasbro with the intention of doing everything I possibly could for every patient, of fixing them, of making them right no matter how messed up their lives or their minds. I would hold futures in my hands, and I would do everything within my power, within the power of medicine and possibility, to help them regain the best life had to offer them." She sighed deeply. "Now, suddenly, I'm thinking about mass euthanasia of a . . . of a . . ."

"Garden?" Nate supplied.

Susan winced as he threw her own word back at her. "A unit," she corrected. "A medical unit."

Nate studied her in the dimness of the windowless room. "Susan, it's nothing new. The R-1s all come to the hospital clinging to their fresh diplomas, eager, curious, terrified to make even a tiny mistake, passionately driven to become the best damn doctor in the history of medicine."

"And?" Susan said, both inquisitive about and afraid of what Nate might say next. Everyone knew a physician so jaded he or she viewed every patient as a bothersome distraction needing to be handled before he or she could go home for the day.

Nate continued dutifully, "Every physician becomes at least a little bit cynical, even the ones used to seeing the glass as full of rainbows." He kept his gaze directly on hers. "Not only does it come with the job, but it's probably absolutely necessary to become the best possible doctor."

Susan felt her features bunch. "How so?"

"Susan, it's not your place to love and care genuinely and deeply for each and every patient. That's the job of the family, and it's the very reason most physicians refuse to treat their own loved ones. When you care that deeply for someone, you can't possibly be objective. I once talked to a pediatrician who was in a near panic over his infant son's one-hundred-five-degree fever. He would have known exactly what to do if someone else brought in a child in the same state, but when it came to his own flesh and blood, logic and reason flew out the window. Part of physician training is to learn how to limit the emotional investment in an individual patient to allow the distance to give him or her the best possible treatment."

Susan understood Nate's point, but she did not know if she wholly subscribed to it. "If my father ever came down with a serious illness, I'd want to be directly involved in his care." She hated to admit she would never wholly trust another physician's judgment.

Nate quoted a familiar adage: "'A physician who treats himself has a fool for a patient.' I believe that applies to loved ones as well."

Susan smiled, and realized she no longer felt like crying. "Thanks, Nate."

Nate sank deeper into the chair. "I didn't do anything. Mostly just listened to you talk."

"Which, as you surely know, is an accepted form of psychoanalysis. I know what I have to do now."

"What?" Nate asked carefully.

"I have to go back there every day for a month. I have to give those patients the best care possible, to make the end of their lives meaningful, even if only to learn the best care for bedsores or mindless pacing."

Susan allowed her thoughts to expand. "It's possible I might find some diagnosis someone else missed."

"It certainly wouldn't be the first time," Nate reminded.

Susan added thoughtfully, "If I can rescue even one patient from that place, find someone misdiagnosed or mistreated who, with the proper therapy, can lead a reasonably normal life, it'll be worth every moment of the time and effort."

"That's the Susan Calvin I know."

And even if I can't find anyone to save, I'll find a way to bring something positive from this experience, whether it's the understanding of end of life, empathy for the patients and their families, or a purpose for the incurably demented. Susan rose with new determination. "Somehow this is going to make me a better doctor, if not a better person."

"Exactly," Nate said. "Now get out there and do what you do best."

"Diagnosis?" Susan guessed, heading for the door.

"Annoying your superiors," Nate corrected.

Chapter 3

S usan entered her thumb into the lock-reader of the apartment she shared with John Calvin, her father. The whisper of a click that followed was apparently enough to clue her father, who whipped open the door and personally ushered her inside. As usual, he gave his grown-up daughter an enthusiastic hug, crushing her cheek to his slender chest. Aside from his height—a couple inches over six and a half feet—he resembled her closely: hair straight and mousy brown, though shorter than his daughter's; eyes blue; chin undimpled and a bit prominent compared with his gaunt neck. "Welcome home, kitten." He glanced at the Vox on his wrist. "You're later than you expected."

Susan did not have to consult her own wrist computer to know it was after seven thirty. "I stopped to talk to Nate."

John's brows rose. Closing the door with a foot, he gestured toward the kitchen to indicate he would make her some food, though the conversation had nothing to do with dinner. "You rode all the way to the hospital to talk to a robot when you have a perfectly good father waiting for you at home?"

Susan responded to the gesture first. "I grabbed a sandwich on the way home." She had considered waiting until she arrived to eat, but it seemed pointless. Her father whipped up some of the most unique and scrumptious meals, but he had not eaten with her, or anyone else, in more than twenty years, not since the death of his wife, Susan's mother, Amanda Calvin. A portrait of the only woman he had ever loved still took up much of the far wall of the living room. As a young child, Susan had thought little of her father's quirk, though she did pine for the days when all three of them had eaten together as a family.

John Calvin did not allow his daughter off the hook, though he did lower his gesturing hand to his side. "And what could N8-C supply that I couldn't?"

"Medical expertise, for one thing." Susan studied her father in the overhead lighting. She had heard of situations where adult children left for a year or two, then returned to find their parents startlingly older. When children returned to school from summer vacation, they always looked so much different to their friends' parents, yet exactly the same to their own. Family members as close as she and her father never noticed the years creeping over their loved ones, so she tried to examine her father through the eyes of a stranger.

He was now fifty-two years old, and Susan thought he appeared younger. Gray hair flecked his temples but had not yet found a toehold in other parts of his scalp. When she looked closely, she did notice a few lines around his mouth, forehead, and eyes. She could think of nothing in his recent actions to suggest he might fall victim to any form of dementia. He still worked full-time at U.S. Robots and Mechanical Men. He showed no propensity for mangling names, forgetting why he entered a room, or mysteriously discovering his wallet in the freezer. Neither of them had ever worn glasses or needed corrective-vision procedures, and he read without the aid of a magnifying lens or adjustment to the focus of his Vox. He had been thin almost to the point of gauntness for as long as she had known him, but he did not act in any way sickly. She had the same tendency to lose track of hunger in times of activity and stress, particularly over the past year.

Given the events of the day, Susan could not help imagining John

Calvin as a patient in the Winter Wine Dementia Facility, requiring full-time care. She had smothered the thought while she toured the unit but could not help conjuring up the scenario several times since leaving it. Now, standing directly in her father's presence, her consideration of the matter seemed more real and confusing than ever. Of course, she would continue to visit him every day he remembered her and responded positively to her presence. Logically, she knew that if he developed dementia, a time would come when he no longer cared if she came or not, could not differentiate her from a stranger. All that would remain was an empty John Calvin–shaped shell, without memory or reason. What purpose did it serve to nurture such a pitiful thing? Whether or not he felt at peace, and she doubted he would, it would prove little more than torture to her.

Susan had learned to ignore what other people thought of her. She had, at times, been a curve buster, a swot, the type of student who appears to value learning over social outlets. She could never win a beauty contest. She would never bow to societal pressures, would not visit a human vegetable, even one who had once been her beloved father, simply for appearances.

John Calvin cleared his throat. "Are you stunned by my ravishing charm?"

Only then Susan realized she was still staring at her father. With a quick shake of her head, she refocused her attention on the familiar furniture: a tan sectional sofa just beginning to fray at the edges, an oblong coffee table nestled into the muted semicircle of couch, and the metal and glass shelving that took up most of the wall space, supporting everything from the television/stereo to her father's journals and a few classical books, mostly physics and mechanics texts. "Sorry. Just lost in thought." She took a seat at the far end of the sectional.

John Calvin also sat. "An enigma already? I wouldn't think there's as much to puzzle over in a dementia unit."

"This is more of a what-if dilemma," Susan admitted. "There's an area devoted entirely to end-stage dementia, and it's got me more angry than stymied."

"Angry?" Susan's father pressed. "'Frustrated,' 'wretched,' 'miserable' seem more appropriate."

Susan sighed. She did not wish to hash over the same ground with her father as she already had with Nate. "The nurses fawn over these patients, speaking to them as if they could understand, treating every ingrown hair and patch of dry skin, vigorously clearing every bit of mucus from the depths of their lungs, styling their hair, and clipping their nails."

John blinked. A moment passed in silence before he said, "Did you want the nurses to verbally abuse them? To beat them? To leave them filthy and unkempt?"

Susan waved the madness away. "Of course not. I would never justify causing suffering." She sighed deeply. "But why do we need to spend scarce health-care resources prolonging suffering when it could be better used battling illnesses we can treat? Or even researching ways to prevent the very dementia that put them in this state, so their descendants, at least, might benefit?"

"Are you talking euthanasia?"

It surprised Susan how swiftly the *e* word came up in these conversations. She shrugged.

"Because some people would call that playing God."

And the G word. "I don't see how allowing nature to take its course is playing God. Perhaps that's why God created pneumonia and bedsores, to end the suffering of people like those in Winter Wine's End-Stage Dementia Unit. I could maintain that forcing these empty husks to go on breathing for as long as humanity-created technology allows is playing God."

John smiled, and Susan suddenly realized he had been baiting her more than actually arguing. They were not going to resolve an argument as long-standing as politics itself in an evening.

"And since when do you concern yourself with God? We don't go to any church, at least not since Mom died."

John explained, "I only made the point that some people would consider it playing God. Not that I necessarily did." He scooted over to sit directly beside her, then put an arm across her shoulders. "Kitten, if I'm ever in Winter Wine End-Stage Dementia Unit, feel free to pull the plug."

Susan found tears in her eyes and could not wholly explain them, which sparked more irritation. For the past week, her emotions seemed to be acting irrationally, of their own accord. "Unfortunately, there aren't any plugs to pull, Dad. Dementia eats away the brain, but it doesn't affect the heart and lungs at all. That's what makes it so singularly awful."

"Yeah, well." John stroked his chin. "Feel free to put a pillow over my head, then. And don't visit. I could never live with the thought I might become a burden or cause pain to my daughter, assuming I could still think in any capacity. Getting on with your own life would be the best thing you could do for me in such a situation."

Susan winced. She did not want to think about the matter any longer, though she did feel a kinship with the families of the patients she would be tending for the next month. They went through a private hell she hoped she never had to deal with, never had to bear. Until that moment, she had focused wholly on the patients, on their lack of future, on their discomfort and inability to beg for mercy. Now she considered the lot of the loving caretaker and could not imagine anything more confusing or exhausting, more testing of a person's stamina, resilience, and grief. No wonder people responded so differently: the demanding son who berated an overworked nurse for not tending to his mother's hair quickly enough, the daughter who came up with myriad excuses not to visit, the brother who sat weeping over a patient without tending to his own needs, the grandchildren standing in stunned boredom, the neighbor who sat and stroked a comatose man's hand for hours. All of them coped with an impossible situation in their own way. A tear rolled down Susan's cheek.

John Calvin said softly, "You're thinking of Remy, aren't you?"

Susan did not believe that to be the case, nor could she see where her father had come up with his theory. "What?"

"You're imagining your life, had the explosion destroyed his brain but left his body intact."

Susan could not deny the thought had occurred to her; she had said as much to Nate. She brushed the tear from her cheek. "I don't like thinking about that possibility." She could not help asking, "Is it . . . immoral to be glad he died instead?"

"I don't believe so." John Calvin reached behind him to pull a bulky envelope from the shelves. "I thought you might want this." He dropped it into Susan's lap.

Susan had no idea what it might contain. She hoped it was not his will; she had contemplated his mortality enough for one day. Opening the flap, she pulled out a professionally framed, glossy 8-by-10-inch photograph.

Susan recognized the site in the picture immediately: a concrete bench just outside their building, beside an immense playground. If she walked out on the terrace and looked down, she could probably see it almost directly beneath them. What held her spellbound were the figures on the bench. She sat on the right, her attention riveted to the man beside her, looking as content and comfortable as she could ever remember appearing. The wind carried a strand of her hair; her open and genuine expression softened her features until they looked almost pretty. It was the best picture of herself she had ever seen. Beside her,

Remington Hawthorn looked as suave and self-assured as always. Dressed in casual khakis and a T-shirt, he studied Susan with a look of obvious adoration. The familiar dark blond curls swept across his fore-head and barely missed eyes that held Susan's gaze longer than any other feature. In the picture, she saw genuine affection. No one could feign that depth of feeling. As he had stated that day, while they sat on the bench together, he had truly loved her.

"Oh, my God," Susan whispered. She could no longer slow the tears bunching in her eyes. They ran down her face in rivulets. "Oh, my God." She tore her gaze from the picture to meet her father's stare. "Where? Where did you get this?" She had no idea such a picture existed.

"Old Ms. Crabtree." John Calvin jerked a thumb upward to indica-tion their upstairs neighbor. "She said she saw you sitting there, and you looked so happy she snapped the picture with her Vox. She forgot about it until last week, when she took some other snaps in for enlarge-ment and found it. I took it to the art store for framing and picked it up after work today."

Susan's attention returned to the photo. "It's . . ." She did not know what to say. "Perfection" seemed immodest. "Beautiful" did not do it justice. ". . . wonderful. Thank you." She clutched it to her chest, the metal frame cold on her arms.

John shifted his position so he could comfortably keep his arm around his daughter's shoulders without interfering with her special moment. "I've been thinking."

Susan wiped away her tears, and a glimmer of joy slipped through. She remembered the conversation on the bench, the first time she had told Remington she loved him, the first time any man, other than her father, had spoken those words to her. They had made plans for her to lose her virginity to him that night but were interrupted by a visit to USR, which had led to a string of harrowing events and, ultimately, to his death.

Although Susan had not acknowledged her father's words, he continued what he had to say. "It's clear something special was happening on that bench."

Susan nodded but did not go into details. It was not the sort of conversation a daughter had with her father. Realizing she needed to say something, however, she nodded. "It was."

John pushed on, "With Remy being buried in his hometown, does it bother you that you can't . . . commune at the gravesite? Put some flowers on the marker now and then?"

Susan forced out a chuckle. Neither she nor her father were spiritual people, although they did make a twice-yearly pilgrimage to Amanda Calvin's grave. "Dad, if there is a heaven, we know they sent a limo for Remy. Whether there is or isn't, there's no real purpose to visiting the place where the empty shell was placed. Even if ghosts existed, I couldn't imagine Remy's hanging around his coffin, waiting to see who visited his rotting corpse."

John Calvin quirked an eyebrow, shrugged. "Surely you don't really think people visit gravesites to appease the ghosts of their loved ones. It's a great place to sit and think about the person who died, regardless of your religious beliefs, a quiet place to reflect and remember or to privately say all the things you wish you had managed while they were still alive."

Susan rubbed the last of the tears from her cheeks. "I know that. I really do. It's just hard to justify the time and cost of flying to Ohio on my rare days off just to visit a gravesite. It's not like I know his family, either. I never laid eyes on them until the funeral." The Hawthorn family seemed nice enough, but they could not possibly understand how close their son had become to her in the short time they had known one another.

"That's what I was thinking," John explained. "We can't be hopping planes or trains to Ohio on a whim. But that bench . . ."

Susan studied the picture again. Ms. Crabtree had clearly taken it from behind the playground structure, where scores of preschool children had been playing. "You do know that's the bench right outside the building, right?"

"Of course."

"Well, one could hardly consider that a place of"—Susan tried to think of words that described the typical gravesite—"serene seclusion."

John grinned. "Well, no. But it's symbolic, isn't it? We could share fond memories of him there with no one the wiser. Even though it's filled with children during the day, the kids are too busy having fun and the parents too busy watching their kids to notice a person enjoying a spiritual experience. And if you do need quiet, it's always empty after dark."

Though Susan liked the idea, she could not help adding. "Empty . . . except for the muggers."

John smiled at the facetious comment. "Well, there is that. But I doubt you need to carry a mess of valuables to visit a dead guy." Gingerly, he took the framed photograph from Susan's hands and placed it on the wall beside the one of Amanda Calvin. Apparently, he had planned that as well, as a preplaced hook anchored the picture at the exact same height and an eye-pleasing distance from Susan's mother.

Susan did not have to force a smile. She appreciated what her father had done for her and wished she had not turned his thoughtful idea into a joke. "Thanks for memorializing the moment, Dad. It means a lot to me." She tore her eyes from the picture to add sincerely, "And for the idea of using the bench as a spot to connect with my memories and grief. It is a great symbol, though I don't think I'll leave any flowers unless I get a hankering to provide preschool kids with bouquets for their mothers."

John tipped the frame this way and that until he found the perfect balance, then straightened Amanda as well. Finally satisfied, he returned his gaze to his daughter. "Just because Remy's picture's up there with Mom's doesn't mean you get to go doolally, like I did."

Susan understood the reference, having confronted her father only a year ago about what she had decided were neuroses. He had not dated in the more than twenty years since Amanda's death, and he dined only when alone. John had reminded Susan he had survived the same accident that had killed her mother, a fact Susan's young age and denial had allowed her to forget. Neurological impairment affecting his senses of smell and taste, as well as sexual desire and function, explained his peculiarities. "Nerve damage is different from neuroses." She gave him a sly wink. "And most of my ilk require an actual psychosis to diagnose someone 'doolally.'"

"All right, a bit nutty, then. My point is you have to start dating again, Susan. Someday I want grandchildren to spoil."

Susan quirked an eyebrow. "You got anyone in mind for the father?"

"How about that redhead you keep talking about? Kendall Stephenson."

"Kendall Stevens." Susan corrected, shaking her head. She had met Kendall the same day as Remington, the first day of their residencies, and had never thought of him as anything more than a friend.

"He's funny, right?" John persisted. "And you could use some humor in your life. Is he seeing anyone?"

For the first time, Susan thought about the possibility of she and Kendall becoming a couple. She had never seen him with a woman who could pass for a girlfriend, and he had not mentioned dating anyone she could remember. They spent enough time together that, had he engaged in even a casual relationship in the past year, she ought to have known about it. "Not to my knowledge, Dad. But he's never shown that sort of interest in me, either."

"No good man would. You were seeing Remy," John Calvin reminded her. "Then Remy died. Not a good time to cozy up to any woman."

Susan found herself unable to imagine Kendall and herself in a relationship. "He's a good friend, Dad, but only a friend. We have a good thing going. Why complicate it with . . ."

"Sex?" John filled in.

Susan felt her cheeks heat up, and it surprised her. She thought medical school had inured her to embarrassment. In the presence of her father, however, she reverted to the mental status of an eight-year-old. "Dad!"

"What? You asked me about my sex life, and turnabout is fair play. Right?"

Susan did not see the comparison. "But I'm a doctor, a budding psychiatrist. And you . . . were acting . . ."

"Doolally?"

This time, Susan did not quibble with the terminology. "Yeah. And master headshrinker that I am, I thought I had all the answers." She rolled her eyes. "Only to discover I didn't even have the questions right."

John laughed. "You know, when I was young, my best friend was a woman."

"Really?" Susan could not help asking, "How did that work out?"

John grinned nearly from ear to ear. "I married her."

Susan realized she had walked right into his trap. Her demeanor softened, and she could not help looking at the picture of her mother she had memorized over the years. "And I'm glad you did. Otherwise, I wouldn't exist." She leapt to her feet. "And now I've got some research to do. There aren't many treatable causes of dementia, not a whole lot of differential diagnoses, either. But, if I can save just one patient from the hellhole that is Winter Wine Dementia Facility, I will consider this rotation worthwhile." She headed toward the palm-pross in her bedroom.

"That's my Susan," John said to her retreating back.

T he rancid odor of the dementia facility pervaded Susan's nose, and she wondered how long it would take to become so accustomed she ceased to notice it. She had spent as much of the morning as possible poring over the patients' charts, trying to find some small clue to suggest a misdiagnosis. Every few moments, her study was interrupted by a nurse seeking fresh orders, asking her to medicate an agitated patient, or assessing some blemish, erythematous area, or scratch that might indicate an impending wound infection or bedsore.

Once again, the hopelessness of the place invaded Susan's soul. Though she hated the interruptions to her examinations and thought processes, she did appreciate the dedication and caring of the nursing staff. She marveled at their ability to see these shambling bodies as the human beings who had once inhabited them. Tireless and strangely upbeat most of the time, the nurses performed their duties without grumbling or complaining, without screaming or crying, with the patience of Job. Though they dealt with the same issues day after day, month after month, year after year, they treated the patients as individuals and answered the identical questions of concerned, angry, desperate, and grieving relatives as if each case were fresh and new, unique and special. They had a knack for this type of work, and the patients and families had little idea how lucky they were to have found these forbearing angels.

And then Susan saw him. He was just one aimless, meandering man among many, an average-sized adult with spiky gray hair, a medium build, and the typical parkinsonian masklike face. Susan was not even sure what had caught her notice, but she found her gaze riveted to him and she drifted toward him. She was on Unit 2, the second step in the three-stage shuffle, which meant he might still have enough of his faculties to carry on the reasonable facsimile of a conversation.

Susan moved directly in front of him, and he stopped. He stood hunched over, his limbs trembling beyond his control, weaving back and forth as if he might fall at any moment. Yet he remained standing, almost rigidly at attention. His face revealed little expression, but his eyes drifted upward to find her own. They were brown, soft, and sad, but at least they did not stare through her. "Hello," she said. "I'm Dr. Susan Calvin."

"Hello," he returned in a hoarse voice that suggested he did not use it often. "I'm Chuck." His eyes rolled, and he repeated, "Chuck, Chuck, Chuck." She did not know if he had echolalia or was searching for a last name somewhere deep in what remained of his memory. She knew she would need more than "Chuck" to find his chart and examine his history.

"Do you know what you're here for, Chuck?"

"Chuck," he repeated. This time, he parroted her. "In for." His facial expression did not change, but she thought she saw a bit of effort in his eyes, as if he was using repetition to gain time to find a more rational answer. "I'm lost," he finally said. "I was on my way to the bathroom."

Susan could see the telltale bulge of an adult diaper beneath his slacks. If he was seeking the restroom, he clearly made a habit of not reaching it on time. "Come with me, Chuck. I'll take you there." She headed toward the patients' toilet. When he did not follow, she turned to face him again. Chuck had not moved. His eyes revealed confusion bordering on panic, and Susan did not want to pressure him. Pushing demented patients often resulted in a violent backlash.

Susan returned in a gesture of harmless concession. "Nice meeting you, Chuck."

"Nice meeting you," he said, though whether to complete the ritual or as more echolalia, she could not tell. His face revealed nothing. He paused for several moments, focused on the floor, as if his brain could not convince his feet to begin moving again. After a few seconds of this, he continued his awkward facsimile of walking, and Susan observed his ambulation from the side and the back, certain his movements were what had attracted her attention in the first place.

Chuck had clear bradykinesia, slowness of movement; his steps were short, his slippered feet barely clearing the floor, and his ankles rotated outward.

One of the nurses, a woman named Asha, left her patient to approach Susan. "That's Charles Tripler," she explained. "He goes by Chuck. He's sixty-six years old. Used to be a plumber. Parkinson's disease for ten years and dementia for the last two."

Susan acknowledged Asha with a nod and a "thank you," but kept her gaze on Chuck. If she had had to guess his diagnosis, she would have gone with Parkinson's, but not everything about his movements was typical for the disease. Pressing the Record button on her Vox, she settled into a chair, planning to observe Mr. Charles "Chuck" Tripler until her next interruption.

Chapter 4

Susan knocked firmly on Dr. Reefes' office door, excited but uncertain about her findings and conclusions. Beside her, Kendall shifted his weight from foot to foot, clearly uncomfortable with disturbing their attending, yet too curious or gallant to leave her to present the patient alone. They had become accustomed to the routine of Manhattan Hasbro, where humorless attendings insisted on daily rounds with every patient, quizzing the residents mercilessly and demanding they remain informed on every aspect of each patient's care.

On a chronic unit such as the Winter Wine Dementia Facility, Susan had not expected the same type of precision. The patients did not require moment-to-moment care. There was little hope for improvement, their medications rarely changed, and their conditions remained stable on a day-to-day basis, with only a gradual and anticipated slide toward oblivion. Still, Susan had expected their attending to show some interest in the new residents, to listen to their plans, and to take an active role in their work.

Reefes' gruff voice barely wafted to the residents, though he was probably shouting to be heard through the door. "Who is it?"

Susan tripped the latch and toed the door open a crack, enough for sound to carry easily without violating any privacy. "It's Susan Calvin and Kendall Stevens, sir. We'd like to discuss a patient with you."

"Come in. Come in." Reefes sounded more harried than upset. "What can I do for you?"

Kendall pushed the door open, and the residents stepped inside. While he closed the door behind them, Reefes gestured toward a single chair in front of his desk. He sat behind the desk, a massive computer screen in front of him. Framed pictures hung from the walls, mostly hand-painted still lifes and photographs of a woman and four children Susan assumed were his wife and offspring. The desk held a snow globe with zoo animals inside it, a box of tissues decorated with crayon scribbles, a large old-fashioned laser printer, and a sleek multilined telephone.

Susan took the proffered chair, leaving Kendall to glance around, shrug, and slouch beside her. "I'd like to talk to you about Chuck Tripler."

"Chuck Tripler." Reefes tapped his fingers on the full-sized keyboard, then sat back, reading. "Charles C. Tripler. Sixty-six-year-old man with a ten-year history of Parkinson's disease. Currently on Unit 2." He looked up. "What about him?"

"Well, sir, I've been watching him." Susan rose and stepped around the desk, tapping her Vox. "May I?"

The gesture had become universal. Reefes tapped out his sequence code to allow her to connect the information on her Vox to his larger system. A grainy video of Chuck shuffling around the unit appeared on the screen.

Kendall came around to join them.

Susan got right to the point, "I think he's been misdiagnosed."

Reefes sat back with a sigh. Like most attendings and nurses, he had probably grown accustomed to hotshot residents arriving each month with personal theories, trying to demonstrate their genius by unearthing a brilliant diagnosis overlooked by their superiors and predecessors.

Susan tapped the proper buttons on her Vox and brought up a Med-Vid of a patient with Parkinson's disease, walking. "This is a typical chronic Parkinson's walk before L-dopa treatment." She tapped a series of buttons to highlight her points as she made them. "It's slow and shuf-fling, but the cadence is actually increased so that the overall velocity remains essentially normal. The steps are short, the posture flexed and rigid. He tends to freeze in place, with hesitation at the start." She backed up to the start of the MedVid to emphasize the point. "The step width and height, however, are nearly normal, and you don't see any rotation angle to the feet."

Reefes sat back. He wore his dark hair short, with bangs dangling over a broad forehead. His narrow green eyes followed the picture on the screen. Full lips currently held a smirk, though he said nothing, silently waiting for Susan to make a valid point.

Susan switched to another MedVid. "This is a patient with normal pressure hydrocephalus."

Reefes groaned loudly, gripping the edge of his desk. "Not again."

Susan froze the video. "Excuse me, sir?"

Reefes shook his head with stiff efficiency. "Sorry, I know you mean well. But this happens every month. Some resident zeroes in on a pros-pect and becomes convinced he has one of the rare forms of treatable dementia, almost always NPH, and tries to make a case for it."

As Susan had intended to find a treatable patient and did intend to make a case for normal pressure hydrocephalus, she could hardly claim Reefes was wrong. However, in this situation, she believed she had a strong argument. "Please let me finish."

Reefes rolled his eyes and started to rise.

Kendall stepped in closer. As he clearly intended to speak, Susan braced herself. Seriousness was not in his nature, and his humor often held an edge. "Sir, I'm sure you see this all the time, but Susan is a special case. Families grovel at her feet. Nurses festoon her with balloons.

Researchers throw flowers in her path, and the hospital attorneys seek out her legal advice."

Susan glared at her companion. She had made some good catches in the past year and she had a decent eye for diagnoses, but exaggeration to the point of absurdity was not going to help her cause. Reefes turned a withering look on him.

Kendall reined in his hyperbole. "Honestly, sir. In our first week of residency, she sent home three PIPU lifers, the staff threw her a party, and Doctors Goldman and Peters asked for her by name to assist in their research." The latter were well-known as the premier psychiatry researchers in the state; their names topped many prestigious articles in the journals all psychiatrists read. Susan tried not to cringe at the high praise. Though true, Cody Peters and Ari Goldman had requested her because of the nature of the research, not her brilliance. They had a robot-related study and knew her father from previous projects. "On the Adult Inpatient Unit, she cured a patient catatonic for fourteen years, rescued a subdural hematoma from lifelong bipolar therapy, and found a pheochromocytoma masquerading as panic attacks. If Susan sees something out of the ordinary, it's worth examining."

Reefes sat back, lips pressed firmly together. "Fine." He made a grand gesture toward the screen. "Enlighten me."

Susan restarted the MedVid. "Watching the man with normal pressure hydrocephalus walk, we see he has the same slow, short steps, flexed posture, and freezing on the first step. Except, on closer inspection, it's clear the freezing is more incessant and profound in the NPH patient. It's not just the first step, but he wrests every step from the ground, as if his iron shoes have to overcome an enormous underground magnet."

"Magnetic gait," Reefes supplied. "That's the technical term, in case they hadn't taught you."

"Yes," Susan said, ignoring the taunt. Many university specialists saw themselves as superior to private practitioners, disregarding so-called outside docs as too far removed from cutting-edge research and set in old-fashioned ways. They sometimes referred to private practice as cookie-cutter medicine. The private practitioners often considered the university doctors arrogant, dependent on technology, and incapable of truly understanding human emotion or observational diagnoses. Susan did not wish to get dragged into that long-standing conflict.

She continued, "Unlike the Parkinson's patient, the one with NPH doesn't increase his cadence to make up for the shorter steps. He simply moves much more slowly. His step width is more open, and his feet are externally rotated, suggesting more balance issues than you see with the Parkinson's gait. The arm swing is essentially normal."

Reefes stared at Susan. "All right. That sounds like it would make an interesting study, had it not, apparently, already been done. But we all know people's illnesses progress at different rates, their reactions span the gamut, and there is no absolute uniformity between patients with the same problem. The days of relying solely on our eyeballs for diagnoses is long gone. According to his chart"—Reefes tapped the right upper square of his computer monitor—"Chuck had a positive alpha-synuclein test when first diagnosed. That means he has Lewy bodies in his brain." He spread his arms. "Ergo, Parkinson's, not NPH."

Susan nodded her agreement. She had read over Chuck's chart thoroughly before bringing her ideas to Dr. Reefes. She was always most careful with the first patient, the one who formed the basis for the attending's opinion of her and her competence for the rest of the rotation. A decade earlier, the alpha-synuclein assay was a relatively new and highly heralded laboratory blood test that obviated the need for invasive brain biopsy. Prior to that time, Lewy bodies generally were not seen except on postmortem examinations. "Lewy bodies aren't pathognomonic for parkinsonism. And I'm not suggesting Chuck has a pure form of NPH, either."

Reefes' eyes narrowed. Clearly, he was on shaky ground now, the technicalities Susan had chosen to highlight beyond his zone of comfort. Kendall put his foot on top of Susan's and pushed down lightly in warning.

Susan ignored her fellow resident to put the grainy images of a walking Chuck back onto the screen. "Now, if we watch Mr. Tripler, we get an unusual picture." She touched buttons on her Vox to highlight different areas. "If I had to diagnose him solely on the basis of gait, I couldn't do it."

"Nor do you have to," Reefes pointed out.

Susan nodded assent. "Nor do I have to. But if you read the old texts, a competent neurologist could distinguish Parkinson's disease from normal pressure hydrocephalus more than ninety-five percent of the time, without a single lab test." She continued before anyone could interrupt. "Chuck's gait is almost, but not quite, a hybrid of the two entities. He demonstrates the magnetic gait, though inconsistently. He has the bradykinesia of both, the flexed posture of both, the rigidity. His feet practically skim the floor, but he can step. He has an inordinately wide-based gait with significant rotation, which favors an equilibrium problem, like in NPH. Additionally, he has some features that don't fit either syndrome." Susan highlighted the proper areas. "His gait is stilted, with a pronounced foot drop, more prominent on the right."

Now Kendall added his two cents to the diagnosis. "You can see foot drop with parkinsonism, and it's not necessarily symmetrical. But the stilted . . ." He moved in closer. "That's pain, isn't it?"

Susan bobbed her head vigorously. "I think the man is experiencing nerve-root pain. And there's one other issue." She left the repetitive image of Chuck walking on the screen. "There are four parts to the idiopathic Parkinson's disease diagnosis. Number one, there are the symptoms, which he clearly demonstrates. Number two is the presence of Lewy bodies, which has been satisfied. Number three is the exclusion of other disease processes, which is exactly what I'm debating. Number four is a documented response to dopamine therapy."

"Which we have," Reefes pointed out, leisurely leafing through the chart by moving his index finger across the screen.

"Anemic, at best. If we go back to the first MedVid, you'll see the same patient after L-dopa. His gait becomes almost normal. Chuck never had anywhere near that impressive a response."

Reefes waved a nonchalant hand. "Which can be easily explained by the fact that different patients respond differently to disease entities and to therapy. How else can you explain how my mother died of ALS ten months after her diagnosis while Stephen Hawking lived with the same disease for longer than five decades?"

Eighty percent of patients with amyotrophic lateral sclerosis died within five years of receiving their diagnosis, and ninety percent survived fewer than ten years. The oddity of the theoretical physicist's prolonged survival assured he would remain one of science's most examined phenomena for decades to come, and comparing a rarity to the norm did not prove a point. Susan suspected they could have had a monthlong discussion on that particular matter, but she did not want to get into it now, so she conceded the point. "Agreed. But when you're using response to a specific medicine as a criterion for diagnosis, that response in any given individual becomes much more germane."

Reefes shook his head and rolled his eyes simultaneously. Susan had a feeling she was rapidly reaching the end of his patience. "Fine, I'll give you that one. But in this case, we have a positive alpha-synuclein. Lewy bodies are seen in exactly three diseases: Parkinson's, dementia with Lewy bodies, and Alzheimer's. Now, of the three, Parkinson's is the most treatable, and that is the diagnosis Mr. Tripler carries. The dementia seen in those three diseases is not distinguishable, at least therapeutically. In other words, they are treated exactly the same way: supportive therapy until death, which is forthcoming and inevitable." Apparently thinking they had finished, Reefes gestured toward the door and tapped the code into his desktop, unlinking it from Susan's Vox.

Kendall started for the door, his movements a bit hesitant. Surely he had expected something better from Susan Calvin.

Susan had to make her case now. "Unless . . ."

Reefes glanced back up, looking surprised to find her still in the room. "Unless?"

"Unless Mr. Tripler has secondary parkinsonism. Perhaps related to NPH, which might explain the oddity of his gait."

Reefes laughed, not cruelly but clearly involuntarily. "NPH causing Parkinson's. That's a new one." He gestured more vigorously to the door. "Please get back to work."

Susan started to obey, then stopped. She turned back to face Dr. Reefes and found him looking at her as well. "I'd like to get an MRI."

Reefes' brows rose in increments, and crimson tinged his face. "Susan, I applaud your effort to try to help an otherwise hopeless patient, and I appreciate your desire to discover something that wiser, more experienced heads might have missed. But you surely know an MRI is an expensive and difficult procedure. It would be uncomfortable for Mr. Tripler, who would have to be sedated. It would waste the time of our staff, who would have to transport him there; the MRI staff, who would have to deal with a confused patient; and the nurses, who would need to prepare and assist him. And it would squander our scarce resources. The taxpayers do not need to be burdened with an expensive study that will not change our therapeutic approach one whit."

Susan knew arguing would prove fruitless. "Can I at least perform a lumbar puncture on Mr. Tripler? That's simple, inexpensive, and wastes only my time and that of a single assistant, who could be the least-paid person on staff, if you wish. I could do it with a janitor steadying him for me."

Reefes stared daggers at her. Susan could no longer hope he

harbored one shred of appreciation for her. "Denied." He thrust his fingers toward the door. "Now *get out!*"

Susan and Kendall scrambled through the door, pulling it carefully closed behind them.

The instant the door clicked closed, Kendall huffed out, "Well. You seem to have made another friend, Calvin. But this time, I'm not sure your ability, or your tongue, can save you." He lowered his voice to a stage whisper. "You may have to castrate this one with a scalpel."

"Funny," Susan growled. Ignoring the patients and milling nurses, she wound her way into the charting room and dropped into a chair, fuming. It was not the first time an attending had chosen not to listen to, or even to belittle, her. Accustomed to gung-ho young doctors, they had heard it all and developed a jaundiced eye, a practical bent that did not allow for wishful guessing. The logical principle of Occam's razor existed in medicine specifically for the fresh faces; patients did not come with labels. Symptoms could suggest many competing diagnoses, and the simplest and most common nearly always proved the correct one.

There was a reason why one of the most enduring aphorisms in medicine was "When you hear hoofbeats, think horses not zebras," and the obvious tautology "Common illnesses occur commonly" was bandied about by attendings, probably through millennia. Medical novices were predisposed to make rare diagnoses for many reasons: the desire to contribute in a substantial and memorable way, because striking diagnoses remain lodged in memory longer and more thoroughly, the excitement of plucking something special from the mundane. Most people chose the medical profession for altruistic reasons. It also attracted people who took joy in learning and lived for the epiphany that came so rarely in science and in life.

Susan rose, opened the door, and surveyed Unit 2 of the Winter Wine Dementia Facility. Without much effort, she picked Chuck out from the group. He sat in one of a line of padded chairs, lips moving silently, staring uncomprehendingly around the unit. Every part of him trembled violently, and she wondered if his sensory system had fully adjusted to it or if the world seemed to jump like an early twentieth-century movie. She tried to put herself in his place, a victim of a degenerating neurological system, adrift in a world that gradually lost all sense or feeling.

Kendall stepped up beside her and spoke softly. "What's your plan, Dr. Calvin?"

Susan bit her lip, grimaced, steeled herself. The answer slipped from her mouth before she had a chance to consider it. "I'm going to perform an LP." She headed toward the procedure room to set up her supplies, calling over her shoulder, "Would you like to assist me?"

Kendall trotted after her, smiling. "Calvin, I thought you'd never ask."

With Kendall's help, the lumbar puncture went off without a hitch. Apparently accustomed to working with and around Dr. Reefes, the ancillary staff did not bother him, or either of the residents, in the ten minutes it took to complete the procedure. Not wishing to involve innocents in their deception, Susan personally delivered the tubes of fluid to the lab, noting only that the cerebrospinal fluid color seemed yellowish instead of crystal clear. Called xanthochromia, it usually alerted a physician to the possibility of a subarachnoid hemorrhage, which was not a logical concern in this case.

Susan knew other causes of xanthochromia existed, including bilirubin abnormalities, such as liver disease or generalized red-blood-cell breakdown, elevated protein, increased numbers of red blood cells in the cerebrospinal fluid from clots or subdural bleeding, or even an unrealized traumatic tap. She also knew eyeballing the cerebrospinal fluid for coloring, the gold standard prior to the last decade, was unreliable, and the lab would use a spectrophotometer to determine whether the xanthochromia was real or a trick of light and background.

As soon as Susan returned, Kendall gripped her arm and guided her into one of the small staffing rooms. For an instant, dread flashed through her, and she wondered if Dr. Reefes had caught wind of her betrayal. He could not get her expelled, but he could contact the director of the residency program and put a blotch on her record. It would not negate all the good she had done, but it automatically put her beneath those with spotless records and could cause a problem when put together with the time she missed while recuperating from her injuries.

But Kendall only thrust a palm-pross into her hands, with information on a patient named Thomas Heaton. "Take a look at this one."

Susan scanned the information. According to the record, Thomas Heaton was a sixty-two-year-old black male with a one-year history of deterioration of mental function. The problems began shortly after an accident in which a falling stage light hit him in the back of the head while he performed his job as an orchestral conductor. At the time, there were signs of soft-tissue injury but no skull fractures or internal brain hemorrhages. He was diagnosed as having sustained a concussion, was treated with over-the-counter pain medications only, and returned to work the following day. The concerning behavior started two weeks later. Initially, it was described by family members as odd and atypical while at home, but essentially normal when at work. His wife first noticed that he quit reading entirely, avoided the Internet, and broke his palm-pross in an apparent fit of pique. Brain imaging did not show any sign of late bleeding or other problems, and neurological tests were normal. He gradually became increasingly confused and agitated until he could no longer function at work, either. For a while, he would respond positively to music, which calmed him and made him more compliant with requests. In the past month, however, even music had failed to reach him.

Kendall took back the palm-pross before Susan could read more. "What do you think?"

Susan shrugged. Based only on that information, she could scarcely begin to narrow down the possible diagnoses. "Let's see him."

Apparently, Kendall had already done an exam, because he knew exactly where to find Thomas Heaton. He took Susan to Unit 1, the location of the newer admissions. In addition to the open common area in the center, private and semiprivate rooms branched off like spokes, more akin to a standard hospital, except the middle was not an arrangement of nursing stations and hallways but an open room, similar to the ones on the other two units. A video screen took up the entire north wall, currently showing the most recent *Cocoon* remake. Chairs facing the screen filled most of the area. A few patients chatted in small groups, but most stayed to themselves, watching the screen or staring off into space.

Kendall took Susan to a slender, dark-skinned man sitting in a chair against the wall. Dressed in a crimson-and-white bathrobe, he kept his arms clenched to his chest, rocking back and forth, humming a complicated tune. He seemed not to notice their approach.

"Mr. Heaton," Kendall said loudly, "I'd like you to meet Dr. Susan Calvin, my partner."

Susan supposed "partner" worked. The words "fellow resident" might be misunderstood, especially in an institution setting. "Pleased to meet you, maestro." Susan held out her hand.

Thomas' eyes rolled up to meet her gaze, but he otherwise remained exactly as he had been, rocking rhythmically with his arms folded. His expression was lax, empty, emotionally flat. His dark eyes looked watery, older than their years, and utterly devoid of passion of any kind.

As he made absolutely no move to shake her hand, Susan retracted it.

Kendall defined what Susan saw in medical terminology. "The poster child for flat affect."

"Catatonia?" Susan suggested, knowing full well it did not fit.

Catatonia was most often associated with schizophrenia, which usually developed in the late teens to midtwenties. Sixty was not impossible, but extremely unlikely—a classic zebra. To ascribe other causes of catatonia meant stretching well beyond the given information.

Kendall shook his head, then grasped Thomas' arm at the wrist. Raising it to above head level, he let it fall suddenly. The arm flopped bonelessly to Thomas' lap, as if it was too much effort to resist, nothing like the waxy flexibility consistent with catatonia. Those patients would leave their limbs exactly where someone placed them for hours or days on end. "Can't find anything infectious or metabolic. Lab tests all completely normal."

Susan bobbed her head. Considering the prior normality and high functioning of the patient and his sudden deterioration, the medical teams must have extensively ruled out a physiological cause for Thomas Heaton's behavior. "Anything at all on his neurological studies?"

"Nothing." Kendall tucked the palm-pross under his arm and headed back toward the charting area to discuss the patient in private.

Susan followed silently, waiting for Kendall to elaborate, which he did once they stepped inside and closed the door.

"Shortly after the accident, they did a neurological exam. No muscular weaknesses. No changes in sensation. Cranial nerves two through twelve all intact. He could name the last five presidents, count backward by fives and threes from a hundred, balance with eyes open and closed on either foot, touch his finger to his nose, name letters and numbers. And they found no papilledema."

A tumor, inflammation, or other obstruction could have caused an increase in intracranial pressure often visualized by ophthalmoscope as swelling of the optic discs, called papilledema. More relevant to the injury, a subarachnoid hemorrhage could also cause papilledema, but the symptoms described did not fit the picture. "And later? When the symptoms developed?"

"Still normal on all counts."

"So . . . physiological causes completely ruled out. It's definitely psychological." Susan knew from experience that differentiating mechanical, physical, and biochemical processes from mental health issues could be intensely challenging. However, in the case of a man like Thomas Heaton, she knew no doctor would send him here unless all possible physical issues had been fully addressed.

"Definitely psychological," Kendall confirmed. "Although, for completeness' sake, there was one finding on the head CT. One tiny hypodense area in the left occipital lobe."

Susan tried to seize on that, but it seemed more of a red herring than a useful fact. Light areas on CT usually indicated pus, blood, cysts, or tumors. "What did Neuro make of it?"

"Bit of blood from the injury or, possibly, a hallucinoma." Kendall used a slang term for an artifact, a lesion seen on a scan that does not actually exist and was usually due to a misinterpretation, a bit of misplaced material, or a smudge. "A follow-up scan six months later didn't show it."

Susan suggested another possibility. "Posterior cerebral artery stroke."

Kendall rolled his eyes down to Susan's, speaking with clear reluctance. "Considered," he admitted. "I had to look that one up. How did you know off the top of your head?"

The realization was painful, and Susan wished Kendall had not asked. "I was dating a neurosurgeon, so I brushed up on my neuroanatomy fairly recently."

"Right." Focused wholly on the patient, Kendall did not seem to notice Susan's discomfort. "They did think of posterior cerebral artery stroke, but the findings on physical exam didn't match. No homonymous hemianopsia, for starters."

Practically diagnostic for posterior cerebral artery strokes, homonymous hemianopsia consisted of complete loss of either the right half or the left half of the visual field in both eyes. Patients with these less-common types of strokes often had little or no loss of speech or muscle control but, instead, ran into walls, furniture, or people that did not appear to them to exist. They could see the world from the outside of one eye and the inside of the other eye, seeming to make a complete picture, but they were entirely blind on the opposite side.

Susan nodded, making no further suggestions and allowing Kendall to voice the next idea. She had thoughts, but nothing firm, and she did not want to steal his thunder.

Kendall did not disappoint her. "I'm thinking the near catatonia has to stem from severe depression. He has no prior history of psychiatric disease and no manic episodes, so it's probably a pure depression. Until we get him talking again, I don't really see we can do much for him."

Again Susan nodded. Given his age, the new onset of primary depression seemed unlikely. To determine a secondary cause, whether physical or emotional, they needed the patient's cooperation to evaluate him. "I'm assuming he's already on antidepressants, correct? This is Last Resortville, and I can't see anyone sending him here until he's failed Neurology, followed by Inpatient and Outpatient Psych."

Kendall hesitated, then swept a jumble of individually packaged gauze pads to the side before placing the palm-press squarely on the desk. He pressed a couple of buttons. "Antidepressants were tried." He sounded disappointed. "Without success."

Susan quoted Dr. Hansen, one of the attending psychiatrists she had worked under at Manhattan Hasbro. "Probably at wimp's doses. We could try something that might actually work."

Kendall could not help laughing. "And if it's toxic to him?"

Susan flushed. "I'm talking high normal doses, not overdoses. And I'm not saying you should use Hansen's approach most of the time. Not even Hansen uses Hansen's approach on every patient. But it seems appropriate in a case like this one, where standard therapy has failed and we might have a reachable person with a treatable problem buried in an overwhelming depression. Especially here." She waved an arm to remind him of the hopelessness of their surroundings. While a significant number of patients did leave Unit 1, the other two units were essentially long-term sentences of deterioration and death.

Kendall chewed his lower lip and followed her gesture with a roll of his eyes that did not appear to take in anything. He was clearly deep in thought, if evidenced only by the fact that his mouth remained closed and no jokes emerged. Susan suddenly realized his wisecracks had become fewer and farther between since Remington's death, and, to her surprise, she missed them.

"Some might argue Hansen's approach is wiser *because* of the risk of extrapyramidal side effects. Maybe it brings them out early, instead of waiting until a patient's been on the drugs for years, when the effects are more persistent. When caught early in treatment, those side effects almost always subside with simple discontinuation. When they develop years later, tapering the drug can actually make the condition worse." It was an argument Susan had considered many times since Hansen had presented it. She shrugged. "Hansen's no spring chicken, his patients love him, he's respected in the field, and he has no lawsuits against him. That's anecdotal, but it does suggest his approach is not the catastrophe many of our professors believe."

Few things happened quickly in medicine. Cowed by regulation and lawsuits, companies put new procedures and drugs through rigorous testing in multiple stages. Doctors worried to change established practices because "deviation from standard of care" was the gold standard for malpractice litigation. Even if correct in every way, a bold doctor risked losing everything: his reputation, his possessions, his livelihood.

Susan often wondered if balance was even possible.

Kendall caught and held Susan's gaze, as if watching for some evidence of approval or indication he had made a mistake. "So, we bombard Mr. Heaton with Hansen's doses of one of the fourth-generation antidepressants and see if we can bring him around enough to find the root cause of his mood issues."

Susan forced a grin. Those also came few and far between in the last year. "That sounds like a perfect plan." Then, as Kendall still seemed to be studying her, seeking reassurance, she added, "Exactly what I would do."

That seemed to satisfy him at last. He let out a pent-up breath, and the corners of his mouth twitched upward. "So it is written; so let it be done." He turned to his palm-pross, typing in new orders for Thomas Heaton. "What do you think of getting some earphones on him playing symphonies? As he comes out of his depression, music may reach him quicker than anything else."

Before Susan could reply, a solidly built nurse whose name she had not yet learned approached. Susan turned her attention to the woman, encouraging her to speak.

"Chuck's results are back. I thought you'd want to look at them right away."

Susan nodded with a smile. "Thanks. I do." She hooked another palm-pross with her index finger and pulled it in front of her. Quickly, she typed her code and brought up Chuck's information. The results from the lumbar puncture were on the first page. The official reading confirmed xanthochromia, a yellow tinge to the fluid. The cause was immediately obvious: a protein level of 3280 mg/dl, while the normal range was 15 to 60. Few things could explain a level that high, and only one seemed plausible.

Kendall's fingers froze on the keys, and he turned in Susan's direction. Apparently, she had made some sort of sign or motion, because he crooked one eyebrow and said out of the side of his mouth, "Raining in paradise?"

"Chuck Tripler needs an MRI." Susan looked at her Vox, which already read 5:07 p.m. She doubted an after-hours expensive test would go over any better than her earlier suggestion. She rose, determined despite the attending's negativity, despite the hour, despite her irritation. She looked at the nurse, who still stood there, awaiting her decision. "And he's going to get it ASAP."

"Dr. Reefes has gone home," the nurse informed Susan.

"Hang Dr. Reefes." Susan meant the words more literally than she ever had in her life. "I'm authorizing it, and I'm going with him."

A grin wreathed the nurse's face. Though it flew fully against regulations, undermining the chain of command, she made no protest. "I'll call Hasbro and Transport. Realistically, it'll probably take forty-five minutes to get everything arranged and moving."

"That's fine," Susan said. It took her a moment to think like a person accustomed to regular hours. The shift change would occur at seven, which meant someone would either have to stay late for several hours or the MRI order should not go out until after six fifteen. Based on their earlier conversation, Susan knew that paying overtime wages would not please Dr. Reefes.

Chuck Tripler had waited years for this diagnosis; he could certainly last an additional hour. Yet Susan's conscience and curiosity could not. "I'll go with him. We won't need any staff, just a driver."

With barely a nod, the nurse rushed from the staffing room to make the appropriate calls.

Kendall had had plenty of time to read the results of the cerebrospinal fluid analysis. "Tumor, huh?"

Susan nodded dully. "Obviously slow growing. Probably benign."

"So . . . how do you explain the Lewy bodies? The parkinsonism? The NPH symptoms?"

Susan had a theory, but she wanted to search the literature, make sure it made logical and coherent sense before presenting it to Dr. Reefes. "I'm . . . not sure. I want to see what the MRI shows first."

"The *forbidden* MRI," Kendall reminded her unnecessarily. "How are you going to get that past the powers that be?"

Susan smiled. "I don't think I'll need my rapier tongue for Reefes. The MRI will say it all."

"Let's hope so." Kendall slammed shut his palm-pross.

"See you tomorrow?" Susan planned to finish up her charting while waiting for the transport shuttle and driver.

"Tomorrow!" Kendall gave a greatly exaggerated look of effrontery, hands mashing his narrow waist, arms formed into indignant triangles. "Did you really think I'd let you have all the fun? I'm coming with you."

Susan might have protested had she not so much appreciated his company.

Chapter 5

Arranging the MRI, meeting with the busy on-call radiologist to go over the results, and returning Chuck Tripler to Winter Wine Dementia Facility had taken until the wee morning hours. Susan and Kendall had spent the night at Kendall's apartment, only a three-block walk from work. There he had collapsed, fully dressed, onto his bed, while she spent the next several hours researching, on his palm-pross and her Vox, the findings on Chuck's MRI and how they might mesh with the history and physical examination.

So Susan found herself exhausted and fuzzy-headed when Dr. Mitchell Reefes finally arrived the following morning and sequestered himself in his office. Rereading the same page of the palm-pross for the fourth time, Susan glanced toward Kendall, who gave her a sheepish shrug. "Time to face the music, Calvin."

With a sigh, Susan rose. "You coming?"

Kendall consulted the whiteboard in the Unit 1 staffing area, which contained a new name: Jessica Aberdeen. He looked back at Susan and smiled. "I wouldn't miss it for the world." Leaping to his feet, he followed Susan toward Dr. Reefes' office.

The short journey took longer than it should have, and Susan realized she dreaded the confrontation. She stopped to examine her Vox twice, to ascertain it still held the tiny image of Chuck Tripler's MRI.

The second time, Kendall glanced over her shoulder. "It hasn't miraculously flipped to your grocery list or the doggy-style porn network, has it?"

Startled, Susan glared at him. "There's a network?"

Kendall rolled his eyes. "How would I know? Do I look like a pervert?"

Susan declined to answer, but she paused long enough to indicate the possibility might have crossed her mind. "I'm just . . ."

"Stalling?" Kendall suggested.

Susan had been about to say "making sure," but she realized Kendall was probably right. "Fine, I'm stalling. Sue me. I don't want a bad review, but I can't help loathing the man."

"And you're afraid you might castrate him." Kendall nodded thoughtfully. "I could see where that might just get you a bad review."

"Whatever." Susan crossed her arms over her chest, then rechecked the Vox, concerned she might have pressed buttons with her gesture; but the MRI picture remained. "Could you stop referring to my verbal altercations as castration? People will get the wrong idea."

"Not the ones who know . . . either of us."

"They're not the ones I'm worried about." Susan recognized even this conversation as a delaying tactic. "Now, let's get this over with." Raising a hand, she knocked at the door.

"Come in." As always, Dr. Reefes sounded distracted.

When Susan did not immediately obey, Kendall nudged her. "You okay?" he asked softly, so his voice would not penetrate the door.

Susan nodded, though the movement intensified her dizziness. She could function well enough, but her thoughts seemed to require extra time to form, and a permanent fog appeared to have descended over her mind. It wasn't the first time she had pulled an all-nighter, but this time it bothered her more, perhaps because she currently wanted her thoughts to be entirely clear. The MRI findings were complicated, her theories on the situation much more so, and her relationship with her attending dicey at best. She twisted the knob and opened the door.

Without bothering to look up, Dr. Reefes waved the residents into the room. Both entered, Susan leading, and Kendall paused to shut the door behind them. The attending did not wait for either of his charges to speak. "You need to look at this MRI on Chuck Tripler."

Susan took the chair in front of Dr. Reefes' desk, trying not to look too smug. "We've seen it."

Dr. Reefes did not seem to hear her. "Look at this. There's a big, honking tumor at the L2 vertebral level."

Susan clarified, in medical terminology, "Intradural extramedullary growth in the cauda equina." She referred to the bundle of nerves that occupied the spinal column below the termination of the spinal cord, so named because of their resemblance to a horse's tail. "Intradural" and "extramedullary" referred to the location of the tumor, within the confines of the membrane, or dura, surrounding the spinal cord but outside of the cord itself. "Almost certainly benign and, odds on, either a schwannoma, a neuroblastoma, or a meningioma."

Dr. Reefes said irritably, "According to the radiologist's report, yes." Clearly, he intended to suggest Susan had taken all of her information from the report, thereby belittling all of her knowledge and research. Susan had not read the radiology report because she had discussed the matter directly with the radiologist shortly after the MRI. Apparently, Dr. Amani Sharna had used much of their conversation in her commentary.

Susan could feel her blood warming, heat rising to her cheeks, but she suppressed her anger and stepped to Dr. Reefes' side to look over his shoulder. The screen was filled with spinal images demonstrating osseous erosions and a hypodense mass that became hyperdense on the T2 weighted images. Susan reached around him to hit the keys, bringing up some of the other MRI images until she found the brain slices she wanted in the middle cranial fossa. "The temporal horns of the lateral ventricles are disproportionately enlarged." She highlighted them. "At least when compared to the sulci, which are normal-sized."

Kendall took the seat Susan had vacated, the only one in the room other than Dr. Reefes' own. "A benign tumor of the cauda equina doesn't cause ventricular dilatation. It's too far removed to cause direct obstruction."

Susan fought a smile. Kendall was deliberately setting up her hypothesis. She appreciated that he was going to allow her to deliver the coup de grâce. "It has to be normal pressure hydrocephalus." They had returned to Susan's original point, that Chuck Tripler had one of the rare treatable forms of dementia. She did not add that the reason she knew the pressure was normal was because she had performed the forbidden lumbar puncture.

Dr. Reefes sat back, practically mumbling. He seemed to be speaking to himself more than the residents. "Tumors of the cauda equina don't cause NPH."

Susan knew he would not have the answer. Practically no one who had not done the research on the rare situations she had undertaken the previous night would. "But they can cause massively elevated protein levels, which increases the turbidity of the CSF. Sludging could block the ventricles and lead to NPH."

It was not common knowledge outside of neurology, but Dr. Reefes accepted the premise without comment.

Slouching in the chair, Kendall helped Susan out again. "But what about the positive test for Lewy bodies? Are you suggesting Mr. Chuck Tripler just happens to have NPH, a tumor of the cauda equina, *and* Parkinson's disease simultaneously, without any connection? That seems like an amazing coincidence." He gave her a mock-hopeful look and a broad wink.

Susan suddenly wished she had not discussed the explanation with

Kendall on the way in to work that morning. He was turning a serious medical discussion into an infomercial.

"They all have to be related," Dr. Reefes said.

Susan considered remaining silent and putting their attending on the spot. She doubted he would come close to finding a logical explanation, at least not without scouring medical journals on the global web for the rest of the day. Even then, she did not know if he had the understanding or skill to pull it all together. However, trained to always protect the dignity of an attending, she explained, "NPH could potentially cause parkinsonism by dysfunction of the circuits linking the cortex, basal ganglia and thalamus, or due to periventricular ischemia, causing a vascular form of parkinsonism."

Susan looked thoughtfully at Dr. Reefes. It was his turn to say something, to validate her actions and logic, to admit his mistake, if only on a subtle level.

Dr. Reefes rose. Without missing a beat, he turned on Susan Calvin. "Which is why, when I tell you to perform a test, you do so right away. You don't argue with me."

"What?" The word was startled from Susan's mouth.

Reefes continued, his stance growing more rigid, his face purpling. "Chuck Tripler could have been evaluated by Neurology two days ago if you had done the lumbar puncture when I asked you to instead of waiting until it was convenient."

Susan shook her head, trying to clear it. She could not believe what she was hearing, certain she had gone schizophrenic overnight, beset by auditory and visual hallucinations. This could not be happening. "I . . . but you didn't . . ." Suddenly realizing she was about to say something vulgar, she clamped her mouth shut.

Dr. Reefes seized her by the elbow and steered her toward the door, opening it with his other hand. "I'll be transferring Mr. Tripler to Hasbro Neurology." He used a condescending tone that suggested he chose to do it himself because he did not trust her to do it. "Now get back to work, Susan, and try to keep on top of things." He shoved her through the opening.

Susan stumbled once, then whirled. Rage flashed through her, igniting her blood into a bonfire. Never in her life had she so wanted to strangle somebody. Her fingers balled into bloodless fists. She would have coldcocked him had Kendall not appeared suddenly in front of her and slammed the door behind him. Even then, she raised a fist to bang on the wooden panel standing between her and the man she fully intended to kick to a painful and immediate death.

Kendall stepped between the door and Susan's hand, catching it before it could land on the door. "He's not worth it."

"Shit, you mean?" Susan spat out.

"He's not worth having to wipe off the bottom of your shoes," Kendall affirmed, fitting eerily into her kicking-to-death scenario. "Verbally cast–" He caught himself. "–igating surgeons is one thing. Murdering an attending will almost certainly get you canned."

At the moment, Susan did not care. She could feel her fingernails biting into her palms.

"And imagine having to look at his gloating face in a courtroom while he sues you for assault."

That did it. Susan dropped her arm to her side, whirled violently, and stormed toward the nearest staffing area. Kendall followed her, step light and cautious, as if he feared the slightest noise or action might set her off again or turn her rage against him.

Susan threw herself into a chair, still fuming. "You know what that moron's going to do?"

"Of course I do." Kendall's face twitched. He was obviously fighting a grin. "He's going to call Neurology, present your case, and act like he came up with it all on his own."

Susan paled. She had only been thinking he would use some

unflattering comment like "lazy" on her evaluation. That would upset her, but would probably get lost among the larger number of glowing reports. Not that every superior appreciated her style. A few had labeled her "distracted" in the months following Remington's death. Others had referred to her as smug or overconfident, although all had appreciated her diagnostic acumen. Somewhat of a perfectionist, she found every criticism irritating, but the unjust ones gnawed at her. Dr. Reefes had no right to refer to anyone else as lazy. The realization that Kendall was right only reignited the fire.

"Then he'll get the"—Kendall put his palms together, then tipped his head against the back of one hand and assumed a falsetto—"'My, aren't you just so clever.'" He batted his eyes as he spoke, then dropped his hands to his sides. "And the balloons in the hallways. And the ticker-tape parade."

Susan wanted to slap him, but in her current mood, she was afraid she might hurt him. "Ha, ha, ha," she said, her tone dripping sarcasm. "All that matters is Chuck getting the treatment he needs. Who cares who takes the credit?"

"Who, indeed?" Kendall had made his point, then his brow furrowed. "What the hell is ticker tape, anyway?"

Susan sat back, glad for the distraction. "It's just confetti thrown from windows over a parade. Originally, it was bits of—" She looked up to find Kendall studying her, brows raised in anticipation. "Rhetorical?"

"Of course." Kendall chuckled. "But leave it to Susan Calvin to have the answer on the tip of her tongue."

Kendall had become Susan's closest friend, and she wondered why she so often felt like doing him grievous bodily harm.

"So." Kendall flopped down into the chair beside Susan. "The good news is, when you've started the morning with a superior taking credit for your hard work, then upbraiding you for not doing exactly what you did, nothing worse can happen to you the rest of the day."

Susan nodded at the new twist on the Mark Twain quote about eating a live frog. "What's in store for us?"

"Two new admissions." Kendall tapped some keys on the nearest palm-pross. "You want the young newbie? Or the old woman who keeps bouncing in and out of here every few months?"

Susan had learned the previous year to let others do the choosing. She tended to cure her patients and cared little for the innuendo that she selected them solely to make herself look more competent than her peers. In some cases, she had gotten lucky, but, mostly, she had a keen eye and ear and knew how to put knowledge and diagnostic details together. "You pick."

Kendall shrugged. "Fine. I'll take Barbara Callahan. She's the bouncer. Reefes put up a fight about taking her at all, and you don't need any more confrontations with him." He shoved a palm-pross toward Susan. "You get Jessica Aberdeen."

Dutifully, Susan typed in her identification and passcode. "We came in together. How did you find out about the new patients?"

"Musica filled me in." Kendall gestured randomly, but Susan knew he meant one of the young nurses. "I went to check on Thomas Heaton first thing, and she corralled me."

Susan teased, "Maybe she has a thing for you." Her conversation with her father two nights ago flashed to the fore. She had mentioned to John Calvin that she had never seen Kendall date anyone. Now the reason became instantly clear. Within two weeks of their first rotation, Remington had died and Susan wound up in intensive care. Kendall partially blamed himself, and it made sense he had not resumed whatever social life he might have had prior to starting his residency. She had not had any interest in pursuing a relationship since the trauma, either.

Kendall did not hesitate. "I doubt it." He twirled a lock of his ginger hair around his index finger. "Lots of men have a thing for redheads, but women . . ." He shrugged. "Especially when you have freckles, they see you as a romantic prospect about as serious as Howdy Doody."

Susan's brows shot up. "Ticker-tape parades? Howdy Doody? Have we been transported back a century? And how do you expect women to take you seriously when you're always joking?"

Kendall ignored the last part of her point for the first. "This place is getting to me," he admitted. "Immerse me in a world of senile ninety-year-olds, most of whom are still living in the 1960s, and my references get a bit . . . stale."

Susan was pretty sure real ticker-tape parades and Howdy Doody predated the sixties, but she did not argue. "And the constant joking?"

Kendall shrugged. "A great sense of humor tops nearly every list of what women want in a man."

Susan could not help ribbing. "That's assuming your joking around is actually funny."

"Oooow." Kendall clutched his chest and screwed up his face. "You've shot me right through the heart."

"Sorry," Susan said, knowing she did not sound it. Though they had put the morning's events behind them, they still colored her thoughts and actions. She typed "Jessica Alberdine" into her palm-pross and gleaned nothing. She showed the error message to Kendall.

"Aberdeen," Kendall corrected. "No *l*, and 'deen' with two *e*'s."

Susan retyped the name, and a description in medical terminology, written by the transferring doctor, popped onto the screen: "J.A. is a forty-four-year-old white female with progressive memory loss and disorientation six months post skull fracture with complete recovery."

Susan assumed the referring physician meant Jessica had completely recovered from the skull fracture, not from the progressive memory loss and disorientation. She continued reading: "Family history positive for breast cancer in the maternal grandmother, mother, and paternal aunt. There is also a strong family history of early-onset Alzheimer's disease in paternal grandfather and two uncles, one of whom died in his late thirties. Social history negative for smoking, alcohol, or illicit drugs. She takes no medications. Brain MRI shows generalized mild atrophy, with no discrete lesions. Alpha-synuclein test is negative, ruling out parkinsonism or Lewy body dementia. Diagnosis: early-onset Alzheimer's versus post-traumatic dementia. Treatment: transfer to Winter Wine Dementia Facility."

Susan sat back, her encounter with Dr. Mitchell Reefes receding to the back of memory, an irritation lost beneath consideration of her new patient. Nothing in the presentation suggested Jessica Aberdeen would not take her proper place among the residents of the dementia facility, moving from one unit to the next as the years passed. Neither early-onset Alzheimer's nor post-traumatic dementia had viable treatments. She would go on the usual assortment of cholinesterase inhibitors and NMDA receptor antagonists until they no longer helped to slow the process; then it would take her like all the others.

Susan sighed heavily, suddenly wishing she had chosen the older patient. The horrors of dementia, the desperate slide into oblivion surrounded by hopeless patients upset Susan enough without having to visit with one so inexplicably young. Jessica would not be the youngest patient at Winter Wine; Unit 3 had a twenty-seven-year-old with variant Creutzfeldt-Jakob disease, and Unit 2 held a nineteen-year-old with Neimann-Pick. Still, the idea of giving up on a forty-four-year-old woman rankled. *Maybe, just maybe, I'll see something on physical examination that gives me hope for something treatable.*

Susan shoved the palm-pross aside, sighed, and rose. She glanced around, but Kendall had already left to tend his own patients. Susan headed for Unit 1. The board indicated Jessica occupied private room number 8, so Susan headed for the door and knocked.

To her surprise, a happy female voice sang out, "Come in!"

Surprised to find any patient here so lucid, Susan opened the door to discover a skinny, middle-aged woman propped in the bed, and the young nurse they knew as Musica arranging a portable dining table. Apparently, it was the nurse who had responded, because Jessica barely acknowledged Susan's presence by rolling her eyes in the doctor's direction. Musica, however, greeted her cheerily—"Good morning, Dr. Calvin"—in the same cadence as the earlier communication. "I was just about to serve Jessica some lunch. Would you like me to wait?"

Susan's gaze drifted to the tray, which contained a series of plastic containers that did not resemble the standard hospital-issued items. "Did she pack it in?"

The nurse hesitated a moment, then followed the direction of Susan's gaze. "Oh. No, of course not. She's on a special diet."

Susan continued to study the containers. One held a white liquid, apparently milk. The other was a bowl filled with some sort of casserole. Susan could make out green beans, mushrooms, and wide noodles. She could not, however, fathom the nurse's words. As Jessica's physician, Susan would specify the woman's diet when she wrote the rest of her orders. "Special diet? Who authorized this?"

The nurse set her jaw, but her gaze dodged Susan's. "I . . . Dr. Reefes . . . said it would be . . . all right."

At the moment, Susan did not feel kindly disposed toward her attending. She wondered why he had decided to involve himself in a patient's food preferences when he rarely bothered with anything else about them, including appropriate care. "Where did this food come from?"

"Her father brought it." Musica shifted from foot to foot, clearly uncomfortable. "He's a naturopath. The whole family's vegan, and he was quite insistent . . ." She finally looked directly at Susan.

Susan did not mean to intimidate the nurse. "Okay." She had nothing against vegan diets, in principle, although she could not help thinking of her militant colleague, Nevaeh, who considered anyone who ate

meat a murderer. Realizing that her irritation with Dr. Reefes had probably entered her tone and manner, she tried to soften them. "So, what's
on the menu for Jessica?"

Musica managed a smile, pointing to the objects on the tray. "Vegetable noodle casserole, a slice of zucchini bread, and a nice, cold cup
of soy milk." She indicated each object in turn. "And I get to help her
eat it, but not until after you've examined her, if you prefer."

Susan considered taking the offer; doctors' schedules usually took
priority over the ancillary staff. Here, however, Susan felt like the inter-
loper. Given Dr. Reefes' mostly hands-off approach, the nurses performed most of the patient care, suggesting courses of action he normally
simply okayed, often without bothering to examine the patient, at least
not the ones on the higher-number units. Besides, Susan suspected vegetable noodle casserole would taste a whole lot better still warm. "No,
you go ahead." She waved at the food and turned to leave. Then, a
thought came to her, and she stopped midstride. "Don't we have other
vegetarians in the facility?"

"Quite a few." Musica pulled the lid off the container and stirred
the contents with a plastic fork. "We handle several types of special
diets on Unit One." She waved the fork vaguely toward the other units.
"By Two, the families are pretty much resigned to let them eat whatever we can get them to take. By Three, they're all on the same mushy
mixture of essential nutrients." She puckered up her face. "We call it
Soylent Gray, which is apparently some reference to an old movie."

Susan chuckled, then did her best Charlton Heston imitation,
"'Soylent Green is made of people! You've got to tell them. Soylent Green is
people!'"

Musica watched her curiously, then laughed. "Well, I'm sure Soylent
Gray isn't made of people. I don't think there's anything organic in it."
She fed a forkful of the casserole to Jessica, who chewed it indifferently.

"It looks and smells like paste, but the patients don't seem to care." She gave Jessica another mouthful. "Of course, by that stage, they don't care about anything."

Susan brought the conversation back to her concern. "Can't the kitchen handle vegan food?"

Musica did not follow Susan's sudden backtrack. "For Unit Three? They choke on invisible lumps. You think we'd risk a plant fiber?"

Susan shook her head briskly. "No, I mean for Jessica. Why does her family have to bring her food? Can't the kitchen make vegan fare?"

Musica set down the bowl. "Would you like a drink, Jessica?"

Jessica nodded, and Musica lifted the soy milk to her lips. The patient took a few small sips; then the nurse removed the cup. A line of white drool rolled off Jessica's bottom lip, and Musica wiped it away with a napkin.

The nurse switched back to Susan's question. "Oh, sure. I mean, they've made vegan before, but her family insists she's allergic to all kinds of additives and preservatives. They make all of her food, and they don't want her having anything they didn't personally prepare." She returned to feeding Jessica. "If you ask me, it sounds like a lot of work. Their entire life must revolve around food preparation."

Susan nodded absently, her mind several steps beyond the conversation. She knew many vegetarians, and their reasons for choosing a meat-free diet ranged from cultural to religious, from ethical to health conscious, always well intentioned. Much like their omnivorous counterparts, however, their execution of their chosen diet varied from the sublime to the idiotic. The healthy ones learned how to build balanced meals that incorporated the necessary vitamins, minerals, and amino acids. Those who survived on Pop-Tarts, Ho Hos, and corn did their minds and bodies more harm than good.

Musica apparently read something in Susan's expression. "Are you going to want to change her diet? Because I think you'll have a fight on your hands if you do."

"I don't doubt it." Susan had no intention of taking Jessica off her family's preferred diet, simply adding to it. The standard-admission laboratory studies included a complete blood count, which Susan suspected might help explain Jessica's decline, and a general profile that gave a nonspecific picture of liver, kidney, and circulatory function. "Could you hold the labs for a bit? I have a few extras I want to tack on, and I'll need to write them down." Susan knew exactly what she needed but did not want to rattle off a bunch of specialized labs without knowing the capacity of Musica's memory.

Clearly, Jessica's family physician had not fully explored the details of her diet. He had likely and understandably focused on the family history of early-onset dementia. Since the fortification of breakfast cereals, breads, cow and soy milk, and salt, nutritional deficiencies of any kind had become exceedingly rare in America, and most of those stemmed from individual metabolic errors. The father had probably assured him Jessica's diet was nutritionally sound and had nothing to do with her current condition, but Susan suspected otherwise. She needed confirmation from the examination and laboratory tests, but she had a feeling she knew exactly what was causing Jessica Aberdeen's dementia.

Chapter 6

By late afternoon, a dense and inescapable fatigue enveloped Susan, and she felt as if she were performing patient care in an unthinking trance. The Winter Wine lifers functioned best with a stable routine the nurses had perfected over many decades. With residents around most of the year to handle the rare problems, changes, and new admissions, Mitchell Reefes had little to do. Susan could understand how he had developed his laissez-faire attitude toward his patients, though she would never condone it.

Startled by a shaking of her arm, Susan turned to face Kendall Stevens. "Asleep on the job, Calvin?" he asked with an insolent smile.

"Just resting my eyes." Susan gave her grandmother's favorite reply after being caught snoring in front of the video screen. She did not believe she had actually fallen asleep; she could not remember losing her train of thought or dreaming. "I'm waiting for some labs on Jessica Aberdeen. What do you need?"

"Just being a pest." Kendall sat down beside Susan. "The usual." He ran a hand solidly through his hair, leaving the carrot-colored strands sticking straight up in clownish patches. "I think the antidepressant blast is already doing Thomas Heaton some good. I put headphones on him, playing Beethoven symphonies, and he's moving his arms. It's too uncoordinated for conducting, but I think that's what he's trying to do.

Also, he looked straight at me today, and I even saw a hint of actual sadness rather than yesterday's statue face."

"That's encouraging." Susan managed a weary smile of her own. "Is Beethoven his favorite composer?"

Kendall hesitated. "I don't actually know. His family hasn't been around to ask yet. Have you ever met an orchestraphile who didn't love Beethoven?"

Susan did not know any orchestraphiles or even if there was any such word. Kendall was not above making up any word he thought sounded funny. "I've met dog lovers who don't care for Labradors and wine aficionados who compare Château Lafite Rothschild to minty fruit juice, so I imagine every enthusiast has biases that might surprise us."

"Speaking of families . . ."–Kendall turned Susan a hopeful look–"I'm about to meet with Barbara Callahan's. Want to come?"

At the moment, Susan would have appreciated nothing more than a nice, warm bed. However, the idea of getting caught sleeping by Dr. Mitchell Reefes rankled, and she thought it best to find something, anything, to make her appear busy. "Yeah, all right. Can I read the chart first?"

"I'll give you the highlights." Kendall cleared his throat. "Normally sweet woman well into her seventies. She spent a week in here about three months ago, improved without any significant treatment, and returned home. She bounced back last month, completely demented, and stayed for eleven days. By the time of discharge, she had her full faculties again." He looked up. "And I do mean full. She could do complicated math problems and was reading romance novels in large print." He continued his recitation. "Now she's back, deeply demented again."

"Anything interesting on examination?"

Kendall shrugged. "She apparently thinks it's 1982."

"How so?"

"Ronald Reagan is president, and Princess Diana just gave birth to a male heir."

"Princess who?"

Kendall smiled. "I looked it up. Trust me; it's 1982. Counting by sevens backward from one hundred, she gave me: ninety-two . . . ninety . . . thirty-six . . . seven . . . three. And her clock has ten numbers, all of them on the right-hand side."

"Aaah." Susan recognized those as unmistakable signs. "Clearly not the gradual slide you expect from most forms of dementia."

"Clearly not."

"Something in her environment?"

"That's what I intend to find out."

"Hmmm." Susan wished she did not have to struggle past exhaustion just to think. "I'm game. Let's start asking." She hoped hopping up from her seat would put her in a more energetic mood, but it only managed to make her dizzy. Groggy, she followed Kendall from the staffing room, through the proper series of doors, to the family meeting area.

The small room had meticulous white walls, a long table for large family conferences, and multiple chairs. A tiny kitchenette took up most of one wall, with spigots for hot water and packets of hot chocolate, several types of tea, and instant coffee. A refrigerator sized for a college dormitory contained sealed cups of a multitude of juices, and an open cabinet held packages of saltines and graham crackers.

Two people currently occupied chairs at the table on the side opposite the door. As Susan and Kendall entered, the couple rose, a balding man in his early fifties and a narrow-faced woman who looked a few years younger. Both wore standard work khakis and dress polos, indicating they had come straight from their jobs. The woman's short-cut tresses were muddy brown, matching what remained of the man's hair, and they both studied the newcomers through similar blue-green eyes.

Kendall strode in with impressive confidence, one hand extended.

"I'm Dr. Kendall Stevens." He shook hands with the man, who was closer. "And this is my colleague, Dr. Susan Calvin." He released the man's hand to take the woman's.

Susan nodded to each, closing the door behind them.

The woman spoke first, Kendall's hand in hers. "I'm Bambi Amber-sod, and this is my brother, Caden Callahan. We're Barbara's children."

"Pleased to meet you." Kendall pulled up two chairs across from the couple and sat in one. Susan accepted the other chair, and the children of Barbara Callahan returned to their own seats. "We'd like to ask some questions about your mother, and I'm sure you have some for us as well."

Caden's voice was a low rumble. "The first of which is why she keeps ending up here. Is this a common way for Alzheimer's to present?"

"Your mother does not have Alzheimer's," Susan said with authority, then wished she had kept her mouth shut. As every eye turned toward her, she no longer had the option of tossing the lead back to Kendall, who deserved it. Barbara was his patient. Susan sat up straighter. "Symptoms of Alzheimer's don't fluctuate much from day to day. The disease starts off with mild short-term memory loss, then progresses. You never see wild swings from frank dementia to normality and back."

Kendall added, "Migraines can occasionally cause sudden bouts of bizarre mental deterioration, but they rarely last longer than a couple of hours."

Susan could think of a few other exceedingly rare problems, but none fit Barbara Callahan's picture, so she did not mention them. It suddenly occurred to her she had a distinct and irritating tendency to blurt out her observations, which might explain some of the reasons peers considered her an irksome know-it-all. Not for the first time, she wondered why Kendall sought her out as a coworker when most of the others avoided her, and realized it probably had less to do with her charm and more to do with his own insecurities.

Bambi perked up considerably. "So . . . this isn't the start of . . . of . . . Alzheimer's?"

Susan kept her mouth firmly shut.

"Definitely not," Kendall said, with as much authority as Susan had used earlier. He had known all along, of course, had not needed Susan's input, but it clearly buoyed him. "That's not to say she can't ever develop the disease; anyone can. But it won't have anything to do with her current episodes of intermittent dementia."

Caden tipped his head. Clearly not one to show a lot of emotion, he did breathe a subtle sigh of relief. "So, what's causing this to happen?"

Again, Susan pursed her lips, allowing Kendall to speak for his own patient. She intended to do that a lot more often in the future. Kendall needed her to do that, to learn to rely on his own vast intelligence and store of knowledge. And she needed to learn how to listen more and talk less.

As if to advance her theory, Kendall glanced at Susan before continuing, "Given the episodes come on suddenly at home and resolve relatively quickly here, I think the cause is environmental."

Bambi suggested, "Mold? A radon leak? Pollution?"

Susan shook her head and spoke before she could stop herself. "Extremely unlikely. Does she take any medications?" *Damn it. Couldn't make it two minutes before opening my big mouth.*

Caden shrugged a shoulder in apparent ignorance. Bambi looked thoughtful for a moment. "She's always been very active, very healthy. She took some multivitamins for a while, but her doctor took her off them after the first episode. She might take an Advil now and then, a Tums, but she's not on anything regularly."

Neither of those was known to cause dementialike symptoms, even as an idiosyncratic reaction. "What about antihistamines? Does she have intermittent allergies?"

Caden looked at his hands; he clearly did not know his mother as well as his sister did. Bambi shook her head. "Mom lives alone, since Dad died six years ago. She prefers to remain independent. Since this started, I've thought about taking her home to live with me, but we're already taking care of my husband's mother, who's in fragile health, and they don't get along." She glanced meaningfully at Caden.

The brother knotted his fingers. "We're not in a position to take her in, either." He did not elaborate. Susan felt certain Bambi was pressuring him to do so. Though she surely meant well, not everyone had the patience, time, or ability to handle a senile loved one. If Caden could not take care of his mother for any reason, bullying or shaming him into accepting the burden would do no one any good and could cause great harm.

Realizing she had not gotten the answer to her question, Susan asked it again. "Antihistamine use?"

"I don't believe so," Bambi said. "She's certainly never complained about those types of symptoms, and I don't recall her sniffling, except with normal colds, of course."

Susan nodded thoughtfully. Long gone were the days when people gulped down worthless antihistamines, antibiotics, and decongestants for upper-respiratory symptoms. She recalled the other medications that risked causing dementialike reactions in the elderly were given for chronic conditions like seizures, depression and anxiety, cardiac diseases, and inflammatory illnesses. Kendall would have told her if Barbara suffered from any of those.

"Where does she live?" Kendall asked. "Does she have any idiosyncrasies, unusual hobbies, pets?"

"Upper East Side." Bambi answered the string of questions in turn.

"Nothing weird. She likes to cook, read romance novels, and knit. She has a cat, Mr. Tibbs, who's got to be fourteen or fifteen now. Dad hated him."

"Dad didn't hate that cat," Caden inserted. "He just pretended to hate that cat. Whenever I came by, Tibbs was in Dad's lap getting petted. As soon as Dad saw me, he'd push the cat onto the floor, always gently, and pretend it had just jumped on him. Somehow, though, it always managed to leave him covered in gray and white hairs."

Susan did not believe the elderly cat had anything to do with Barbara's problems. A bird or reptile might raise the specter of a nonclassical infection, but a cat who had lived with her for many years was not likely to cause something new and unusual or even trigger a late-life allergy.

Bambi added thoughtfully, "Maybe we should have you talk to Emma. She's Mom's neighbor. She's younger—in her thirties, I think. Maybe early forties. A few years ago, I started paying her to check in on Mom once a day or so. Gradually, they've become good friends. I think she'd visit Mom even without the money, but I know she can use it. And Mom adores her." Bambi reached under the table. "In fact, when she found out we were coming, Emma gave us a few things she thought Mom might want during the hospitalization." Bambi pulled out a zippered cloth tote stuffed with at least one oversized item of clothing.

Kendall rose to accept the bag, set it on the floor between him and Susan, then sat again. He heaved a thoughtful sigh. "Unfortunately, environmental triggers can be notoriously difficult to pinpoint. Witness the number of people who say they're allergic to *something*, but have no idea what." He sighed again. "Given the severity of your mother's symptoms and the fact it's happened three times now, we can assume it's not just going to go away without treatment or explanation."

The children of Barbara Callahan nodded glumly. "What's the plan?" Bambi asked.

"The plan," Kendall repeated. He looked at Susan.

Susan wisely said nothing, forcing him to continue.

Kendall complied, "You search your mother's apartment and see what you find. Focus on the bathroom, kitchen, and pantry: medications, supplements, herbal teas and coffees, that kind of thing. Susan and I will talk to the neighbor and, when she's more lucid, we'll grill Mom. How does that sound?"

"Perfect." Caden rose. "Thank you, Doctors."

"Thank you," Bambi repeated, also standing. "I'll let you know if I find anything. I'm sure you'll do the same."

Still enveloped in a mental fog, Susan remained seated as Kendall walked the siblings out the door, chatting. She lay her head on her arms for a few moments, listening to the distant buzz of conversation, the clatter and scrape of Unit 1's patients, the occasional calling of the nurses for one another. Then, realizing if she did not do something she would fall asleep, Susan hooked the handles of the tote and drew it toward her.

Susan unzipped the bag, and a soft fleece sweatshirt spilled out, accompanied by a few personal effects: a well-worn brush with some missing bristles, clearly an old favorite; a grinning stuffed monkey probably won at a carnival; and a faded pair of jeans. A sweatshirt seemed like an odd necessity for a summer admission, but Susan knew the elderly residents tended to overdress for the weather. Her grandmother had often worn a pink wool sweater around the house when Susan and her father felt comfortable in shorts and tees. Barbara's sweatshirt was red and fuzzy, worn smooth in places, with an embroidered Mickey Mouse over the left breast.

Waiting for Kendall to return, Susan bunched the sweatshirt in her arms and rested her head on the fabric. It made a comfortable pillow, the fabric smooth, sweeping, cushiony against her cheek. The smell of it filled her nostrils, almost choking her with an odd, pungent aroma half burning leaves, half oily musk. She jerked her head up, shoving the offending object away, then drew it back for another tentative sniff. She knew that unique aroma, but her memory refused to process it for several moments. She took another whiff, cautious and necessary, and the answer finally came to her.

With a chuckle, Susan shoved all the items back into the bag, grabbed the handle, and took off after Kendall. As he reentered the room, she checked her headlong rush, barely avoiding a collision.

Kendall staggered against the door frame. "What the hell, Susan? Late for the racetrack?"

Susan regained her balance, grasped the sweatshirt, and hauled it from the bag. She shoved it into Kendall's face. "Smell this."

Kendall took a delicate whiff, then a deeper one. His features screwed into a caricature of disgust. "Phew! What is that? Skunk whiz?"

"I think it's marijuana."

"What?" Kendall looked at Susan as if she had gone stark raving mad.

"Marijuana," Susan repeated. "Smell it again." She shoved it deeper into Kendall's face.

Kendall pushed the offending cloth away. "It doesn't do any good to wedge it up my nose. I've never smoked the shit."

The denial made Susan defensive. "Neither have I, but I've smelled it. That unique, indescribable odor. That's marijuana." She stuffed the sweatshirt back into the bag.

Kendall's features remained bunched. "I'd hardly say 'indescribable.' It smells like burnt skunk urine. Why the hell would anyone inflict that crap on their innocent, irreplaceable lungs?" Realization suddenly flashed through his eyes. "Are you saying Grandma's a junkie?"

Susan laughed. "Probably more like an occasional user."

Kendall looked over his shoulder. "Obviously, we have to stop her. So why do I feel like a snitch ratting her out to her . . ."

"Parents?" Susan supplied.

"Well, in this case, her kids." Kendall waved in the direction Caden and Bambi had taken. "Isn't it weird how the trends go? Just when you start thinking every generation has to do everything ten times nuttier than its predecessors, you find one making healthier choices, living more fit and sensibly. My grandparents thought nothing of eating double-fried, lard-filled doughnuts on a stick and similar things that make me puke at the mere thought, combining that toxic ball of grease with a gallon of supercharged soda, then lighting up a nicotine-filled tube of death and blowing the smoke into other people's faces."

As if in answer to Kendall's rhetorical question, Nurse Musica poked her head into the conference room. "Ah, there you are, Susan. Lab wanted you to Vox up the results on Jessica Aberdeen."

"Thanks." For an instant, Susan wondered why the lab had not just sent a signal directly to her Vox, then realized another interesting trend. Now that they could reach nearly anyone with anything at any time, people sometimes hesitated to do so, for fear of interrupting something important with a buzz, ring tone, or vibration. Quickly, she tapped up Jessica's results.

Kendall tried to look over her shoulder, an action the tininess of the screen rendered intimate. "Don't tell me we're going to solve three hopeless cases in a day. That's got to be a record."

Susan lowered her arm. The results were no surprise. "Jessica has macrocytic anemia, though it's surprisingly mild given her symptoms and the dirt-bottom low of her cobalamin level." She extended her wrist toward Kendall.

Seizing her arm, Kendall studied the Vox, then whistled. "That's the lowest level I've ever heard of." He let go of Susan. "What do you think, Calvin? Intrinsic factor deficiency?"

Susan shook her head gloomily. She hated cases like this one. "Rigid vegan diet. She's probably never had fully adequate stores of B_{12} in her life."

"Well, then, Calvin." Kendall patted her on the back. "Another opportunity for you to bring around a hopeless case. A couple of stiff injections, and she's perfectly normal. Chalk up another miracle for Susan Calvin."

Susan narrowed her eyes and turned to face him. "Have you ever actually seen a case of B_{12} deficiency?"

"No," Kendall admitted. "It's a zebra. Rare."

"Do you know why it's rare?"

Kendall hesitated only a moment. "Because . . . it's not 1763?" He took on the voice of a stereotypical crusty pirate, "An' . . . argh . . . we're not all scurvy dogs."

Susan yawned. "Scurvy is vitamin C deficiency."

Kendall continued his pirate imitation. "Argh! Twelve's a high 'nuff B, it might's well be vite-min C." He added in his own voice, "My point's valid." .

Susan rolled her eyes. "Valid, indeed, if your point is the federal government fortifies our food so deficiencies have become a thing of the past, except in cases where disease states impair our ability to absorb or process them."

"But?" Kendall tipped his head.

"But," Susan inserted, "we have a forty-something woman still living with her extremely controlling parents, who are dietarily militant."

Kendall tipped his head still farther, to an exaggerated degree. He looked like he might fall over.

"She's probably been B_{12} deficient all or most of her life. God knows how much of the neurological damage we can reverse at this stage."

"You're saying it's not just a matter of pumping her full of B_{12} and sending her on her way."

Susan shook her head sadly. "Not that I won't. We'll start her on a thousand micrograms per day IM. I'm sure we'll see some improvement, possibly significant improvement, but it's not going to be the hundred-percent miracle we're all hoping for."

Kendall chuckled.

Susan turned him a sour look. "What's so funny?"

Kendall's laughter grew so uproarious, Susan found it difficult to pin him with her gaze.

"What's so damn funny, Kendall?"

Kendall waited until he fully caught his breath to reply, "Only the great Susan Calvin would characterize a patient going from frank dementia to significantly functional as a failure."

"Yeah, yeah." Susan punched his arm a bit harder than a friendly tap. "It bugs the crap out of me when people do stupid things to themselves, then expect us to fix it. But it makes me homicidal when people ruin the lives of their children, even if it's well-meaning." She added to her own surprise, "Especially when it's well-meaning."

Kendall stared. "Wow, you're in a mood today."

Susan did not care. "And why shouldn't I be? I haven't slept in about thirty-two hours. I wiped myself out saving a man's sanity, only to be treated like dirt for my efforts. And now I get to clean up the mess made by a couple of morons who worship diet as a religion to the point of turning their daughter into a vegetable."

Kendall chuckled, and Susan rounded on him. "What's so damn funny about destroying a child's brain?"

"I'm sorry," Kendall said, not sounding it. "You just essentially said that eating vegan turned her into a vegetable. Gives new meaning to the phrase 'You are what you eat.'" He laughed again, shaking his head, and put an arm around her shoulder. "Come on, Susan. You're deliriously tired, and you need to go home right now."

Susan knew Kendall was right, but that only annoyed her further. She shrugged off his touch.

"Everyone is irrational about something. You've run into this a million times in medicine, and you've always managed to handle it." Kendall raised his hand again, as if to place it on Susan's shoulder, then dropped it to his side. "You'll find a way to educate them."

Susan suspected she had about as much chance as talking a Christian Scientist into a blood transfusion or a priest into an abortion. Kendall was right about one thing: She needed to go home.

More cautiously, Kendall put an arm around Susan's waist and steered her toward the door. "I am sending you home, and I'm not going to hear any protest. Reefes already left; he won't even know. The nurses and I will cover for you."

Susan knew they all would, too. She trusted them at her back. "Fine. I'll leave as soon as I get the orders written for Jessica Aberdeen."

"Do you need me to get you on the right glide-bus?"

"What?" It took Susan an inordinate amount of time to understand the obvious question. "No, I can handle it. I've been doing it since I was three."

"Well, see that you do." Kendall headed toward the charting room. "Because if you're still here in ten minutes, I'm carrying you out, kicking and screaming and ranting about dietary extremism as religion."

Susan turned Kendall a withering look. Though taller and heavier than she was, he clearly had little more than a nodding acquaintance with gym equipment. "I'd like to see you try."

Chapter 7

Susan awoke with no memory of where she was or how she had gotten there. She opened her eyes, trying to orient herself to the ceiling, a broad expanse of mottled off-white with a generic overhead fixture, currently turned off. Gaining too few clues from that, she rolled her gaze across her near surroundings. She lay on a patterned couch, her head resting on one arm. In front of her, she found a low table with an untidy array of palm-prosses. The scene finally coalesced into the familiar tableau of the first-floor Manhattan Hasbro charting room, where she usually met with Nate.

"Good morning, sleepyhead." The robot's voice cut through Susan's confusion, and the events of the previous evening came rushing back. Instead of going straight home, she had headed to the hospital to talk to him. She had found a couple of residents in the room, discussing a difficult patient, but no sign of Nate. She remembered lying down on the couch to wait for him, her last conscious decision.

Susan sat up suddenly. "Oh, my God! Am I late for work?"

Nate sat in a chair parallel to and at the head of her couch. The residents had left hours ago. "Only if you have to be at work by four twenty-six a.m."

The pressure off, Susan sank back into the cushions, yawning. "My father's probably frantic."

"I already contacted John Calvin. He knows where you are and that you're safe."

Susan blushed. She should have done that. "Thank you. That was very kind."

Nate shrugged. "It was little effort, and only what needed to be done."

The events of the previous day returned to Susan's memory, and she groaned.

"Bad day?" Nate guessed.

"How did you know?"

"The noise you just made was a giveaway, even if I ignore the fact that you chose to come here after a job you characterize as gardening, fell asleep, and didn't wake up until the wee morning hours."

"Bad day," Susan admitted. "Bad two days merged into one really long, rotten day."

"Would you like to talk about it?"

Nate's tone was sincere, but Susan could not help laughing.

Nate looked positively wounded by her mirth. "What's funny? What did I say?"

Susan lay back down on the sofa, using the armrest as a pillow. "I just got a flashback to when I first met Lawrence Robertson. He asked me when I'd be joining the staff of U.S. Robots." She chuckled at the memory. "He was just being polite to the daughter of one of his workers, and I made a joke about robotics corporations not needing psychiatrists. There followed a bit of banter and a joke about a robot lying on the couch, spilling his lack of guts." She deliberately did not think too long about the joke itself; Remington had made it.

Nate continued to study her curiously, clearly wondering where she intended to take the conversation.

Susan twisted so she could see his face. "So, instead of me becoming a psychiatrist for robots, I'm lying here getting analyzed by a robotic psychiatrist. It just struck me as hilarious turnabout."

Nate smiled but did not seem to find the same amusement. "Except I'm not a psychiatrist, robotic or otherwise."

"Well, you're serving a therapeutic purpose for me." Susan turned her head back to stare at the ceiling. "And that's good enough for a joke at four thirty a.m."

"Hmmm," Nate said, sounding very much like a classical Freudian. "So, what brings you to Dr. Nate?"

Susan sighed again, all of the humor draining from her in the instant she pulled her thoughts back to reality. "I think lack of sleep is amplifying everything. I went to work with renewed enthusiasm after our last talk, found a patient who appeared to have been misdiagnosed, and presented him to our attending in order to get permission to perform a few tests."

"Naturally," Nate said, "he refused."

Startled, Susan glanced at him. "How did you know?"

Nate chuckled. "Because if he had said, 'Sure, Susan. Go right ahead,' you wouldn't be making noises like a wounded rabbit and require the services of a robotic psychiatrist."

Susan folded her arms over her chest, stared back at the ceiling, and laughed. "Well, yes, then. He refused, all right." She muttered under her breath. "Arrogant, demeaning jerk."

Nate made a thoughtful noise. "This sounds familiar."

That caught Susan off guard. "How so?"

"Well, I seem to remember a first-year resident bringing me a similar dilemma almost exactly one year ago. She had a patient who needed reevaluation by Neurosurgery, but no one was brave enough to accuse the greatest neurosurgeon in the world of having made a mistake."

Susan remembered quite well. "Well, this time, my attending expressly forbade me from doing the tests, even though I was pretty sure we would find something significant, something we could treat that might improve or rescue the man's sanity and, ultimately, his life."

"You did the tests anyway," Nate guessed.

Susan sat up. "My mood told you *that*?"

"Your being Susan Calvin told me that," Nate responded simply, as if no other explanation were needed. "And these tests were, indeed, abnormal."

"Yes." Susan did not press Nate's knowledge again. It would result only in compliments to her diagnostic acumen, and she did not need anyone, least of all Nate, to remind her of her talents. They often seemed as much a curse as a blessing. "And when I presented my findings to my attending, he acted as if *he* had made the discovery against *my* protests and chided me like an errant child right in front of my peers." She amended, "Well, my peer. Singular."

"Wow." Nate went silent a moment before asking, "What did you do?"

Susan said soberly, "I punched his eyeballs through the back of his skull."

"What!" Nate stared in horror, then sat back. His tone turned doubtful. "You did not."

"Well, I wanted to," Susan confessed. "I probably would have if Kendall hadn't stopped me. Then kneed his privates through the roof of his mouth and surgi-stripped them to his ears." Susan suddenly realized she might be making Nate distinctly uncomfortable, not because the image of traumatized testicles would upset any man, but because she doubted his wiring even allowed him to imagine the scenario she had created. "You know, at that moment, I actually wished I was a robot. Then the First Law would have constrained me, and I could not have even considered injuring a human being."

Before Nate could analyze the thought, Susan added carefully, "Of course, if I were a robot, I couldn't have helped my patient, either. I'd be constrained by the Second Law."

"Susan," Nate said softly. "I would have done nothing different than you did."

Now, Nate had Susan's complete attention. "What?"

"The First Law states, 'A robot may not injure a human being or, through inaction, allow a human being to come to harm.' The Second Law officially states, 'A robot must obey orders given it by human beings–'"

Susan interrupted. "And my attending ordered me not to do those tests. And he's a human being . . ." She added under her breath, "Barely."

Nate finished his thought as if Susan had not interrupted. "'–except where such orders would conflict with the First Law.' In this case, the order given would conflict with the First Law."

Susan considered, puzzled. "How so?"

"Because," Nate explained, "in this case, doing nothing, as ordered by your attending, would cause harm to the patient, who is also a human being. That conflicts directly with the second part of the First Law, which takes precedence over the first part of the Second Law."

Susan ran the wording through her mind again. "'Or, through inaction, allow a human being to come to harm.'" She could not help adding, "Wow." She studied Nate. "I knew the Laws of Robotics allowed more insight than most people imagined they could. They fit together like a flawless and beautiful tapestry." There was an inherent perfection in the whole of the Three Laws, the way they meshed, that went even beyond their creator's realization. Lawrence Robertson had wanted safe, loyal robots. What he got was a cleaner, better breed than mankind could ever be, stronger creatures, more faithful and useful than himself and wholly devoted to him. How could anyone not see the value of this incredible creation, this thing of steel and gears and positrons that lived in secrecy because the mankind he served so lovingly was so foolish as to fear him?

A thought came to Susan that seemed so obvious, she wondered why she had never asked before. "N8-C," she whispered.

Nate turned her an all-too-human glare. "You know I prefer Nate the same way you do Susan. *Dr. Calvin.*"

Susan ignored the jibe. "The eighth in the NC model line, you once told me."

"Yes," Nate admitted. "What of it?"

"Is there an N7-C? An N1-C?"

"No. Those prototypes were disassembled to make me."

"Really?" That surprised Susan. When it came to the creation of any type of electronics, the more units produced, the cheaper the cost per unit. Technology was one of the few classes of production in which higher demand ultimately tended to decrease the price of the goods.

Nate explained, "My parts alone are worth millions. The biological technology that allows me to appear so human is far beyond its time, priceless, with dozens of patents pending. The positronic brain . . ." He hesitated, and Susan studied his expression. Judging him as human always seemed fraught with peril, though so far it had worked well. He appeared more at a loss for words than confused or deceitful. ". . . is still relatively young. The NC line went far beyond what USR could or should reasonably expect at this point in the evolution of robotics. We're out of sync or sequence, especially when you consider it's only been seven or eight years since scientists developed the technology for speaking robots."

That triggered a memory of Susan's own. "I once wrote a paper on a speaking robot." She smiled at the recollection, unimpressive and long buried. "It had to be longer than seven or eight years ago, because I was still in high school. Physics One," she recalled. "We did a small unit on robotics. As part of the research, I spent three hours at the Museum of Science and Industry observing a so-called talking robot in a children's program." She shook her head at the memory.

The Talking Robot, as the signs had aggrandized it, could not hold a candle to Nate. It had been an immobile, formless mass of wires and coils covering some twenty-five square feet of floor space and did nothing more than answer simple questions. It was, essentially, an oversized computer with voice-recognition and -transmission software. Most of the children who came to the exhibit owned personal electronic gizmos more impressive than the Talking Robot.

What had caught Susan's attention was a small girl who had entered the room alone between showings. She had had an air of anxiety about her, a desperation, and she had addressed the ungainly and impractical device with a respect it had not deserved. "A little girl, maybe seven or eight years old, broke the thing with an innocent question." Susan recalled the details. "She asked it about another robot, one she described as looking like a real person but who couldn't talk. The Talking Robot apparently wasn't programmed to wrap its thoughts around the concept of its existence in regard to other robots." She remembered the incoherent spluttering, the acrid smell of burning coils, the warning shrill of impending implosion. "It turned out to be the best material I got for the paper. Earned me an A."

Nate shook his head, frowning. "That Talking Robot wasn't one of USR's, but the girl had to be Gloria Weston and the nonspeaking robot she was seeking was Robbie." His frown deepened. "Although saying he looked like a real person is a bit of an exaggeration. He had a head, but it was shaped rather like . . ." Nate's fingers flailed around his face for a moment, as if to form the three-dimensional shape from thin air. "Well, I don't know of anything in common usage shaped like a parallelepiped."

"I remember geometry," Susan said dryly, picturing six parallelograms fused together the way the same number of squares could form a cube.

Nate continued his description, "He had red eyes with metal-film eyelids, a flexible stalk for a neck, then a much larger parallelepiped for a torso. His shoulders were flat, with arms hinging off them, and he had the proper number of legs. His entire outer shell was chrome-steel, nothing anyone could mistake for human." He smiled ever so slightly, like a mother watching her child do something clever. "Though, to Gloria, I'm sure he seemed utterly human."

"Seemed?" Susan did not like his use of the past tense. "So, she never found him?"

Nate's smile grew. "She found him, all right. She spent seven more years with her best friend, in addition to the two they shared before they got . . . temporarily separated. Robbie was programmed and built exclusively to serve as a companion to a child. The idea was that once other parents saw the incredible bond between robot and girl, the wonderful job Robbie did, robotic nursemaids would become the rage."

Susan knew what had to come next. "Except for the Frankenstein Complex." She shorthanded the generalized phobia that seemed to strike otherwise normal human beings when it came to robots, especially those most resembling themselves. Entire organizations existed that were dedicated to the goal of preventing robots from becoming a regular part of society. At least one of these groups was prone to violence as fearsome as anything Susan could imagine a horde of robots inflicting. The Society for Humanity was behind several explosions, including the one that had killed Remington and nearly killed her.

Nate nodded gloomily. "Many believe innocent, harmless Robbie—and, more properly, the neighbors' reactions to him—were directly responsible for the ordinance passed in 2025 forbidding any robot on the streets of New York between sunset and sunrise." He made a grumpy noise. "As if great, bellowing gangs of robots owned the city prior to that time. Five years later, robots were banned from all of Earth, except for scientific experiments."

Susan recalled her father telling her that as well. "So, what happened to all the robots? Did they join the Mercury expedition?" She laughed alone.

"Actually, we do have robots on Mercury. I think that's where they sent N12-C."

Susan brushed hair from her face, wanting to take the conversation in twenty different directions. She had multiple questions and limited time, so she focused with laserlike intensity on the topic most interesting to her. "So, there's an N12-C?"

"There was," Nate responded carefully. "Susan, I told you the NC model line was way ahead of its time. That happens sometimes with inventions; an object gets created that predates anticipated technology and attitudes. In its own time, it may seem useless or, in my case, practically anachronistic."

Susan could think of a few herself. "In the fifteenth century, Leonardo da Vinci made detailed sketches of helicopters, tanks, and underwater breathing apparatuses."

"And parachutes and retractable landing gear," Nate added. "Scuba equipment was placed into operation four hundred fifty-eight years later, helicopters in 1907, tanks in 1917, and retractable landing gear not until 1933. As far as parachutes, their use predated planes. The first jump was from a hot-air balloon in 1793."

Susan knew Nate would have more detailed facts at his command, and she appreciated it. In the past year, she had considered the many potential uses of robots and the foolishness of the human race in general, in ways she had never worried about in the past. Everyone had beliefs uniquely their own, and Susan had been raised to appreciate all of them. Yet in the past year, she had become vastly more cynical. During her high school unit on robotics, the teacher had distributed the results of a poll in which 87 percent of respondents admitted to being moderately or severely suspicious of intelligent robots, and a full 23 percent stated that they were actually afraid of them. At the time, Susan had dismissed the results as ludicrous. Now she was not so certain.

Nate ran with the tangent. "The first workable computer was

designed in 1834, but the inventor, Charles Babbage, was unable to procure funding because the government could not see any use for such a thing. In 1877, Thomas Edison invented the phonograph, but the first LP record wasn't created until 1948. Frank Sprague completed a fully electric railway seven years before the invention of the electronic loco-motive. Bar codes were created twenty years prior to the technology capable of reading them."

"Uncle!" Susan cried.

Nate looked at her curiously. "What?"

"I get the point," Susan explained. "What I want to know is why the NC robot line was created and how many of you still exist."

"Three," Nate said simply.

Susan rubbed the sleep from her eyes. They had been conversing for nearly an hour now, and she needed to start thinking about going home to change and prepare before work. "Three . . . NC robots exist?" she guessed.

"Me, Nick, who is N9-C, and N12-C, which, I gather, was the one they settled on for whatever purpose they chose to make us in the first place. One through seven were scrapped and the parts reused to create us later models. Ten and eleven were also destroyed, as I understand."

"Where is Nick?" Susan wondered aloud.

"Nick bounced around a few businesses and finally landed at Upper Manhattan VA Hospital, where he has run into many of the same prob-lems I have when it comes to completing his work. As far as I know, he's still there."

"As far as you know?" Susan tipped her head sideways. "I would think you'd keep in touch."

"It's not like he has a blog." Nate sighed heavily. "We're supposed to keep our profiles low until people become more accustomed, more accepting of us. I'm serviced quarterly by a USR technician. All I know is what he's willing to tell me."

"And you think N12-C is on Mercury." The thought did not sit well with Susan. "What possible reason could they have for placing a robot so human on Mercury? Given the external dermal layers, the hair, the eyes, wouldn't he need the exact same protections as a human astronaut?"

Nate shrugged once, said nothing, then shrugged again. "I'm not privy to every conversation or what's in the minds of my creators. I know only the intention of the NC model line seemed to be constructing a robot so apparently human, it could pass for a man in essentially every way. What purpose that serves, beyond freaking out the local populace and triggering the Frankenstein Complex, I have no idea."

"A goal hardly worth hundreds of millions of dollars and hours, I wouldn't think." Susan had every intention of finding the truth. Her days of accepting what her father said without question were over. She had lost the only man she had ever loved, and nearly her own life, to USR's cause. *No more secrets. At least, not from me.*

Nate made a thoughtful noise but added nothing else useful.

Susan suddenly recalled something else Nate had said. "Robots were banned from Earth?"

"In 2030, yes."

Susan thought back on the past several years. In addition to her high school physics unit, she had taken a cybernetics course at Columbia, much to John Calvin's chagrin. He had long feigned ignorance about the inner workings of U.S. Robots and Mechanical Men, Inc. For most of Susan's life, he had convinced her he held a desk job having little to do with the actual robotics projects. She had discovered the truth only in the past year, and he had explained the reason for his deception: parental love and fear the Society for Humanity, or another desperate antirobot organization, might harm her.

It had turned into a more-than-reasonable concern, as the events of a year ago could attest, and it made Susan even more curious about the purpose of the NC line. Its sole intent seemed to be to aggravate the SFH to the homicidal fury that had already resulted in Remington's death. "Well . . . robots continued to exist on Earth after 2030."

"For scientific purposes," Nate reminded.

Susan shook her head. "Theme park animatronics, military drones, corporate assembly lines." She waved an arm to indicate Manhattan Hasbro Hospital. "There are displays in this very building of robotic toys through the years."

Nate bobbed his head in surrender. "It all depends on how you define robots, doesn't it? Even the law didn't do a great job of it, but one thing was abundantly and absolutely certain: Anything containing a positronic brain qualified as a robot, whether or not it resembled humanity in any way or even performed functions in a humanoid manner. And as USR owns all the patents on that particular product . . ."

Susan finished the thought quietly. "It was hit hardest by the law." She marveled anew at the pure genius of Lawrence Robertson. He had managed to turn all the decades of work on artificial intelligence on its ear when he created the positronic brain path from a spongy glob of platinum-iridium. Until that time, true, strong AI was a distant concept. So many scientists had contributed through the decades to the ability of mechanical creations to move in a useful or human manner, to manipulate objects fluidly, to perceive the world around them. The computational power of computers had progressed at light speed for many years, then slowed to a crawl as the number of transmitters reasonably placeable on an integrated circuit dwindled.

Intelligence was so much more than the integration of billions of facts. The ability to imbue a man-made object with true intelligence— common sense, planning, social understanding, creativity, deduction, reasoning, problem solving, and the like—had frustrated scientists since the beginning of time. Even the most ancient cultures had the myth of the golem or statue that comes to life and acts with reason, for evil or good. Bronze figures in man shape had existed as long as the humans who created them. But until Robertson's mysterious and amazing innovation, fast, intuitive judgment; the ability to intermingle experience, emotion, and idea; and the default reasoning that defined humanity were entirely in the realm of nature.

Susan asked the obvious question. "How did you and Nick get around the ban?"

"Scientific purposes," Nate reminded her for the third time, apparently thinking the early hour had muddled Susan's thought processes.

Susan yawned and stretched again. "I'm not seeing the science in using multimillion-dollar prototype robots as gofers." She leaned back, placing her arms behind her head, elbows bent. "I mean, I see the science that got the nanorobot study okayed. We were experimenting for a potential cure to a scourge on mankind."

"And the worldwide ban on earthly robots expired in 2034."

"Really?" As far as she could tell, nothing had changed in regard to robots in the past couple of years. "So, why hasn't USR flooded the market with positronic robots?"

Nate crooked a shoulder and an eyebrow simultaneously. It surprised Susan how much that gesture reminded her of Kendall. "You'll have to ask Dr. Robertson. If I had to hazard a guess, I'd say it's either money or caution."

Susan nodded thoughtfully. She could understand both of those eventualities. Surely USR had borrowed most of the cost of producing the NC line, in addition to their other projects. She also knew the scientists, including her father, had pitched in the bulk of their own savings. Surely they had some government grants as well. Still, the enormous price tags for their goods had to slow the process. As far as caution went, she could understand that as well. If a simple and harmless nursemaid had led to global bans, she could understand why USR might want to accustom the world to their products more slowly in the future. The only illogical part of the sequence was the development of the NC line.

Susan forced herself to rise. She could discuss these matters with Nate all day, not only to distract herself from work she had grown to despise, but also from overwhelming interest and curiosity. However, if she did not leave soon, she would forfeit any chance for a shower and change of clothes, let alone the possibility of catching her father before he left for work. She did not intend to broach the issues raised by Nate with John that morning. She needed to catch him after work, when they both had time to discuss the situation in sufficient depth. "I need to go, but I'll be back."

Nate grinned. "About that, I never harbored a single doubt."

Chapter 8

Determined to turn around her mood and her luck, Susan Calvin swept into Winter Wine Dementia Facility with an air of hopefulness bordering on cockiness. By the time she had arrived home from Manhattan Hasbro, her father was leaving for work. They exchanged brief but heartfelt hugs and hellos, and as Susan prepared for another day of treating the untreatable, she made some important decisions about the remainder of her rotation. She scribbled John Calvin a note, promising to return home that evening and to talk, though she did not get specific with the details of the forthcoming conversation. He had spent most of her life hiding the extent of his involvement with the projects of U.S. Robots and Mechanical Men, Inc. She did not want to give him the opportunity to prepare, to create clever dodges to her questions. The less he knew about what she had learned, the better.

The nurses seemed to notice the change in Susan's manner. They always traded greetings with her and Kendall, but those had gotten more cautious as Susan's interactions with Dr. Reefes had grown more venomous. She had never taken out her irritation on them directly, but she supposed she had become more terse, less open, and decidedly quieter. Now they grinned happily at her and met her with a cheery "Good morning, Susan."

Susan visited Jessica Aberdeen first, uncertain how quickly the cobalamin shots might work. To her delight, she found the woman sitting up in her bed, carrying on a conversation with a nurse named Farrah. Wanting to observe, Susan remained silent in the doorway, examining the woman from a distance. Once again, she was impressed by the small, birdlike dimensions of Jessica Aberdeen. Her thin, ever-pale face was surrounded by a halo of stringy, mouse-colored hair. She had a smile on her face, though, and her dark eyes followed Farrah around the room with an interest she could not have managed even one day earlier.

Susan strained but could not make out the specifics of the conversation. To hear, she would need to reveal herself. Rather than mince inside, trying to eavesdrop, she strode in with the confidence she would need to display to convince Jessica and her family of her competency. "So, how is Jessica Aberdeen today?"

"Okay, I suppose." Jessica's voice emerged reedy, exactly what one might expect from her appearance. "Are you another nurse?"

Farrah intervened, "This is Dr. Susan Calvin, Jessica. She's your doctor. Remember? She saw you yesterday, and we told you about her again this morning."

For a moment a blank look crossed Jessica's face. "Doctor?" she said. "Why do I need a doctor?"

Farrah explained to Susan, "She's a lot better, but she's still confused. Clumsy, too."

Jessica rejoined the conversation. "I've always been . . . awkward. My whole life." She added, as if it were a deep confession, "I drop things, and I've always sucked at sports."

"May I?" Susan asked, pulling out her reflex hammer. Jessica did not resist as Susan tested several deep-tendon reflexes, including the biceps, brachioradialis, and patellar, all of which were notably brisk but equal from side to side. In contrast, the tendocalcaneal reflex at the ankles was absent. The primitive Babinski and Rossolimo reflexes in response to specific stimulation of the feet were both abnormally, if only slightly, positive.

Susan exchanged her reflex hammer for a tuning fork. Blind testing demonstrated that Jessica had almost no vibratory sensation awareness, and her proprioception, the ability to mentally locate a body part in space, was severely impaired. Her responses as to whether Susan had raised or lowered her big toe were little better than random guessing. When asked if touches to various parts of her body felt normal, Jessica always answered that they did.

A light touch to her right arm was perceived the same as a similar one to the left. However, Susan did elicit a vast difference in the response to stimuli applied to Jessica's hands or feet and those applied to her face and torso. A pinprick to her shoulder resulted in a yelp of pain and a request that it not be repeated, while she acknowledged a sharp poke to the top of any toe as a touch.

It soon became clear to Susan that Jessica had distal neuropathy of both hands from the tips of her fingers to just past her elbows and from her toes to her ankles. Most people would define what Jessica called normal as a pins-and-needles tingling or burning sensation of the hands and feet with decreased sensation overall, as if they were wearing gloves and socks. Apparently, Jessica had suffered the problem since childhood, because she considered the neuropathy completely normal. That alone could explain her lifelong clumsiness. It might also explain why the neuropathy had escaped the notice of doctors for so long. Unless a physician had strong suspicions, as Susan did, the diagnosis of neuropathy depended on patient complaint and description. Few doctors, other than neurology specialists, bothered to check routinely for vibratory sensation and proprioception anymore; they saw little cause for wasting time on such a low-yielding and time-consuming test in otherwise normal patients.

Making sure the door was closed and curtains pulled, Susan performed a complete physical examination. The relatively subtle findings on neurological testing turned out to be the most striking problems found on examination. Jessica's hair was a bit brittle and thin for Susan's taste, but she had seen no other genetic family members for comparison. The woman's breath was unwelcoming, and her dental hygiene marginal at best. Closer inspection revealed multiple crowns, implants, and veneers. She was still confused, though far less so than on admission. Prodded to walk, Jessica stumbled about dizzily, quickly became short of breath, and masked her discomfort beneath a sudden and intense irritability that sent doctor and nurse scuttling from the room.

Once outside, the door shut, Farrah rounded on Susan. "What do you think, Doc?"

Susan forced a weak smile. "I think a couple of lean-beef burgers, a glass of whole milk, and two or three hard-boiled eggs would perk her right up."

Farrah looked horrified. "You'll never get the family to agree to that, Susan. They're on God's Ideal Diet. It's vegan and a hundred percent raw."

Susan headed toward the privacy of the charting room. "Well, God's Ideal Diet may work for angels, but it's destroying Jessica Aberdeen's neurological system." Remembering a promise she made to herself that morning, Susan disengaged without further denunciation and headed more firmly toward the charting room.

Before she got there, Kendall hurried up, hooked her sleeve with a finger, and hauled her toward the staffing area. "Good morning, Susan. How's tricks?"

"Tricks?" Susan repeated, mock scandalized. "So now I'm a hooker to you?"

"Sailors," Kendall pointed out, "also call their shifts tricks." He unhooked his finger briskly, propelling Susan toward a chair while he spun one directly in front of himself. "And I think you know the expression really just means 'How's life treating you?'"

Susan took the proffered seat. "Well, as you know, life is spitting all over me. But you're not going to see me mooning over that anymore."

"Oh?" Kendall's gaze was so absolute he clearly, genuinely wanted to know the reason.

Susan looked for a way to word her new decision. "From now on, you might want to call me Su."

"Sue?" Kendall gave her a sideways glance. "Short for Susan, obviously; but I've never heard anyone call you that. Not even your father."

Susan elaborated. "Not Sue. S-U 2."

Kendall straightened suddenly. "What?"

The reaction was not what Susan had expected. "S-U 2. As in the second unit in the Susan update line. S-U, Su. Like N8-C is Nate."

"So," Kendall guessed, "you're a robot now?"

"Think of the advantages of living life by the Three Laws of Robotics." Susan had considered it the entire way into work, which gave her an enormous benefit over Kendall, who had the idea dropped on him cold and without context.

Kendall gave her a bemused look. "You mean, emotionless, apathetic, and calculating? Calvin, I've heard of maintaining professional distance, but isn't that overdoing it a bit?"

Susan was seized by a sudden urge to slug him. "After all we've been through, that's your take on robots? Apathetic? Calculating?"

"Well," Kendall started slowly, but he had to know he was treading on thin ice. "I admit Nate's absolutely amazing, but I'm not to the point where I'm ready to trade in my human brain for coils and wires."

Susan did not bother to correct his misconception of the makeup of the positronic brain, especially since she had only a superficial understanding herself. "I think we could exchange half the existing human brains for positronic ones, and it would only improve the world. We'd have fewer people believing in spirits and ghosts and a lot more trusting in proven science."

Kendall added, "That may be so, but yours isn't one of the brains we should be replacing, Calvin."

Susan continued as if he had not spoken, "We'd double the average IQ, halve the rate of illness, and people would treat one another a lot better."

Kendall did not seem as enamored of the idea as Susan. "What's the point? It's not as if those features would be passed on to future generations. Only the actual humans could procreate. All our faults would survive, and you'll have to convince me that's a bad thing. Art, music, poetry all arise from our flawed human minds. We may be stupider than our robotic counterparts, but it took our imperfect minds to conceive of and create them."

It was an undeniable point, one Susan had not previously considered. "I'm not suggesting we replace humans entirely. I just think there's some advantage to my taking on a robotic persona for the remainder of this particular rotation."

Kendall nodded stiffly, clearly in agreement at last. "If you were forced to observe the First Law, it would probably rescue our attending from slow disemboweling." He chuckled. "Though I'd love to see you try to follow the Second Law. I don't think you could obey orders given by human beings, even if you agreed with them. You have too much faith in your own competence and too little in that of most other people." He added quickly, "With good reason, of course. But even if the order was sound, you'd question it. You're a contrarian by nature."

"I am not!" Susan retorted, while Kendall laughed so hard, he nearly cried.

She had just proven his point, and Kendall had no need to speak a word in explanation. He merely turned on his heel and headed out of the charting room, leaving Susan alone to contemplate her mistake.

I am not a contrarian. Susan rolled her eyes at her own reply, then managed a laugh of her own. *My father and Nate are right about one thing:*

Kendall gets me. And, at the moment, he's exactly what I need. She tried to imagine herself dating Kendall Stevens. He was not stunningly handsome in a Remington Hawthorn sort of way, but neither was he wholly unattractive. He was a bit ginger for her taste, but that was not a deal breaker. The idea of kissing him did not repulse her. He did have a great sense of humor, if over the top on more than one occasion. Intellectually, he had graduated medical school in the middle of his class, which made him nearly enough her equal. He embarrassed her sometimes, but he always had her best interests at heart, even when she did not realize it. They had a great working relationship, and, after her father, she considered him her closest human friend.

Susan opened the palm-pross and checked Chuck Tripler's information. Transferred to the neurosurgery service at Manhattan Hasbro Hospital, he had undergone resection of a large cauda equina neurinoma, a benign spinal tumor of nerve-cell origin. Time would tell how much permanent damage had been done by the long-term compression of brain tissue by his dilated ventricles, but she felt certain he would have a far better future than what he had suffered the past few years. At least he had a reasonable chance for a partial or near-full recovery.

Susan wondered about Thomas Heaton and Barbara Callahan, but she did not want to interfere with Kendall's patients. So many times he had watched her succeed beyond expectations. She wanted him to experience the delight and excitement of having cured someone who seemed hopeless. He did not seem to mind sharing the credit with her, even looked to her for guidance, but she suspected he would appreciate it more if he managed a few triumphs on his own. *He's more than capable, but strangely insecure.* His near-constant need to resort to humor proved the thought. Susan wondered if she would ever elicit the root cause of his self-doubt.

While Susan looked over Chuck's recent history, Hazel Atkinson approached her. Susan would never forget the CNA receptionist, the first person she had met at Winter Wine Dementia Facility. Hazel handed Susan a manila envelope containing something hard, flat, and square.

Susan accepted it, curious. "What's this?"

Hazel pressed wrinkles from her scrubs with her hands. "Thomas Heaton's wife said you'd asked for it. It's some of the music he conducted."

Susan remembered. She had mentioned the possibility the first day she had met the addled conductor. "Thanks. This is great." She leapt to her feet and went searching for Kendall, and found him almost immediately in Barbara Callahan's room. The elderly woman sat up in bed, a stupid grin plastered on her features. She wore a pair of stretch jeans and a T-shirt displaying a basket full of Chihuahua puppies. She bobbed from side to side with a sinuous movement that started in her head and moved down her neck to her shoulders.

"Interesting," Susan said.

Barbara's gaze found Susan, but Kendall was the one who replied. "Positive urine test for cannabis. Negative for everything else." He glanced at his patient. "She's actually a bit better today. She's in the right century, anyway."

Barbara continued to study Susan. "Caden, introduce me to your girlfriend."

Kendall rolled his eyes toward Susan but nodded indulgently. "I'm not Caden, Barbara. Remember? I'm Dr. Kendall Stevens, and this is my fellow doctor, Susan Calvin."

Barbara bobbed her head. "Caden, Kendall—what's the difference?"

Susan chuckled. "Nice to meet you, Barbara. I've talked to your children."

Barbara stopped her odd movements and put both hands over her face. "Oh, I embarrass them."

Susan continued to smile. "All parents do. I'd worry if you didn't."

Barbara lowered her hands. "Really? Oh, I'm so glad you understand. You're like that nice neighbor of mine. Do you know Emma?"

Kendall looked moderately pleased. "Earlier, she'd have assumed you were Emma."

Barbara turned to him curiously, "Emma who, Caden?"

As Barbara seemed less confused when speaking with females, Susan perched on the edge of the bed. "Tell us about Emma."

"Emma?" Barbara repeated in evident confusion. She tipped her head in consideration, then her features brightened. "Oh, Emma, my neighbor. Sweet girl, isn't she?"

"I don't know her," Susan reminded gently. "Tell us about Emma."

"Emma's my downstairs neighbor. I just adore her. Anything I need, she gets for me, sometimes even before I know I need it." A beatific smile crossed her face. "She got me a kitten, gray tabby, looks just like my Mr. Tibbs. I didn't realize how much I missed the old fellow." The grin left her features suddenly, and she turned to Kendall again. "You did feed Tibbs. Didn't you, Caden?"

Barbara seemed so concerned, Kendall simply answered, "The cat has been fed."

Susan appreciated that the straightforward reply, though possibly untrue, forestalled a long discussion about a kitten that might or might not exist. She made a mental note to make certain an animal had not been forgotten in the old woman's apartment.

Kendall made a desperate attempt at an answer. "Barbara, does Emma ever bring you any . . . brownies?"

Barbara rocked her head in a noncommittal fashion. "She comes for tea every day. I usually supply the pastries." She added happily, "I like apple tarts best."

Kendall and Susan exchanged looks. The obvious avenue had not panned out. At least, not yet. It seemed unlikely they would get any useful information that day, and prudent to wait until Barbara had regained more of her senses.

Susan rose from the bed, displaying the envelope for Kendall. "I've got something for you."

Apparently thinking Susan had addressed her, Barbara clapped her hands with delight. "Thank you, Emma. Do you have some more of those wonderful cigs?"

Susan froze in midmovement. Kendall's double take could have graced the most primitive cartoon. "Cigs?" Susan repeated. "Do you smoke, Barbara?"

"Smoke?" Barbara made a pained face. "Heavens, no. Nasty, dangerous habit. No one does that anymore." She turned Kendall a severe look. "And I'd better not find out you've started smoking, young man."

"Never," Kendall promised. "I'm more concerned about you. Has Emma been bringing you"—he used Barbara's own words—"wonderful cigs?"

"Emma who?" The confused expression crossed Barbara's face again, and her eyes went limpid. She closed them, rolled onto her side, and appeared to drift off to sleep in an instant.

The residents tiptoed from the room, Susan still carrying the envelope and her palm-pross. As the door shut behind them, Kendall exclaimed, "I think we have a pretty good idea what's going on here. But why would someone take tea with an elderly woman just to poison her with wacky tobaccy?"

Susan saw the situation differently. "I don't think there's any deliberate attempt to harm anyone. The way Barbara and Bambi describe it, Emma's a good friend. She just has a certain way of . . . of relaxing, let's say. I'm betting Emma has no idea her wacky tobaccy is the cause of Barbara's dementia. In fact, I'm betting she thinks what she's supplying is medicinal."

Kendall groaned. "What I am supposed to tell Bambi and Caden?"

He made a broad gesture, as if gathering kindergarten students into a huddle. "Kids, I'm afraid your mum's a bent-A stoner."

"No," Susan said. "Definitely not."

Kendall continued to pay attention to Susan's response, which she interpreted as a request for real help.

"THC is known to compete with acetylcholinesterase and helps prevent amyloid beta-peptide aggregation. In the early part of the century, it was considered and discarded as a possible treatment or preventative for Alzheimer's." Susan shrugged. "Emma probably read that somewhere and thought she was helping Barbara stay young and focused."

"Or," Kendall suggested, "Emma has an addiction and thought she'd share it."

Susan could not deny the possibility. "I think we're better off taking the first approach. Marijuana as a cause of dementialike symptoms in the elderly is well documented, but, used sparingly, there's no indication it actually causes long-term dementia. If we make it clear to Barbara, her family, and Emma that Barbara is having acute, toxic reactions to the stuff and needs to completely avoid it, I think we can keep all the friendships intact and our patient permanently out of harm's way."

Kendall nodded vigorously. "I like that. If the kids believe Emma meant well, they're unlikely to uproot Barbara or ruin a treasured friendship."

"Unless it happens again," Susan pointed out.

"In which case, she should be uprooted and the relationship ended. There's no real danger to her having another episode. Correct?"

Susan managed a lopsided grin. "Correct. As long as Barbara hasn't become pathologically attached to her wonderful cigs."

Kendall added, "Or doesn't replace them with some wonderful pills or snorts."

Susan rolled her eyes. She doubted Barbara Callahan would discover the joys of hallucinogens at the ripe old age of seventy-six. "I'm pretty sure this will solve the problem, but you're welcome to lecture Grandma Barbara on the dangers of home baking methamphetamine for the grandchildren."

Kendall put his hand out, palm up. "So, are you ever going to give me that thing you promised? Or are you holding out for money?"

"What?" Confused, Susan stared at Kendall, watching his gaze fall to the arm at her side. Noticing the manila envelope still clutched in her fingers, she put it into his waiting hand. "Sorry about that. I forgot that's why I came in."

Kendall shook out the tiny disc. "What's on this?" He examined it closer, reading the miniscule print on the label. His eyes widened, his mouth curled upward, and a light crossed his features. "This is great!" He glanced around, finally noticing that Susan clutched a palm-pross as well. "Bring that. We're going to visit Thomas Heaton next." He swept away.

Caught up in Kendall's excitement, Susan followed. She passed the palm-pross to Kendall, tuning her Vox to catch the audio signal. In tandem, they trotted down the hall, followed by the gazes of curious inpatients and staff, and burst into the conductor's room. He sat up in a chair, covered in a hospital-issue blanket, headphones over his ears, his arms weaving in staccato patterns.

Kendall shoved aside the remains of Thomas' breakfast, a discarded hospital gown, the call button, and a single shoe to plop down the palm-pross in the middle of the bedside table. He inserted the disc, adjusted his own Vox, and tugged the headphones off of Thomas Heaton. With a grand gesture, he tossed them aside and hit the Play key on the palm-pross.

For a moment, nothing happened. It abruptly occurred to Susan neither of them had actually listened to the disc. For all she knew, it might contain a grocery list or a Satanic sermon, or a series of swear words directed at their patient. Then, just as she felt certain it was entirely blank, she heard the tap of a baton on a podium and a hush, followed by the sweet sounds of a symphony orchestra playing a romantic piece Susan did not recognize. Every sound emerged crisp and true, an ancient wonder in an era of synthetic and simple music. The quadriphonic quality created by the palm-pross's dual speakers and the individual Vox made the music seem to come from every direction at once.

The change in Thomas Heaton was gradual. The glaze melted from his eyes, granting them a new and lifelike glimmer. His head slowly lifted, dissolving what had seemed like a permanent double chin. His gestures, initially inhibited and jerky, smoothed as the first piece progressed so that by the end, they became noticeably fluent, strong strokes cleaving the air with sure precision.

Susan did not have to close her eyes to imagine the woodwinds blowing, fingers flying over the keys; the chirpier quality of the strings, bows dancing; the blaring of the brass, their horns gleaming golden in the subdued lights; and the intense focus of the percussionists keeping it all in proper rhythm. She could imagine this broken man in his prime, robust and professional, at the head of it all, lashing them into their finest performance.

As the final strains of the first piece trickled to silence, Kendall turned down the volume while Susan crouched in front of Thomas Heaton and chased his gaze until he had no choice but to physically cover his eyes or look at her. The latter required less energy, apparently, because the tired, dark eyes finally met hers. There was a glow this time she had not seen before, and she wanted to catch it before it disappeared again. "Maestro, please. Talk to us. We only want to help you."

For an instant, nothing happened. Then broad shoulders heaved beneath the crimson-and-white bathrobe and a great sigh escaped him. It was a terrible noise, filled with the all the pain and wretchedness of the universe, yet it was also an enormous improvement from his previous near catatonia.

Susan glanced at Kendall, who continued the music at a lower volume and gestured for her to continue.

Susan did not know what else to do, so she took both of Thomas' hands in hers. He had strong hands, lightly callused, larger and colder than her own. Brown lines etched deeply into his pale palms. She continued to hold his attention until it became more difficult to dodge her than to stare. "Maestro, please. We're doctors, and we've seen everything. Whatever it is, we can help you."

Thomas' lips moved, but no words emerged.

Susan dropped to her haunches, wildly frustrated. She looked at Kendall again.

Kendall stepped to her side and crouched down beside her, also studying Thomas Heaton. When the conductor made no further attempt to speak, Kendall did what he always did best. "Mr. Heaton, do you know the difference between a bull and an orchestra?"

Susan froze and turned her head hurriedly toward Kendall. This sounded suspiciously like the opening to a bad joke, and, if not, then to a grave insult. Either way, she doubted it would help. "Kendall," she started.

Thomas made a strangled noise. Then abruptly he let out a sudden bray that seemed to clear a long-plugged throat, followed by a rush of air.

Kendall carefully began the punch line. "A bull has the horns in the front . . ."

Thomas finished in a rusty tone, "And the asshole in the back."

Both men laughed as if they had just collaborated on the most brilliant comedy ever written. It did not surprise Susan that Thomas knew the ending; likely he had heard every conductor joke in existence. What shocked her was both Kendall's knowledge and the other man's reaction. As the realization came to Susan that Thomas had just referred to himself as a nasty part of bovine anatomy, she chuckled along with them.

As the chortles died out, Susan worried Thomas Heaton might lapse back into the depths of his depression, into his stony and imprisoning silence.

Kendall must have thought the same thing, because he pulled out another joke. "What do you do with a clarinetist who can't play?" Kendall responded before the other man could. "Put him in the back, give him two sticks, and make him a percussionist."

Susan wondered why Kendall had run over his own punch line without giving Thomas time to answer, but then Kendall continued.

"But what if he can't do that right either?" This time, he waited for Thomas to reply.

A slight grin came to the corners of the man's broad mouth, but he clearly had to figure out the answer. "Take away a stick, put him in the front, and call him the conductor."

Again, the two men laughed. This time, Susan watched life trickle into the older man's eyes. Responding appropriately to jokes demonstrated a command of memory, reason, and humor, all higher functions of the brain. Clearly, as they had suspected, the depression was the cause of his sudden slide into apparent dementia. It only remained to find the underlying cause, and Susan suspected it had something to do with the opaque spot on his MRI. She went back to her original thought: posterior cerebral artery stroke. "Maestro Heaton, are you having trouble with your vision?"

Heaton reluctantly pulled his gaze from Kendall to plant it on Susan.

Susan cringed, wishing she had not killed the mirth so quickly. Kendall had had a great idea that worked, one Susan would not have thought to try in this situation. "Do you find yourself startled by things that come upon you unexpectedly? Are you tripping or falling frequently?"

The conductor looked at Kendall, as if the male resident could explain the odd series of questions. There was a wariness to his manner, as if he might disappear back into his funk at any moment, irretrievable.

Susan tried the direct approach. "Maestro, please tell us what your symptoms are. We want to help you."

It turned out to be exactly the wrong thing to say. Thomas buried his face in his palms. His body slumped into the chair.

Susan watched him for several moments, while Kendall cringed, head shaking. The conductor did not make a single motion. He did not even appear to breathe.

Susan released his hands and rose, scurrying to find a different approach before it was too late. "Maestro, I have some musical questions that have been bothering me for some time. I wonder if you could help me."

Kendall froze in midmovement, head slightly cocked, as if he simultaneously suffered hope and fear for what Susan might say next. She wondered if he knew how many times she had worried for what might come out of his mouth.

Thomas' head bobbed ever so slightly. Susan hoped she had not imagined the movement.

"My father and I have argued a long time over the correct pronunciation of"—she continued, letter by letter—"B-E-E-T-H-O-V-E-N."

Thomas stiffened all over. Gradually, his head rose. "That's Beethoven."

"Ah." Susan pretended to consider the response. "Dad insisted on pronouncing it 'Beet Oven.' I thought he was teasing, but he sounded so sure of himself." She added, "And C-H-O-P-I-N?"

Thomas gave the name its proper French pronunciation. "Frédéric François Chopin."

Susan nodded, as if taking mental notes. "So, not 'Choppin.'"

Thomas managed a rusty laugh.

Susan tried one more. "B-A-C-H."

Thomas accommodated that request as well. This time, Susan did not try to come up with a weird, phonetic response. She set down the palm-pross on a level surface, then retrieved a crumpled bit of paper and a pen from her pocket. "I'm going to look something up. I wondered if you'd save me some time by writing my grocery list while I'm doing it."

It was a wretched attempt at casual behavior, but the conductor gamely smoothed out the paper and accepted the pen. While Susan did a quick search of the Net, she dictated: "Avocados, pecans, tomatoes"– she hesitated as the item she had sought came onto the screen, then continued–"canned cat food, a round pan, a birthday cake, and"–she tried to think of an appropriate addition–"celery."

Clutching the pen, Thomas turned Susan a thoughtful look. "Would you like me to pick up your laundry next?"

Susan chuckled, taking the pen and paper and placing it in her pocket absently. She turned the palm-pross to face the conductor. "What's this, exactly?" The answer was clearly marked at the top of the screen in bold letters above a complicated musical score.

Thomas hummed the first several bars, one hand waving dramatically. He grinned suddenly. "That's Bach's *Brandenburgische Konzerte*, Number Three."

"Is it, now?" Susan said, as if the screen bore no label. She punched a few more buttons. "How about this one?"

Again, Thomas hummed several bars, waving grandly, before declaring it Franz Liszt's *Orpheus*.

Susan tried another tack. She brought up an image on the computer. "Do you happen to know who this is?"

Thomas glanced at the picture and answered almost instantly. "That's Leonard Bernstein."

"Is it, now?" Susan examined the picture more closely. "Looks like my Uncle Justin." She found another online portrait. "Who's this, then?"

Thomas had no difficulty naming the obscure composer. "That's Francesco Malipiero."

Susan turned the palm-pross around to examine the screen and made a thoughtful noise. "So it is." She touched a few more buttons. "I have one more identification for you." She brought up an image and turned it back to Thomas Heaton.

The conductor laughed. "That would be me."

"I knew that," Susan said, as if admitting a secret. "But I'm wondering what you're doing there."

Thomas studied the picture, the smile plastered in place, as if forgotten. "I'm clearly conducting the Manhattan Symphony Orchestra." He leaned in closer. "That's the score from Mozart's Fourteenth, which means that picture was taken in 2029."

"How do you know you're conducting?"

Thomas Heaton turned Susan a look of withering disdain. "First, that's what I do. Second, why else would I have a baton in my hand and an audience at my back?"

Susan turned the screen around to look at it. "Baton? You mean that pink-and-green stick in your hand?"

"Pink and green?" Thomas grabbed the edge of the palm-pross and pulled it back around. He gave Susan another queer look. "Are you color-blind, Doc? It's clearly white with a bit of red at the tip. One of my favorites at the time, if I remember correctly."

Susan accepted the palm-pross back. "Why, so it is. White with red at the tip. Maybe the illusion of movement made me see pink, but green? Where'd I get that from?" She put her hand in her pocket, trying to make the gesture look absentminded. "Well, we need to be going now, Maestro. Is there anything we can get you to make your stay more comfortable? I'll add it to my list."

"Thank you, but that's not necessary."

Susan pulled her empty hand from her pocket. "Darn it, I seem to have lost the list." She drew out the pen but left the paper in place. "You don't happen to remember what I had on it, do you?"

Thomas considered. "I recall avocados, pecans, birthday cake"—he thought a moment longer—"and celery. There were a couple of other things, but I'm blanking on them."

Susan glanced at Kendall with a slight head shake, concerned he might jog the older man's memory, but the other resident had taken a seat on the only other chair and seemed content to watch Susan work.

Susan feigned discovering the list deeper in her pocket. "Ah, here it is." She scanned the list, written in small, neat print. "I'm sorry, I can't make this one out. Can you tell me what this says?"

Susan placed the list over the palm-press keypad and pointed to the words "canned cat food" that Thomas Heaton had previously written.

The effect was dramatic. His smile wilted into a deeply scored frown of irritation. All humor left the conductor's features, his body language grew tight and tense, and his gentle stare became a solid and angry glare. "I thought you had to leave, Doctors."

Susan acted as if she had not heard him. She pointed to the word "celery." "Also this word, if you please. I can't quite read your writing."

Thomas' head sank back into his palms. His body seemed to shrink before her eyes. "Get out," he said feebly. "Leave me alone."

Susan had all the information she needed. "Good day, Maestro," she said, then scurried from the room. She waited until Kendall exited behind her before shutting the door. Without speaking, they fast-walked to the staffing area, where Kendall collapsed into a chair, laughing. "What the hell was that, Calvin? Some bizarre sort of surreptitious mini mental-status exam?"

"Bingo." Susan dropped the palm-press to the table. "The posterior cerebral artery version."

"Sounds like a computer game."

"It wouldn't be the most boring one I've ever played." Susan explained in more detail. "Remember Diesel Moore?" The case was a year old, but she felt certain Kendall would remember the boy.

"Ten-year-old with Prader-Willi syndrome."

"Not exactly." Susan had been following the child in her outpatient clinic, so she had more recent updates. "He appeared to have Prader-Willi syndrome, but the test was negative. He actually had the syndrome of optic nerve hypoplasia. It just presented like PWS because he had normal vision coupled with the hypothalamic problems that often accompany hypoplastic optic nerves."

"Yeah." Kendall sprawled across his chair, one arm thrown over its back. "So?"

"So, that case made me realize any disease process presents as a constellation of symptoms that can vary between individuals."

Kendall raised his brows. "That's the first time you realized it? Isn't that elementary pathology?"

Susan sighed. "Of course, Kendall. But my point is, we naturally shortcut the symptoms to those displayed by the greatest number of people with the particular illness." She used a more straightforward example. "When I was on Pediatrics as a student, we had a toddler present with intractable seizures accompanied by clouding of the cornea and excessive tearing."

Each of those features, in and of itself, was rare and interesting. Kendall sat up. "Injured the eyes during one of the seizures?"

Susan bit her lower lip. "That was assumed. It took a week before anyone suspected glaucoma."

Kendall snapped his fingers. "Glaucoma." Taking the next appropriate step, he asked, "And what did the child ultimately turn out to have?"

"Sturge-Weber syndrome."

Kendall slumped in the chair and gave Susan a searing look. "Well, anyone could have made that diagnosis, if you hadn't left out the most significant detail. Why didn't you mention the gigantic reddish-purplish splotch across the face?"

"Because," Susan emphasized, "she didn't have the classic port wine stain."

"Okay, what made this particular port wine stain so hard to see?"

"It didn't exist, Kendall. She didn't have a port wine stain."

"But I thought all—"

"Ninety-eight percent of infants with Sturge-Weber syndrome have the port wine stain, which leaves two percent to the whims of diagnostic suspicion. A hundred percent have leptomeningeal angiomata, which she did turn out to have. Eighty-three percent have seizures." Susan winced at the memory. "Because of the delay in diagnosis, this little girl wound up blind. Had doctors diagnosed the glaucoma earlier, she might have had a chance for at least some vision."

"Might," Kendall emphasized. "But doctors aren't perfect, and when the disease presents without its primary feature . . ." He trailed off as understanding struck him. "What's the percentage of people who suffer a posterior cerebral artery stroke who develop homonymous hemianopsia?"

"Not sure," Susan said. "It's the classical symptom, so we all look for it. When someone presents without it, or any obvious motor dysfunction, or even apparent memory impairment, we overlook it."

"We," Kendall repeated smugly, "meaning anyone but you."

Susan dismissed words Kendall probably meant as a compliment. "I, and you, have the benefit of hindsight."

"Do we?" Kendall planted his feet firmly on the floor. "Most physicians would have accepted the previous doctor's diagnosis, that Thomas Heaton had developed dementia, and he would have become lodged here for the rest of his life, albeit short."

Susan merely shrugged.

But Kendall had not finished. "Calvin, I'm tired of you couching your successes in terms suggesting anyone could have figured it out. Everyone could *not* have figured it out, or someone else would have done so."

The conversation discomfited Susan for reasons she could not wholly explain. "Fine, I'm brilliant. I'm the smartest woman in the world. Does that make you happy?"

"No," Kendall admitted. "Mostly because you're being sarcastic while I'm trying to . . ."

"Butter me up?" Susan tried.

"No." Kendall's face assumed an exaggerated leer. "Although the image is somewhat satisfying." His tone dripped with innuendo. "I could lick off the butter—"

"Enough!" Susan stopped him before he could say anything lewd, thus wholly changing their association in an instant. Apparently, he had given upgrading their relationship at least as much thought as she had. "I have one talent: a knack for taking handfuls of facts and putting them together in the proper order." She added carefully, "And a good grasp of human nature and behavior."

"And yet," Kendall pointed out, "earlier this morning, you wanted to be a robot."

Susan bobbed her head pointedly, "Perhaps that's exactly why I wanted to be a robot."

The point apparently bothered Kendall, who shivered and flopped back into his sprawled-teen posture. "All right. I'm still waiting for the mental-status exam explanation."

Susan appreciated leaving the discussion of her personal strengths and weaknesses to focus on helping Thomas Heaton. "The self-conducting scene responses were the most revealing to me. He was able to examine the picture and integrate its parts into a cohesive interpretation, thus ruling out visual simultanagnosia."

"Visual simultaneousnesseses." Kendall deliberately mangled the long Latin term. "How the hell did you remember how to pronounce that, let alone what it means?"

Susan ignored the question, not wanting to go off on another tangent. "Thomas was able to easily and properly name a baton, which ruled out both apperceptive and associative agnosia."

"The difference between those being?"

Susan was not sure whether Kendall did not know or if he tested her, but this time, she deigned to answer. "In associative agnosia, the ability to draw or point to objects named by someone else is preserved, while both forms of agnosia inhibit the patient from naming even the most common objects. It's usually tested with keys. You have the patient try to name them by sight, then by sound or touch." She paused a moment for further questions before continuing. "He corrected my false colors of the baton, which means he hasn't developed either color-blindness or color anomia, which would keep him from naming colors even though he could still perceive them."

Clearly entertained, Kendall gestured for Susan to continue.

"Having him identify Mozart and the like tested for prosopagnosia, or inability to recognize faces. He could write beautifully, so he doesn't have agraphia. Or, for that matter, optic ataxia, because it's tough to write actual words when you've lost hand-eye coordination."

Kendall had clearly been paying attention. "It sounds like you've completely ruled out a posterior cerebral artery stroke."

"Actually, just the opposite. He definitely suffered a stroke. I think with a little research, we could figure out the exact location of the damage."

Kendall leaned forward, intrigued. "How so? What did you note on testing that I missed?"

"Thomas Heaton has pure alexia, Kendall."

Kendall heaved an enormous sigh and plumped his chin on the

back of the chair. "For those of us who truly are doctors but don't remember every esoteric Latin word for situations we haven't actually seen, can you translate into medical English, please?"

Susan said simply, "He can't read."

"What?" Kendall's eyes narrowed as he considered the information that had brought her to the conclusion. "You mean, he's illiterate?"

"I mean, he used to be able to read, but now he can't. I mean, English words now look like Chinese pictographs to him."

"No wonder he's depressed." Kendall's eyes remained slitted. "Are you sure? He didn't seem to have any trouble pronouncing composer's names when you spelled them out to him."

Susan bobbed her head. "That's not unusual. Patients with pure alexia often retain the ability to formulate a word and its meaning if spelled out to them verbally or traced, letter by letter, on their hands."

"Weird." Kendall had surely seen weirder, or would in the future.

"It's actually a positive prognostic sign, because it bodes well for his ability to learn to read again, though laboriously and slowly, letter by letter." Susan continued, "The symphonies were tests of this, too. He didn't seem to notice they had titles at the top. He had to hum them aloud to identify them."

"That's true," Kendall said carefully, apparently lost in his own thoughts. "Calvin," he started, then stopped in consideration. "Do you think being enmeshed in music might help him? That the proper therapist could use his thorough knowledge of music as a segue to learning how to read again?"

Susan honored the idea with lengthy contemplation. "I would imagine it's quite possible. Usually, people with pure alexia either never learn to read again or do so with great difficulty. Obviously, a straight substitution wouldn't work, especially since musical notes only go up to G."

Kendall ran with the idea. "If he can instantly name a mouthful of symphony by humming the first few bars, imagine what he might do by associating sound with word by blending chords or stringing passages." A brilliant thought followed. "He clearly kept his ability to absorb music as a whole entity, rather than as a string of individual notes. If we could rechannel reading through that particular mechanism, one most people never develop to his extent, he might actually learn to read again as fluently as in the past."

Through the doorway, Susan caught sight of a man striding purposefully toward Jessica Aberdeen's room. A stab of discomfort lanced her stomach, accompanied by an imminent feeling of dread she could not wholly explain. "That's an amazing idea. In fact, I think you should work out a detailed plan with his occupational therapist when you discharge him . . . today. I've never heard of such a thing being tried, and this might well turn out to be a reportable case."

Kendall's response came from behind her. "I'd appreciate you looking at me, preferably with adoring eyes, while you're calling me a genius."

Susan suddenly realized she had her attention fully on the passing man and had craned her neck to watch him turn the corner. "Excuse me, Kendall. I think Jessica Aberdeen's father just arrived, and I'd better go talk to him."

"Good luck," Kendall said, and Susan did not think she imagined the trepidation in his voice. For the first time all day, he did not offer to accompany her.

Chapter 9

Chase Aberdeen was a swift walker, and Susan did not catch up to the man until he had stepped into Jessica's room. A tall man, in clear and vivid contrast to his tiny daughter, he had a bony face that reminded Susan of a ferret. He was lanky and slender, though not emaciated, and his skin had a grayish cast, suggesting low blood-oxygen saturation and probably anemia. As he entered the room, he flung his long arms about like one accustomed to people taking notice of him at all times. Despite his bold manner, his voice emerged tinny, thin. "Good morning, Jessica. How are you feeling today?"

Farrah looked up from the IV infuser, and Jessica turned to her father with a weak smile. "Much better, Dad. Thanks for asking."

Chase seemed to grow taller in that moment. "So glad to hear it, darling. We'll have you home in no time."

Susan stepped into the doorway. "Another week, at least. Most likely two."

Chase whirled on his heel, a motion that nearly uprooted him. He fixed his eyes on Susan, green with golden flecks that seemed to flicker in the low light of the dementia room. "And who is this young woman who seeks to countermand me?"

Susan took an instant disliking to the man and appreciated that

Farrah spoke before she could say something she might regret. "This is Jessica's doctor, Mr. Aberdeen. Dr. Calvin, this is Jessica's father."

Susan did not waste time with small talk. "Mr. Aberdeen, your daughter was suffering from severe vitamin B_{12} and calcium malnutrition."

Chase Aberdeen nodded, though a frown scored his features. He clearly took Susan's words as a direct assault. "She's not a fan of raw nori, and the tempeh clearly wasn't enough. I knew it was only a matter a time before the combination finally worked."

Susan shook her head. She kept her tone level, her timbre conversational. She needed to enlighten without confrontation. "What worked, Mr. Aberdeen, was the intravenous addition of vitamin B_{12} and calcium to her system."

His grin was predatory. "Let's agree to call it a combined effect." He turned back to tend Jessica.

Susan would have loved to do so. It would make things so much easier, so much smoother. Though it incorporated ignorance, it was a compromise she could live with. Unfortunately, Jessica Aberdeen could not. "With all due respect, Mr. Aberdeen, I can't agree to that. Nori and tempeh do contain B_{12} analogues, perhaps even active B_{12}, but it's not in a bioavailable version."

Chase jerked his attention to Susan. Color eased onto his face. And while it probably indicated the raw stirrings of anger, it gave his face a rosy, more friendly, hue. "Are you a vegan, Dr. Calvin?"

"No," Susan admitted. "But, like most people, I explored vegetarianism for a few years. It did not suit me."

Chase snorted in clear derision. "So you're a fizzer. I should have known."

Susan allowed her brows to inch gradually upward as the silence became heavier between them.

At first, Chase Aberdeen met her gaze, but he soon turned his attention back to his daughter. He spoke loudly. "Don't worry, darling. I'll have you out of this terrible place." He emphasized, "Today."

Susan did not allow herself to speak until she could keep all of the irritation from her voice. "So, is this the famed vegan compassion I've heard so much about? Apparently, compassion for animals doesn't extend to people."

Farrah's eyes widened. The man stiffened in every part before stating coldly, "'Fizzer' is merely a descriptive term, not an insult."

Susan did not point out the preceding snort nor the venom that had dripped out with the term. "I wasn't talking about what you said to me. I was talking about what you said to your daughter."

Chase lost it. "I love my daughter. That's why I want her away from this"—he gesticulated wildly—"this . . ." He did not seem to have a functional term that would not prove Susan's point about compassion. If he used her word, "garden," he would denigrate all of the inhabitants and his own chosen diet simultaneously.

"Hospital?" Farrah supplied helpfully, hiding a grin of her own.

Chase added pointedly, "And what does a fizz . . . a failed vegetarian know about nori and tempeh?"

Susan had done her homework. "Nori is an edible seaweed, a species of red algae from the genus Porphyra. It's usually used as a wrap for sushi or onigiri. Tempeh is a fermented whole soybean product that originated in Indonesia. The fermentation starter contains bacteria known to produce active B_{12}."

Chase frowned. "Okay, so you know—"

"Unfortunately," Susan finished, "it is not bioavailable cobalamin when consumed by human beings such as Jessica. There are only two sources of useful vitamin B_{12}: animal products and supplements."

Chase stood his ground. "You're wrong, Doctor. There are at least two million practicing vegans in America alone, and they aren't demented. If the whole world practiced raw veganism, we'd double our lifespans, quadruple our food supplies, and end war entirely."

Susan could not think of a single military conflict that had arisen from a disagreement over recipes or the contents of a dinner plate. Nor could she name a two-hundred-year-old human, vegan or otherwise. Anecdotally, if raw, plant-based diets made people more docile, she was not seeing that espoused in the hostile person of Chase Aberdeen. However, that particular line of argument was not harming anyone, so she did not bother to refute it.

"Mr. Aberdeen, I'm not condemning vegetarians in general or vegans in particular. Many of my friends and colleagues choose not to consume animal flesh or products for a variety of legitimate reasons. As I've said, I've tried it myself." She sighed deeply, seeking a careful way to assuage a man whose emotional and philosophical identity was so intricately intertwined with his diet.

"Unfortunately," she continued, "facts do not conform to desire or faith. The great majority of vegans obtain vitamin B_{12}, and other necessary nutrients, from supplemented soy milk. As you produce your own soy milk, it lacks this supplementation. Thus, Jessica's diet, and your own, is deficient in vitamin B_{12}. Probably for very similar reasons, Jessica is also deficient in calcium, which explains the deplorable state of her teeth."

Chase Aberdeen's face obtained even more color, a vast improvement, though probably, once again, for negative reasons. "Bad teeth run in my family."

Unnecessarily. Susan did not argue the point. "Heredity can be a strong factor in many illness and conditions. In some cases, we can escape our genetic fate; in others, we can't."

"Exactly," Chase trumpeted. "Which is why, despite the near-perfection of Jessica's lifelong diet, we could only delay the dementia."

Susan worked hard to make absolutely certain she caught Chase's full gaze with her own. "Mr. Aberdeen, there isn't one shred of evidence Jessica is suffering from early-onset Alzheimer's."

Chase allowed her to hold his gaze, though, as he tipped his head, Susan found her own moving with his. "So . . . her previous doctors are wrong."

"All wrong," Susan said. "At least anyone who diagnosed her as having early-onset Alzheimer's."

"And heredity?"

"Is what it is, but it has nothing to do with Jessica's current problems." Susan finally glanced toward Jessica, who seemed to be watching the exchange with an expression mingling interest with horror. Clearly, she had never heard anyone stand up to her father.

"So, you know better than everyone else in the world, young Dr. Calvin?"

Susan had tired of hearing it. "It's not a matter of knowing better. It's a matter of performing the right tests, Mr. Aberdeen. And tests don't lie." She leaned in carefully, lowering her voice. "Jessica is deficient in cobalamin and calcium. And probably in other micronutrients as well."

Chase Aberdeen leaned in even closer. "Then we will have to put more bok choy, broccoli, and okra on her plate. More nori and barley grass."

Susan knew the vegetables he named did contain adequate amounts of calcium, but the nori and barley grass would not help the situation. "Mr. Aberdeen, you can solve the entire problem by using commercial, supplemented soy milk in the future. And it wouldn't interfere with your veganism whatsoever."

Chase rolled his eyes, as if he found Susan singularly uninformed. Apparently, her knowledge of tempeh and nori had not convinced him one iota. "I'm not going to stoop to commercial preparations. They add artificial preservatives. Sugar, salt, starch. Colorings and supplements."

He shook his head with obvious disgust. "The food manufacturers process all the positive nutrients out of our food, add all kinds of poisons, then they expect us to cheer when they supplement it with a bit of what they squeezed out in the so-called refining process." He shook his head harder. "No way I'm feeding that toxic waste to my only child."

Susan stifled a sigh. She had seen a case like this before: A woman pathologically afraid of her own weight gain had literally starved her toddler nearly to death. The doctor had taken custody of the child, who had subsequently bounced between home and foster care multiple times until she became old enough to feed herself. By then, she had developed an unhealthy relationship with food that left her in a constant struggle with obesity, all of which could have been avoided had her mother just taken a more evenhanded and casual attitude toward food.

Susan knew what she had to do. She raised her head to hold Chase's green gaze again. The golden flecks seemed to shimmer and snap in the lighting. "Mr. Aberdeen, you don't understand. Jessica is frail, fragile, with severe neurologic damage due to chronic vitamin B_{12} deficiency."

"She's always been frail and fragile," Chase insisted, disengaging from Susan's stare. "That's why she needs this special diet. It's the only thing that's kept her alive this long."

Susan walked all the way around Jessica's bed to reassert her position. She would not allow the man to look away. "Mr. Aberdeen, Jessica is not frail and fragile despite your ministrations. She is frail and fragile because of them."

Chase's jaw clenched. The flecks in his eyes became positively hyperactive. His words boomed, echoing through the room and spilling out into the hallway. "Are you saying I've neglected my daughter? That I've abused her?" His fists knotted, and he tensed as if to pounce.

"Not deliberately." As Susan now fully held the man's gaze, she shifted left to readjust the position she had taken. She wanted the bed between her and Chase Aberdeen and the door at her back. "The road to hell is paved with good intentions, Mr. Aberdeen, but consequences don't evolve from what we want or feel to be right. No matter how much we desire it, dirty diapers will never smell like roses."

Chase's brows rose farther, until his eyes seemed as wide as golf balls. "So now you're saying I stink."

Farrah rose suddenly. "That's not what Dr. Calvin said, Mr. Aberdeen. I know you could have a rational discussion, if you'd just calm down—"

Susan cringed, but only inwardly. She could think of few worse things to say to an angry person. No matter how heartfelt or carefully worded, suggesting to someone in the pique of emotion that he was behaving irrationally always sounded patronizing. Still, Susan could hardly blame the nurse for stoking a fire she, herself, had kindled and nurtured.

Chase's features purpled, and he gesticulated so wildly that, had Farrah not scrambled out of the way, he would have struck her. "No person in the history of the universe has loved a human being as much as I do my daughter. And no one eats a healthier diet than Jessica."

Susan was not at all sure the near-miss was accidental. "I'm just saying it's possible to get too much of a good thing. To a man with a blood sugar of five hundred, insulin is lifesaving. But too much will drive him into a hypoglycemic coma."

Chase scoffed. "You can't overdose on natural substances any more than you can on clean air."

"Insulin *is* a natural substance," Susan pointed out. "And you *can* overdose on clean air. In addition to the explosive potential, exposure to excessive amounts of oxygen is known to cause oxidative damage to cells, collapse air sacs in the lungs, constrict blood flow to critical areas of the brain, induce seizures, and cause blindness, especially to infants."

Chase glared. "You're quite the know-it-all, aren't you, Dr. Calvin?"

It was clearly a rhetorical question, so Susan did not bother with an answer. In the past year, she had finally learned it was often better to keep her mouth closed than to risk escalating the situation with some comment, wise or not. As she watched a vein jerk and throb in Chase's neck, she realized she needed more time to hone her technique.

When Susan did not answer, Chase continued, "I have spent the better part of my life studying and learning about the vegan lifestyle, far longer than you've been alive. You're not going to convince me it's anything but the healthiest, most natural, most compassionate, and most environmentally friendly way to eat."

Susan sidestepped the worthless argument. Even assuming every word he spoke was bare truth, it did not change her approach to the situation. "Mr. Aberdeen, I apologize if I'm repeating myself. I'm not suggesting there's anything wrong with eating vegan, nor am I asking you to give up your lifestyle. I am simply stating Jessica needs B_{12} supplementation in her diet, and it would be in your best interest to do the same with your own."

Chase lowered his head, the movement bringing images of striking snakes to Susan's mind. No longer loud, his tone went flat, dangerous, indicative of barely controlled rage. "Dr. Calvin, I will be removing Jessica from your care immediately and treating her nori deficiency as I feel appropriate."

Susan set her jaw. "I can't allow that."

His face became a sneer. "And just how do you intend to stop me?"

Susan did not flinch. "With every medical and legal option at my disposal." With that, she turned on her heel and marched from the room.

The request for her to visit Dr. Mitchell Reefes' office did not surprise Susan; only the fact that an hour and a half had passed since her encounter with Chase Aberdeen did. She had spent most of the interim researching her options in regard to Jessica. The best course of action clearly involved Jessica herself. If the woman expressed the desire to remain at Winter Wine Dementia Facility, her demand for autonomy would take priority over her father's wishes. Susan believed she could talk Jessica into staying, but doubted her influence could counteract the pressure Jessica's lifelong caretaker could assert. Confused and accustomed to obeying her father, Jessica would likely cave to his demands.

Under normal circumstances, Susan would do almost anything to avoid creating a rift in any family, especially one where one member remained so obviously dependent on another. In this case, however, she suspected Jessica would have done far better had someone ripped her free of the unhealthy relationship with her father in childhood. Regularly supplemented, Jessica had a chance to regain some of the neurological deficits lost to her chronic B_{12} deficiency. Thrown back into her previous state of existence, however, she would ooze into a dementia that might not prove nearly as amenable to treatment a second time. To complicate matters, the injected B_{12} would remain in Jessica's system long after supplementation, so her decline would not happen quickly. Chase could credit his nori for her improvement and blame the gradual slide back into dementia entirely on heredity.

Lost in her thoughts, Susan found herself at the office door all too soon, knocking peevishly.

"Enter," Dr. Reefes said coolly.

Susan did not bother to brace herself before entering. Whatever her feelings for her attending and his competence, she felt certain she had the words to explain her position and convince him of its righteousness. Whatever else, he was a trained and studied doctor. Surely even he would not condemn a woman to brain death when the solution was so simple and close at hand.

Reefes gestured for Susan to sit in the chair in front of his desk, and she complied. He wore a pair of half-glasses she had never previously seen on his face, and he peered at her over his oversized computer and the straight-cut top of the lenses. "I discharged Jessica Aberdeen."

Susan's blood ran cold. She could not believe what she had heard. "What?" She did not allow a hint of emotion to enter her tone.

Reefes twirled his glasses by one stem. "I said, I discharged Jessica Aberdeen to her father's care."

Susan kept her voice flat. "You can't do that."

He leaned forward. "I can and I did, Susan. This is my facility, and I have every right to do so."

Susan had to believe Reefes was baiting her, that he had only told her this lie to measure her reaction. She clarified, heart pounding, "I didn't mean you physically can't do it. I meant you morally can't do it. At best, it's misfeasance."

The glasses stilled in Dr. Reefes' hand. "Are you, a second-year resident, actually accusing me, an established professional, of medical malpractice?"

Susan wished people would stop putting inflammatory words in her mouth, even ones as true as this. "I used the term 'misfeasance.' That is not the same as malpractice."

Reefes leaned across the desk. "Enlighten me."

Susan dutifully explained, taking care to avoid the second-person pronoun "you." "When *someone* takes an inappropriate action, it is misfeasance. For malpractice to have occurred, *someone's* failure to follow generally accepted professional standards must cause a breach that is the proximate cause of harm." She met his smoldering gaze. "When Jessica slips back into a demented state, as she will, and we can't extract her from it the second time, only then malpractice will have occurred. Until that moment arrives, releasing her into the care and custody of an idiot is simply misfeasance."

Reefes stared at Susan for a full minute before speaking. "Mr. Aberdeen is correct. You are a mouthy know-it-all."

"Thank you" did not seem an appropriate response, so Susan remained quiet.

"As Mr. Aberdeen, who you so glibly refer to as an idiot, has assured me, he will fully supplement his daughter's diet with foods containing the appropriate nutrients, in this case B_{12} and calcium, I see no harm in releasing her to his care. We have no evidence she's losing these nutrients through her gastrointestinal system. Correct?"

Susan spoke through gritted teeth, forcing herself to answer only the question on the table. "Correct. Her deficiencies are wholly dietary. But–"

Reefes stalled her with a raised finger. "The standard of care would be several more days of injected cobalamin, but I am certain we have reasonably replaced her stores so oral sources can provide her with an adequate daily supply. There was absolutely no reason to insult and belittle Mr. Aberdeen."

Susan made a thoughtful noise. "And those dietary sources of B_{12} would be?"

Reefes frowned. "I assure you, Mr. Aberdeen has the situation well in hand. He's studied the various nutrients in all types of exotic plant sources, and he was able to show me studies proving certain varieties of seaweed and algae contain more-than-adequate amounts of cobalamin."

Susan had reviewed those studies and seen the flaws in them. "There have been studies demonstrating nori tests positive for vitamin B_{12}. Unfortunately, further studies have demonstrated most of that activity comes from inactive cobalamines and corrinoid analogues not bioavailable to the human metabolism. Dried nori doesn't contain any active B_{12} or analogues, which suggests the source of the cobalamins found in the nori in the study was probably bacterial contamination."

"The exact source doesn't matter." Susan noted Reefes did not argue about the research itself. Likely he had not read it, only the bit Chase Aberdeen had shoved under his nose.

"No," Susan admitted. "Unless the eater takes the unprecedented step of washing it!" She was angry now and finding it harder to hold her tongue. Even the robotic mind-set ceased to help. There was nothing in the First Law preventing a robot from hollering at an impossibly dense human being. "Or if the particular nori being eaten wasn't lucky enough to become contaminated with B_{12}-producing bacteria."

"Don't take that tone with me! I'm your superior."

Superior moron. Susan kept the evaluation to herself, tired of arguing with people who seemed incapable of logical thought. "Jessica could have been entirely normal, with a life all her own. Instead, she's saddled with a father insistent everyone in the world must behave exactly as he does, despite proof it's damaged his daughter's brain. Why do some people feel their viewpoint is valid only if they inflict it on as many people as possible?"

Mitchell Reefes did not look amused. He had replaced his glasses during Susan's tirade and stared at her again over the tops. "Susan, you're being every bit as rigid as you claim Mr. Aberdeen was. There are more things in heaven and Earth than are dreamt of in your philosophy. I believe that's from the Bible."

Susan had to bite her tongue to keep from laughing out loud. "That's from *Hamlet*, sir." She wanted to continue, to explain that when Hamlet said those words to Horatio, he was attempting to justify the reality of a ghost that might or might not exist only in his mind.

Susan's comment served only to further irritate her superior. "Susan, when you *grow up*"—Reefes emphasized the last two words, clearly intending to offend—"you will realize 'getting more flies with honey than vinegar' is not just a folksy saying. It's often better to indulge your patient's beliefs, no matter how unscientific, in order to maintain her confidence and get her to listen to your advice when she might otherwise discard it."

Susan knew the best thing to do now was to practice what he had preached, to thank him for his great advice and to leave the room with a shred of dignity intact. But her conscience would not allow her to leave until she had rescued Jessica Aberdeen from irrevocable insanity. "Sir, I really do appreciate your advice. I want to assure you I don't go around haranguing people about their points of view, no matter how irrational. However, I did take the Hippocratic oath, and I feel bound by it to ensure that my embracing of another's mind-set, whether tacit or aloud, causes my patients no harm. It was exactly this type of mute acceptance that resulted in the deaths of several thousand babies and toddlers at the turn of the century, when pediatricians avoided warning about the significant dangers of co-sleeping because it 'offended' some parents."

"My wife and I co-slept with our children until they each turned six. They turned out perfectly fine."

Susan could not help saying, "Anecdote and scientific proof are two very different things."

The throbbing in Reefes' neck increased, and his eyes narrowed appreciably. "I know the difference between anecdote and proof. I was merely pointing out—"

There was no legitimate way to finish that sentence, so Susan left him to struggle without assistance.

"That . . . that . . . making bold statements can . . . offend the very person you're trying to convince." It was disingenuous. Had that truly been his original point, he had no reason to point out the outcome.

Susan remained silent, seeking the words to save Jessica without digging herself a deeper hole.

"Susan." Reefes leaned across his desk, rubbing his eyes with thumbs shoved over the glasses, slipping them down his nose a bit. "I spoke with Manhattan Hasbro."

Susan went utterly still. Dr. Reefes had no right to do that. She had done nothing wrong.

"They informed me you've been under an extreme amount of stress this past year, over and above your residency duties."

Susan waited for the other shoe to fall.

"Because of that information, I'm not going to dismiss you from this rotation." Reefes paused, apparently waiting for appreciation he was not going to receive. When Susan remained silent, he continued, "I am, however, going to suggest you take the rest of the day off and evaluate whether or not you're really temperamentally suited to being a doctor. Not everyone is, and there's no shame in it. No shame at all."

Stunned, Susan could not find words she dared to speak aloud. She could not believe this lazy lummox, who scarcely deserved the title of doctor, was lecturing her on her suitability. Replies crowded her mind, but as none of them would do anything but worsen the situation, she swallowed them. Doing so left a bitter taste in her mouth and a queasy feeling in the pit of her stomach. The First Law of Robotics popped into her head, and the simple morality of the Laws struck her once again. *If I walk away, Jessica will come to harm. Yet,* she realized, *nothing I say now will change that. It will only wind up harming both of us.*

Without another word, without acknowledging Mitchell Reefes' suggestion, Susan left the room and Winter Wine Dementia Facility.

Chapter 10

S usan rode the glide-bus home, her thoughts so invested in Jessica Aberdeen's predicament she missed her stop and had to ride the complete cycle a second time. When the doors finally hissed open at the west edge of Tompkins Square Park, she exited in a fog of rage and despair, jaw set, fists clenched, mind overflowing with thoughts that ranged from the quiet peace of an afternoon nap to barbarous and bloody murder committed upon the person of Dr. Mitchell Reefes. If Chase Aberdeen happened to get injured in the mayhem, so much the better.

Sunlight streamed through the myriad skyscrapers, glinting off metallic surfaces and enhancing the direct rays already spilling through what remained of the park's sacred elms. Susan had never before noticed how blinding that reflective cacophony became, probably because she left for work before sunup and rarely came home prior to twilight. As a medical resident, she worked most weekends, too. She usually spent her downtime sleeping or, when possible, interacting with John Calvin.

Thoughts of her father finally brought some inner peace, and Susan found herself smiling for the first time in hours. John would still be at United States Robots and Mechanical Men, performing the job Susan now knew had less to do with paperwork and more to do with the development and construction of robots. She looked forward to spending time with him that evening, discussing the information Nate had given her, and it bothered her that she had missed the opportunity to have these conversations with her father in her youth. He had always dodged questions about his job to focus fully on the trials and achievements of his only child. Even now, he never volunteered information. When she wanted to know something, Susan had to figure out what to ask and press him directly.

Glad to find herself finally capable of concentrating on something other than her confrontation with her attending, Susan suddenly realized the reason she spent so much time with Nate. She liked him, of course, and he had helped her through some difficult moments. It had never previously occurred to her she might also appreciate that Nate handed her topics of new conversation with the father she adored. The positronic robot had opened the door to glimpses of John Calvin she would not otherwise have had, and it had brought the two Calvins, always close, even closer. *I'll have to remember to thank him the next time I see him.*

Tompkins Square Park was strangely full this Thursday afternoon. Children's laughter and squeals rang over the underlying buzz of myriad conversations. They swarmed the playgrounds like ants over a discarded candy bar. She could scarcely see the grassy spaces for the masses of adults on blankets and towels, some conversing, and others lying silent in the sunlight. As Susan walked down Ninth Street toward her building just off Avenue C, she found herself winding through hordes of pedestrians, far more than she ever remembered encountering on a weekday in the past.

At first, Susan's mind dismissed it as the difference between walking home at 2:00 p.m. rather than 6:00 or 7:00 p.m. However, it soon became clear this could not explain the teeming masses of people, which continued past Avenue B and outside the park. Most of the crowd seemed set on going in the exact same direction as Susan. She considered what might make the day so special. *Monday was the first, which makes today the fourth.* She finally understood. *It's Independence Day, and normal people not enmeshed in residencies have the day off.*

At length, Susan found herself irrevocably entwined in a jam of people, unable to make any forward progress or see over the vast sea of human heads. Every few moments, someone would push his way backward through the crowd, saying, "Excuse me" repeatedly, to head in a broad tangent around the milling people. This allowed Susan and the others a bit of occasional forward motion. *One block,* Susan reminded herself. *Then I'm home and out of this nightmare.*

Another step down Ninth Street allowed Susan to catch sight of multicolored lights strobing off the metal and concrete surfaces ahead, alternately striping the spectators in shades of patriotic red, white, and blue. A news helicopter swept over their heads, low enough to ruin conversation in a broad area, creating a massive breeze that stole ball caps and ruined hairstyles. *What is going on?* Susan had seen her share of Macy's fireworks shows, but she could never recall anything July-Fourth-related happening so early, particularly so close to home.

Only then it occurred to Susan to tap her Vox. She flashed through news feeds until she came to the one matching the logo on the newscopter, a black silhouette of a galloping horse. Finding hearing difficult, she muted the sound and read: ". . . a breaking story. Police have cordoned off a Lower East Side apartment complex in Alphabet City. Our eyes in the skies see no structural damage to the building, but a crowd has gathered. Police procedure, and ambulances standing by, suggest the possibility of a death or serious injury to at least one occupant of the building at Ninth Street and Avenue C. More details when they become available." The feed launched into commercials, and Susan tapped it off her Vox.

Susan recognized the location immediately, and a chill spiraled through her. *Home.* Her thoughts went immediately to her father, and the realization that he should be nowhere other than at work sent a wave of relief through her. With that concern firmly pushed from her mind, she considered the lot of their neighbors. A few were home-bound, and several others had retired years earlier. One of those elders might have suffered a medical complication that required emergency services. Susan had just started considering the plight of individual neighbors when something nagged at the edges of her thoughts. She rarely watched police dramas and knew little about their procedures, but she felt fairly certain they did not cordon off an entire apartment building to evacuate a myocardial infarction or cerebral infarct. A single ambulance with an experienced crew of EMTs would perform the job admirably.

Susan inched her way closer to the front of the line, dodging the writhing shoulders and flying elbows of people intent on becoming a part of infamous history. She finally worked her way close enough to ascertain it was, indeed, her apartment building at the center of the cordon and to catch occasional glimpses of the barricades and glowing neon crime-scene tape keeping the crowd at bay.

Susan's arm buzzed. For an instant, she thought one of the lookie-loos had zapped her with a prod. When it happened a second time, she finally recognized it as the all-too-familiar sensation of her Vox. She tapped the face, surprised to see Lawrence Robertson's name come up. She could think of no reason why her father's boss, the founder of U.S. Robots and Mechanical Men and creator of the positronic brain, would be calling her. Despite the simple routine of a Vox call, she felt her heart skip a beat and a lump form in her throat. The last time he had called her, they were chasing a mad bomber. And Remington had died.

Knowing she would not hear anything Lawrence said over the sounds of the helicopter and the crowd, and he could not possibly hear her replies, she nudged the switch into text-translation mode: "Susan. Susan?" The device translated only his words, not his tone, but Susan sensed urgency.

She hit the Kwik-set key for "Dr. Susan Calvin here."

There was a pause, followed by more text: "Are you at work?"

Susan tapped out pidgin shorthand. "Lft early. Crowd o-side apt blding. U no y?"

The subsequent pause left Susan light-headed. The translator should turn words into text instantaneously. If nothing came from the other end, it meant Lawrence Robertson had stopped speaking.

"???," she sent.

Finally, words scrolled from the other end, "Is John OK?"

Susan could feel her chest tying itself into knots. "He w/ u!" She indicated her father should be at USR with Lawrence at the present moment. She added fiercely, "??" *Please be there, Dad. Why wouldn't you be there?* Her thoughts raced. *At least don't be here!*

"Susan, your father went home an hour ago. Damn . . ." The text line filled up with random marks as Lawrence Robertson either muffled the Vox to talk with someone else or muttered something unprintable.

Susan slammed in a few more question marks of her own.

Lawrence took infuriatingly long to reply. "Susan, go directly to the police." She could almost hear the sudden, irritating calm in his lack of voice.

"Y?" she demanded.

"Tell them everything you know."

"No nothing!"

Lawrence gave the last answer she expected: "Perfect. Stay with the police until you're sure you're both safe. Let me know what happens."

"But . . ." Susan started, but Lawrence's words rolled over her own.

"Please, Susan. Erase this conversation immediately, and don't show it to anyone. Lives may depend on it." He added maddeningly, knowing the intense bond between father and daughter, "Especially John's."

Irritated as much as terrified, Susan texted back. "No erase til u tell me smthng uzful!"

There was a faint click, all but lost beneath the noises of the crowd; then Lawrence Robertson was gone.

Susan stared at her Vox a moment, uncertain what to do. Impotently, she shook her arm, as if this might bring back the signal. It seemed futile to call back Lawrence Robertson. Her father and Lawrence had been college roommates, had trusted one another since long before her birth. Her father trusted him, believed him the most brilliant human being who ever walked the earth, and her father's judgment was always spot-on. Reluctantly, she erased all traces of her last conversation before shoving violently into the crowd.

The people in front of Susan turned dirty looks on her, but something in her demeanor must have cued them, because they did not fight back as she cut through them without apology. Frantic for her father, Susan paid no heed to shouts, prods, and curses. She knew only she had to get to the front, had to talk to the police, had to ascertain nothing bad had happened to John Calvin. *Home in the early afternoon the same day I'm home early, the same day the police show up at our building.* It all seemed too much for coincidence, and Lawrence's call only worsened her suspicions. Susan's discomfort flared immediately to panic. *It's Dad! Oh, God, it has to be Dad!* Susan flailed through the crowd, no longer worrying whom she might strike in blind panic.

Miraculously, a pathway cleared in front of Susan. Without any memory of how she managed it, she found herself at the crime-scene tape and, a moment later, addressing an officer who was engaged in conversation through a standard-issue Ear-mite clipped to his left lobe.

"Please," Susan said, seizing his arm. "My father's in there."

Susan half expected him to shrug her off and send her reeling back into the crowd, so it surprised her when he turned his full attention to her. He had a weathered face, relatively young but prematurely creased, with a well-healed scar running from the outside corner of his right eye to the middle of his cheek. He stood only a few inches taller than Susan, with eyes the same dark blue as his uniform, a broad mouth, and a sturdy figure. "What floor?" he asked with a casual air that conveyed only mild interest. He had surely asked the same question multiple times.

"Tenth," Susan said. "Apartment 10B."

The officer stiffened, though whether at Susan's reply or at something coming over the Ear-mite, she did not know. He raised his hand to Susan and spoke into the air. "Travis, hang on a mo. I found 10B." He paused a moment. "The daughter, I think."

Susan did not like the sound of that. The officer did not seem particularly excited; he might simply have been relaying the apartment number of a random person who lived in the building. Still, to Susan's worried mind, they had been searching frantically for her.

The officer turned his full attention on Susan, and the crowd hemmed in, clearly eager to hear the conversation. He glanced at his Vox. "Is your name Calvin?"

Susan felt as if icy fingers had invaded her chest. She supposed the police had easily acquired a list of every person who lived in the building, but it still bothered her that he brought up her name so quickly and easily. "Yes. Susan Calvin."

"Daughter of John Calvin, same address."

"Yes, yes." Susan could stand the suspense no longer. "Is my dad okay?"

"Come with me, please, Ms. Calvin."

"That's Dr. Calvin," Susan corrected, hoping the title might make him less condescending and more talkative. She added, a bit more forcefully, "Is my dad okay?"

"We'll explain everything. This way, please." With a hooked plastic rod, the officer scooped a piece of the crime-scene tape high enough for Susan to slide under without ducking. When she did so, he dropped it back into place and ushered her along the familiar sidewalk. In the playground directly below their balcony, she saw a smaller crowd and recognized several of them as neighbors. The benches were full of nannies and stay-at-home mothers with children on their laps, while others milled around or chatted quietly among themselves or into Vox.

Susan expected the officer to mix her into the herd. Instead he took her to the front door of the apartment building. There he stopped and gestured for her to wait.

Again Susan obeyed silently, her heart pounding in her chest and her patience waning. It bothered her that he had taken her somewhere different than where the other inhabitants of the building were. She felt as if a thousand eyes followed her and, when the policeman left her side to talk to others at the entrance, she glanced back at the crowd. The prickles at her back proved true; everyone seemed eager to see what happened to her. Even the newscopter buzzed lower, and she heard the muffled click of Vox-cams.

Not a fan of mystery, Susan allowed the police a few moments of private conversation before approaching them. As she came within earshot, they grew eerily quiet, all attention focused on her. "If you don't tell me something about my father, I'm going to go hysterical on you."

The officer to whom Susan had already spoken headed back to his post. A new one took her arm and coaxed her to the door. This time, she had the wherewithal to glance at his badge, which read "Freeman." "Ma'am," he said carefully, "I'm not privy to all the information. The detective in the lobby will tell you all you need to know."

Susan suspected the officer knew exactly what she needed to know but preferred not to be the one to tell her. Seized by an irrational urge to grab him and shake loose everything in his head, she found herself incapable of any action but following dumbly along behind him. Her throat closed, making even speech impossible. John Calvin had sat vigil at her bedside through the aftermath of two bombs. He had survived the accident that killed her mother, though it had required months of hospitalization and rehabilitation. Susan would do whatever it took to make him better. After all the storms they had weathered together, no one could steal him from her now.

The lobby looked exactly as it always did, except the security doors were propped open. She recognized the six civilians seated on the padded benches lining the walls near the elevators as other occupants of the tenth floor. Mike and Linda Cready from 10G, a retired couple in their eighties, sat together, talking softly. Gray-haired Gary Stolty, the widower from 10D, sat nearby, head bowed, face in his hands. He was a friendly man, semiretired, performing odd jobs for the building manager as well as for his neighbors. He never asked for money but always took what they gave him graciously.

Ashley Terrance from 10E was sobbing. She worked in retail but was currently home, nursing a viral infection. Aldius Maynard, a chronically unemployed slacker who lived with his parents, stared into space, wide-eyed; his girlfriend, Rochette Holley, was rocking and crying hysterically beside him. She wore a blanket over her heaving shoulders, and a detective stood in front of the pair, talking softly. Notably missing was Sammy Cottrell, a thirty-two-year-old mother of three who lived in 10C. She was nearly always home, tending two highly active sons and a daughter with special needs.

Officer Freeman took Susan to a man wearing a suit and tie and standing near a stairwell, speaking into the air. "This is Detective Hollinger. He's the one you need to talk to."

Susan tried to thank the officer but could not squeak out a single word. A cold wave of discomfort washed over her, and she suddenly lost all urgency for information. Her medical training made her calm in a crisis, which allowed her to think clearly. At the moment, she wanted to avoid her thoughts; panic might have seemed welcome.

The detective stood nearly as tall as her father, about six and half feet, and so slender he looked as if he might break in a solid wind. He wore his blond hair in a buzz cut that might have made him seem military if not for the baby-faced features accentuated by the need to remain professionally clean-shaven. He looked more like a high school basketball player or high jumper than a detective, even with the obvious gun holstered at his left hip.

Freeman waited for the detective to stop speaking before finishing the introduction. "This is Ms. Susan Calvin."

The detective nodded solemnly, and Susan stuck out her right hand. "That's *Dr.* Susan Calvin," she corrected.

Detective Hollinger clearly had paid more attention than Officer Freeman had. "Doctor," he said with a nod, and clasped her right hand in a strong grip, then released it nearly as quickly. "What kind of doctor are you, Dr. Calvin?"

"Medical," Susan said.

The captain gestured at Freeman, who promptly left, then to an empty corner that held the only open seats, a small and weathered bench. If they kept their voices reasonably low, no one else would be able to hear them. As they headed toward it together, he said, "Your father is a doctor also?" It was more question than comment.

Susan dutifully stepped to the indicated corner and sat on the far end of the bench, hands clasped in her lap. She focused on the detective's use of the present tense in reference to her father. That buoyed her spirits remarkably, despite the fact it had never consciously occurred to her that her father might not be alive. "My father is the PhD kind of doctor. Robotics."

Hollinger remained standing in front of her. "He worked at U.S. Robots, didn't he?"

"All my life," Susan replied. "USR was incorporated the year I was born, and he was there from the start." Still attuned to verb tenses, she furrowed her brow. "He still works there, at least he did as of this morning."

The detective cocked his head, apparently listening to something on his Ear-mite. The technology was still in its expensive stage, but she doubted it would take long for everyone to have the ability to listen to conversations without the need for text or the possibility of others over-hearing. "Excuse me a moment," he said to Susan, then into the air. "I'm talking to her now."

A moment of silence followed, then the detective continued, "Susan Calvin, yes. The daughter." He paused. "Yes, she's also a doctor." He rolled his eyes and glanced at Susan as if they shared a joke, though he never smiled. "No, a *real* doctor. MD."

Susan wondered how often her father heard the "real doctor" crack and if it ever bothered him. She supposed most people with PhDs grew accustomed to the misconception or deliberate ribbing, but she knew some stodgy doctorates became positively apoplectic.

"Not yet. Give me a chance." He turned his attention directly on Susan. "Sorry about that."

Susan wiped her palms on her khakis, surprised to find they left an obvious smear of moisture.

Hollinger cleared his throat, and Susan's breath caught. She had delivered enough bad news to recognize stalling. "Aren't you off a bit early, Dr. Calvin? I thought young doctors like you worked crazy hours."

Susan could not think of a topic she would less like to discuss, especially when she still had no idea of her father's fate. However, she knew lying to cops, or even withholding information, was rarely a good idea, especially for an innocent person. "My attending and I weren't seeing eye to eye on a patient, and we both decided it was a better idea for me to go home than to deck him."

Hollinger loosed a strained chuckle. "You don't look like the violent type."

"I'm not," Susan assured him. "But this guy could incite Gandhi." She thought she might get another chuckle, but Detective Hollinger gave her nothing. He clearly had a sense of humor, so Susan made the obvious leap. Apparently, something troubled him enough to make laughing inappropriate, and it likely concerned whatever news he needed to give her. "I'm not sure why my father came home early, but I know he did. He was in that building when . . . whatever happened . . . happened." She tried to keep her tone firm, stifling worry, making it clear she deserved some information.

The detective clearly got the hint. He glanced longingly over his shoulder, as if hoping someone would relieve him of his duty or an even more urgent call would come over the Ear-mite.

Susan pressed, "I'm sure whatever you have to tell me can't be any worse than what I can imagine." It was a well-known phenomenon in medicine. No news was generally good news; laboratory personnel alerted doctors to abnormalities while leaving the normal results to arrive over time. Doctors, too, were far more likely to sit on routine matters and handle the critical ones first. Still, the longer patients waited, the more they imagined they, or their loved ones, had something disfiguring and fatal the doctor could not bear to pronounce. She wondered if police ever got to deliver good news.

Hollinger dropped to a crouch to look Susan directly in the eye. "I'm very sorry to have to tell you this, Dr. Calvin." He took a breath that seemed to last a lifetime. "Your father is dead."

It felt as if all the blood drained from Susan's body in an instant, replaced by a sudden flood of icy water. She found herself incapable of speech, thought, or movement. She knew nothing but the sting of a deep and entrenching cold seeping through her every part. Had she been standing, she probably would have collapsed. Far beyond meaningless, the pronouncement was impossible. She finally managed words, "Are you . . . sure?"

They were words, but not intelligent ones. Susan felt certain the police knew dead when they saw it, just as she did. They did not require a second opinion from her or any other physician. She tried again, "Murdered?"

"It would appear he was shot." Hollinger kept his attention on her face, apparently looking for clues to her mental state. "Several times."

Susan doubted the police considered her a suspect. More likely, the detective wanted to make sure she was not going to topple over, run screaming, or mindlessly attack him in her grief. She was accustomed to death, used to being the messenger, and she knew how difficult a job it was, regardless of how many times, how many ways. Susan remained calm; her training would not allow otherwise. "How?" She looked Hollinger straight in the eyes, surprised to find them moist. He was crying.

"Perhaps you'd be more comfortable . . . ," he started, but Susan stopped him with a firm shake of her head.

"Can I . . . see him?"

"No."

The answer startled her. It was always the first thing doctors did, a quick cleanup, if necessary, then a walk to the bedside to cement the reality of death for the survivors. But this was not a long-suffering grandparent fading into routine darkness. This was a crime scene, ugly, brutal, probably bloody. It was silly to think they would allow her access before they examined every clue.

The detective explained, "They've already taken the body away. When they're finished upstairs, I'd like you to accompany me to your apartment. We'll need help figuring out what's out of place, putting all the pieces together, finding answers."

Still strangely cold, Susan felt as if someone had dropped a boulder on her chest. Yet still the tears did not come to her own eyes. "Tell me everything you know. What happened to my"—to her surprise, she had to force out the final word—"father." And, once spoken, it released the floodgates in an abrupt and violent sob. Her eyes filled so quickly, she was blinded, and the tears ran down her face. *Not Dad.* Her thoughts flashed backward a year to the agony of losing Remington. *Not Dad, too.*

Hollinger put his arms around Susan, holding her close and tight. Susan wondered if he did so against regulations, if he risked charges of misconduct, but it was exactly what she needed. She clung to him, sobbing into his chest, appreciating his warmth and support, his loss of decorum, more than anything else he could possibly have done. It meant a lot to know someone cared about her pain. Whether or not he fully understood it, he appeared to. And, for the moment, that was enough.

Susan did not know how long she cried in the detective's strong arms, but he made no move to pull away, never rushed her, remained in place until she finally regained control and broke the embrace. Only then he stood up and pulled a handful of crumpled tissues from his pocket, his dress shirt darkened by her tears. Silently, he handed the tissues to Susan, his pale eyes filled with genuine concern. They were grayish green, Susan noted, and they probably changed color depending on light and background. "I'm sorry," she said, wiping her nose and eyes.

"Sorry for what?" he said.

Susan knew he did not expect an answer. Both of them were trained to remain composed and in control at all times, yet the idea of doing so now seemed beyond abnormal. "Tell me what happened. Please? I have to know."

Hollinger studied Susan briefly, as if to ascertain she could handle the news. "All we know for sure is there were two bodies: a female in the tenth-floor hallway and a male in apartment 10B."

A trickle of hope arose. "Are you sure it's my father?"

Hollinger cocked an eyebrow. "Would you expect other bodies in your apartment?"

"I wouldn't expect *any* bodies in my apartment." Susan continued to wipe away tears. "My father should have been at work, but he came home early." That reminded her of the Vox call she had received from Lawrence Robertson. For some reason, the director of U.S. Robots did not want the police to know about that call, and, for now, she would honor his wishes. However, if it interfered with finding her father's killer, she would violate them in an instant. "I presume you performed a retinal scan?"

Hollinger chewed his lower lip, fighting a scowl. He had probably grown tired of civilians watching detective and forensics programs, then telling him how to do his job. "Dr. Calvin still had his wallet, and the fingerprints matched."

That puzzled Susan a bit. She had thought the on-scene retina scan was the swift and simple gold standard of their age. Few people managed to avoid the database. Most parents had their children scanned and printed for security reasons. Public schools required it for all students in case of accidents and in order to activate lockers. Anyone missed in childhood was nearly always picked up when they joined an organization, purchased a door or safe lock, or committed a crime. Fingerprints worked as well but required the scanning of multiple digits as opposed to a single eye.

"Do you want me to ID him?" Susan did not relish the job, but she did want to make absolutely sure. Somewhere in the deepest recesses of her mind, she dared to hope they had made a mistake. Though surely born only of desperation, she could not wholly banish it. Everyone had heard stories of a person pronounced dead who woke up screaming in the morgue. Such things did not happen anymore, at least she had never heard of an actual case, certainly not in the United States of America. The stories were either old, from a third-world country, or apocryphal.

Hollinger looked distinctly uncomfortable. Susan supposed anyone would feel ill at ease discussing such matters with a family member, especially so soon after announcing his untimely death. "That won't be necessary, Dr. Calvin."

"Susan," she suggested.

He barely nodded an acknowledgment. "There'll be an autopsy, of course. To determine the cause of death."

"The cause?" Susan looked at him curiously. "I thought you said he was shot."

"I said he appeared to have been shot. You'd be surprised at how many times the obvious cause of death isn't . . . the"–the detective fidgeted, obviously even more uncomfortable with the turn the conversation had taken–"cause. . . . Are you sure you want to talk about this right now?"

Susan knew she definitely did not want to focus directly on the hard, cold reality of her father's death, the cavernous hole it would leave in her life, the grief threatening to overwhelm her the instant she opened her mind to thoughts of him. The longer she questioned the details, kept herself in professional mode, the longer she could avoid the ugly reality of her father's death and what it meant for the future. "Please continue."

"Every murder warrants, and gets, an autopsy."

"Of course."

Apparently looking for a reason for Susan's sudden focus on the autopsy, Hollinger tried, "When they're finished, they put everything back together. Any incisions are carefully hidden. You can still–"

Susan waved him off. She had given the speech herself to families concerned an autopsy would preclude an open casket ceremony. "I did my pathology rotation in med school. I know the drill. I really want to know where he's going, to know he's in competent hands, to be able to find him to make . . ." Grief threatened to overwhelm her again. She swallowed hard. ". . . arrangements."

"Excuse me a moment," the detective said, then spoke into the air. "No, we're not quite finished yet. Probably a few more minutes. I'll let you know."

Hollinger switched back to Susan without losing the thread of the previous conversation. "I'll let you know where they took him as soon as I know. If there's space, he'll most likely go to Hasbro. They're the best."

Susan had no idea the hospital served as a morgue in addition to performing the standard medical autopsies on patients who died in the hospital with uncertain or suspicious diagnoses. Then again, she had never needed that information. "I'm doing my residency at Hasbro, so it would be foolish of me to disagree with your assessment."

The detective sat down next to Susan on the bench. "Not pathology."

"Psychiatry," Susan said. "But we're still the best."

"Undoubtedly."

A tremor rushed through Susan's hands, then encompassed her entire body. Still chilled in every part, she felt herself shivering uncontrollably. She glanced at her Vox, reading the temperature at a balmy 76 degrees. The arm above her Vox resembled plucked gooseflesh, and a wave of nausea swept through her.

Hollinger studied her, then gestured to someone near the elevator. "The scene is secured. They want to know if you're feeling up to examining it."

Susan nodded. The more she had to do, the less she focused on her own pain, on the realization of a desperate loss. "Let's do it."

Hollinger spoke into the air again. "Mel, I'm bringing Dr. Calvin now. Are you ready for us?" He glanced at Susan, whose stomach roiled, then tipped his head to listen for the distant answer she could not hear.

Susan had a sudden urge to crawl into her own safe bed and take a long nap, fueled by the absurd notion that, when she awoke, everything would return to the way it was that morning. Maybe if she approached Chase Aberdeen more tactfully, if she ignored Mitchell Reefes' stupidity, a deity in whom she did not believe would restore the world to its proper order.

Apparently unaware of Susan's inner turmoil, the detective continued, "I'd like to get your take on the scene while it's still a safe place
to go."

Focused on her father, Susan had not considered that. "The killers?
Did you catch them?"

"Not yet." Hollinger's tone made it clear he saw no possibility of failure. "They were gone before we arrived, apparently. As far as we can
tell, they killed your father first. The woman probably surprised them
in the hallway, and they shot her, too."

Guilt flashed through Susan, worsening her nausea. A person of good
character would have worried for the other victim as well as for her
father. She had completely forgotten about the woman. "Who?" Her
mouth had gone painfully dry; the single word was an effort.

But Hollinger understood the question. He headed for the stairs.
"Samantha Elizabeth Cottrell, age thirty-two. Do you know her?"

"Neighbor," Susan forced out, then realized something important.
"She has three young kids. Are they all right?"

The detective nodded. "I apologize for the walk. We shut down the
elevators trying to catch the . . . killers."

Susan sensed he had stumbled over jargon. The climb suited her. It
would give her time to prepare herself for a fresh look at no longer
familiar surroundings. Also, she hoped the exercise would warm her
up and decrease the queasiness threatening to overtake her. Hopefully,
exercise would channel the blood flow from her digestive system to
her limbs.

Detective Hollinger led the way at a fast and steady clip, and Susan
followed him closely. She found herself obsessing over the word "apparently." *They were gone before we arrived, apparently. Apparently.* But what if
they remained somewhere, hiding in the building? What if they were
waiting for all the police to leave before claiming more victims? The
idea of blithely sleeping in the place her father was murdered became

unbearable. She could imagine herself lying in bed, alone with her thoughts, sobbing uncontrollably while the killers made short work of her as well.

Again Hollinger seemed to read her mind. Susan supposed he had enough experience to figure out relatives' concerns at a time like this. "I highly recommend you find somewhere else to stay for a while, preferably with a good friend or relative. Do you know someone who will let you do that?"

Susan nodded dumbly, certain Kendall would let her stay with him. If not, there were other residents to ask and always the hospital on-call room, or even the couch in the charting room in a pinch. She did not relish the thought of a quiet, empty hotel room.

Though in reasonably good shape, Susan was panting by the time they reached the tenth-floor landing. She took a bit of solace from the realization that even the slender police detective had some trouble speaking wholly normally. He turned to face her, his hand on the knob. "I want to prepare you . . . a bit. The second body . . . landed near . . . the stairway. The body's gone, but there's still . . . evidence of what happened. I assume, Doctor . . . you're not squeamish."

Susan frowned and shook her head. As a medical student, she had watched two members in her class faint when confronted with their first surgical patient. Both men, they had suffered for their temporary weakness for the remainder of the rotation. Most doctors would rather die than appear delicate to peers; but, at the moment, Susan felt she could be forgiven for losing her nerve, no matter what form it took. "I can handle it," she growled, not at all sure she could.

Detective Hollinger turned back to the door, and Susan closed her eyes. When she opened them, she knew, the world would never be the same.

Chapter 11

Susan kept her eyes squeezed shut; it stung too much to open them. The familiar sounds of New York City night surrounded her: the hiss of glide-buses, the not-quite-discernable conversations of debarking passengers, the occasional loud honk from a disgruntled driver, and the intermittent shouting of people arguing, too drunk or foolish to realize the lateness of the hour.

Susan opened one eye a crack to glance at her Vox. It was 4:23 a.m., a time when wise and normal people were sleeping. She could hear Kendall's deep, rhythmical breathing beside her, and she shifted to her back carefully to avoid waking him. She had an excuse for missing work the next day. So did he, but she doubted his would garner as much sympathy, and Mitchell Reefes would likely throw a tantrum if neither of his residents showed up and he actually had to deal with a patient directly.

Susan managed to open both eyes, examining the off-white ceiling through painful slits. Hours of crying had swollen her lids to three times their normal size. She had always thought of her father as the ideal man and assumed all other daughters felt the same way about their own. Not until middle school did she discover that emotions toward the paternal parent, for those who even had one, spanned the gamut.

John Calvin had always been protective without being suffocating, had nurtured Susan's dreams and never demeaned them, had steered her constantly in positive directions. His advice was sound and logical, but he never inflicted it upon her, allowing her to go her own way, to make her own mistakes. She could never remember him losing his temper or his cool even when life handed him unfair or difficult situations; and she could not recall him uttering the words "I told you so" in any circumstance.

Quiet dignity defined John Calvin. Always there to solve Susan's problems, he never visited his own on her or, to her knowledge, on anyone else. He helped anyone in whatever way he could, avoiding ill-tempered or -willed individuals without uttering a single negative word about them. An obsessive reader and listener, he never seemed to forget anything, yet he indulged Susan's desire to watch favored programs repeatedly. Though wholly committed to Susan, he never asked the same of her, never deliberately made her feel uncomfortable or guilty for living her own life. She could not imagine anyone ever wanting to harm him.

Yet harm him they did, and it was clearly no accident. Whoever killed her father had done an extensive search, slashing mattresses into useless rags, flinging the stuffing from the sofa, scattering the contents of the cabinets, and tearing all the shelves and pictures from the walls. Clearly not common thieves, they had left gutted electronics, her father's wallet, and the pearl necklace Susan had inherited from her grandmother, the only valuable piece of jewelry she owned. They had taken John Calvin's palm-pross and Vox, all of the VFDs, anything on which any kind of media could be recorded. Other than that, Susan could not tell what was missing.

The body was gone by the time the police brought Susan on the scene. She had looked diligently for the standard chalk outline that seemed to magically appear in every police drama she had ever seen, but she never found it. Apparently, the crime-scene investigators relied solely on pictures of the body before they removed it. Susan had also prepared herself for huge amounts of blood. The female body in the hallway had left a scarlet pool, so the sparse splatters on the carpet and across the shredded sofa in their apartment surprised her. Her medical training had kicked in, despite her personal relationship to the corpse. The best explanation for the paucity of blood was a spine shot, which enraged her. The killers might have shot her father in the back while he was trying to cooperate with their demands. She supposed wounds in the lower torso would not bleed as much as those nearer the heart, but every head wound she had ever seen bled profusely.

By the time the police had finished with Susan, Kendall had come to collect her. Exhausted, she had gone with him quietly, taking the glide-bus to his apartment and spending the next several hours sobbing in his arms. To her surprise, he proved a gallant and competent consoler, remaining silent most of the time but sneaking in the right words at the appropriate moments. Her father had been right about one thing; Kendall knew her better than anyone else, understood her circumstances, and cared deeply for her.

When Susan found herself emotionally drained, unable to say another word about her father, they had naturally switched to all topics deeply personal. She had learned a lot about Kendall, things he usually hid behind an impenetrable mantle of humor, his interests and fears, his early history, his most exhilarating and embarrassing moments. She also discovered Kendall had received many of the same unsubtle hints from friends, coworkers, and family that the two of them belonged in a relationship together.

That had naturally led to Susan's admission of virginity, how she had finally found Remington, a man she cared for enough to end it for, only to have him snatched from her life forever just hours after they had decided to consummate their love. Kendall had confessed to being nearly as inexperienced as Susan. Their shared pain, their closeness, physically and emotionally, had made the next step inevitable. They had made love amid the explosions, pops, and whizzes of the Independence Day fireworks, flashes of multicolored light intermittently sailing past the bedroom window.

And now Susan lay awake, wondering how an act so boring and uncomfortable had toppled kingdoms and civilizations, driven otherwise normal men and women to break sacred vows, supported the highest-grossing industry of all time. Had their purity rendered them clumsy and self-conscious, or was one or both of them simply bad in bed? Did they lack the necessary chemistry for lovers, or was she neurologically or endocrinologically abnormal? Perhaps she was undesirable, unattractive; Kendall had seemed to have great difficulty keeping focused on the task. Or maybe the medical problem was his.

Susan sighed, confronting the inescapable logic she would rather avoid. The guilt of seeking pleasure on the night of her father's murder had, most likely, stolen any joy she might have garnered from the act of lovemaking. Or, perhaps, she subconsciously worried about dishonoring Remington's memory.

Susan rolled toward Kendall to study him in his sleep. He looked boyish and innocent, strands of orange hair flopping over one closed eye, features slack, lips slightly parted. His face did not remind her of angels, as slumbering faces often did to lovers in romance novels and movies, though moonlight slipping through a gap in the shade did bring out blond highlights in the otherwise clown-orange hair. She had never had a particular attraction to redheads, had never pictured her husband or children that way. Even when she had contemplated making changes to her own appearance, she had imagined herself as a blonde or raven locked, perhaps even auburn, but never copper or carroty. Freckles had never occurred to her, either. She neither loathed nor loved them; they were simply not on her radar.

Eyes desperately stinging, Susan closed them again, holding them tightly shut. The pain brought back clear memories of the day before. She relived the puddle of blood in the hallway, surrounded by spilled garbage, the carpet stained deeply red, the side wall splattered with rusty brown patches. Even with the body removed, there was no question about the means of Sammy Cottrell's death. Something moving at high speed had struck her, splashing her blood across the wall, and she had exsanguinated swiftly on the floor.

Susan imagined Sammy had emerged from her apartment, headed for the incinerator, leaving the children inside, hopefully napping. Fleeing the Calvins' apartment, the killers must have run into her. Susan could imagine the young mother glancing toward them to apologize, realizing their strangeness, perhaps even screaming, before a well-placed gunshot ended her life. Susan could not help putting herself in Sammy's place—the sudden terror, the agony of a bullet tearing through her skull, then darkness as she collapsed to the ground. She hoped only that the children had remained inside, blissfully sleeping, unaware of what had happened until neighbors or police carried them safely, blindly past the gore.

Without her scream or, perhaps, the thud of her body, the police might not have known about John Calvin until after Susan returned home and discovered his body. By then, there would have been no chance of catching the murderers; the trail would have grown cold.

Susan could not get the same vivid picture of her father's end as she did of Sammy Cottrell's. There was just too much she did not know, could not know, until after the full investigation. She wondered why understanding his last moments meant so much to her. Did it really matter whether he spent them battling his attackers or falling calmly and silently to their attack, whether he attempted to follow their demands or oppose them, whether he even saw it coming? Was it better to die oblivious or to know your attackers and their motives? Thus far, she had only hoped he had not suffered. Now she needed to know so much more.

The police had warned Susan about that. They had made it distinctly clear that days or weeks might pass before they delivered any more information to her. They promised they would tell her as soon as they knew anything, that calling sooner would only frustrate everyone.

Susan opened one eye a slit to glance at her Vox again. It was now 4:36, only thirteen minutes since she had last looked. She sat up, eyes still tightly closed, careful not to awaken Kendall. She needed to know something, anything, and, if the police would not tell her, perhaps she could learn something from Lawrence Robertson.

Susan slipped from the bedroom into Kendall's tiny living room. She already knew her way around the familiar and simple décor, and dodged a coffee table by memory to flop into the well-worn checkered armchair. She considered sending a text, then remembered how he had left her hanging, and placed the call instead. He did not deserve the luxury of a leisurely reply.

To her surprise, and despite the hour, Lawrence answered immediately. "Susan?"

"This is Susan," she confirmed. "Did you expect someone else to call you from my Vox?"

There was a catch in Lawrence's voice. "Are you . . . alone?"

"Not completely," Susan admitted. "I'm at a friend's house, but he's asleep in the other room."

"Susan," Lawrence said. "Are you sure you're safe?"

Susan wanted to shout, "Of course I'm not sure. My father was murdered in our secure apartment in the middle of the day. How can I ever be sure of anything again?"

Lawrence's voice dropped to barely above a whisper. "I'm so sorry. We're so sorry, Susan." She finally recognized the oddity in his voice and timbre. He, too, had spent a long time crying.

"What was he doing home in the middle of the afternoon?" Susan tried not to sound accusatory, but she doubted she wholly managed to hide her anger. He should not have been home. He loved his job; he was never home on weekdays, not even on the Fourth of July. He had never considered any day a holiday unless Susan also had it off, which was rare.

Lawrence sighed. "It was his idea, Susan. We tried to talk him out of it."

"Why?" Though soft, it was a demand. Susan did not specify whether she wanted to know why her father left or why they tried to stop him. She needed both answers.

Lawrence complied. "We got a tip, not particularly reliable, but we took it seriously. We always take threats seriously. John insisted on going home, packing some things, then personally picking you up when you finished work."

Susan assumed Lawrence meant by cab, as they did not own a car.

"We suggested staying together in a safe place or getting a police escort, but he was sure no one would try anything in broad daylight."

Susan wondered aloud, "Was it a threat against USR? Or against my father specifically?"

Lawrence Robertson cleared his throat. She could tell he did not want to answer. "We had reason to believe John was the target."

"How?" A more significant question arose, and Susan asked it without waiting for an answer to the first. "Why?"

The founder of U.S. Robots and Mechanical Men went very quiet.

"How and why?" Susan repeated.

"We don't know."

It was a lie, and Susan knew it. She also dared not press too hard. Lawrence Robertson did not have to tell her anything, and if she challenged him, she might lose the little information she could coax from him. Quite possibly, he did not want to relay certain details until he had her in a more secure location. "Dr. Robertson . . ."

He cleared his throat.

"Lawrence," Susan substituted, guessing he was about to remind her he preferred a first-name basis with his best friend's grown daughter. Coming across as an equal might also encourage him to speak more freely. "Am I in any danger?"

"We don't know," Lawrence admitted. "They obviously can't use you to get to him anymore, so that should get you off the hook. Unless . . ."

Lawrence Robertson could not have trailed into silence at a more frightening time. "Unless," Susan repeated.

"Unless we're reading this completely wrong." Lawrence finished quickly, sounding frustrated. "Susan, we just can't be sure. It's best for you to lay low, stay safe. If you can get police protection, so much the better. If you can't, get out of the city. Find a relative, a friend, a loved one–"

Susan interrupted, suddenly angry. "A relative? They're all dead. A loved one? Dead, too. My mother, my father, Remington, my grandmother."

"Your grandmother died from cancer."

"She's still dead," Susan pointed out. "The operative state for anyone who loves me is *dead*."

"I love you," Lawrence pointed out.

"Not enough, apparently," Susan said sullenly. "Or you'd be dead."

"Snap out of it," Lawrence ordered. "Your life may be in serious danger. You need to find a safe place to go, to hide. It's better you don't tell anyone where you're going, not even me. Keep contact to a minimum. You never know who can trace what."

Susan would have none of it. She was not going to cower in a dark hole of ignorance while her father's murder remained unsolved and utterly senseless. "Now hear this, Dr. Lawrence Robertson. My father didn't raise a coward. I'm not going to let a thug stop me from completing my residency. I'm staying right here in Manhattan. And if you don't want to know where I am, hide your own damned self!"

"I'm not going anywhere," Lawrence said in an oddly reassuring voice.

It took Susan a moment to realize his intentions. He was trying to let her know he would be nearby if she needed him. That assuaged much of her rage, and she suddenly felt drained and tired. "Lawrence, who killed my father? Was it the Society for Humanity?" The name of the organization tasted bitter on her tongue. She wanted to spit it out, to stomp on it.

"We believe so, and that's what we told the police when they questioned us."

Susan appreciated that. When patients injected with nanorobots had detonated bombs in the city, he had begged her to keep the information from law enforcement for a time. Susan had spent many hours considering whether involving law enforcement earlier might have saved the lives of Remington and a mall security guard. It had taken a lot of thought, and even more soul-searching, to realize the request had saved many more lives in the long run. Lawrence could not have anticipated Remington flinging himself into harm's way to save others.

"I want you to know when I asked you to erase our conversation, I wasn't hiding anything from the police. I just didn't want anyone tracing and connecting the two of us, at least until we have a better idea what we're facing."

"And now?" Susan pointed out. "We're connected again."

"If you're intent on staying in Manhattan, some association is necessary. At the least, it's important for me to know you're safe. However, I plan to erase any communications on my end so they can't find you through me." Lawrence did not request the same security for himself from her. "I'd appreciate knowing any information the police pass on to you."

"And vice versa," Susan insisted.

"And vice versa," Lawrence agreed. "Stay safe, Susan. Please."

"I'll try. And you, too, Lawrence. You, too." With that, Susan cut off the connection and erased the call. Wearily, she leaned into the plush contours of the armchair and succumbed to exhaustion.

S usan awakened sprawled across the chair, her eyes less swollen and no longer painful. A heavy shade covered the terrace door, preventing any penetration of light directly into the living room, although tendrils of sunlight oozed from the bedroom, allowing her to easily make out the gray lumps of furniture. She glanced at her Vox to find it later than she expected: 10:34 a.m. Susan rose and pulled open the drapes, allowing light to flood the otherwise dreary room.

In front of the checkered armchair in which Susan had slept, the coffee table held her personal palm-pross with a square, orange sticky note on the cover, a vase of plastic daisies, and a large figurine of a monkey. Shelves held an entertainment system and an assortment of VFDs: movies, games, shows, and novels.

A sofa took up most of the left wall space, with paintings and pictures above it. Between the overhead spot-lamps in the ceiling dangled a mobile with ceramic circus clowns in various positions ranging from the merely goofy to the bizarre, most with rust-colored hair and bulbous scarlet noses, a perfect complement to Kendall's quirky humor. Smaller simian figurines sat in most of the empty shelf spaces, including a trio in the classic "see no evil, hear no evil, say no evil" positions, except the first was peeking through his fingers over the words "I see you," the second had hands cupped behind his ears with the caption "I hear you," while the third was using his hands to form a makeshift megaphone and shouting, "I'm going to tell!"

The one oddity of the scene finally penetrated Susan's sleepy, overactive brain. She returned her attention to the sticky note, pulling it off her palm-pross to read it: "Went to work. If you can find anything resembling food, help yourself. Call if you need anything." It was signed *KS*.

Susan stared at the note longer than necessary, trying to read things in it that did not exist. Despite their intimacy the previous night, nothing seemed to have changed. He had not suddenly started referring to her as "darling" or, worse, "snugglebear" or "snooky-ookums." Knowing Kendall, he was probably waiting to do so until the right moment for maximum hilarity for everyone around them. In the heat of the moment, at her most vulnerable and personal, Susan had not considered the effect a failed relationship might have on their friendship.

Susan was glad Kendall was not privy to her conversations with Lawrence Robertson. Her fellow resident would never have left her alone had he known she might be in any danger. As much as she had appreciated a friendly shoulder the previous night, she needed some time to herself to sort out her future. One thing she knew for certain: She was not going to lounge around Kendall's apartment, mooning over her loss, feeling sorry for herself, and waiting for the police to feed her crumbs of information. After a quick shower, some fresh clothes she had grabbed from home, and a bite to eat, she headed for Manhattan Hasbro Hospital to visit her father at the morgue.

Susan had visited the Pathology Unit many times at the various hospitals serving Thomas Jefferson Medical School, usually to examine tumor or marrow cells from a patient not yet diagnosed. She had even attended a few autopsies of patients who died while under the care of fellow medical students and residents and even, once, under her care. She vividly remembered the overwhelming odors of formaldehyde and other preservatives, the chill bite of the refrigerated room, and the echo of voices and whispers from her colleagues. Her patient had died from overwhelming infection after a marrow transplant intended to rescue him from the aggressive chemotherapy necessary to extinguish an osteosarcoma, a tumor of the thighbone.

Susan could never get the image of his face out of her mind. He looked peaceful enough, his eyes closed, his features slack, his limbs still at his sides. The endotracheal tube, cut short, still jutted from his lips, and an intravenous central line catheter remained taped to his chest, reminders that his was not a natural death at home. It seemed impossible she had chatted with him the previous day, discussing his favorite video game and laughing over a well-meaning, colorful get-well card in which his younger sister had declared him a "sweat bother she luffed."

When the pathologist had made the first incision, Susan found herself sobbing against her will, unable to banish memories of the nights on call she had spent with him, the days of agony she had suffered with his family, the terrible decisions she had presented and faced with them all together. They had known the transplant option was a long shot, but the possibility of a permanent cure seemed worth risking several months of a slow and withering death. She had always wondered if they regretted losing those last several weeks together when the end had come so quickly, all a horrible disaster.

Susan knew where to find the Manhattan Hasbro Pathology laboratory, the usual well-camouflaged first-floor location. She had passed it many times in her travels between units, barely acknowledging its existence as she flew past it on another mission. She knew it had separate areas for tissue and cell examination, bodies headed for mortuaries, and those requiring full or partial autopsies before dispatch. Anyone who died under suspicious circumstances would require a full autopsy, and murder certainly qualified as suspicious circumstances.

As boring and innocuous as the staff entrance appeared, Susan knew there must also be a more dignified door for families of the deceased.

She did not bother to look for it. She knew too much of the process to be lulled by somber, tasteful décor. She had learned to react to death with clinical detachment, no longer amazed by the way anything living could go from a breathing, vibrant individual to a lifeless shell in an instant. Susan had even once seen a woman look the attending physician in the eye, squeeze his hand, and state, "I'm going to die now," immediately fulfilling her pronouncement with astonishing accuracy.

Susan had no idea whether she could maintain her professional composure at the sight of her father lying cold on a mortuary trolley beside an electric reciprocating saw, let alone the other trappings of an autopsy. She had sobbed unabashedly at Remington's funeral, but she had not had to glimpse him through a mantle of clinical formality, as a pathology specimen prepped to have every cavity of his body probed and examined. There she had played the appropriate role of mourner. Here she would have to confront the situation as a doctor, not a daughter, or she had no business using the staff entrance and areas.

Uncertain if she could handle the situation, Susan steeled her features, seized the knob, and turned it. The door opened onto a hallway. There was no desk or receptionist, this being a part of the hospital that did not anticipate visitors, at least not through this particular entrance. A sign on the wall pointed out the pathology laboratory to her left. The right hallway led to the mortuary and autopsy area. Straight ahead, a sign declared, led to the family and waiting areas. Susan turned right.

The hallway opened onto an enormous unisex lavatory area, with showers, lockers, changing nooks, and storage bins filled with disposable gowns, aprons, booties, and masks. Susan heard a distant toilet flush, but it otherwise looked empty. She donned the appropriate gear, leaving the mask dangling from her neck in case she blundered into an ongoing autopsy.

Footsteps dampened by the paper booties, Susan moved almost soundlessly into the only other exit from the restroom, a storage area containing empty stainless-steel gurneys polished to a reflective sheen and multiple cabinets that surely contained the tools of the pathology trade. There were three additional exits from the room, none of them labeled. The first door was noticeably colder than air temperature, which suggested she had found the morgue. Susan pushed the door open into a room with a sloping concrete floor and an enormous drain in the center. Plastic handles jutted from three of the four tiled walls, and lines between the tiles revealed them as drawers that could easily accommodate multiple bodies. Every handle had three rings inset over it, and plastic tags dangled from several of these.

High above where the cabinets clearly ended, spacious windows admitted natural light, though Susan suspected vision could travel only one way. No hospital would allow passersby to look into any pathology area. The fourth wall held a sink and multiple built-in cabinets for object storage. A well-tiled hole allowed the passage of samples through it, presumably into the middle room, which would contain microscopes and chemicals for examining and preserving bits of viscera, skin, and organs. In the ceiling, lights and colossal fans lay recessed behind plates of plastic to allow for easy cleaning.

In the center of the room sat two tables, each over seven feet long and four feet wide, with drainage grooves, mounted spotlights, embedded scales, and a spigot. No bodies currently lay open on either table. Aside from a couple of deeply entrenched stains, they both gleamed to a shimmer that easily reflected Susan's face.

On a broad ledge beside the sink lay an oversized bound book, the type of thing a fairy-tale giant might keep in an old-fashioned castle. Crossing the room, Susan headed for it, opening it to a random page. Apparently built specifically for the book, the ledge accommodated the open cover perfectly. The two pages she examined had typed titles in a variety of boxes, the remainder of the area filled with neat handwriting. Clearly a logbook for bodies and autopsies, it contained areas for such things as name, weight, length, hair color, eye color, and distinguishing features, as well as check boxes to confirm the means of identification.

Apparently, the pathologists preferred using the book to risking smearing body tissues and microorganisms onto a keyboard. A book, at least, could survive the sterilizer. Suddenly aware of the possibility of teeming bacteria in such a setting, Susan hoped it had done so recently.

Still not fully certain if the coroner had brought her father's body here, Susan shifted the bulk of the pages toward the front of the logbook. She thumbed cautiously through it, backward, until she found his name written in black marker. Susan closed her eyes, not quite ready to read a piece of paper that would reduce her father to a few vital statistics. Then, steeling herself with a slow, deep breath, she opened them.

The page was mostly blank, which meant the autopsy had not yet been started. That did not surprise Susan; in a busy morgue, it might take a week or longer to get around to an individual body. His name, John Woodrow Calvin, was written fluidly in the appropriate area. Beside it, someone had marked the fingerprint box in the "absolute identification" area. There was also a check in the "presumptive iden-tification" area, indicating the presence of a picture ID. For length, they had written 5'10"; for weight, 174 pounds. Both gave Susan pause. Her father stood an easy 6'8", and though he sometimes struggled to keep meat on his slender frame, he usually weighed in at a solid two hun-dred. Susan felt sure she would have noticed if he had dropped twenty pounds. *Obviously an error.*

Susan supposed blood loss could account for the difference in weight, although she would have expected the scene to have appeared far more gruesome. Perhaps the body had, somehow, fully drained of any remaining bodily fluids on the trip to the morgue. The length dis-crepancy seemed far more perplexing. It would take a careless exam-iner to make a ten-inch mistake and not repeat the measurement. The eye and hair color boxes were empty, which also seemed odd given the meticulousness of pathologists in general and what she had seen so far in the logbook.

Or misidentification. Hope trickled into Susan's thoughts, despite her best attempts to squelch it. A misprint in the morgue would not bring her father back to life. She glanced at the last box the attendant could fill in without actually opening the body, labeled "distinguishing features." The box contained a single word, one that froze Susan's blood so abruptly it lanced through her like physical pain. A shiver racked her, then grew into a relentless, irrepressible trembling.

Then a voice came from behind Susan, loud and accusatory. "Hey! Who are you? And what are you doing?"

Susan whirled to face a woman of Amazonian proportions, dressed in olive-drab scrubs with a white apron, a paper hairnet, and comfortable boots that looked more suitable for fishing than hospital work. A head taller than Susan, she glared down at the psychiatry resident through sharp hazel eyes, her broad lips pursed, and her hands clamped to shapely hips otherwise lost in the layers of scrubs and apron.

"Dr. Susan Calvin, R-2." Susan waited for a return introduction before continuing.

The woman regarded her like an unidentified thing found deep inside a body cavity. She made it clear she did not feel fully satisfied with half an answer, though she did oblige with her name and title. "Dr. Twilla Farnaby, chief resident." She cocked her head, awaiting the rest of Susan's explanation.

Susan never took her eyes from the other woman, whom she found unnerving. She suspected most men, however, would consider her strikingly handsome. She was not wearing any rings, but Susan suspected no one did in the pathology area. If not an outright rule, it would be understood that wearing rings and earrings risked trapping decomposing tissue beneath them. "My father was murdered yesterday. I wanted . . . more to the point, I *needed* to see the body. I also hoped you might have some findings that explained . . ." Susan trailed off. *Explained what? Why some heartless goon killed him?*

Twilla's expression softened, probably about as much as it ever did. "If it happened yesterday, we wouldn't get to him for another couple of days." She hesitated a moment, making the appropriate connection. "Calvin, you said. As in John Woodrow?"

Susan nodded briskly.

The pathologist's expression changed, but Susan found it unreadable. She had exotic features, indicative of mixed heritage, her nose strong, her cheekbones high, her eyes mildly canted, and her generous mouth enhanced with lipstick. Her skin had a rich olive hue. Her hair strained the confines of the paper hat, suggesting long, full locks that cascaded in private life. "I understand your desire to hurry things along, but these things take time." Her tone was patronizing. "Next time, Dr. Calvin, you should use the visitors' entrance."

Susan tipped her head, wishing she had Kendall's ability to cock a single eyebrow. "I'm hardly a visitor to Manhattan Hasbro. I practically live here."

"Not in the Pathology Department."

Susan continued to stare. "And I suppose if a beloved family member of yours was rushed to Neuro in status epilepticus, you would strictly adhere to visiting hours? I suppose you would allow some nurse practitioner to steer you to the waiting room?"

"Well, I wouldn't get underfoot."

Susan glanced around, as if she had not already fully grasped the scene. "Am I interfering with an ongoing autopsy?"

"Not yet." Twilla could hardly claim otherwise, given the clean tables wholly devoid of bodies. "But I'm about to start."

"On my father?" Susan's throat tightened as she spoke. She had to focus to keep from squeaking out the question.

"Not yet. He's third in line." Twilla sucked in a deep breath, then let it out slowly. "Susan . . ." They had apparently switched to a first-name basis. "Susan," she repeated, and her tone became soft, almost matronly. "I don't know what the police have told you, but this is not the way you want to remember your father. When I'm finished, I'll make things as neat and clean as possible before sending him on to whichever funeral home you choose. Once he's dressed and tended, he'll look so much more . . . dignified. So much more . . . as you remember him."

Susan swallowed hard. She would not be denied. "Look, Twilla. I appreciate your trying to spare me, but I'm not some soft-handed florist unaccustomed to death and disfigurement. I want to see my father."

Twilla's jaw clicked shut. She was clearly unused to anyone disobeying her commands. Susan could imagine men snapping to attention at her beck and call, women intimidated by her size, appearance, and self-assured manner. She had probably never received a ticket of any kind in her life. "I think you should leave."

Susan folded her arms across her chest. If Twilla wanted her out of the autopsy room, she would have to physically remove her. Susan suspected she might prove capable of it but doubted she would dare.

For a moment, they stood in perfect stalemate. Then Twilla reached into her apron pocket for her personal Vox. "I'm calling security."

"Okay." Susan kept her tone flat and did not budge.

"I mean it."

Susan shrugged. "Mean it in all sincerity. I certainly haven't done anything destructive or violent. I haven't threatened you in any way, and I'm certified to be in any medical-service area of this hospital as long as I'm wearing the proper protective gear." She shook an edge of her paper gown. "What are you going to tell security that won't make you look like a heartless, mean-spirited harpy?"

The pathologist's look went positively predatory. "Was that a threat?"

"Merely a description. Had I added that I savor eviscerating harpies and scooping out their brains to sprinkle over my cereal, that would be a threat."

Twilla took a step backward, which seemed wholly unconscious. "Is *that* a threat?"

"A clarification," Susan said, remaining calm. The conversation was taking an uncomfortable turn. "Look, Twilla. I'm not going to do anything to you or this facility, other than to wait here until you allow me to see my recently deceased father. Professional courtesy demands you allow me to do so, even if not graciously or against your medical advice. Security might be able to remove me, but if they try to prevent my immediate return, I will flash my bona fides."

Apparently unfamiliar with the term, Twilla looked scandalized. "Flash your what?" Her gaze strayed to Susan's chest.

Susan could not help noticing when it came to such things, Twilla probably had some impressive "bona fides" hidden beneath the layers her job demanded. "My identification. As I've stated, as a resident employee of Manhattan Hasbro, I have a right to be in all the medical-service areas of this hospital. That includes pathology."

Twilla's eyes narrowed, obviously uncertain whether Susan spoke the truth. Susan was not wholly sure herself, but she suspected hospital security would balk at removing a medical doctor from any part of Hasbro. Finally, Twilla slumped, defeated, at least for the moment. She put the Vox back into her pocket, an unusual storage site. Once affixed, few Vox ever left their owners' wrists. Twilla's action reaffirmed Susan's suspicion that either rule or convention kept pathologists from wearing jewelry or other items that might contaminate themselves or their work. "Susan, I swear I'm only trying to protect you. Your father is not in a state fit for viewing by loved ones."

Susan swallowed hard, suddenly forced to focus on the written word that had startled her just before Twilla's arrival. "I know," she forced out. "He's been . . . decapitated." Again, Susan felt the rush of ice water through her veins. The word seemed abruptly strange, weirdly foreign, a Latin holdover as ridiculous in modern vocabulary as "defenestrated." She doubted many people off the street knew the meaning of either word, and why should they? How often did one need to speak of headless bodies or objects thrown from windows?

"You know." Twilla no longer looked intimidating; more like a fellow resident in a difficult position. "And you still want to see?"

Susan thought it best not to reveal the truth that she had arrived without the knowledge and had gained it only by reading the logbook. It was probably something the police hoped the family would never have to know. Twilla might blame herself if she discovered the means of Susan's knowledge. Better for the Pathology chief resident to believe the police the source of Susan's information.

Abruptly, most of the previous blanks in Susan's mind became filled. Decapitation explained why the police had used fingerprints instead of retinal scanning, why the pathologist had measured him at only 5'10", and even the missing weight. Two things remained a mystery. The first, she could explain. If a gap of time existed between the killing and the removal of John's head, the blood could have fully clotted, leaving the scene relatively clean. This was also a bit reassuring, as it meant the severing of John Calvin's head was not the brutal and horrible cause of his death. The bigger question remaining was why anyone would hack off a man's head after his death.

Nausea bubbled into Susan's throat, and she forced herself to swallow the bitter-tasting fluid. After her stalwart demands, she could not back down now, and she would surely regret it if she did. She would not likely get a second chance. "I have to see him. I won't sleep until I do." She avoided the "closure" cliché, though it seemed apt. Too many people had come to hate the word.

"Very well." Twilla stepped around Susan to one of the drawers, started to pull it open, then slammed it suddenly shut. She whirled to face Susan, her back pressed to the enormous drawer. "I'm sorry, Susan. You really are going to have to leave."

Susan let out a noise of irritation. "Haven't we already done this? Because if not, I'm suffering a severe case of déjà vu, and I'm completely out of patience."

Twilla left all emotion from her words. "Please believe me. It's best for everyone if you leave. Right now."

Susan shook her head briskly. "I'd sooner sleep on the dissection table. I'm not leaving until I see my father."

Twilla's nod had an air of inevitability. "Then you're here for good." She pulled open the drawer amid a small cloud of condensation as refrigerated contents met the warmth of the room. Two bodies lay neatly inside, neither of them John Calvin's. The third tray was empty, only a smear of dark, dried blood to indicate it had ever held a corpse. "John Calvin's body has gone missing."

Chapter 12

Susan discussed the day's events with Kendall over a take-out grilled chicken dinner in his apartment. They sat at the kitchen table, surrounded by stainless-steel appliances and built-in wooden cupboards, at a rickety portable table that seemed wholly out of place. In no other room did it seem quite so obvious that the equipment and storage areas came with the apartment, while Kendall had supplied the furniture and embellishments. At least he kept them clean and polished. He covered his sorry excuse for a dining table with a festive tablecloth decked out with circus animals on a brilliant red background. They ate off reusable plastic plates with flimsy tableware that had taken too many rides in a hot dishwasher.

"The body was missing," Kendall repeated, fork stopping halfway to his lips. He placed it back on his plate, untouched. "Are you sure it wasn't . . . misplaced?"

Susan was not in the mood for silly questions. "Well, I hardly thought it had risen from the slab and lumbered off, seeking human brains."

"Give me some credit, Susan. I wasn't going to make a crude joke about your recently deceased father. I just meant, did you search the other drawers?"

Susan also stopped eating. It was not squeamishness that stopped her; she had chowed down after Human Anatomy with the odor of formaldehyde still nestled in her hair. It just seemed dishonorable to casually shove food in her mouth while discussing her father's decapitated and purloined corpse. "No sign of my father, headless or otherwise."

Kendall's features crinkled. "What did the Pathology chief resident think?"

Susan could not help recalling the stare of stupid panic that had lodged itself on Dr. Twilla Farnaby's face. "Clearly stunned. She assured me no body had ever gone missing before, and I believe her. Who would steal a corpse?"

Kendall had answers, if not particularly good ones. "Some crazed necrophiliac?"

Susan finished the thought as if it were an open sentence: "—wouldn't choose a mature, headless man over a supple young woman with all her parts intact."

"The murderer or murderers? To prevent discovery of the means of death because it might . . . implicate them."

Susan considered the possibility, though it seemed farfetched. It might explain why they had taken the head; if, for example, they had left a bullet from an identifiable gun lodged inside it. But Sammy Cottrell's body still lay on its slab in the morgue, probably dispatched with the same weapon. Until they left the Calvins' apartment and blundered into Sammy, the murderers had aroused no suspicion. They had had plenty of time to dismember the body or toss it off the balcony. Splattered on the pavement ten stories below, the body would have given the police and coroner a much more difficult puzzle.

Appetite fully lost, Susan ignored her plate.

Kendall studied her. "Susan, did you talk to the police about this?"

"Of course." Susan's mind wandered to the oddity of that conversation, apparently for several moments, because Kendall prompted.

"And?"

Susan reluctantly abandoned her thoughts for words. "I mentioned only the missing body, not the decapitation. They had to know about that already, and I wanted to see if they would finally tell me."

"And did they?"

"No. And when it came to the missing body, the first officer I spoke with seemed surprised. He fobbed me off on a second guy, who switched me to a third."

Kendall demonstrated no impatience, though he clearly wished Susan would get to the point. Anyone would, but he seemed to realize she had a reason for everything she said. In this case, Susan wanted his reaction to what seemed like odd and inappropriate evasiveness. "You can certainly understand their being a bit blindsided. It can't be often a family member drops a bombshell like that. If the pathologists didn't even know until you insisted on seeing the body, how could the police?"

Susan continued, "The third guy informed me the body never went to Manhattan Hasbro. He said they planned to send it to Hasbro but chose the office of the chief medical examiner instead."

Kendall nodded thoughtfully. "That would explain it. Even the great Dr. Calvin can't be in two places at once."

Susan was not wholly sure to which Dr. Calvin Kendall referred, and the realization her father's body and his head were certainly in two separate places made the comment seem unintentionally morbid. "Except it doesn't make sense. I mean, they sent Sammy Cottrell's body to Hasbro. Why would they want to split up the investigation of two victims of what appears to be an extension of the same crime?"

"Second opinion?" Kendall suggested.

Susan rolled him a critical look. "On a dead man? Who does that?"

Kendall absently shoved a forkful of coleslaw in his mouth and chewed thoughtfully. "Maybe there just wasn't enough room, or the wait was too long. Maybe they wanted to examine your father right away, but they felt the woman could wait."

Susan planted her elbows on either side of her plate and placed her chin in her hands. "Reasonable thoughts, as long as you discount the fact that the body was logged in, physically received at Hasbro. The police said nothing about moving the body, and I gave them every opportunity. I didn't mention I looked in the logbook; I wanted to see what they said. Also, he was clearly tagged and bagged there. His name was on the drawer door, and the slot where he belonged was empty. The chief pathology resident was at least as shocked as I was to find him missing."

Kendall swallowed, the implications of Susan's point obvious. "So . . . the police . . . lied?" He looked squarely at her, his dark eyes more serious than she could ever remember. The previous year, he had never seemed serious, even at the most urgent and critical moments. Now she could scarcely remember the last time he had cracked a joke.

"I don't know." Susan drooped in resignation. In the past few months, nothing made a lot of sense. "Maybe?"

"Why would the police lie about something like that?"

"Because there's something they don't want me to know."

Kendall huffed out a sigh. "Duh, Susan. That's the purpose of a lie. But why would there be anything the police wouldn't want the deceased's closest family member to know? You hear about cases solved because the police kept the details a secret, hoping to trip up a suspect who reveals something only the killer could know. But I've always believed the family is given the truth." He added carefully, "And what possible purpose could there be to lying about the location of the body to any-one?" He stiffened suddenly. "You don't think you're a suspect, do you?"

Susan supposed, at the moment, everyone was a suspect. However, she doubted the police would consider her for long. She had an airtight alibi and a long history of a close, loving relationship with her father, and she doubted anyone would believe a young woman would have the intestinal fortitude to carry out such a brutal crime. "No," she said firmly. "I can't imagine so. Besides, if I had stolen the body myself, I certainly wouldn't have called them about it."

Kendall muttered thoughtfully, "Murderers have done stranger things." Apparently realizing the implications of what he had just said aloud, Kendall amended, "Not that I'm suggesting you're the murderer. Obviously, that would be impossible."

"Obviously." Susan wondered if Kendall could dig himself a deeper hole.

Kendall changed tactics. "I'm guessing they don't want to admit you surprised them. They don't want you to lose confidence in their ability to solve this case, so they tell you something to appease you until they have a real answer."

That made more sense than any of the other ideas they had raised between them. Susan said, out of the blue, "I'm going with you in the morning."

Kendall looked up suddenly. "What?"

"I'm going with you. To work."

Kendall ran his tongue around his mouth before speaking. "Are you sure that's a good idea? I mean, you've just suffered a horrible catastrophe. Shouldn't you take at least a week or two to work through it emotionally?"

Susan did not bother to shift her head. She merely flicked her eyes toward Kendall. "What for? So I can wallow in my own grief? So I can think about how awful my life has become, how I've lost all my closest loved ones and would be better off joining them?"

Clearly growing ever more uncomfortable, Kendall bit at his lower lip. "Susan, a few sessions with a grief counselor might do you good."

"Call me Calvin."

"What?"

Susan leaned forward. "You've always called me Calvin, then cracked some usually offensive joke. I like you better as yourself than as my mother."

Kendall sat up straight. "I hardly think I can be mistaken for any-one's mother. I just think you've suffered a ridiculous number of catas-trophes in a one-year span, more than the entire population of most small cities do in a lifetime. You should see . . . someone." He avoided the title that had bothered her a few moments earlier.

"Like a psychiatrist?"

"Not a bad thought."

Susan sat back, arms crossed. "I see two every day, and that's enough."

"Funny."

Susan tried to explain, "Look, Kendall, that's not going to help me. I know all of our tricks, and I'm just going to spend my time trying to counteranalyze my analyst."

"Call me Stevens."

That derailed Susan's thoughts. "What?"

"If I have to call you Calvin, you have to call me Stevens. Oddly enough, both first names in their own right."

Susan finally managed a chuckle. "Nowadays, everything is a first name in its own right." Not wishing to get sidetracked, she returned to her explanation. "In the past year, I've come to realize, for me, wallowing in small problems is harmless venting, but wallowing in large ones par-alyzes me. I do better when I'm busy, distracted. I want to go back to work, and tomorrow seems the perfect time. It's Saturday, so it'll be slow, and we get to leave at noon if our work's finished. I can grieve without toppling into a bottomless pit of despair, and I won't awaken from this nightmare to find myself impossibly far behind in my training."

Realizing she had left something else unaddressed, Susan added, "And you don't really have to call me Calvin. I was just hoping you'd find it funny and get back your sense of humor."

Kendall turned her a crooked expression nearly approximating a smile. "Really? You should probably leave the jokes to me; that one went right over my head. And I'd kind of hoped calling you Susan would remind you our relationship has . . . changed a bit."

Without thinking, Susan repeated, "Changed a bit?"

Kendall could not resist. "Was the nookie that memorable?"

"I remember," Susan said quickly, not wanting to go into a rehash of it. At the moment, she felt a bit embarrassed by the whole thing, and the euphemism only heightened her discomfort. "Best I've ever had."

This time, Kendall laughed. "I'd take that as a compliment if I didn't know you were a virgin." He sighed. "The truth is, I was anxious and distracted."

"Same," Susan admitted. To her relief, Kendall returned to the original subject.

"You're sure you want to come to Winter Wine tomorrow?"

"Definitely."

Kendall shook his head. "Reefes is still there, you know. And he hasn't gotten any less . . . lazy. Or irritating. Are you sure he's something you want to deal with right now? You're well within your rights to skip the rest of the rotation. You can make it up someplace else and not have to deal with him at all."

Susan had never run from her problems and did not intend to do so now. "I'm going with you tomorrow, Kendall," she said with what she hoped was finality. "Geez, I've never met a resident more selfish about sharing patients."

Again, Kendall chuckled. Although the attendings suggested having call every other night meant missing half the good cases, most residents still preferred quiet nights and small caseloads. "Fine. You're coming, you're coming."

Appetite returning, Kendall dug into his food. Even Susan managed to eat.

A lthough Susan had missed only a day and a half of work, Winter Wine Dementia Facility already seemed strange and she had to adjust to the odor of it again. The first hour dragged. Loath to bother Susan, the nurses took most of their concerns directly to Kendall, and she found herself shadowing him to keep the entire staff, including Kendall, from tiptoeing around her. Chuck Tripler was gone, recovering in the Neurosurgical Intensive Care Unit, and Thomas Heaton had gotten transferred to a therapy facility with specialists assigned to help him relearn written language by equating it with musical notes. Barbara Callahan remained on Unit 1 as the cannabis slowly left her system. The drug normally had a long half-life, and her age further delayed its secretion. Discharge planning was already in the works, and Susan doubted the frequent bounce-back patient would ever return to the facility.

Left mostly to her own devices, Susan focused on discovering other patients with treatable forms of dementia. After several false leads, she finally discovered Kado Matsuo. His age attracted her attention first. At forty-three, he fell into the early-onset category, although Susan quickly noted he did not carry the diagnosis of actual dementia but of post-traumatic psychosis, which fit his symptoms of sudden-onset delusions and hallucinations after a divorce. Reading through his chart, Susan noted other clues: night terrors in which he would wake up screaming and agitated, then return to sleep with no memory of the event, insomnia, and generalized odd behavior, including extreme hyperactivity, irritability, and even aggression. The latter symptom had kept him in Winter Wine Dementia Facility for about two months.

Kado was a thin, disheveled man of Japanese descent who fought Susan, forcing her to do a quick and abbreviated examination. She noted no obvious abnormalities. His senses seemed acute, he moved all his limbs fully, and his heart and lung sounds were normal. His only abnormal finding was hyperactive bowel sounds, which led her to check on his eating and toilet habits.

Over the months, the nurses had noted persistent vomiting, though not in excessive amounts. He also had bouts of diarrhea. He drank water and refused juice. When offered a veritable smorgasbord, he demonstrated a strong preference for fatty meats. He appeared unnaturally slender but not skeletal, and Susan noted no signs of dehydration. Anorexia was not an uncommon finding in confused individuals; they sometimes forgot to eat or whether they had eaten, which could result in under- or overnourishment. However, Susan did not think she would see anyone malnourished in a fully staffed facility like Winter Wine.

Susan looked over Kado's chart more critically. Previous physical examinations had noted nothing abnormal, no signs to indicate anything other than an internal brain disorder. Still, the persistent vomiting and dietary oddities stuck in her mind, sending Susan to her palm-pross for research.

An hour later, Kendall found her in the charting room, hunched over her keyboard. He dropped to a crouch beside her and spoke softly, "Calvin, there's an old friend to see you."

Susan glanced up, anxious despite Kendall's bantering tone. She waited for him to explain.

"One of your patients has returned." Kendall batted his lashes at Susan. "I'll give you three guesses which one."

Susan had sent out only a couple of patients, and only one of those had gone home. She sucked in a sudden breath, then groaned. "Jessica Aberdeen." The news did not surprise either of them. A sudden flash of anger suffused her, an emotion she had not experienced since

Lawrence Robertson had suggested she cower from her father's killers. It felt bizarrely good to suffer a feeling strong enough to displace the grief that had colored her every moment since she had gotten the news of her father's murder. "I can't believe they brought her back here. I wouldn't think her father would dare show his face here after the last conversation we had."

"He dared, and he did." Kendall sucked air through his teeth, then shrugged. "He's in there now, dictating feeding instructions, so he doesn't seem to have learned anything from her relapse."

Susan's hands balled to fists. She could handle anything medical, except dealing with Chase Aberdeen.

Kendall seemed to read her mind. Still crouched, he balanced on his toes. "Would you like me to take her this time?"

Though not unheard of, it violated one of the basic rules of residency. Bounce-backs to the same service returned to the resident of record, even if admitted by someone else on call. "No, Jessica's mine."

"But under the circumstances . . ."

Susan ignored him, rising suddenly and walking from the room. There was no hurry to examine the woman. The nurses would need time to settle her in, and Susan could wait until the father left before writing orders. Still, curiosity drove her, and the need to understand what had caused Jessica's swift return loomed high on the list of priorities. Without knowing the interim history and without hearing Chase Aberdeen's reasons, she could not provide the best possible medical care, but arguing with Jessica's father served no positive purpose. Either Susan's line of reasoning and the ensuing course of events had convinced him of the medical facts, a decision she quietly needed to support, or he remained rabidly adherent to his own point of view, in which case nothing she said would accomplish more than upsetting him.

Susan could hear Kendall's trailing footsteps, but she did not look behind her. She knew he worried for what her fragile emotional state might cause her to say. Even she was not wholly certain she could maintain her cool. Braced for the worst but prepared to remain calm and upbeat, Susan swept into Jessica Aberdeen's room.

Jessica sat up in the bed, silently studying her surroundings, glancing from walls to floor to ceiling. Her features were flat, revealing no thought or emotion. A nurse stood at the bedside, typing information into a palm-pross on the portable table. Seated in the only chair, Chase Aberdeen looked up at Susan's entrance. His greeting was cold. "Oh, it's you. I specifically asked for a different doctor."

Kendall came in behind Susan. "That would be me," he said before Susan could do or say anything in reply. "Kendall Stevens, MD." Though he introduced himself, he did not proffer a hand and remained at Susan's side. "My first order of business is to examine the patient and elicit a confirmatory opinion from the most brilliant clinician I know." He tipped his head toward Susan. "Dr. Calvin."

Susan turned a snort of suppressed laughter into a cough.

Chase Aberdeen clamped his mouth into a line, obviously miffed. "Am I going to have to request a third doctor?"

"Sorry," Kendall said, moving toward the bedside. "All out of doctors."

The man fairly snarled. "Unless you prove a bit more ... educated in nutritional matters than your colleague, I'll have to move Jessica to another facility."

Susan glanced at Jessica. A moment earlier, the woman had seemed entirely unfocused. Now a slight smile played over her lips, and her stillness suggested she was taking it all in. Susan played a hunch. "That decision isn't up to you, Mr. Aberdeen."

Kendall shut his mouth abruptly. Apparently, he had been about to say something about changing facilities being the man's prerogative.

Chase Aberdeen's brows shot up. "Excuse me? Jessica is my daughter."

"Your *adult* daughter," Susan pointed out. "Old enough to make her own legal decisions." She looked directly into Jessica's eyes, exploring their depths. Deep inside a glaze of confusion, she saw something alive and burning. "Jessica, do you want Dr. Stevens and me to continue treating you?" She took the woman's clammy hand in her own.

Jessica wrapped her fingers around Susan's. "Help me," she managed to say, barely above a whisper.

Kendall flicked his gaze to the father's. "That's clear enough."

"Clear as mud!" Chase almost shouted. "She's addled. She doesn't know what she's agreeing to."

"She's addled," Susan pointed out, "because you keep her in that state. We've so far proceeded on the assumption it's due to a misguided but well-meaning belief that you're helping her." Still allowing Jessica to clutch her hand, Susan turned her body slightly to confront Chase Aberdeen directly. "However, if you insist on unraveling and impeding her recovery, we'll have to assume your intentions are deliberate and mean-spirited. And that's a crime." She added in a clipped tone that robbed the title of respect, "Mr. Aberdeen."

Fire flashed briefly through Chase Aberdeen's eyes, then disappeared. For an instant, Susan thought he would leap bodily upon her and wrestle her to the floor. Instead, he slumped, all fight extinguished, at least for the moment. When he finally spoke, his voice was thin and reedy, almost pleading. "Why would I want to harm my daughter? I love Jessica more than anything in the world."

You're not acting like it. Susan kept the thought to herself. People had widely different ways of showing love, not all of them healthy. "Prove it by allowing us to help her. If we're wrong, a little bit of food you consider unwholesome won't do her any long-term harm. However, if we're right, and you continue fighting us, you're risking losing your daughter." She pinned him with her gaze. "Mind, heart, and spirit."

Once the choice was framed in that context, Chase Aberdeen could not refuse it and still stand by his assertion he loved and wanted the best for his daughter.

Susan worried saying anything more might back the man into a corner, driving him to attack. Yet Kendall managed to add something quiet but laced with underlying threat. "Mr. Aberdeen, we will help Jessica, and we would like to do so in a therapeutic environment that includes her father as a willing, if skeptical, partner. I know you're contemplating legal action—"

Chase Aberdeen opened his mouth.

Kendall spoke over him. "Don't bother to protest; anyone would consider it. Before you waste your money on a lawyer, I want you to understand I know the legalities of this situation like the back of my hand." Kendall stabbed a finger into his palm. Even at his most serious, Kendall could not always resist a pratfall. "Please don't make us take emergency guardianship of your adult daughter or restrain you from visitation. It's not in anyone's best interests, but it's better than the alternative."

Jessica's grip on Susan's hand loosened as she drifted into sleep. That suited Susan, who wanted to leave the room as soon as possible. She did so, and Kendall followed. They walked with silent decorum until they reached the security of the nearest charting room and pulled the door closed behind them.

Both residents plopped into chairs simultaneously and turned to face one another. "Very impressive," Susan said. "That's the most forceful I've ever heard Dr. Kendall Stevens." She could not help adding, "Though I thought I'd lose it when you misidentified the back of your hand."

Kendall smiled wearily. "You inspire me, my love."

A trickle of dread coursed through Susan. He had never called her that before.

"Apparently, I've watched you perform enough emasculations, I'm becoming an expert in my own right."

Susan turned him a withering look. "Just don't accidently do yourself."

Kendall clasped his hands under his chin, batting his eyes at her. "Oh, you care."

Warning bells filled her mind; their encounter had clearly meant more to Kendall than to her.

The chime of Susan's Vox startled her. She jumped so suddenly, she nearly jabbed a finger in her eye.

Kendall chuckled softly as Susan looked at the source of the call. It was a text from Dr. Mitchell Reefes. Even before she read the message, her heart sank, and the actual words flashing onto the screen only made things worse: "Come to my office stat!"

"What do you suppose he wants?" Apparently, Kendall had read the words upside down and from a distance, an impressive feat. "You don't suppose Jessica's dad already complained."

Susan shook her head. "Too quick. He's still reeling. Besides, if that were the reason, I think Reefes would call us both on the carpet." She rose, prepared for the inevitable.

"Maybe he's just concerned about you. I mean your father did just–"

Susan interrupted Kendall before he could use some humorous euphemism. She was not in the mood. "Impossible. Reefes has ice chips in his chest and sawdust in his skull." She headed for the door.

Kendall looked longingly after her. She knew he wanted to go with her, but he had no reasonable excuse for doing so, nor did she have a right to ask him. "See you, SU-2," he said, shorthandedly reminding her of her "can't harm human beings" robotic status. Not that it did much good. Susan was not at all certain she could classify Dr. Mitchell Reefes as human.

Chapter 13

Susan entered the office of Dr. Mitchell Reefes, shut the door, and waited for him to look up from his palm-pross. It took inordinately long for him to do so, and when he finally did, it was with condescending slowness. He studied her with the same predatory expression she imagined a hyena might have after stealing a meal from a hungry cub.

Reefes gestured toward the chair in front of his desk.

Susan followed the motion with her eyes but made no move to act on it. If he wanted something from her, he would have to use something more than hand motions. They made her feel like an obedient dog.

After a moment in stalemate, Reefes said, "Sit."

Susan accepted the chair, perching stiffly on its front edge. She regarded him with what she hoped was an emotionless expression. She had no intention of making this easier for him.

"So," he said at length. "Jessica Aberdeen's back."

Susan continued to study her attending. As he had not asked anything, she felt no particular need to respond.

Mitchell Reefes cleared his throat. When Susan continued to stare at him impassively, he continued, "Susan, you're making it difficult for me to help you."

"Help me?" Susan repeated, having no idea what he meant.

Reefes purposefully closed his palm-pross. Apparently, he wanted to give the impression his focus was wholly on Susan. "You know I have to write your evaluation. Thus far, you've made some mistakes that can only be described as ... well, dangerous."

"Dangerous?" Susan had intended to answer only to direct questions, but the word was so unexpected it was startled from her lips.

Reefes ticked off the cases on his fingers. "First, you argue against transferring a man to Neurosurgery, despite a whopping spinal tumor on his MRI."

Susan's mouth fell open.

Reefes appeared not to notice. He thrust out a second finger. "Then you discharge a malnourished woman back into the care of her deluded father. Had he not returned her, she would probably have developed irreversible brain damage. She might even have died."

Suddenly, Susan wished she were a robot, the kind with ten-foot-long, thrusting blades and no understanding of the Three Laws. "What are you talking about? I'm the one who sent Chuck Tripler to MRI, against your orders. You're the one who discharged Jessica Aberdeen."

Mitchell Reefes muttered something under his breath. He shook his head, his entire face creased. "I'm sure you'd like to remember it that way, young lady. But that's not what happened."

Susan studied her attending's face. She saw nothing suggesting deception, just a raw hint of anger. Either he really believed things had happened the way he said or he was a master liar. Which one did not really matter. He held all the power, and he clearly intended to use it against her.

Rage seethed through Susan like a living thing. She could imagine herself leaping from her chair, burying her fist in his holier-than-thou face. She could practically hear the crack of cartilage, feel the warm blood from his nose coursing between her fingers. Anything she did or said would only make the situation worse.

Dr. Reefes' voice took on the phony tone of concern Susan heard from people who wanted to seem compassionate when they really did not care at all. "Susan, I know how difficult it must be to lose your father. My parents got divorced when I was six, and I never really got over—"

Susan could not bear to hear another word of it. "I didn't lose my father; he didn't wander away in a grocery store or fall out of a hole in my pocket. He was viciously murdered." Her field of vision turned a spectacular scarlet, and her head buzzed so loudly the sound filled her ears, muffling her own words. She needed to explode like a volcano, violently thrashing out tons of molten rock, hurling irrevocable statements of fact and feeling, in an instant. She was on her feet before she realized it, fighting the compulsion to fling herself at him, instead turning on her heel and marching toward the door.

"Susan, sit!" Reefes called after her.

Susan ignored him until she reached the door, fingers tensing around the knob. There she paused, trying to dredge some reasonable thought from the swirl of homicidal noise pounding through her head.

Apparently assuming he had her attention, Reefes said, "If you leave, I'm going to fail you for this rotation."

Susan suddenly realized that was the worst he could do. She could make up the extra time at the end of her residency, could chose a different elective, one that did not have her working with a madman. No matter what happened from this moment on, she had no chance to salvage a positive evaluation. Susan whirled suddenly to face him, her glare so intense it caused her actual, physical pain. For the first time in her life, she really wished looks could kill. Without another word, she whipped open the door, strode through it, and slammed it closed behind her.

Kendall was waiting in the hallway when she stormed past him, dimly wise enough to keep his mouth shut. He caught up to her in the residents' area as she gathered up her palm-pross and miscellaneous belongings. "Calvin," he said cautiously. "Go back to my apartment. I'll cover here."

Susan went utterly still, head low, struggling with rage. Her mood had nothing to do with Kendall, and he did not deserve to suffer for it. After what seemed like an hour in that position but was surely only a few moments, Susan regained enough control to look at another human being without tearing him into pieces. "I'm sorry to dump everything on you, but I'm not coming back."

Kendall laced his fingers, clearly uncertain how to approach the situation. "Ever?"

"Ever," Susan confirmed, then gradually realized Kendall worried more for whether she was giving up medicine than Winter Wine Dementia Facility. "Not the whole residency. Just here."

Kendall visibly relaxed but remained silent. He knew better than to say something that might sound even remotely like "I told you so." He had cautioned her to take some time off, that she was not ready to return to work, but she had chosen to ignore him.

Susan felt confident she would have done fine on any other rotation. She had even taken Reefes' personality into account; she just had not expected him to flat-out lie. She clearly could not stay; yet, as her ire cooled, she suffered guilt at the knowledge that Kendall would have to work doubly hard and that she was essentially abandoning her patients, even into his capable hands. Susan reluctantly sat. Not only did she want to get out of the environment as soon as possible, but she knew if Mitchell Reefes attempted to speak to her again, she could not account for her actions. "Before I leave, would you like me to go over my patients?"

Kendall shook his head vigorously. "I know them all well enough. Anything I don't know, I can get from the chart." He added helpfully. "And don't worry about Jessica Aberdeen. I can handle her father."

That being obvious, Susan tried to smile but found it impossible.

"There is one other patient I'd like you to check on. His name's Kado Matsuo."

"That young Asian on Unit 2?"

Susan supposed "young" was appropriate for a man in his forties at a dementia facility. "Consider citrulinemia."

"Citrulinemia?" Kendall's features crinkled. "Isn't that one of those weird baby diseases they test for at birth? Krebs cycle or citric acid cycle—something to do with ATP or NADH or some other alphabetical energy source we had to memorize in microbiology?"

Susan finally managed a slight smile. "Citrulinemia is a defect in the *urea* cycle. You need to draw plasma levels of ammonia, citrulline, arginine, threonine-to-serine ratio, and pancreatic secretory trypsin inhibitor. If you can get consent, you'll want to send out some blood to the genetics lab to identify a possible biallelic mutation in the SLC25A13 gene."

Kendall stared. "God bless you."

Susan had no idea what he meant. "What?"

"Was that a long sneeze or did you just start speaking in tongues?"

"Speaking in . . . ?" Susan was still in no mood for games. "What are you talking about? I was just telling you how to handle diagnosing a patient using basic medical terminology. What did I say you didn't get?"

"I missed everything after 'plasma levels of.'" Kendall gave her a suspicious look. "I'm sure I know what all those things are; I just wouldn't remember them all at once and spout them off so easily. Are you sure you're not really a robot, SU-2?"

Susan snagged a piece of paper and wrote out the necessary tests. "I'd suggest you type that into something or at least rewrite it in your own handwriting before you take it to"—it took all the restraint she could muster not to refer to Mitchell Reefes by an expletive. Even then, she could not force out his actual name—"our esteemed attending. If he thought it came from me, he'd kill it on the spot, along with the patient." She handed the paper to Kendall, who shoved it into his pocket without bothering to read it. "After you've drawn the labs, I'd start him on arginine and sodium pyruvate, which should buy him some time before you can talk . . . you know who . . . into allowing a curative liver transplant."

Susan heard footsteps in the hallway. Worried they might belong to Reefes, she snatched up her palm-pross again. "See you this afternoon." She glanced furtively out the door, seeing only one of the nurse's aides passing by. Relieved, she scuttled into the hallway and away from Winter Wine Dementia Facility. If she so much as glanced at her attending now, violence was almost a certainty.

T he call, an innocuous buzzing of Susan's Vox, came on the glidebus. The display flashed a message from the police station, and Susan answered immediately. "Hello?"

"Dr. Susan Calvin, please." The voice on the other end was youthful, male, and unfamiliar.

"This is Susan," she acknowledged softly, directly into the Vox.

"This is Detective Jake Carson, NYPD. I'd like to talk to you about the investigation of your father's death."

Susan sat bolt upright. "Yes. What have you found out?"

"We're closing the case, ma'am."

Confused, Susan considered what to say next. "Closing it? You mean you've caught the murderer?"

"Not exactly, ma'am. We've determined there was no murder. Your father died of natural causes."

No words could have surprised Susan more. "What?" She did not care that she positively screamed out the word, attracting the attention of the sparse passengers on the bus. "So . . . bullets are now considered natural?"

"Bullets? No, ma'am. No bullets."

Susan was confused on so many levels, she did not know where to start. "They told me he was shot. Several times, in fact."

"No, ma'am. The ME's report was quite conclusive. Natural causes, ma'am."

"But . . . but . . ." Realizing she was sputtering, Susan tried to regather her wits. Still seething from her encounter with Dr. Mitchell Reefes, she found it impossible to integrate information that seemed to make no sense at all. "The apartment was trashed. And there was blood"–she remembered thinking she had not seen as much as she should have in the apartment–"and a second victim in the hallway, Sammy Cottrell."

"Her case is still open, Dr. Calvin."

Susan grasped at the only bit of logic thus far. "She was shot, wasn't she? What kind of absurd coincidence is that?"

The detective listened patiently until Susan paused to breathe. "I'm not at liberty to discuss that other case, I'm afraid. Not with anyone outside her family."

Susan continued to piece together information that made his pronouncement implausible, if not wholly impossible. "Dad's body disappeared from the morgue. How can you have a medical examiner's report at all?"

Apparently stunned silent, Jake Carson said nothing for several seconds. If not for the faint sound of his breathing, Susan would have thought he silently disconnected. "I'm not sure where you got that information, ma'am, but it's wrong. I have the ME's report right here in my hand. Natural causes, it says. A brain tumor, apparently. It sent him into some kind of wild, uncontrollable convulsions, resulting in the tearing up of the apartment."

Susan grasped for sense in a preposterous situation. She had seen the pathology log, had spoken with Hasbro's chief resident in the morgue. She wanted to scream at Detective Carson, to call him a filthy, flaming liar, to demand the explanation of how a brain tumor could cause decapitation. But, wisely, she held her tongue. Accusations and hysterics would only drive him into worthless silence. Perhaps the pathology lab had misidentified the body or some innocent explanation existed for the discrepancy. Even if it did not, Susan would gain far more information by listening and pretending to go along than by confrontation, at least for the moment. Unlike those of Mitchell Reefes, Jake Carson's errors, whether deliberate or accidental, did not immediately risk a human life.

Why would the cops lie? Building on the presumptive honesty of Detective Carson's claim, Susan tried to think of a malady that could present in the manner he had described. If her father had been harboring a brain tumor, she should have seen at least a few soft signs prior to such a major event. Seizures did not cause the kind of complete and methodical destruction she had seen, nor sudden and instantaneous death. Fighting to hold accusation from her tone, Susan demanded, "Read me the ME's report."

That clearly caught the detective off guard. "It's mostly medical jargon. I doubt I could even pronounce it."

"The 'doctor' in my title is not decorative." Susan kept her tone flat.

"I'm not trying to be evasive, Doctor," Jake said in his most reassuring tone, which only served to reawaken memories of Reefes' condescension. "It's mostly a bunch of organs and their weights—that sort of thing. If you'd like to come down and read it yourself, I'm at the Ninth Precinct. Homicide division."

Susan would not be deterred. "Read me the cause of death, Detective Carson."

Jake cleared his throat. "I'll do my best, ma'am. It says: 'traumatic brain injury with internal bleeding, increased intract crynal pressure . . .'"

"Intracranial pressure," Susan corrected.

"'. . . and massive seribral eedeema . . .'"

"Cerebral edema."

"'. . . secondary to large gly-oh-blast-amah multiform . . .'"

"Glioblastoma multiforme." Again, Susan provided the correct pronunciation.

"CK levels consistent with massive and sustained convulsions, status epilepsy-tykus."

"Status epilepticus."

"Clearly, that means more to you than it does to me. As it was explained to me, he had an enormous brain tumor that caused wild seizures, and ultimately hit his head on something, or several somethings. Death was from massive head trauma."

Susan had to admit, it did fit together neatly. Seizures were often the first sign of a brain tumor, at least in the general public, where people were not trained to notice subtle signs of abnormality. Perhaps the tearing up of their apartment had only seemed methodical because she had assumed it the work of a determined human hand; she had not considered the possibility of sudden, intense confusion and convulsions. That could certainly also cause intracranial injury extensive enough to kill someone, if not immediately, then after voluminous internal hemorrhaging.

Except that, in another way, none of it made sense at all. Susan could discount some of her findings as errors or misinterpretations, but certain facts remained and wholly contradicted the information she had just received. She knew people often found it difficult to accept that people beloved or of great stature died in the same direct and lowly fashion as the rest of humankind. Seventy-five years after the assassination of President Kennedy, people were still inventing and rehashing vast conspiracy theories to explain his death. Elvis Presley would be a century old had he survived his overdose, yet people continued to spot him, or obvious progeny, at various places around the country.

Maybe someone switched Dad's living but injured self with a decapitated body to fool his would-be killers into thinking he was dead. Susan did not want to fall into the trap of believing only things that substantiated her hopes that her father might somehow, miraculously, still be alive. On the other hand, she had no intention of falling prey to trickery. Pinning people down by Vox was not working for her. She was trained to read people, their gestures, their expressions, their actions. None of these came through during a strictly verbal conversation.

"Dr. Calvin. Dr. Calvin?" Detective Jake Carson's tone held an urgency suggesting he had repeated her name far more than just two times. He probably thought she had collapsed in some terrible or public place.

Susan considered disconnecting, leaving him to worry, but that seemed counterproductive. In the future, the police would never relay any information over Vox, forcing her to come to the station for every little piece of information. *Although with the investigation closed from their standpoint, they have no real reason to call me anymore.* "I'm here," she reassured him. "I'm just thinking." It seemed futile to demand more information, but she did need a few additional answers only he could give her. "I'll be down to see that form. In the meantime, could you tell me the name of the ME who signed off on it?"

Several moments passed, which only made Susan more suspicious. It should only take an instant to read off a name.

Finally, Jake replied. "I'm sorry, but I just can't make out the signature. I do know the body was delivered to Foder and Massey Funeral Home at 152 Twelfth Street. You should be able to make arrangements there."

"All right." Susan prepared to disconnect, but had one last question. She tried to sound matter-of-fact. "Just out of curiosity, which morgue performed the autopsy?" This time, the detective could hardly claim difficulty reading it. The name would surely appear at the top of the form in large-print letters. She half expected him to say Manhattan Hasbro Hospital, to catch him in an obvious lie.

"It's stamped Milton Helpern Institute of Forensic Medicine at New York University and bears the seal of the New York City Office of the Chief Medical Examiner."

"Thank you," Susan said, not knowing enough about mortuaries, morgues, and medical examiners to make any assumptions about the information. She disconnected and flopped back into her seat, considering her next step. Was it really possible her father had grown a massive brain tumor without her noticing a single sign? She tried to recall a laughed-off stumble, a lapse in memory, words garbled or misspoken, any indication he suffered from headaches or nausea.

Susan could not recall even one incident, could not remember her father ever acting sick in any way, at any time. He had always been extraordinarily healthy. In fact, other than the year he spent in rehabilitation after the accident that had killed Susan's mother, she could not recall him suffering from sniffles or sneezes or ever visiting a doctor, other than for routine checkups. He was either the healthiest person she knew or just good at hiding his aches, pains, and maladies. Still, could a person, even one accustomed to hiding discomforts, control lapses in judgment, speech, and memory, as well as gradual balance imperfections and changes in mood or personality?

As the glide-bus charged smoothly onward, Susan discovered other obvious and glaring inconsistencies. If the body had gone directly to the county medical examiner's office, why was it logged into the Manhattan Hasbro system? Was it a police error? Had they somehow tagged another man's decapitated corpse with her father's name? Either way, why did the chief Pathology resident remember the body coming in but not leaving? Was it possible the body had gone to the county morgue first, the head was removed to examine the extensive injuries and the tumor, then the remainder of the body was accidentally taken to Manhattan

Hasbro? Was the disappearance of the body an attempt to cover up a foolish mistake, an effort to preserve the integrity of the investigation? It seemed like an impossible coincidence that the same day John Calvin received a credible threat and left work early, he abruptly died of natural causes in strange circumstances, ones in which another person was inexplicably shot and killed.

Susan shook her head. The information she had thus far received did not fit together in any logical way. Clearly, she needed more information, and she had every intention of getting it. The irony reached her at that moment. This time last year, she had found herself enmeshed in a deadly plot, wanting desperately to call the police but prevented from doing so by her father's loyalty to Lawrence Robertson and U.S. Robots. This time, Robertson wanted her to involve the police as much as possible, yet they had closed their investigation. She would receive no further assistance from them, at least not without presenting them with enough evidence to reopen the case. To do that, she needed to perform some serious sleuthing.

Susan departed from the glide-bus at the next stop and switched smoothly to the one that would take her back to the home she had shared, until two days ago, with her father.

Caramel-colored walls with neutral still-life paintings enclosed simple but elegant, red-cushioned chairs in the waiting area of the Foder & Massey Funeral Home. At Susan's entrance, a young man looked up from an alcove desk, a wistful smile on his slightly off-kilter face. "Good afternoon, ma'am. It would be my pleasure to assist you."

Susan doubted it, but had to marvel at his ability to so carefully balance tone, expression, and movement. Either from training or instinct, he had the perfect manner for an attendant at a funeral home. She wondered if he radiated more warmth in his personal life. He seemed too young to have engraved such somberness into his psyche . . . yet. "I'm here to see my father's remains."

"So sorry for your loss." The young man sounded sincere. "Can you tell me your father's name, please?"

"Dr. John Calvin."

The receptionist stepped behind the desk and touched the keyboard multiple times. While he examined the screen, an older man opened a door beyond the alcove and peered out at Susan and the receptionist. "Is that Dr. Calvin?"

The young man stopped typing. "Dr. Calvin's daughter. Yes, sir."

The older man stepped up behind the receptionist. He had a headful of fine white hair that hugged his scalp, a heart-shaped face, and watery, dark eyes. "Also a doctor in her own right, as I understand." He held out a hand to Susan. "I'm Chris Massey. I wish we could have met under more fortuitous circumstances."

Susan did not imagine this man met many people in any but the worst of circumstances. She clasped his hand and found her own enveloped in an enormous, firm grip. "I've come to see my father and make . . . arrangements."

"Yes, of course. Please step into my office." Chris motioned Susan down a short hallway broken by several other doors and an open showroom, through which she could see several caskets, grave markers, urns, and memorials on shelves. She stepped inside a neat office with a single desk, multiple white chairs that looked brand-new, and a few tasteful pictures of animals. A shelf full of books and knickknacks lined one wall. Chris Massey motioned for Susan to sit in one of the chairs, and he selected one catty-corner to hers rather than retiring to his desk. Susan appreciated that. Her memories of confronting men from behind a shielding piece of furniture were not currently pleasant.

The funeral director got right down to business. "Are you planning a wake, a memorial service, or a funeral?"

The question surprised Susan, though it should not have. She had not given the matter any thought, having been more focused on the details of the death itself. "Well, actually, right now I'd really just like to see the body."

Chris Massey stared at Susan longer than politeness dictated. Apparently catching himself, he shook his head and cleared his throat. "Excuse me?"

"I'd like to see the body first," Susan explained. "I'm still trying to figure out how he died."

Chris leapt to his feet, face reddening. "I'm so sorry, Dr. Calvin. I thought the police had already informed you . . ." He headed toward his desk, clearly mortified. "Usually either the doctors or the police handle all those details and—"

Susan stopped him with a dismissing wave. "The police did talk to me. I just want to see for myself."

Chris mumbled something under his breath before plopping into his seat behind the desk and tapping at the touchboard of his desktop computer, ignoring several nearby palm-prosses. "It says here natural causes." He looked up at Susan. "Prolonged seizures . . . brain tumor?"

Susan sighed deeply. "I heard all that. I just want to see the body for myself." She thought she had conveyed that information directly enough, so it surprised her when Chris remained silent behind his desk. "Mr. Massey?" she prompted. "Surely I'm not the first to want to see a loved one before the funeral."

"Of course not." Chris seemed to regain his composure. "But you're the first to ask to see the body *after cremation*."

Susan was standing before she realized she had moved. "Cremation!" She did not know much about the funeral business, had never had to deal with arrangements before, but she could not believe she did not get a say in how her father's remains were disposed of. "Who decided that?"

Chris turned the computer screen around to show her a legal page titled "Cremation Authorization Form."

Susan did not bother to scan the information, her gaze falling to the signature blank where her own name nestled in the same handwriting she used to sign off on medical reports. She collapsed back into her chair. "That's my signature," she admitted. "But I never saw that form, never signed it. How . . . ?"

Chris Massey moved swiftly to her side, took her hand, and gave it a gentle squeeze, just right for comforting. He had done this many times. "Dr. Calvin, it's not uncommon in times of stress to forget–"

"I didn't sign that form."

"No one could blame you for doing things in a bit of a trance. After all, your father died, which is bad enough. But with the circumstances and the police and . . ." He didn't seem to know how to end that sentence. Instead, he dropped to a crouch in front of her and waited for her to speak.

Susan latched onto the pertinent. "So . . . it's done. Nothing left but ashes."

Chris tightened his grip on Susan's hand. "I'm sorry. You can still choose a casket, if you wish. Many people do." Apparently misinterpreting the cause of her consternation, he added, "We also have a beautiful assortment of urns."

Susan wondered if being possessed of the urge to grab nearly every person she had spoken to that day and shake them until their brains rattled was a form of insanity. Here it would do her no good. Clearly a fraud had been perpetrated, but she had no reason to believe this man had had anything to do with it. He had simply followed the same orders he did every day. Threatening him, physically or legally, would not reconstruct her father's body. "I need some time to process this. I'll come back when I've given it more thought."

Chris also rose, dashing to her side before she could exit the office unaccompanied. "Again, I'm so sorry for your loss, Dr. Calvin. Please call before your next visit so I can make certain to be here for you."

"I'll do that," Susan promised, walking briskly back into the entryway and out the front door.

Despite repairs in the past year from a nearby bomb blast, the unmarked building housing U.S. Robots and Mechanical Men still managed to appear drab and wholly gray. Susan ignored the simultaneous palm and retinal scanner her father had used to open the doors on her previous visit and tried to block out the details of that fateful day, since they revolved around the two men she loved most in the world, now both dead.

Instead, Susan stood in front of the door and pressed a button resembling an old doorbell from the days before mini intercoms and the need for expert security systems on businesses not open to the general public. A female voice blared crisply from an invisible speaker. "Can I help you?" Then, apparently recognizing Susan through an equally invisible camera, she added, "Oh! Dr. Calvin." The door whisked open to reveal a large, semicircular desk, behind which sat a sophisticated woman Susan's father had introduced as Amara. As before, an enormous computer console partially obscured the secretary's overly made-up face. She was shoving a piece of paper that read VISITOR into a plastic holder hung on a lanyard.

Now live, the intercom voice greeted Susan pleasantly. "I'm so very sorry about your father. He was a brilliant and special man—one of the kindest I've ever known. The world is a far, far colder place without him."

Susan stepped inside, and the door whisked closed behind her. She accepted the badge from Amara and put it on. "Thank you," she said politely, gaze sweeping the foyer. Familiar with the five-door configuration, she pinned her gaze on the second one, which bore the name LAWRENCE ROBERTSON. "I need to speak with Lawrence."

"Of course you do," Amara said. "Just let me let him know you're here." She pressed a button behind the desk. "Lawrence, Dr. Calvin here to see you."

Amara tipped her head toward her left earspike, apparently listening to a reply. She spoke aloud, "Dr. *Susan* Calvin, sir. The daughter."

Amara met Susan's gaze again. "He said to go right in."

Susan had expected nothing else from Lawrence Robertson. Her father's college roommate, the genius behind the positronic brain, had always treated her kindly. She suspected he was like that with everyone, an unpretentious prodigy with not only a stellar scientific intellect but an equally bright social aptitude. Those two did not always go together, but they did in both Lawrence Robertson and John Calvin, which probably made them well suited as roommates as well as coworkers.

Susan stepped around the desk and reached for the latch. Before she could trip it, the door opened to reveal Lawrence Robertson standing in the opening. He wore a friendly smile, clipped by circumstance, and more gray seemed to have blossomed around his temples since she had last seen him nearly a year ago. He had the same dark, wavy hair, large mouth, and rugged complexion.

Susan closed the door. The instant she did, Lawrence caught her in an embrace. For several moments, they stood clamped together like father and daughter, no words passing between them. When the appropriate amount of time had passed, they released one another, and Lawrence waved vaguely toward several chairs. Susan accepted one, and Lawrence scooted another directly across from her, rather than sitting behind his desk.

"How are you?" Lawrence asked.

"Fine," Susan said, knowing he would see through such an obvious lie. "Considering the circumstances."

Lawrence sighed deeply. "I'm devastated, Susan. I can only imagine you feel doubly so."

Susan simply nodded. She knew how close the two men had been, how her father had always looked upon Lawrence not only as a partner, but as a great man and a loyal friend. They had known and respected one another longer than she had lived. "Where's Nate?"

"What?"

Susan had a natural ability to read expressions and tone that had steered her into the psychiatric profession. Further training made her certain she had heard a hint of disingenuousness in an otherwise startled question. "I can't find N8-C. I thought you might know where he'd gone." After visiting the funeral home, she had gone immediately to Manhattan Hasbro to seek out her mechanical confidant.

"Gone?" Lawrence repeated, not quite casually enough. "He's not relegated to a closet, you know. He's probably off helping one of the doctors on a research project or with some paperwork."

"Is he doing that?" Susan asked directly, chasing Lawrence's gaze.

Lawrence remained evasive. "Why would you think I'd know that? I have no connection to the hospital."

"You don't," Susan agreed, "but I do, and I can't find him. You do, however, have a connection to N8-C." She was done playing games for the day, maybe forever. "He's here, isn't he?"

Lawrence hesitated.

"Don't lie to me, Lawrence. I swear, I'm going to shoot the next person who lies to me, and I don't want it to be you."

"All right. He's here." Lawrence finally met Susan's gaze. "I was concerned about his safety."

"Why?" It was less a question than a demand.

"Because the threat information we received about your father included Nate."

"The Society for Humanity," Susan guessed. The antirobotic technology group had shown itself more than capable of deadly violence in the past.

"Yes," Lawrence stated, rising. The office had three doors: the one through which Susan had entered, another on the opposite wall, and a third on the wall between them. The last one had a standard turning knob, which suggested it was a closet or restroom. Lawrence walked to that last one and turned the knob. "And that's why I want you safely away from here. Clearly, they're the ones responsible for John's death, and that's exactly what I told the police, and you by Vox."

The door opened to reveal a small, clean restroom. Nate peered out. A grin split his all-too-human face. "Susan!"

"Nate." Susan could not help smiling as well, though the expression felt weird and inappropriate after the prior events of the day. She wanted to talk to the robot, but she would not miss the opportunity presented by Lawrence's last remark. "Lawrence, do you think it's even remotely possible my father died of natural causes?"

Lawrence flinched, clearly startled, then rolled his gaze to Susan. "No," he said abruptly. Then, as if to soften his delivery, he explained, "He was healthy as a horse, your father. Always." His brow wrinkled. "Why are you asking? You think he had a heart attack from the stress of the threat?" Lawrence's gaze flicked in so many directions, Susan could scarcely follow it. He licked his lips, rocked from foot to foot, all signs the conversation made him increasingly uncomfortable. Finally, he managed to focus. "Susan, I do not believe it's possible your father died of natural causes. Why do you ask?"

Susan watched him closely as she delivered the news. "Because that's what the police just told me."

The look Lawrence turned her was transparent. Surprise and puzzlement freely mingled, then turned to deep contemplation. "Based on . . ."

Susan obliged. "The alleged medical examiner's report."

"Medical examiner's report," Lawrence repeated, a finger stroking his lower lip. He looked up suddenly. "Then I suppose we have to believe ..." Something in Susan's own expression stopped him. "Did you say 'alleged'?"

Susan glanced at Nate, who stood utterly still aside from his eyes, which moved from Susan to Lawrence and back in turn. "The ME's report is a fake."

"A fake." Lawrence seemed condemned to repeat Susan's last words. His eyes flickered around the room, landing everywhere except Susan's face. "Are you . . . are you quite sure?"

Susan was. "Not at first. They created an almost reasonable scenario involving a brain tumor and a prolonged period of seizures."

Lawrence sat back in his chair and crossed his legs. It was a casual gesture executed too casually. It indicated an unspoken discomfort, an effort to pretend to accept information he had discarded only a few moments earlier. "Could he have had a brain tumor without us knowing it?"

"It's plausible." Susan addressed only the direct question. "As I said, they created an almost reasonable scenario, something even I might have believed, despite the fact it would force me to accept I had missed subtle signs in the person I loved most in the world, signs I never would have overlooked in any patient." She paused for breath. "The problem is, it completely contradicts the obvious evidence."

"Which is?"

This time, Susan took a roundabout route to the answer. "I was almost ready to believe my father's body arrived at Hasbro headless because the extent of his injuries and suspicion of the tumor caused the medical examiner to want the skull and its contents studied at a separate facility from the body. I might even buy the idea the funeral home accidentally cremated his body, then forged my signature on the papers to cover their mistake. Perhaps, if I suspended all my disbelief, I might come to accept that the chief Pathology resident at Manhattan Hasbro, one of the best hospitals and teaching programs in the world, had a lapse of memory in regard to the receipt of, and the disappearance of, a corpse in her care.

"Stretching that even further, I could just barely grasp the possibility of a woman murdered in our hallway on the same day my father died being just a phenomenal coincidence. Maybe my antigun father secretly owned an antique revolver and, in the throes of an unreasoning convulsion, shot her himself." Finally, Susan got to the point. "However, when I finally went home and examined the scene—"

Lawrence interrupted in a voice so stern it sounded almost angry. "You went to the apartment today? Susan, that's horribly dangerous. Why would you do that?"

Susan finally managed to pin down his gaze again. "If he died of natural causes, what danger could there be?"

Lawrence looked away again, though not far. He trained his attention fanatically on Susan's upper lip. "The threat against your father was real."

"So, what are they going to do? Use me to get to . . . a dead man? Murder or natural causes, John Calvin is dead." Susan suddenly realized the possibility still existed that the body was misidentified. She had never actually seen it. She started to tremble. "Isn't he?"

Lawrence did not immediately answer.

"Isn't he?" Susan repeated more forcefully. She needed to know, had every right to do so.

Lawrence scooted his chair closer and put his arms around Susan again. "Susan, there is no doubt about this: Your father is dead."

Susan looked at Nate and found him blurry behind a curtain of her own tears. He pursed his lips, and his eyes held longing and hope.

"Tell her," the robot said, "what you told me."

Lawrence turned his head toward Nate, and Susan could almost feel the heat of the glare she could not see. She tried not to let her hopes rise. Lawrence had not said "John Calvin is dead" as he might if he had changed her father's name and sent him somewhere safe temporarily. He had specifically stated, "Your father is dead."

"Shut your mouth," Lawrence instructed Nate, and the robot obeyed, as the Second Law stated he must. But his gaze found Susan's again, and it spoke volumes.

Susan shoved off Lawrence, until she created enough space between their seats that he could no longer hold her, could no longer keep his face hidden, could no longer avoid her searching gaze. "Lawrence, you can silence Nate, but not me. Whether you like it or not, we're in this together."

Lawrence sighed. "Susan, you're misunderstanding. There's nothing I can tell you that will change anything. You have to understand that."

Susan would not let go. "The only thing I understand is I'm missing a crucial piece of information that might tie this all together. Until I have it, I can't focus and I can't rest. And if you don't give it to me, I'll have to find it out myself, even if it means significant risk to USR, to you, and to my own life."

"She has a right to know," Nate said.

Lawrence looked sharply at the robot. "Didn't I tell you to shut your mouth?"

"Yes," Nate admitted. "And I did." He smiled ever so slightly, clearly for Susan's benefit. "Then I opened it again."

Susan winked at Nate but continued addressing Lawrence. "Lawrence, there are at least a dozen bullet holes in my walls. Nearly everything I own was cut or torn open and strewn across the floor, far too methodically for seizures to explain it. What are the odds my father managed to destroy every single thing we own before hitting his head on some object so hard it killed him?" Susan shook her head; she had considered all of this on her way to United States Robots and Mechanical Men. "Nothing fits, because I'm missing important information." She rose and stared intently into his face. "I deserve to know the truth."

To Susan's surprise, Lawrence quailed beneath her gaze. He did not try to rise; merely clasped his hands in his lap and dropped his gaze to them. "Susan, what if something I say changes your relationship with your father? What if it quakes your very foundation? What if it destroys your confidence in yourself and everything you've ever accomplished?"

Susan sat back down, giving Lawrence's questions their due consideration. She allowed several full minutes to tick past while thoughts raced through her mind. She did not try to guess what Lawrence might say, because that would undermine the purpose of his questions. She considered herself strong and capable, despite the events of the past year. Before starting at Manhattan Hasbro, she never would have believed anything could unnerve her. Now she knew otherwise. "Lawrence," she said, with all the sobriety the request deserved. "I can't quit searching until I know the whole truth. You can either let me find it on my own, whatever the danger, and deal with any consequences by myself. Or you can help me."

"Tell her," Nate said. Though he scarcely moved, there was a forcefulness about his stance and tone that made him seem more master than creation. Then, more softly, "Tell her."

Lawrence Robertson sucked in a deep breath, as if prolonging the moment indefinitely.

Susan understood his reluctance and did not press. Knowledge sometimes had its price, including the realization that, once learned, it might never be forgotten.

Chapter 14

They sat in Lawrence Robertson's spacious office at U.S. Robots and Mechanical Men, Lawrence's and Susan's seats facing one another while Nate pulled a chair up beside Susan, close enough to put a supportive arm around her or hold her hand, if either became necessary.

At the moment, Susan found herself more intrigued than concerned or frightened. So much had happened in the past year, she doubted Lawrence could say anything that would upset or truly surprise her, though she felt certain he was going to delve into all the worst moments of her life. In that, he did not disappoint her, beginning with the most horrible time of her existence.

"Do you remember, Susan, when you were a little girl of three or four?"

Susan knew exactly where Lawrence was going. "When my mother died in a horrible accident, and I nearly lost my father as well. My life changed dramatically from that moment onward. Nothing was ever the same."

"Yes." Lawrence glanced at Nate as if to beg the robot not to force him to continue. Of course, Nate had no power over his creator, so nothing he said or did truly mattered. He was only the voice of Lawrence's conscience, albeit one who could compute complex mathematical riddles in an instant and had grown to know Susan's psyche far better than her father's best friend. "And for more reasons than you know."

Susan cocked her head to indicate interest. She steeled her emotions, not wishing to reveal any hurt or distress, to give Lawrence any reason to abort his story. "My mother died more than twenty years ago. You're not opening any fresh wounds here, Lawrence."

"Maybe," Lawrence did not sound nearly as certain as Susan. "Except I need to change the details a bit, present it to you a different way."

"All right." Susan looked directly into Lawrence's face, wanting to reassure him nothing he said would bother her. Her father had not handled the death of Amanda Calvin well. He had avoided talking about it, dodged questions, and generally changed the subject to the point where Susan learned not to broach it with him at all. She suspected denial had suited her as well, crushing the horrible memory of losing her mother into the deepest recesses of her brain and allowing her to focus solely on the happy times.

When John had spoken of Amanda, he did so with all the love in the universe and always in superlatives. To Susan's knowledge, he had never so much as dated since her death. It had taken her until last year, until she found Remington, to question her father about his private life. Only then, with his assistance, had she dredged up enough cobwebbed images to remember he had gotten severely injured in the same accident, sustaining wounds that left him with permanent neurological damage and little desire or capacity for sexual entanglements.

"Amanda was a brilliant woman, Susan, dedicated to her work with USR."

Susan caught herself stiffening. Her father had never mentioned her mother also worked for U.S. Robots. He had always downplayed his own role there, too.

"Surely John told you I invented the positronic brain."

Susan nodded vigorously. John Calvin had shown the same breathless, reverent awe whenever he mentioned the name Lawrence Robertson and his staggering creations.

"It was your parents, Susan, who meticulously crafted the wording of the Three Laws of Robotics, with input from me and Alfred, of course." Lawrence waved vaguely toward the office of Alfred Lanning, a stocky man he had once introduced as his head of research. "But it was wholly John and Amanda who came up with the coupling, the indelible and inseparable process of eternally linking the Three Laws of Robotics and the positronic brain, so one could never exist without the other."

That brought Susan's thoughts back to a day when she and Remington had visited with Nate and, during the discussion, came up with a theory that the Three Laws were the very thing sabotaging the Society for Humanity's attempts to use nanorobot-infused, mentally ill humans as mindless bombers. Nate had insisted, "The Three Laws of Robotics are the basis from which all positronic brains are constructed. Without them, there is no positronic brain, no thinking robot. U.S. Robots has made the Three Laws so essential to production that such cannot be undertaken without them." John Calvin had later added, "All USR robotics begin and end with the Three Laws. It would be utterly impossible to build a positronic brain without the Three Laws or to remove them without permanently disabling the robot."

It never ceased to amaze Susan how her father could so easily bypass any mention of his own hand in the events he described with such assuredness and admiration.

"It's rare to meet two people so ideally suited to one another as Amanda and your father. They wanted to remain together during work, after work, night after night. And they lavished attention on what they considered their greatest joint endeavor."

"The Three Laws of Robotics," Susan guessed.

Lawrence managed a laugh, though the situation strained it. "I meant you, Susan. They considered you their monumental achievement. They used to take you almost everywhere, and it was a stroke of luck you were with your grandmother when . . ." He stopped suddenly, his next word garbled by a lump in his throat.

"The accident," Susan filled in. Too many years had passed for her to surrender to emotion about it, especially in front of Lawrence.

"It was no accident." The words emerged softly, conversationally, yet they struck Susan like a physical blow.

"Dad's always described it as an accident." Lawrence's words made no sense. "Are you trying to say . . . he crashed the car on purpose?" Lawrence had warned Susan that knowing the truth might change her opinion of her father, but she would never believe he had intentionally killed her mother and, nearly, himself.

"No car," Lawrence corrected. "No crash." He closed his eyes deliberately, slowly, and held them shut. "Susan, your parents were gunned down."

Susan's mouth fell open.

"By the Society for Humanity."

Susan could not believe what she was hearing. "Gunned down," she repeated. "My parents?"

Lawrence opened his eyes. "I told you it would quake your foundation. I can stop here, if you wish."

Susan shook her head vigorously. She had to know it all, for her safety if for no other reason. "Why target my parents? Why not . . . the creator of the positronic brain? Why not"—in her rush to get the name out, she momentarily forgot his official title—"Alfred Lanning?"

Lawrence sighed, lowered his head, and sighed again. "Believe me, I asked myself that question a million times. Why them? Why not me? Why? Why? Why?" He fell silent, apparently questioning the universe again, as if this time he might get the answer. "USR was only a few years old at the time, barely on the SFH radar. I had revealed the positronic brain at a few symposiums, and there was some buzz, some early excitement."

A strangely serene look stole over his features; the memory of simpler times, with everything fresh and new, briefly carried away the burdens of the next two and a half decades. "Calvin was the one who anticipated the Frankenstein Complex. . . ."

Susan had never heard Lawrence call her father by their last name before, and it seemed jarringly out of place.

"And it was his attempts to assuage it that ultimately led to his death."

Susan remained quiet but tried to keep an inquisitive look plastered on her face. She did not want Lawrence to see any of the building turmoil in her own thoughts. She worried he would hold back on those parts of the story he thought would most upset her, the very ones that could make the difference between appropriate wariness and abject panic. She needed to know what dangers she faced without false reassurances or gaps in her knowledge. "Hence their work on the Three Laws."

"Yes." Lawrence studied her features intently. If he could read below the superficial game she played to keep him talking, it did not stop him. "Amanda and Calvin believed that if they could convince the public of the safety of the positronic robot, they might get past the irrational fear. But the announcement did not go as they planned. Somehow the emphasis fell squarely on the security of the bond between the Three Laws of Robotics and the positronic brain."

Susan noted the oddity again and could not help commenting on it. "I've never heard you call my father Calvin before. Now you've done it twice."

Lawrence bobbed his head. "Calvin was your father's name." He added carefully, "His *first* name."

Susan supposed the information ought to startle her, but it did not. It only made sense to let the killers believe they had accomplished their goal, that her father was a different man, by changing his name. Otherwise they would go after him again. Susan now understood what must have happened. On or about July 4, 2036, the SFH had finally seen through the deception, more than twenty years after their quarry had survived their deadly barrage.

Lawrence anticipated Susan's question. "Unfortunately, Calvin had a bright daughter who reveled in her ability to write the names of herself and the two people she loved most in the world. No amount of gentle or coercive steering could get you to give up those three names: Susan, Amanda, and Calvin." He smiled ever so slightly. "And Calvin was adamant that, no matter what happened to him, things be as normal for you as possible."

Susan had to admit he had done a marvelous job, miraculous by some standards. She did not like that he had lied to her about the car accident, but she understood why he had needed to do so. Now his reasons for avoiding talking about it made even more sense. Had Susan known the truth as a child, she could never have kept it secret, and any revelation would have placed her father, and probably her, in lethal danger.

Lawrence finished answering her question. "Luckily, you couldn't handle the last-name part yet. Just 'Susan,' 'Amanda,' and 'Calvin.' We simply added 'John,' moved 'Calvin' to the end, and everything worked out." He added quickly, "It wasn't the name that tipped off the SFH this time."

Susan knew she needed to explore that, but the issue of why the SFH had targeted her family in the first place still remained on the table. She wondered about her original last name but saw no real reason to know it, since she could never safely use it. "So, they targeted my parents because they were the ones speaking publicly about positronic robots."

Lawrence frowned and shook his head. "That might be part of it, but I've come to agree with Alfred. What put Calvin and Amanda in SFH's crosshairs was a comment they made about the Three Laws. The reporters had become utterly relentless and refused to accept that the Three Laws would keep mankind safe from a robotic revolt because, somehow, the sheer brilliance of a brain capable of learning would allow robots to uncouple themselves from the restrictions placed upon them. Repetition wasn't working. Even their insistence that the two were inseparably linked, that any attempt to uncouple them would render the positronic brain nonfunctional, didn't do the trick.

"It somehow got into the public consciousness that a secret formula existed that could separate the two, and the questions became even more unstoppable about how USR would keep that information out of the hands of the robots or some other malevolent force. In exasperation, Amanda said something to the effect that if such a formula existed, it would die with the two of them, because not even I knew it."

It was obvious to Susan where this was going. "So, the SFH tried to kill them to keep the formula from ever getting used."

"It would appear so," Lawrence said miserably. "For no reason at all, really, because no such secret formula ever existed. The truth is, Susan, there isn't and never was any such possibility. The positronic brain and the Three Laws are inextricably intertwined."

Despite Lawrence's forceful statement, Susan found herself strangely uncertain, left wondering if he was lying to keep her safe. If there was an uncoupling mechanism, she doubted Lawrence would tell her anything different than he had. Perhaps her parents had told the truth: the knowledge had died with them.

As they reached the end of the story, Susan realized Lawrence was wrong. His revelation had not rocked her foundation; nothing of significance had changed. "So, that's it? The big secret that would shake me up and change my life forever is the accident was actually a murder?"

An expression crossed Lawrence's face, then vanished nearly as quickly. He weighed his words.

Was that relief? Susan refused to let him off the hook. "There's still something you're not telling me."

Lawrence looked away. Nate stared at his creator, as if willing the man to finish what he started.

Susan remained as relentless as the reporters who had driven her parents to make the offhand comment that had, ultimately, destroyed them. "Spit it out, Lawrence Robertson. I have a right to know."

Lawrence sucked an enormous breath through his teeth, then let it out in a long, slow exhalation. "Susan, I've given you all the clues. I haven't withheld anything you couldn't work out if you took some time to consider everything you know."

Susan turned him a withering look. "I spend more than enough time unearthing obscure diagnoses in mistreated patients. There's no benefit to giving me riddles, and no time to waste solving them when you could just tell me"—Susan raised the volume so Lawrence could find no way to avoid it—"*the truth!*"

"Fine." Lawrence could have thrown Susan from his office, if he chose. Instead he settled on doing exactly what she asked, bluntly and without preamble. "Calvin did survive the shooting, but only for a few hours. Long enough to make it clear how he wanted his daughter raised. Understand, Susan, we did everything we could to honor his final wishes, odd as some might find them."

Susan could hardly miss Lawrence's point. "So, John Calvin was not my . . . biological father." She immediately realized it did not matter. "So what? He loved me at least as much as if he were. And it doesn't change how I feel about him, either."

Nate finally spoke. "NC stands for New Calvin."

Those five words made the connection Lawrence had missed imparting with several hundred. Susan found herself incapable of speech, movement, or even thought. That was the moment the earth finally collapsed beneath her feet and yet she felt infinitely grounded, as if she had grown roots that reached deeper than the molten core. When she finally managed to force out a breath, it emerged in a squeaky whine, "John Calvin is N12-C." She did not need confirmation. It all came together in an instant: Nate passing so easily for human, her father's aversion to public eating, his decision to devote himself wholly to his daughter, even to the exclusion of dating, his own happiness. N12-C had a mission that subsumed his every waking moment, the daughter to whom he dedicated himself because his programming made it so. The perfect father was, in fact, a positronic robot.

"Susan!" Susan had no idea how long Lawrence Robertson had been shaking her. "Are you all right?"

To Susan's surprise, she was. She found herself more impressed than upset or betrayed. They had pulled off the deception flawlessly, the only details that might have given him away covered with such plausible lies that even she had believed them. Susan prided herself on noticing details, on putting tiny inconsistencies and bits of information together to create a previously unappreciated diagnosis. She had not missed anything here; rather, the picture was so complete, so perfect, so natural she had never considered the possibility. *Who in their right, or even wrong, mind would?*

As soon as Lawrence had Susan's attention back, he tried to explain, "We incorporated as much of Calvin's genetic material as we could. A simple blood test or saliva test would have matched you as father and daughter. I tried to copy the neural circuitry as closely as possible, worked to incorporate the memories, with only one change: John didn't know about the shootings; we couldn't allow that. We had to get the features near enough for you to recognize him without the SFH becoming suspicious. Your tender age made it easier, as well as the fact that you spent a year in the sole care of your grandmother while your father recuperated. She was provided with progressive pictures to show you to allow for a believable transition.

"Calvin had worried for your future from the moment of your conception, had planned for the eventuality of your losing one or both parents. He kept meticulous journals of his life and Amanda's, every detail of which wound up in the positronic brain of his replacement. He dedicated every spare moment to what he called biorobotics, the science of creating robots of flesh and blood, indistinguishable from people, miraculous beings like Nate and Nick and John. He was obsessed with ensuring your upbringing was ideal, happy, exactly as it would have been if he had lived. As he lay dying, he made me promise, he made me swear a thousand times . . ." Lawrence's eyes grew distant and hazy. He looked as if he might start crying.

Susan could sense her father's desperation, felt certain John Calvin had raised her precisely as the man he replaced would have done if he had had the chance. She harbored no anger, and, more important to her own sensibilities, no regrets, at least not for the moment. Perhaps in a time of lonely contemplation, she would find reasons to condemn the decision, the actions of desperate men acting out of dedication and friendship and love. For now she found herself captivated by the concept, fascinated by the details. Her entire life had become a psychiatrist's dream study: the hapless little orphan raised by a robotic father, the victim of overreaching and evil geniuses.

Lawrence now studied Susan as he spoke, seeking clues as to when curiosity became overbalanced by too much difficult information. "If Calvin had had his way, we would have reproduced Amanda instead of him. Unfortunately, no matter how small the circuitry, no matter how much we scaled down the positronic brain, we could not get it sized to fit inside a woman's head without making her preternaturally big. A man taller than six and a half feet does not draw the same untoward attention as a woman who towers over the world, and it's easier to hide wayward lumps and flaws in the masculine form." Lawrence likely would feel far more comfortable discussing the technical details, but had to realize those things mattered little at the present moment. Perhaps someday Susan would become as fascinated by those specifics as her parents had been when they had chosen to dedicate their lives to robotics.

Susan found herself more concerned with the events of the past few days. "What was the threat, Lawrence? Why did my father leave work in the middle of the day, and what did the SFH want from him worth"– she almost said "killing him over," but the words seemed wrong now–"destroying him for?"

Lawrence sighed again, shaking his head even more briskly. "We try to keep track of the SFH Web sites, their main one but also their social networks, their communication boards, their private sites, when we can get on them. There was some activity suggesting someone might have discovered a connection between Calvin and John, even some credible talk the two men might be one and the same. Threats followed. We thought it best if you and John disappeared for a while. He went home to pack, with plans to go into hiding with you until things blew over. Obviously, it didn't go quite as planned."

Susan realized the truth. "I was the connection, wasn't I? They figured out I was Calvin and Amanda's daughter, and the man raising me resembled my biological father, at least superficially."

Lawrence Robertson ignored the question, an answer of sorts. "The killers who gunned down your parents received life sentences. We originally thought they were rogue operatives, like the lunatics who murdered abortion doctors or the fringe conservationists shooting hunters and scientists in the name of rescuing innocent animals. It wasn't until last year, when the bombs showed up in the hands of the nanorobot study patients, that we realized the lengths to which the SFH would, once again, go. Of course, those people, too, wound up behind bars, so we thought we had disposed of the worst offenders." Lawrence could no longer hold back the tears. "Oh, Susan. If we had had any idea—"

Susan waved him off. She did not hold Lawrence in any way responsible. The information he had given her seemed oddly immaterial. "Do you think" she started carefully, "the SFH knew . . ."

She paused just long enough that Lawrence filled in, "John was robotic?"

Susan nodded once.

"No." Lawrence's lips twisted in a parody of consideration. "Nothing in their communications suggested they even suspected it. If I had to guess, I'd say they surprised him in your home and questioned his connection to Calvin. After that, your guess is as good as mine."

"They must have eventually figured out what he was." Susan did not realize she had spoken aloud until Lawrence responded.

"Not necessarily."

Susan could scarcely believe what she had just heard. Her brow furrowed. "You mean—" She did not know how to finish, so she allowed him to do it.

Nate did so for him. "Biorobotics," he reminded. "We wouldn't resemble real humans so completely if we didn't have a full dermal system. You can't have living tissue without nourishment, so we have a circulatory system to oxygenate blood and pump it to where it needs to go. Wires and electronic pulses aren't that different from the natural human neurological system. An autopsy would reveal the mechanical framework, as would a simple X-ray, MRI, or CT scan. Our limbs can break with sufficient force, our skin can scrape and cut quite naturally, our wounds bleed."

Lawrence bobbed his head, as if someone had inserted a spring in his neck. "All true and correct."

Susan could not remember her father ever becoming sick, though he handled her own illnesses with all the right nurturing, as if he understood the discomforts, the family cures, the scourges of nasal discharge and raw, pus-covered tonsils. She had applied the occasional Band-Aid to the inevitable scrapes and injuries accompanying her father's everyday life. She had noticed nothing odd about them. "So a gunshot wound . . . ?"

"Would probably look grossly similar to a human one," Lawrence supplied. "I'm not an expert on firearms or pathology, but the density of the parts isn't that different from muscle and bone in a human being. Entrance wounds ought to behave similarly. Exit wounds, if they exist, perhaps not. It's possible a wire might protrude or a blast might take out a patch of skin and leave the framework exposed."

Susan became fully professional, blocking out the realization they were discussing her beloved father as if he were a complicated toy. "Are you saying the SFH might have killed a robot and, *to this moment*, still believe he's human?"

"Susan, I'm saying it's possible even the police still believe they're investigating a murder."

Susan knew otherwise, but, for the moment, that information did not seem as significant as what Lawrence had just said. "How could they not notice? They have the body, for Christ's sake!"

"We have the body," Lawrence said quietly.

"What?"

"We swiped it from Hasbro, Susan. We couldn't risk it." Lawrence took Susan's hand. "Can you understand?"

Susan shrugged and bobbed her head simultaneously. There were layers of danger: legal, social, and future implications more important than business profits and losses. She felt certain Lawrence had even considered the problems it would cause her if anyone knew about her upbringing.

Lawrence continued his explanation. "The police don't examine the body all that closely. They're trained to scrutinize the environment, to follow leads and clues, but to leave the forensics to the experts. They let the pathologists take the lead on removal and inspection of the body itself. We had to get that body before the first cut was made. There's only one problem, and it's a doozy."

Susan knew the answer. "You didn't get the head."

Lawrence's jaw fell open. "How could you possibly know that?"

Susan reminded him, "I mentioned it earlier in the conversation, but you were too focused on trying to avoid giving me the information about my father, on letting me believe the 'natural causes' baloney the police concocted." Though the truth, it was not an altogether fair attack. Lawrence had finally leveled with her despite a promise he had held sacred for longer than two decades. "I gave you a list of things I might have believed under different circumstances, including my father's body arriving at Hasbro headless because the medical examiner wanted the skull and its contents examined at another facility."

"That did slip past me," Lawrence admitted. "How did you know?"

At the moment, Susan would tell him anything that might help explain the situation. "I read the Hasbro pathology log. He arrived that way."

Lawrence stiffened and turned away. Clearly, she had told him something he did not know. "We also thought they sent it to a different part of the morgue for special examination."

An idea struck Susan, one she could not possibly wait to speak. "Lawrence, if we can recover that head, could we . . . bring John Calvin . . . back to life?" The idea buoyed her in a way nothing else had in at least a year. She felt giddy and nauseated, excited and terrified, abruptly thrilled with the understanding that her father was not a flesh-and-blood man. A concept that should have appalled her became her one saving grace. Every microsecond it took for Lawrence to answer became a deep and throbbing pain.

Lawrence whirled to face Susan. "No, Susan. No. Please don't pin your hopes on that."

"Why not?" Susan's voice emerged unwittingly confrontational. She sounded to her own ears like a whining toddler. "If the memories still exist . . ."

"That's a big 'if,'" Lawrence reminded. "We don't even know who has his head, what they might have done with it before or after they recognized what it was. The entire process is patented, of course, so information on construction and care is freely available. But even if they intended to keep it safe, to retain access to John's thoughts, that would have been hard for nonexperts to do."

Susan was resolute. "I'm going to find that head."

"We have to," Lawrence agreed. "We can't leave a positronic brain in the hands of the SFH. Who knows what they might learn, what they might do, what they might use it for?"

Susan had a completely different take on the matter. "If there's any chance whatsoever of bringing back my father . . ."

"Susan, no." Lawrence's tone grew sharper. "You're not thinking clearly. How could you possibly explain your murdered father rising from the dead? Even if you found a plausible explanation, what would keep the SFH from exposing him? Or killing him again more permanently?"

"We can deal with that issue after we recover him." Susan wanted her father with a desire so raw and deep she would give up anything else to have him.

"Susan . . ."

"We could rework his features and present him as an uncle or a brother. A friend."

"Susan . . ."

Susan did not want Lawrence to finish his sentence, to remind her of all the practical considerations she did not wish to confront at the moment. "We need to find the head."

"I agree with you, Susan." Lawrence tried another tack. "We need to find it, but I don't want your assistance."

That was not what Susan had expected him to say. "Why not?"

"Mostly because of the obvious physical danger, but also because I don't want you emotionally devastated again. I can't have you believing this is a rescue mission, a means of saving your father's life. The truth is, that's an extremely unlikely outcome."

"Why?" Susan demanded.

This time, Nate explained. "Because the positronic memory is volatile. When stored, it requires a source of power to remain intact, and it's sensitive to radiation. That's why I never volunteer to stick my head in a CT scanner, even though it's not supposed to emit enough to damage me. It might violate the Third Law."

Lawrence nodded. "Thank you, Nate. I don't believe the SFH knew John was robotic when they went after him, which means they wouldn't have brought a backup power source, and they wouldn't have hesitated to shoot him in the head multiple times. More likely, they figured out what he was while dispatching him and took the head for study. It's unlikely to have survived the transport intact, and who knows what they might have done to it since."

"Fine," Susan said. "I won't get emotionally involved." It was a promise she could not keep, but she did not allow doubt to enter her voice. "I'll consider this a mission to regain your proprietary information and parts, but you have to count me in. You can't do it without me."

"We can't?" Lawrence might have intended his question to be rhetorical, but Susan had a ready answer.

"You need me because the police won't speak to you. You're not family. For the time being, at least, they still have me assigned to a contact. Either they don't know about the robotics or they don't want me to know, and I can take advantage of both possibilities." Susan looked pointedly, questioningly, at Lawrence Robertson. "So we're in this together."

Reluctantly, Lawrence rotated his head in the vertical plane, robot-like. "I guess we are, Susan. I guess we are."

Chapter 15

It was nearly 3:30 p.m. when Susan arrived at the station and demanded to see Detective Jacob Carson. She was ushered into a small, neat office lined with shelves and cubbies. Each compartment held a packet of e-formation, bound papers, electronic equipment, battery chargers, or folders. No pictures hung on the walls, and no photographs occupied any surface.

The sole occupant of the room, a man of approximately six feet, dressed in a spotless dress suit with perfect pleats, rose as Susan entered. His coat and pants were a dark and solid blue; the shirt lighter with vertical stripes. He was clearly a proponent of the gym, with sculpted pectorals, a slender waist reminiscent of old Ken dolls, and arms that filled out his sleeves. He sported short, spiky hair the color of straw; quick hazel eyes beneath tweezed brows; and a clean-shaven, boxy chin. He appeared midthirties, with just a hint of middle-aged coarsening. She noticed no gray in his hair, even at the temples, and he appeared sleek and stylish, except for the anachronistic suit. No one wore them anymore, to Susan's knowledge. Suits had gone the way of the strangulating tie, replaced by the khakis and dress polos she and her colleagues wore to work.

The man offered his hand across the desk. "Detective Jake Carson. What can I do for you?"

Susan took his hand and gave it a brisk shake. He had a dry and solid grip, and held for only a moment before releasing her. "My name is Dr. Susan Calvin. I'm here to talk about my father's murder."

"Ah." Jake gestured at the chair in front of his desk before turning to pull a folder from one of the cubbies and laying it on the remarkably uncluttered surface. "I spoke with you on Vox, Dr. Calvin. Remember? I told you we had closed the case. Your father died of natural causes."

Susan did not take the proffered chair. When the detective turned, he found himself looking directly into her bosom, which clearly startled him. He immediately flicked his gaze to her face. "Dr. Calvin, please sit."

Susan remained in place. "Detective Carson, I'd rather not."

"Jake," he suggested.

"Susan." She gave the standard response, not at all sure she should have. He had the strategic advantage of being on his territory, in his office. She could have given herself a similar one by remaining on superior ground in the area of titles. "And my father was murdered."

Ignoring her decision to remain standing, Jake sat in his chair and leaned back. "Susan, I know you loved your father. I understand he was a brilliant scientist. When a loved one dies suddenly, it can be hard to believe they were felled by something so strange and unexpected. But the autopsy doesn't lie."

"An autopsy," Susan said coldly, "was never done."

Jake sat up. He studied her. "I assure you it was. I have the report right here." He opened the folder.

Susan did not wait for him to find the proper paper. "The autopsy report is a forgery."

Jake sighed deeply. "Susan," he said firmly. "This must be extremely difficult for you, and I do sympathize. However . . ."

"There are bullet holes in my walls."

Jake crinkled his face, then shook his head. "You're mistaken, Susan. You're misinterpreting what you're seeing."

Susan did not give him time to concoct a plausible explanation or refer to a preplanned cover story. "And decapitation is not a natural cause of death."

Jake froze. He studied Susan for a moment, as if afraid to speak. When he did, the words seemed to blossom from nowhere, blatant non sequiturs. "You're a beautiful woman, Susan. I'd be honored if you'd agree to have dinner with me."

Susan's mouth opened, but no words emerged. She stood there, stupidly staring at him. She wanted to ask him to repeat what he had said, but the idea of stammering out a "what?" only made her feel more stupid. She met his earnest gaze and found nothing akin to desire. Instead she found promise and desperation. Clearly, he wanted to talk to her somewhere other than his office. "All . . . right," she finally managed, the wind collapsing from her sails in an instant.

Jake rose, placed an arm on Susan's shoulders and guided her toward the exit from his office. There was no passion in his touch, just a firmness that forced her to walk in the direction he specified. "Wait for me in the waiting area. I'm off duty in five minutes, and I need to punch out. Then we'll go eat wherever you prefer."

Susan found herself moving without intending to do so. He walked her to the waiting area, then released her and turned back into his office. Susan swung around to watch his retreating back, wondering exactly what had just happened. She had not finished what she needed to say, and she had every intention of doing so. If he harbored any notion of sneaking out a side or back exit and giving her the slip, she would see to it he regretted that decision, even if it meant destroying his career.

Susan need not have worried. As promised, Jake appeared within a few minutes, his hair neatly combed, the file on John Calvin tucked under one arm, a palm-pross under the other. He said some words to the receptionist, then beckoned to Susan with crisp movements of his fingertips. They walked out the door together.

Silently, Jake Carson ushered Susan into the parking lot to a Subaru Sapphire parked perfectly within the lines of its compact space. He opened the passenger's door for her, a gallantry she had not seen outside of movies, and she found herself in a small, clean leather seat that seemed almost to embrace her. She had rarely traveled by anything other than public transportation. Personal cars had been rendered unnecessary, and her father particularly avoided them ever since the accident that had injured him and killed her mother.

Susan discarded that last line of thought, which had risen so naturally. Her father was not a man and probably could not have obtained a driver's license. She now knew Amanda Calvin, or whatever her last name had been, had not died in a crash, either. A car had, in fact, never played a role in the loss or serious injury of her parents. Susan no longer had a reason to fear automobiles, yet she found herself unable to fully quell her long-held abhorrence. She waited until Jake settled into the driver's seat before saying the first inanity that came to her mind. "Nice car."

"It gets me where I want to go." Jake placed the folder and palm-pross into a pull-out shelf, then settled them in place. He looked at Susan. "Before you get the wrong idea, you should know I'm gay as a nightingale."

Once again, Jake managed to render Susan speechless. Though she had never really believed he found her skinny frame and plain features so exquisitely desirable he had to ask her out before even getting to know her, she still had not expected that kind of candor. Luckily, he did not seem to expect a response.

"I just needed to get you away from the recordings. Nothing said or done in a police station is private anymore." He pulled out of his parking spot smoothly and drove toward the street. "Now, where do you want to go? We should probably head for a restaurant, just in case."

"Anywhere's fine. Nothing expensive, please. We're obviously going Dutch."

"I'll pay." Jake responded defensively. "Romantic or not, I did ask you out."

"Wouldn't hear of it." Susan hoped she had the last word. She had not meant to offend him. "I know what policemen make."

"More than medical residents, I'd warrant." Jake inadvertently revealed he knew more about her than she had told the investigators. She had merely informed them she was a medical doctor. "But if you insist, I'm not going to fight with you. I was actually hoping for a home-cooked meal."

"Home-cooked?" Susan did not know what he meant. "Are you taking me to your place?"

"*Your* place. I was hoping you'd show me the bullet holes and allow me to make my own judgment."

"You mean, as opposed to the party line?" Susan could not resist. "Initially, I felt like the police came to help. Now I'm not so sure." She expected Jake to vigorously object, and appreciated it when he remained silently contemplative.

The detective clearly knew the way to Susan's apartment, so she did not bother giving him directions. "So," he said, "decapitation?"

Susan got the feeling he was testing her knowledge of the situation, seeing how much she knew so he could make up a story to explain it. "Prior to his arrival at the morgue, someone separated my father's head from his body. Please don't insult my intelligence by suggesting it just popped off during the course of a seizure."

Jake shook his head, keeping his attention on the road. Modern cars took nearly all of the guesswork out of driving, but competent drivers still remained alert and studied the conditions around them. "Certainly not. Removing a head from a body requires a large, sharp instrument and an enormous amount of brute force. Few things insult my willing suspension of disbelief more than some primitive warrior in a movie sending heads flying with nothing but a copper sword and a bodybuilder's forearms." He glanced at Susan, apparently concerned she might find his casual discussion of decapitation offensive.

Susan was quick to agree with him. "A galloping horse and a finely honed war axe might do the trick, but even that would more likely break the neck than sever it." She looked directly at Jake. "So, you're not suggesting my father tripped over the vacuum cleaner and cut off his own head with a wayward butter knife."

"Of course not."

"So?" Susan pressed.

Jake sighed. "You're absolutely certain he arrived at the morgue . . . um . . . headless."

"This is my father we're talking about. I'd hardly get that wrong. Would I?"

Jake cleared his throat. He licked his lips.

Susan folded her arms across her chest with a snort. "Do I seem like a hysteric to you? I know you want to give me some gibberish about mental states and loved ones and delusions. I'm a psychiatrist, Jake. Believe me, I've seen and heard it all. I *personally* went down to the morgue at Manhattan Hasbro, where they took him, not this phony forensics lab you claimed performed the autopsy. His head did not arrive with him. His body disappeared soon afterward, under mysterious circumstances. One thing I know for certain: It never went to the chief medical examiner's office. An autopsy was never done, and that report you have is fraudulent."

Jake's shoulders slumped. "Susan, if the body disappeared under mysterious circumstances, as you say, how do you know it never went to the chief medical examiner's office?"

Susan shook her head. She could not reveal the source of that information. "Let's just say I know it for a fact, and work from there."

Jake pulled into the familiar parking lot, and Susan's anxiety increased. She knew the area as well as her own name. She had always felt safe there, welcomed, enveloped by her father's loving presence. Now, it seemed sterile and empty, shadowing hidden and lethal dangers. "For someone who wants me to defy my superiors and come clean, you're sure not revealing much yourself."

Susan remained seated in the idling car. "So, you admit you know things about this case that you're hiding from me?"

Jake's brows inched upward. "Ah, a poker game. I assure you, I do know how to bluff. Wouldn't it be better if we both just laid our cards flat on the table, Susan?"

"I'd like that," Susan agreed. "You go first."

Susan did not expect him to comply, so it surprised her when he turned in his seat, propped his knees against the console, and turned her an expression raw with honesty. "Your father did not die of natural causes. Your turn."

Susan dismissed his forthrightness. "Tell me something I don't already know. Something I didn't tell you first."

Jake twisted his lips, as if eating something bitter. "Fine. The head was not on the scene when my colleagues found him." He looked at Susan intently, as if uncertain whether she might lie about already having the information.

Susan wanted to do that, to keep teasing facts from him under the guise of knowing it all, but she was too honest to pull off the scam. "All right, my turn. I know who took the body."

Jake leaned toward her eagerly. "Who?"

"When you tell me who has the head, I'll tell you who has the body."

Conflicting emotions crossed Jake's face and passed. He sighed again. "I understand you're a highly competent psychiatrist."

Susan guessed where this was leading. "Competent enough to know when someone's lying, no matter how well trained to bluff. And if you don't tell me the truth, we're finished."

Jake bobbed his head and tucked his legs more comfortably. She wondered how long he planned to keep her in the car. "Just so you know, I'm also trained to read faces, body language, and other nonverbal cues."

"I would be disappointed if you weren't." It surprised Susan to realize she liked the man and found herself wishing he had not referred to himself as "gay as a nightingale." "Are you really gay or did you just say that to put me off?"

Jake grinned. "You're the incomparable people reader. You tell me."

Susan considered what she knew about Detective Jake Carson thus far. He had a conspicuously macho job, which could represent overcompensation. He did display some stereotypically gay characteristics: painstaking attention to detail, especially in dress and appearance; good muscle tone; a lack of photos on his desk and walls, as if he preferred no one knew his personal business and he wanted to avoid teasing from coworkers. Many years had passed since anyone batted an eye at sexual preferences, but she could see where a gay policeman might feel inclined to keep his proclivities a secret. "It's a bit of a joke that manly men don't buy cars from Subaru's gemstone line, but you don't seem the type to fall prey to pigeonholes."

Jake chuckled. "Subaru calls it their 'hard rock' line, but I'm not sure that makes things any better. And yes, I'm really gay. Cops don't kid about stuff like that." His eyes narrowed. "Clever way to distract me, though. It's your turn to tell me something you've learned about this case. I don't suppose you know who killed your father."

"At least you're admitting he was killed." Susan thought back to the last revealed fact. "And you're the one being clever. It's actually *your* turn to tell *me* something."

Jake opened his door. "How about if I give you a professional assessment of the apartment? I haven't actually seen it yet. I'm relying on what you and the investigating officers have told me."

Jake got out and headed around the front of car, but Susan did not wait for him. She opened her own door and stepped out into the parking lot. "A deal," she said, "as long as I get a fair and honest investigation and not more twaddle."

Jake took Susan's arm, displaying the lost manners of distant predecessors. Susan suspected a greatly loved or overbearing mother had probably drummed them into his head. She rather enjoyed the attention, finding his proprieties flattering, even though he probably executed them more from rote than from any particular intention. Since Remington's death, no man had gone out of his way to perform those little niceties that most women publicly shunned but many secretly appreciated.

Seized with sudden insecurity and a jangling sense of alarm, Susan wondered if she could ever feel normal again after an event of this magnitude. She understood why so many families chose to leave their homes after a death, even one from a lingering disease, during which they had plenty of time to adjust to the inevitable. The building seemed unfriendly, almost hostile, a quiet testament to the abrupt and ugly change the world had taken in the last couple of days. She never remembered seeing such hollow looks in her neighbors' eyes, never recalled her footsteps echoing in the hallways, never realized how dim and poorly revealing the lights in the shared spaces must have always been.

Quite unconsciously, Susan found herself stepping over the place where Sammy Cottrell had taken her last gasping breaths. The body was gone, of course, along with a hunk of carpet that had soaked up the scarlet stain of her exsanguination. Susan did not bother to point it out to Jake, though the detective did kneel to examine the scene while she inserted her thumb to activate the door lock to the apartment she had shared with John Calvin. Man or robot, she still considered him her father.

The lock clicked, and Susan pushed open the door into the wreckage of what had once been their tidy little apartment. She had examined the scene twice before, and it should have looked hauntingly similar, but it did not. The destruction had clearly intensified, the couches and chairs wholly disassembled, their cushions reduced to strips of colored cloth. The enormous picture of Amanda that had filled most of one wall for as long as she could remember now lay shattered on the floor, hacked to bits by a questing knife.

Susan unleashed a shattered moan that brought Jake to her side. "What's wrong?"

Susan pointed. "My mother died when I was just three. That picture used to be of her. It was my father's prized possession."

Jake lowered his head respectfully. "I'm sorry."

"Earlier today, it was off the wall, clearly checked over, but mostly intact."

Jake crouched in front of the remains. "Wait . . . did you say earlier today?"

"I was here before I came to see you. Remember, I told you about finding the bullet holes." Susan's gaze went instinctively to the places she had seen them. Now the wall held myriad gouges, including one that caved in the area where she had noted several obvious bullet holes. "What the hell?" She looked back at the door, which Jake had carefully closed behind them. "I heard the lock click when I triggered it just now. I swear I didn't leave it open."

Jake did not contradict or suggest she might have made a mistake. "There're ways around a simple thumbprint lock. A professional would know them."

"A professional?" Susan looked around the room again. Someone had definitely entered in the hours between her last visit and this one. "You think a professional killed my father? A gangster?"

"No."

It was not the answer Susan expected. She whirled to face Jake Carson. "No? Didn't you just say . . ."

"I said a professional could get past a thumbprint lock. A professional definitely tossed this apartment."

"Tossed?"

"Searched." Jake walked around the room, studying the walls, the chaos that had once been its contents, the wreckage of furniture. "A professional went through here today, but I don't think the person or people who killed your father were professionals."

Susan tried to put together the pieces of Jake's revelation. "So, one murderer or group killed him. A different one rummaged through the apartment today?"

Jake turned to face Susan. "Your turn."

"My turn?" Susan started, then figured it out. "To tell you something. Okay. My father worked for U.S. Robots and Mechanical Men."

Jake rolled his eyes. "The deal was information that's not common knowledge. We've spoken to your father's coworkers; it's always part of an investigation."

Susan doubted anyone at USR had told him John Calvin's true nature. That was a secret they, and probably she, intended to take to the grave, if possible. "Fine. Did you know I spent time in the hospital last year—"

"Recovering from an explosion at the mall from a bomb ignited by a child. Of course we looked into your past. We also spoke with one Lawrence Robinson—"

"Robertson," Susan corrected.

Jake nodded once to indicate he accepted the correction as part of the narrative. "–who believes a group called the Society for Humanity was behind the bombings as well as the death of John Calvin, at least when it was still under investigation as a murder."

Susan turned him a withering look, then headed for the kitchen. Jake followed. "What?"

"You're still standing by the claim my father died of natural causes, some of which included gunshots, decapitation, and another murder." The table had been flipped, the legs disassembled, the appliances strewn around the room. Someone had moved the refrigerator, but it still ran. She opened it, relieved to find some intact food, though an erratic assortment. Her father had a knack for concocting delicious stews and casseroles from the most unlikely combinations.

Susan had always appreciated her father's culinary skills, until this moment. Now she looked at the strange array of fruits and vegetables, the strips of lean chicken, beef, and fish with a new eye. She had already realized John's robotic makeup accounted for his unwillingness to eat more than a bite or two in the presence of other people, including herself. Earlier she had blamed it on a neurosis caused by painful memories of family meals with Amanda. Later, he had claimed the accident caused him neurological damage, that foods lacked flavor or tasted strange and strong to him at inopportune times. He might vomit in a restaurant or at someone's dinner table or have to excuse himself suddenly, not only insulting the host, but also causing everyone present to lose their own appetites.

Now, Susan realized, he had limited capacity for digestion of any kind. She had always loved his cockamamie meals, and none of her friends had ever complained. She wondered if he used some sort of mathematical formulas to create the perfect balance of flavors, if he had a limited ability to taste, and if she had simply become accustomed to weird blends from early childhood so they seemed normal to her.

She wondered how Jake would react to her reproducing one of her father's recipes. Susan set to work on a salad incorporating nearly every intact food in the refrigerator.

Jake looked over her shoulder. His closeness sent a thrill through Susan, something she had not experienced since Remington's death. The irony of its source did not escape her. "What are you doing?"

"I believe you promised me dinner," Susan reminded. "So I'm making it."

"How is that *me* providing *you* dinner?"

Susan shrugged, turning. He was so close, she nearly spun into him. "Do you want to make it?"

Jake back-stepped. "I was about to say you wouldn't want to eat anything I prepared, but I've never seen anyone put plums in a dinner salad before. If it's just a matter of throwing everything in the fridge into a bowl, I can actually handle that."

Susan returned to her work, finding herself using John Calvin's words. "There's more to it than chucking together random foodstuffs. It's a matter of proportion and proper blending, enhancing rather than overwhelming. Taste it and see." *Over time, we discover ourselves turning into our parents, whether we want to or not. What does that mean for me?*

"All right." Jake righted a kitchen chair, tested it with a portion of his weight, then pushed it into a corner. "I think we're safer eating on the floor." He opened one of the cabinets to reveal shards of "unbreakable" crockery. "From the wooden serving bowl." He picked up a couple of forks from the floor and carried them to the sink to wash.

"So," Susan said, sucking a bit of fruit juice from her knuckle. "Last I remember, we were justifying a diagnosis of 'natural causes' from a bullet-riddled, headless corpse."

"Bullet-riddled is a bit of an exaggeration." Jake washed the forks under a steady stream of water, the dish-soap dispenser lying in pieces. "But I can hardly argue the point."

"We agree my father was murdered, then."

Jake shouted over the running water, then abruptly turned it off. He opened the cabinets under the sink, and water poured out onto the floor. "They took apart the pipes." His voice sounded almost awed. "Thorough."

Susan continued working. "Who did? The natural causes?"

"Checkmate," Jake said. "Just between you and me, clearly murder. The party line: natural causes."

Susan whirled to face Jake again. "Why?"

"Why what?"

"Why are they denying such an obvious killing? Why don't they want to investigate?" Susan knew her next words would upset him. "We're taught from infancy the police are our friends, we should go to them in our most vulnerable moments, trust them implicitly. How can I do that when my father's been murdered and they're lying to me, refusing to do anything to help?"

Jake sighed deeply. He did not, Susan noted, have an answer.

"Well?" she pressed.

Jake stopped examining the area under the sink. "Well, what?"

The question was so obvious, Susan saw no reason to repeat it. Nevertheless, it seemed quicker than a staring contest, so she did. "Why are the police lying to me?"

"I wouldn't call it lying, exactly." Jake examined the forks in his hand. "I just shared the information I was given: the autopsy report and the conclusions. I wasn't in on the actual investigation, until you brought me here."

"*You* brought *me* here," Susan reminded.

"Well, yes. Literally." Jake shook the forks to dislodge the water. No clean dishcloths remained. "But I wouldn't have come if you hadn't intrigued me."

"So I'm no longer the hysterical, delusional daughter?"

"You never were," Jake assured. "I've met plenty of those in my time. You don't fit the pattern." He looked around for a place to put the forks, then apparently decided no place could be considered clean, and held them. "Now let's end this silly game and give each other all the information we have so we can solve this mystery."

"Cards flat on the table?" Susan went back to making the salad.

"Cards flat on the table," Jake agreed.

"You first."

Jake laughed. "I should have known not to match wits with a highly educated woman."

Susan forced away a smile and focused more thoroughly on her salad. "Well, we can hardly go simultaneously."

"No, but . . ."

Susan waited for him to finish, but he did not. She chopped carrots noisily with a bent knife. When she completed the task and he still hadn't spoken, she turned to face him.

"I don't know how to phrase this, exactly. Believe it or not, I have a lot more at risk here than you do."

Susan tried not to take offense. "More than the life of your father?"

"No," Jake admitted, "but you don't have that, either. I mean, that ship has sailed, right? I could lose my job, my career, and I don't know how to do anything other than police work."

Susan stifled a laugh. After police work, anything else should seem easy. Safe. "You don't know how to do anything other than put your life on the line for strangers day after day, outwitting criminals?"

Jake shrugged. "It's not all that exciting, but yeah. And I'm not keen on joining the Marines."

Susan topped off the salad with a fruity vinaigrette of John's creation. "There. It's done." She tossed it with a flourish, sending bits of safflower seeds and endive springing from the bowl.

Jake glanced over her shoulder again. "It looks . . . interesting."

"To interesting!" Susan carried the bowl to the clearest space she could find, then sat cross-legged on the floor in front of it.

Jake handed Susan a fork, moved some debris, then sat directly across from her. He stabbed a bit of lettuce, peach, and grilled chicken in the same forkful and studied it dubiously. Finally, he put it in his mouth and chewed thoughtfully. His expression brightened. "This is good!"

"You sound surprised."

"I am, a bit," Jake admitted. "What an eclectic combination."

Susan liked the adjective he picked. "That's my father in a nutshell. Eclectic, at least when it came to food. Guess I inherited a bit of that." She liked her own choice of verb a lot less. She could not have received any genetic information from John Calvin, though Lawrence had assured her they shared enough to fool a paternity test.

Jake ate quickly enough, and in sufficient quantity, to convince Susan he meant the compliment. She enjoyed the salad, too; it reminded her of John Calvin and the simpler life they had lived before she started her residency. She suspected her return home after medical school had a lot to do with the SFH reexamining John Calvin and, eventually, coming to believe her biological father was still alive. And that had, ultimately, turned her blissful existence into an illusion, her childhood into a lie, the bond between herself and her father into a sham.

Susan rerouted that train of thought to wonder, *What power does the SFH have over the New York Police Department?* That did not bode well. When the antirobot organization had made its move last year, Lawrence and her father had begged her not to involve law enforcement until they determined the proper time for it. This time, Lawrence had clearly hoped they could work together, but cooperation now seemed unlikely. *Put the cards flat on the table.* Susan took a deep breath, wondering if she was about to make a huge mistake. "Jake, why is the police department protecting a violent antitechnology cult?"

Jake dropped his fork, then caught it in midair. The tines did not prove as agile, releasing their burden back into the bowl. "What? Why would you think that?"

Susan put aside her own fork. "All I know is my father was killed, and it happened the same day he received a threat from the terrorist group that planted bombs all over Manhattan. The police are turning a blind eye."

Jake adjusted the fork back into its proper position. "I'm here, aren't I? My eyes are wide open."

"Is your mind?"

"Like I just said, I'm here, aren't I?"

"Only after feeding me a false autopsy report and making me believe I could find my father's body at a specific funeral home."

Jake took a couple more forkfuls, chewed, and swallowed before speaking. "Now, just a minute." He waved the fork at Susan. "First, I only told you what was reported to me. I had the autopsy report and the name of the funeral home right in front of me. Second, didn't you say earlier that the body disappeared under mysterious circumstances?"

"That's right."

"And I sent you to a funeral home."

"Where they tried to convince me I had given them permission to cremate my father's body, something I would never do, given that I clearly wanted to examine it myself. I visited the morgue the day he was killed, remember?"

"So you say." Jake licked his lips. He spoke the words matter-of-factly and with proper consideration, not accusatorily.

"Why would I do that if I was going to allow them to destroy the body without allowing me a peek?" Susan shook her head. If Jake tried to answer, it would only annoy her. "That signature was a forgery, more likely an electronic stamp. It will probably perfectly match my patient-charting signature."

"So . . . this is all an elaborate conspiracy."

Susan shrugged. The conclusion was inescapable, at least to her mind.

Jake sighed heavily, then returned to eating. "I'd be lying if I said this was the best salad I'd ever tasted, but it comes very close. It's great."

"My dad's were better," Susan said by way of apology, even though the situation did not require one. "Are you denying there's a conspiracy? That the SFH has somehow managed to convince the police not to investigate?"

"I can tell you emphatically the SFH is not in cahoots with the police."

"How?"

"With my lips, Susan. How else could I tell you? You don't expect me to punch up a document certifying that the police and the SFH don't work together, do you?"

Susan doubted she would have believed it even if such a document existed. She would have given it no more credence then the false autopsy report or the fraudulent consent for cremation. Susan realized Jake had denied only one portion of her accusation. "So, the police are in cahoots with someone other than the SFH."

Jake pursed his lips. He clearly would have preferred not to answer, though he did. "Let's just say we have a hierarchy. We sometimes have to answer to authorities higher than ourselves."

They continued to eat in silence while Susan mulled that bit of information. It was Jake who finally broke the hush. "Are you suggesting the body was stolen in order to cremate it to prevent you from examining it?"

Susan did not like the direction of the questioning. She did not want to reveal Lawrence Robertson's role in the theft. "What better way to keep me from questioning the autopsy results? If I had had a chance to see the body, I would have known for certain the report was faked."

Jake found the flaw in Susan's argument. "Except you didn't see the body, and you're still convinced the report was faked."

"Yes," Susan pointed out. "But only because I did see the pathology log chronicling the missing head, and was present when the pathologist discovered the body was stolen, a fact that whoever tried to pull off this elaborate deception clearly didn't know."

"Hmmm," Jake said around a mouthful of food.

"Hmmm?"

"I'm trying to put this all together, but I think I'm missing some critical pieces of the puzzle." Jake looked pointedly at Susan.

Susan chewed and swallowed her own mouthful. "Apparently I am too."

They stared at one another. There was nothing more Susan felt she could tell him, should tell him. He seemed straightforward, and she had no proof he had deliberately lied to her; but he clearly had some information he did not intend to share. She had a sneaking suspicion he was playing her, teasing out the information she had managed to gather in order to find the most effective way to get her to drop her own investigation. She was not going to give him any more ammunition, and she doubted she could tweeze anything further from him, either.

Jake placed both forks into the empty bowl and placed it into the sink. "I'd do the dishes, but it would only cause a flood."

Susan glanced around the kitchen, despising the destruction, wanting everything back in its proper order. "Is the investigation finished?" She made a motion to indicate the apartment.

"You mean mine? Or the police in general?"

"Both. Either."

Jake nodded. "I've got the general idea. I think I can glean any additional information from the pictures of the scene when the police first got involved. Is there anything else you want to show me?"

Susan could not imagine anyone could get more than the impression of near-complete destruction. "I guess not. I can't think of any-thing."

"Fine." Jake headed for the door. "Thanks for a great and interesting meal. Where would you like me to drop you off?"

Susan made a broad gesture to indicate the room. "I think I'm just going to stay here and try to salvage as much of my dad's security deposit as I can."

The detective hesitated at the door. "Are you sure? I can take you anywhere. Don't worry about it being out of the way."

Susan did not want to admit she had not even considered the pos-sibility she might be inconveniencing him. "I'm fine. I'm going to have to deal with this sometime. I might was well pick up the pieces of my home while I'm picking up the pieces of my life. Put all the grieving together."

Jake removed his Vox from his wrist and proffered it to Susan. She did the same with her own. Each entered his or her number, then returned the proper Vox. As he put Susan's Vox back into her hand, he closed his fingers around hers. "Susan," he said so softly she had to strain to hear him, "I'm on your side; I need you to understand that. If anything happens, if you need anything, call me anytime."

Susan nodded, waiting until he released her hand to restore her Vox. "I'll be all right."

Jake clipped his own Vox back in place. "Be careful. And don't try to handle this alone."

"I have friends," Susan assured him. "And a boyfriend." She did not know why she felt the need to add the last part, perhaps more for her-self than for the self-proclaimed gay policeman.

"Yeah, all right." Jake did not question, though Susan projected the doubt she suspected she would feel in the same situation. If she had a boyfriend, why would she choose to stay in the ruins of her former apartment instead of accepting a ride to his place? In truth, Susan did not know why she preferred to sit amid her memories rather than return to Kendall's far more comfortable apartment. She could convince herself she wanted to mourn by herself for a time, and she needed to escape any mention of Winter Wine Dementia Facility until her outrage fully passed and she could laugh about Dr. Mitchell Reefes. But, the truth was, she could not fully grasp the reasons why she just wanted to spend some time alone.

Chapter 16

It surprised Susan even more when, after the detective left, she found herself missing him. She liked his easygoing manner, sensed competence beneath a quiet exterior, and had even enjoyed the banter, despite usually detesting verbal games. There was nothing sexual in their give-and-take; his initial pronouncement had put an end to that.

After she closed the door, Susan shuffled through the wreckage of the Calvin living room. Bits and pieces of her mother's familiar picture, the one possession John had treasured most and could never replace, lay scattered around the room. Uncertain where to start, she began piling strips of photograph, the twisted metal of the frame, the shattered pieces of the safety glass. She grabbed for a curled fragment sticking out from under a mound of broken wood, and it kept coming, bigger than she expected. In a moment, she held an entire photograph in her hand, and it was not a piece of her mother.

Susan turned it over, confronted by her own smiling self, sitting on the familiar concrete bench below their terrace beside a tall, handsome man with dark blond curls. *Remy.* Memories flooded down on her, not only of the man she considered her soul mate, but of the moment when her father had presented her with the picture and had placed it proudly on the wall beside the one of Amanda Calvin. *Not Calvin. Amanda Whatever-My-Last-Name-Used-to-Be. Amanda, my mother.*

A tear splashed onto the picture. Afraid to ruin it, Susan blotted the droplet away with the bottom edge of her shirt. Quickly but carefully, she rolled up the photo, tucking it into her back pocket. The empty feeling of loneliness became unbearable. She headed for the terrace, tore open the curtain, unlatched the door, and slid it open. She stepped out onto the concrete balcony in time to watch Jake striding across the parking lot toward his Subaru. It was not yet six o'clock, but the overcast and the coolness it brought made it seem later. Susan considered shouting and waving her arms, calling him on the Vox, doing anything to attract his attention and bring him back. As he reached his car, he turned to look at the building.

Susan raised a hand and waved.

Jake's head rose slowly, scanning up the balconies to stop on Susan's. It took him a moment to spot her, but he finally must have, because he returned her friendly greeting with one of his own.

Again Susan considered calling him, but decided against it. The apartment was going to feel uncomfortable for a long time, and she had no right to burden others with her pain. The detective had given her a couple of hours of his off time, more than she had a right to demand. For all she knew, he had an adoring husband and a host of kids missing him.

Susan started to turn to go back into her apartment. Rough hands closed around her arms, ripping them behind her. She felt her Vox stripped from her wrist as dark cloth was shoved over her head and another hand clamped tightly to her mouth.

It all occurred so quickly, Susan barely had time to acknowledge that something had happened before she found herself dragged back inside and heard the door slam shut, the shush of the pulled curtains. She found herself unable to scream, barely able to breathe. Her arms were pinned immobile, so she lashed out with her legs. Debris rolled under her step, stealing all balance, sending her reeling. She fell hard, shards of safety glass and hunks of damaged wood jabbing her in what felt like a thousand places. She was shoved against a wall, and a gruff voice filled her ear. "Be still if you want to live."

Susan froze, sprawled across the wreckage. Panic crushed down upon her. She could feel twine or rope tightening around her wrists, binding them behind her back.

"Sit," the voice continued. "Make yourself comfortable."

The incongruity of the statement penetrated Susan's consciousness like the peal of a code-blue alarm. With it came the slow, calm rationality that accompanied her worst moments in medicine. When a patient's life lay at stake, she always mustered the necessary clearheaded competence to do the right thing. She knew she needed to maintain that same professional demeanor to save herself now. Susan struggled to place her back against the wall, to blindly kick away the chips and splinters.

"Susan Calvin?" another disembodied male voice came from out of the darkness.

She could scarcely deny it. They had her Vox. Susan attempted to make a noise, anything to draw attention to the cloth over her head and the hand still firmly pressed to her mouth.

"Nod or shake your head," the first man demanded.

Susan forced out another noise, one intended to convey urgency. She did not want to suffocate.

Apparently, they understood. The voice in her ear returned, and something cold and hard pressed into her ribs. "Don't scream, don't do anything stupid, or you're dead."

Now Susan nodded.

The hand fell away from the cloth, no longer driving it into her nose and mouth. Then the cover disappeared from her face, leaving her blinking in the subdued and artificial light. A man crouched at her side, one hand behind her neck, the other clutching an oversized handgun, its barrel buried in her side. Another crouched in front of her, a holstered pistol just behind his right hip. Both were of moderate build, well muscled, sinewy, and dressed in black. Both had short, mouse-colored hair; dark, predatory eyes; and unremarkable features. Both were clean-shaven. They virtually defined "nondescript."

Susan had expected a couple of massive, hairy brutes with hawkish noses and weak chins. The clean set of them, the neatness of their appearances, the normality of their movements, unsettled her. They could easily murder her, leave, and blend into the Manhattan crowd without a hitch. Their descriptions were elusive, common, without defining features. Even staring straight at them, she was not certain she could pick them from a lineup. *Assuming I survive this.* It did not seem likely. They had allowed her to see them, which did not bode well for her future.

The nearest one spoke again. "If you cooperate, you live. If you do anything stupid, you die. Understand?"

Susan did not, but she nodded anyway. She had a feeling any other answer would be considered stupid. "Who are you? What do you want?"

"Quiet!" the other man said, softly but with emphasis. Susan flinched away from an anticipated slap that never came. "We do not answer your questions. You answer our questions." His voice had a hint of an accent, Southern American, Susan believed.

Susan's Vox buzzed, startling her. The man in front of her opened his hand and glanced at it. "Steven Kendall." He looked at Susan.

Obediently, Susan said nothing.

"Who is he?" the man asked impatiently.

Susan's mind raced. Could she trick them into answering a call? And, if she did, what would happen? She did not want to put Kendall at risk. Were they testing her? She did not have long to answer. To have a chance of surviving this, she had to play the panicked female willing to follow any command to save her life. "Work colleague."

"What's he calling for?"

Susan wanted to say, "How should I know? Ask him," but knew it would only antagonize. The truth seemed best. If she appeared to cooperate, she might be able to pull off something later. Jake's description stayed with her: *professionals.* "He's covering my patients, and he would have just gotten home. He probably wants to give me an update."

"Leave it," the other man said.

The buzzing stopped, and a tone sounded to indicate Kendall had left a message. The man played it back on conference mode.

Susan tried not to cringe, uncertain what he might say. Kendall's joking might get her into trouble if these men took it seriously.

Kendall's voice came through the speaker: "Calvin, where are you? Thought you'd be here. Call me."

Susan carefully let out a breath she had not realized she was holding. She needed to pay more attention to the cues she gave them. She had to become a blank slate, to reveal nothing except what she wanted them to believe. She needed to become SU-2. And she needed to think faster.

"What did he mean, he thought you'd be there?"

Paranoids with guns. Great. Susan did not want to reveal their relationship; it could put Kendall at unnecessary risk. "I'm on call tonight," she lied. "I told him I'd try to meet him at his place to get the rundown on the patients for tonight." She looked around the room. "There's not a whole lot to keep me here at my apartment."

"Does he know where you are?"

Susan tried to anticipate the reason for the question. Likely, he worried Kendall might come looking for her. She did not want them to feel they had to move her or hurry. Being home did not give her much of an advantage, especially when the destruction made it so alien to her, but at least one person knew her current whereabouts. On the move, she was virtually unfindable; it became too easy to slaughter her and dump her body in an alley. "That's what he asked me," she reminded. "If I don't show, he'll figure I went straight to the hospital. He's not going to come looking for me here, if that's what you're worried about."

The one in front of Susan made a thoughtful noise.

Susan looked from one man to the other, trying to memorize some detail that would allow her to identify them. She had to believe she would survive this encounter . . . somehow. Still, though the question seemed dangerous, she could not help asking, "Did you kill my father?"

"Quiet!" the man said again.

His companion spoke next. "You're a scientist, too, aren't you, Susan?"

"I'm a psychiatrist."

"But you've worked with robots."

Susan tried to guess what answer would keep her alive longest. These men could have killed her on the terrace, but they did not. That suggested she had something they wanted. As long as they believed she had this thing and she did not give it to them, she remained alive. If they discovered she did not have it, or she turned it over to them, she would die. No reassurances from them would convince her otherwise. "Yes," she admitted. "I have worked with robots."

The men looked at one another, and Susan wondered if she had just made a fatal mistake. Perhaps they merely wanted to know if she might continue her father's work, if they should murder her to keep her from doing so. If they believed she knew nothing about his projects, perhaps they might leave her alone. She added, "But I'm not a robot scientist. I'm a psychiatrist who worked on a robotics experiment." She hoped that left things open enough for them to draw their own conclusions, to keep them from shooting her.

For the moment, at least, it did. The man across from Susan still seemed focused on the Vox call. "You're expected at the hospital tonight."

She wasn't, but it was the story she had concocted earlier. An adage her father had often quoted came, unbidden, to her mind: *He that will lie must have a good remembrance, that he agree in all points with himself.* "Yes."

"And if you don't show up?"

Susan thought fast. She had originally lied to protect Kendall, but now she saw a way to use it to her advantage. "Hospitals don't run without residents on call. We're slave labor, and they hold our futures over our heads if we're late. If I don't show up, they'll certainly come looking for me."

The gun barrel dug deeper into Susan's ribs. "Beat it out of her, shoot her, and let's get out of here."

That galvanized Susan. "Wait! I've answered all your questions. Why do you think you need to beat something out of me? Just ask." Her arms throbbed, and she strained at the ropes without budging them.

The man in front of Susan rose, towering over her where she sat amid the wreckage of her home. "You know what we want to know."

"I don't," Susan insisted, honestly confused. "Just ask me."

"We need the formula that uncouples the positronic brain."

So Lawrence was right. Susan hesitated, seeking the best approach. She could create a fake code, but it would do her little good. True or false, they would no longer need her alive. *Why would the SFH want such a thing?* Susan imagined that by releasing the robots from the Three Laws, they could create the Frankenstein's monsters they had warned the world about. Perhaps they intended to demonstrate the danger of robotics by creating that very danger, hiding their hand in the events. It seemed a ridiculous thing to do, especially since it went against all their previous actions. They had, presumably, gunned down Amanda and Calvin to keep the information from ever becoming known or acted upon. Susan had assumed they killed John Calvin for the same reason, in the mistaken belief he had survived their earlier attempt to murder him. Clearly, they had not known he was a robot at the time of the murder. *Given their successes, why would the SFH change tactics so abruptly and completely?*

Susan knew she had limited time to think. She tried to gain more by stalling. "Uncoupling the positronic brain? What do you mean by 'uncoupling'?"

The man beside her made an impatient clicking noise with his tongue. The other watched her cautiously, obviously trying to read her. "We mean detaching the brain from the constraints placed upon it."

Susan blinked, trying to appear clueless. "You want to be able to detach the positronic brain from . . . its power source? From its . . . non-brain functions?" She shook her head, as if trying her best to understand. "You want it to be able to think without the constraints of a preprogrammed agenda?"

"She's stalling," the closer man said.

The other held up his hand, forestalling any action by his companion. "Maybe." He looked directly into Susan's eyes. "Susan, you are playing with us. You know about the Three Laws of Robotics, don't you?"

"I do," Susan admitted, then acted as if she had an epiphany. "You want to know . . . how to uncouple the Three Laws of Robotics from the positronic brain."

Both men nodded.

Susan deliberately gave them the USR party line, knowing they would not buy it. "Can't be done. If the Three Laws are deactivated, the positronic brain cannot function. For safety reasons, they're irrevocably intertwined."

"Unless you have the code. A code that only your parents knew." His eyes narrowed. "A code they gave you. Didn't they?"

Susan shut her mouth firmly.

The men looked at one another. One raised his brows. The other nodded again. They turned their attention back to Susan.

The genie was out of the bottle. Susan knew what she had to do, at least in a general sense. As long as they believed she had the information but refused to give it to them, she lived. The moment she gave them a response, whether true or false, they would likely kill her. "What possible use is that information to the SFH?"

The man in front of her gave her nothing, but the one beside her closed his eyes to slits. If she had to put a label on the expression, Susan would have described it as confusion.

"We're asking the questions," the one in front reminded her again, but he said it with less vehemence than previously.

Susan knew she now had some small measure of control in the situation, though she had to use it sparingly, carefully, cleverly. Physically, they still held all the power; they had her life wholly in their hands. Her own hands, at the moment, lay uselessly bound behind her. Mentally, however, she held the aces now. *I'm a psychiatrist, for Christ's sake. If I can't use that to my advantage, I don't deserve to live.* Susan pursed her lips with exaggerated tightness and looked through the man crouched in front of her.

"Talk!" he barked.

Susan continued to stare penetratingly.

The man dropped to his haunches. The one beside her sighed loudly. "Torture, extract, kill."

Susan did not move a muscle. She had nothing to lose.

The man in front held up a hand. He used a reasonable tone, shifting closer to his prisoner. "Susan, we are not bad guys. We're on the same side here. Honest."

Susan turned him a withering look. "You kidnapped me, then threatened to beat me, torture me, and kill me. You slaughtered my father. With friends like you, who needs enemies?"

"We had nothing to do with John Calvin's death." The man's features softened. "And you can stop playing with us. We know he wasn't your father."

For reasons she could not wholly explain, his choice of words upset her nearly as much as the gun barrel in her ribs. "Oh, John Calvin *was* my father." Truer words had never left anyone's mouth. In every sense of the word but one, the mechanical man who went by that name had been her only parent for most of her existence. He had raised her, loved her, made her the priority of his life.

Susan thought back to the Ansons, the parents of the antisocial little girl who had deliberately triggered the bomb that took Remington's life and, nearly, Susan's as well. The Ansons had adopted Sharicka with impeccable intentions and lavished her with the purest, rawest love in the universe, despite the inherited conduct disorder that made her a demon in child guise. They took understandable offense when people referred to the sperm and egg donors who created her as her "natural" or "real" parents. The Ansons were not babysitters, not "artificial," "unreal," or "fantasy" parents, and John Calvin was not just a chunk of metal programmed to act like a caretaker. He was Susan's father.

Susan bore Amanda and Calvin no ill will; they had clearly loved her. But John Calvin had dedicated every moment of his life to Susan; had given her a moral compass, nursed her through her illnesses, taught her all the important lessons in life; had weathered her adolescent storms, shared her successes and disappointments; had paid for her necessities and indulgences, her education; had done everything possible to mold her into the person she had become. Gears and wires, flesh and blood—what did it matter? John Calvin was her father, and she bore his last name proudly. "John Calvin," she repeated more forcefully, "was every bit my father."

"John Calvin was a robot," the man beside Susan pointed out.

There was only one way he could know that information. "You

murdered my father." Susan fairly spat the words. "You murdered my father!"

The man recoiled slightly, and the gun barrel receded from Susan's ribs.

The man in front of Susan spoke quietly; at least it sounded quiet in the wake of her shout. "The men who shot your father obviously didn't know what he was, even after they left the scene. Susan, by the time we got here, he was already . . . damaged beyond repair."

The man beside Susan cleared his throat. "There's no time for explanations."

Susan needed to hear more. She could not die without knowing the truth of what had happened in her father's last moments. "I have to hear this. I need to know. Give me this, and I'll tell you what you want." She added carefully, "I can buy us all the time we need."

"How?" the side man asked suspiciously.

"Let me call my . . . dispatcher," Susan said, creating a position to handle a nonexistent problem. "If I tell him I'm not coming in for call, they won't expect me."

The man in front narrowed his dark eyes, studying her. "Didn't you say residents were slave labor?"

"I just lost my father," Susan reminded them. "Even residents are allowed time to grieve, to get affairs in order. They offered me time off. I refused it. At the time, I didn't want it. I thought I could lose myself in my job, that if I worked myself to exhaustion, I'd never have to deal with what happened. I now realize how foolishly I acted. No one will be surprised if I change my mind."

The man in front of Susan gestured to his companion. The two moved away, talking among themselves.

Susan did not strain to hear. Instead, she busied herself trying to figure a way out of the situation. Eventually, they would realize she had nothing, no code, no idea of the information they wanted. If they allowed her this phone call, she had to find a way to use it to her advantage. She wrestled helplessly with the ropes binding her wrists. She could not break free, at least not quickly enough. The call was her only reasonable hope.

The men returned shortly. When they stood together, Susan could finally see slight differences between them. The one who had held the gun on her was several inches shorter and a bit heavier than his companion. He had a thicker face and larger hands, and he wore boots to the other man's shoes. He returned to her side, but kept his gun holstered.

The taller man placed Susan's Vox in front of her. "We're going to allow the call, but we're keeping it on conference. You're going to say only what needs saying. If you do anything to alert anyone, not only will you die, but we'll stay here and kill whoever comes to help you. Understand?"

Susan nodded. Her heart pounded. This was probably her only chance, and she had to play it perfectly. "Do I get my hands?"

"No. Just tell us who to call."

Susan fixed her gaze on the Vox, uncertain what to do. There was no such thing as a hospital dispatcher, and she had lied about being on call. She needed to call someone who could not only help her, but would also catch on quickly and play along. It could not be Lawrence Robertson or anyone from USR. The gunmen would know those names and that they were not medical dispatchers. "It's under . . . Jake."

"Jake who?"

"Just Jake." Susan did not know why the detective had not entered his full name on their Vox exchange. A strictly first-name entry seemed inappropriately intimate for a person she hardly knew, a status usually reserved for parents, siblings, or lovers. "We're only acquaintances. It's not like I call him to chat. I don't know his last name."

The man pressed the appropriate buttons, and Susan heard the buzz of Jake Carson's Vox. Her heart rate quickened so suddenly, pain shot through her shoulder. She had no idea how he might answer.

"Hey, Susan. What's up?" The familiar voice came crisply over the speaker.

"Hey, Jake," Susan said, trying to keep her tone level. "I'm not going to be able to make it in to work tonight. Can you find a replacement?" Susan's life hinged on his response. Terror swam down on her, but she kept her face a blank mask, forced herself to breathe evenly.

"Are you all right?" Jake said, with appropriate concern.

It was a hedged answer that revealed nothing. Susan could work with that. "Yeah, I'm just feeling down about my dad."

"Understandable. Do you need me to come by?"

The men shook their heads warningly. Focused on the Vox, Susan could see them only from the corner of her eye. The urge to shout, "No!" seized her, and she had to make herself pause before saying nonchalantly, "No, I've got a couple of friends keeping me company." She made sure not to look at the men as she spoke, trying not to clue them in to the hint she had just given Jake Carson. "Sable's free tonight. She should be able to fill in for me."

"Don't worry about it," Jake said. "I'll handle it. You just take care of yourself."

Susan appreciated that response. Either he got the message or, at least, was playing along. She dared not give him any more hints. "Thanks, Jake. I'll do that."

The man leaned forward and tapped off the connection.

Susan pursed her lips. "Now there's no time limit. No one will come looking for me tonight." She honed in on the man in front of her. "What happened to my father?" Her tone, forceful without a trace of fear, surprised her. She wanted the information too badly to allow anything to stand in the way.

If either of the two men suspected the Vox exchange was anything other than what she claimed, they did not show it. Perhaps her abrupt redirection of the conversation kept her from focusing on it, from revealing what she had done with nonverbal cues, sidelining their qualms.

"He was shot," the man beside her said gruffly.

The one who had spent most of his time crouched in front of Susan turned his companion a withering look. "Can you let me handle this?" He dropped back down in front of her.

"Fine," the other said with a grunt. "You're on your own. I have to take a leak." Without asking for permission or directions, he headed directly for the bathroom.

Susan trained her focus fanatically on the man in front of her. Though still bound and cornered, she felt a strange sense of relief, at least temporarily, at losing the one who had kept the barrel of a presumably loaded gun in her ribs, the one who had suggested torture and death. She wondered if they played a strange and cruel game of good assassin, bad assassin. "My father," she reminded.

"We planned to come and get the uncoupling information from him."

"At gunpoint," Susan spat out.

"If necessary." At least the man seemed willing to discuss the matter honestly. "But we hoped it wouldn't come to that. We thought if we explained we worked for the government, he might choose to cooperate."

Susan saw the flaw in that argument. "But you knew he was a robot."

"Not at the time." The man turned Susan a sincere look, as if it really mattered to him that she believed him. "We had no idea until after we searched the body."

"The body," Susan repeated. "So you killed him, then searched him."

"We didn't kill him," the man insisted, not for the first time. "He was dead when we arrived." He amended, "On the ground, with bullet holes in lethal places. Blood on the floor. No pulse. Eyes wide open. Nearly dysfunctional."

Susan pounced on the important word. "Nearly?"

"We searched him and the apartment, hoping to find the code."

Susan made a thoughtful noise, revealing nothing. She had to maintain the fiction that the code existed, that she had it.

"He opened his eyes, and I almost had a heart attack."

Susan sat up as much as she could with hands tied and back against the wall. "So he was still alive."

"Functional," the man corrected. "Barely. We were able to talk to him for only a few moments. He said you would have the code. And to tell you he always loved you with"–he considered a moment–"how did he put it?" His eyes rolled upward. "With a love as clear and pure . . ."

A movement in front of and to Susan's right caught her attention. She started to suck in a breath and caught herself as the door to the apartment edged slowly open.

Her reaction gave her away. The man in front of her whirled, rising, as Detective Jake Carson shoved the door open, gun in hand. "Police! Don't move."

The man went still, holding his hands partially outstretched, palms up, "Whoa, hold it. FBI. I'm on the job!"

Jake started to lower his pistol.

Susan struggled, trying to get to her feet. "No! He's lying! They're going to–"

The bathroom door slammed open, and shots rang out. Susan heard at least two, saw Jake stiffen. His free hand clutched at the left side of his chest as he stepped to the right and returned fire. The man collapsed into the bathroom doorway.

Susan saw the other thug grab for his gun. She flung herself toward him, managing only to slam into his leg as he moved. Apparently, that unbalanced him a bit, because his draw was sloppy, allowing Jake to get off two shots. Susan could hear the thud of their impact, saw him jerk. The rounds had hit their target, but they seemed to make less impression than her own feeble strike.

Jake lunged forward, firing into the man's face. Blood and tissue splattered Susan, and her captor stumbled backward, sprawling over her. She lay pinned beneath him, drenched with warm liquids and semisolids she did not want to identify. She had seen blood and injuries and death many times before, but never so suddenly, so horribly. She felt her guts churning and swallowed hard. She had never lost her lunch, even during the most invasive surgery, and did not intend to do so now.

Prone beneath the body, arms tethered behind her, Susan wriggled like a fish to get free.

"Any more?" Jake asked.

"That's all of them," Susan reassured him.

The gun still in his right hand, Jake clutched his left over his chest and slumped to the floor. Susan could see him visibly shaking as he thumbed his Vox, "Central, cop shot. Nine-four-five East Ninth and C. Apartment 10 Boy."

Susan could hear a distant voice over the speaker. "Signal 10-13, 945 East Ninth Street and Avenue C, apartment 10B." The voice grew louder, more direct. "Units responding. K."

More noise came over Jake's Vox, sounding like several voices carrying on a conversation in another room. Susan could not hear the exchange, but whatever they said relaxed Jake. He seemed to gain some control over his trembling and pulled his hand away from the wound, revealing less blood than Susan expected. She increased her struggles, freeing her torso and arms, still bound together, from beneath the corpse.

Jake kept his gun trained on the man lying near the bathroom as he spoke into the Vox again, "Manhattan South Homicide, urgent! I have two perps shot, civilian hurt, and a cop shot at this location. Get me three buses and a boss here forthwith."

Susan continued to work her legs from under the weight, deliberately avoiding considering the identity and content of the warm slush she kicked. For the first time ever, her medical training seemed like a curse.

A reply came over the Vox: "Units on the way, Homicide. Any perps outstanding? Where are you hit?"

"Both down, Central," Jake responded. "I'm hit in the left chest."

Susan finally managed to wriggle loose. She dropped down beside Jake. "Untie me."

Jake pulled a knife from a sheath attached to his belt with paracord, and slashed the ropes with a few deft strokes. The instant the ropes fell away, Susan grabbed Jake's hand and pulled it away from the wound. Blood flow, raw agony, rushed back into her fingers. Dizziness swam down on her. The only thing that kept her from collapsing was the realization he might think less of her, that she could not handle difficult situations. "Ow, ow, ow," she said as normal feeling gradually returned and the ache diminished. "Let me get some water."

Carefully clambering to her feet, so as not to risk fainting, Susan headed for the kitchen. Ignoring the water pouring out of the pipes below, she vigorously washed the dead man's blood from her hands, filled up a bowl with warm, soapy water, and grabbed a large shred of relatively clean dishrag.

Jake had his hand clamped to his chest again.

With a glare, Susan pulled it away once more to examine the wound. "Give me that knife."

Jake turned positively pale. "You're not planning to muck around in there, are you? Because 'bus' is slang for 'ambulance.'"

Susan remembered him asking for three buses. "Well, those two

don't need any buses. They can grab the express straight to the morgue."
She took the knife, which slid into her hand, leaving the sheath dangling from his belt by its cord. It had a four-inch-long tanto blade and the brand name, Strider, where the blade met the cord-wrapped hilt.

"Are you absolutely sure? Because our lives may depend on it."

Susan rolled her eyes. "I'm a doctor, but if you'd like a second opinion, you can check pulses yourself." Not that Susan had bothered to do so. A man who had just had his brains blown out the back of his head was clearly no danger. As for the other thug, if the shot through his upper chest had not killed him, the one through the neck certainly had. Susan could see damaged trachea and bone, and no air bubbles emerged from the blood. He was not breathing, and she had no intention of performing a tracheostomy or administering CPR.

Without waiting for a reply, Susan deftly sliced Jake's shirt in half. As the pieces fell away, he defensively covered his wound again. "Don't you think we should wait for the—"

"Paramedics?" Susan gave him a look as sharp as the blade. "So, let me get this straight. You want the trained medical doctor to watch you bleed to death waiting for the transport team?"

Jake did not move his fingers. "Didn't you say you were a psychiatrist?"

Susan resisted the urge to slap him. For all they knew, the bullet had passed clear through his heart, with only rushes of adrenaline keeping him conscious. He could die in front of her eyes. "Are you going to make me dig out my license? I apologize for not having it posted on the damned wall!" She made a gesture to indicate the shattered ruins of her home. "The State of New York granted me a license to practice medicine and surgery. I took all the same classes and rotations as Diego freaking Webster." She named a fictional surgeon on a popular primetime medical show. "Just because I prefer mucking around in people's brains doesn't mean I forgot everything I learned." She brandished his knife. "Now, if you don't move your damned hand, I'm going to cut it apart the same way I did your shirt."

Swiftly, Jake moved his hand.

"And you can put away the gun. Twenty thousand volts couldn't make either of them twitch a muscle." Her motion far gentler than her words, Susan pushed him down onto the floor and dumped the soapy water over the wound. She wiped away the drying blood with his ruined shirt to reveal a minimal amount of bleeding. Either the bullet had not penetrated any vital vessels and organs, or clots had formed quickly to prevent further bleeding. From the shape of the abrasion collar, she could easily tell the angle of entry was oblique. Carefully, she turned him over, examining his back and sides without finding anything abnormal. She checked his vital signs and several pulses. Finally, she superficially probed the wound with her fingers, careful not to sweep blindly.

The sound of distant sirens wafted to them through the terrace door.

Susan looked up, re-creating what she had witnessed in her mind's eye. With the additional information gleaned from her examination, she had no difficulty finding the bullet, which she triumphantly handed to Jake.

The sirens grew louder, closer.

Jake watched everything Susan did in silence. "You do know you're tampering with evidence."

Susan snorted. "I'm not terribly impressed with your precinct's evidentiary sleuthing. We both could have been gunned down, disemboweled with rusty scimitars, and hanged from the rafters, our skulls bludgeoned, and your great detectives would label it natural causes."

Jake drew breath. He probably wanted to argue, but he winced in pain instead. "So, Doc, what's your brilliant diagnosis? Am I going to live?"

Susan had something to prove. "He shot you twice. The first came in here"—she demonstrated on herself—"low and to the left. Went through your shirt; you can see some residue here." She indicated some darkening on his skin. "The second bullet came in this way"—she indicated the angle it penetrated—"struck the point of your tenth rib, and bounced off. You're now holding it in your hand. The X-ray will show the rib is cracked but no other damage. I'm sure it hurts like hell, but you are going to live." She could not help adding, "And the next time I tell you I have a couple of friends keeping me company, take my word for it. You didn't see that guy coming at all. Did you?"

"I didn't expect him from the bathroom," Jake admitted, allowing Susan to wrap a makeshift bandage made from his shirt around his chest. He examined the bullet. "Nine millimeter."

"Is that significant?"

"Well, it is what the FBI uses now, but it's what we use, too. Lighter, faster, cheaper. Short of the military, it's hard to find a government agency that uses anything else anymore." Jake turned pale. "You don't suppose they really were—"

"No," Susan said, more to reassure him than out of any real certainty. "I certainly hope the FBI doesn't kidnap and threaten to kill U.S. citizens."

The sirens grew louder.

Jake grabbed Susan's arm and hauled her toward the door.

After the manhandling she had just escaped, Susan found the touch, though firm and painless, strangely unpleasant. "Where are we going?"

"To the hallway." Jake shoved open the door. "By the way, you need to get yourself a new lock. They've got this one rigged to open for any thumb, including mine."

Susan could not help pondering the simple genius of that strategy. As long as the lock worked properly for him, an owner would likely never consider the possibility. Who tested locks by having friends or strangers try them? She allowed herself to be led into the hall. "Why not wait inside?"

"In these situations, ambiguity is the norm. I'm off duty, dressed in street clothes. Who's the cop? Who's the perp?" He sat on the floor, gun holstered, and gestured for Susan to come down beside him. "When the elevator and stairwell doors open, I plan to have my shield in hand and to say the magic words to keep us from becoming targets."

Susan settled down beside him. She wanted to be as close as possible to the guy with the badge and the magic words.

Chapter 17

Susan visited Jake Carson's room at Manhattan Hasbro Hospital as soon as his well-wishers from the police force had dispersed. She found the detective sitting up in bed, blankets covering his hospital robe and gown. His heart monitor blipped a steady rhythm at a fit sixty-two beats per minute. His breathing was a bit erratic, consistent with the moderate pain the chest-wall motion probably caused him, but his oxygen saturation was 100 percent.

Clearly surprised to see Susan, Jake waved her to the bedside. "What are you doing here? Shouldn't you be all monitored up for observation, too?"

Susan came to his side. She had refused admission, a luxury she had not allowed him. "After a shower, they couldn't find any reason to keep me. None of the blood was mine. A couple quick jabs to protect me from blood-borne pathogens, and I was good to go."

Jake smiled dully. "I got those, too. Along with six X-rays and three consults, the end result being the exact same conclusions you made in forty seconds, under duress."

Susan shrugged. "I had the advantage of being an eyewitness. They had to put the pieces together based on your memory and the results of their exam and studies."

Jake chuckled. "Most people would consider being trussed up at a shootout a *dis*advantage."

"Yeah, well. Panic can make some people a bit distracted." It was the sort of reply Kendall Stevens would have given. Susan wondered if her fellow resident's sense of humor was rubbing off on her, and that made her think of him. She realized she missed him. He was surely worried about her, and she needed to explain her disappearance.

Jake glanced around, then leaned toward Susan, as if he worried someone might overhear. "Susan, who were those men? What did they want from you?"

Susan gave him a wide-eyed look, wondering if the wound had addled him. "How should I know? They obviously weren't friends of mine. Isn't it your job to figure that out and tell me?"

Jake's nostrils flared. The hostility of her response clearly surprised him. "When's the last time you psychoanalyzed someone without any input from the patient? Come on, Susan. I can't question those men now, can I? How am I supposed to figure anything out without knowing what happened?"

Jake had an irrefutable point, but Susan was not yet sure who to trust. The police, specifically Jake Carson, had lied to her about her father's death and the disposition of his body. Clearly, they had an agenda besides ferreting out the truth. "Two men, strangers, grabbed me, tied me up, and threatened me. What more do you need to know?"

Jake lay back with a sigh. "I'm assuming my colleagues have already questioned you."

"Nope."

Jake rolled his eyes to Susan again. "No? They didn't have a single question for you?"

Susan remembered the whirlwind of activity when the police had arrived at the building. They had focused on Jake, barraging him with questions, packing everyone off into ambulances, and rushing them to Manhattan Hasbro. Susan guessed the police had intended to descend upon her hospital room, if she had taken one. She imagined they had a million questions, most of which she could easily anticipate and none of which she wished to answer until she understood the motivations of the people sworn to serve and protect.

Susan had turned off her Vox. It would not make a sound, would not alert her in any fashion, but it still informed her she had twenty-seven messages waiting in her queue. Three or four of those, she guessed, came from Kendall. Another one or two might be Lawrence Robertson. The rest, she felt certain, were attempts by colleagues of Jake to piece together what had happened during the time between his leaving her apartment and returning to kill two gun-toting strangers who, at least at one point, claimed to be agents of the United States government.

Were they? Susan could scarcely believe she was considering the possibility. When she ran back through her memories of the encounter, she could not help finding the moments when they claimed as much. Snippets came to her mind in the voice of the man who had crouched in front of her: *"We are not the bad guys. We're on the same side here. Honest." "We thought if we explained we worked for the government, he might choose to cooperate." "FBI. I'm on the job!"*

Were they government agents? Susan asked herself again. *Is it just possible?* She could not wholly deny the possibility. The man had denied killing John Calvin, a claim she had not believed at the time. Even if he had spoken the truth, he clearly had a hand in trashing their apartment, and had obviously sawed off and retained the head, stealing the positronic brain and making it virtually impossible to revive her father.

When Susan did not speak for several moments, Jake intervened again. "Listen, Susan. I'm sure they're looking for you. It's imperative you go to the station and talk to them."

Though she had no intention of doing so, Susan simply said, "Okay."

The response clearly did not convince Jake Carson. "Susan, it may not seem like it, but we are trying to help you, to do what's best for the investigation."

"I said okay," Susan repeated with a hint of vehemence. Jake's words sounded too close to the ones her captor had uttered. Now that the excitement had died down and pure adrenaline no longer coursed through her veins, she felt exhausted, spent. The last thing she wanted to do was waste hours answering the endless questions of second- or third-shift police officers just waiting for her to slip up and say something foolish. "Get some sleep. I'll come back to visit you in the morning."

"You'd better." Jake looked tired, too. "You're the best doctor on my case."

Susan turned with a parting wave, not bothering to correct his misconception. She had nothing to do with his medical care any longer. Even in the highly unlikely case his attending physicians wanted a psychiatry consult, she was not on the right rotation to accept it. She left the room, with no clear idea where to go next. She finally decided on the first-floor charting room, even though she knew she would no longer find Nate there. She did not have the courage to return home or the energy to explain all of the night's events to Kendall.

S usan awoke disoriented, her mouth gluey and her back stiff from lying on a couch never designed for overnights. A general-surgery resident sat in a chair on the opposite side of the room, a palm-pross balanced on his knees. Susan glanced at her Vox. It read 12:46 p.m. and blinked to alert her to forty-six messages waiting in the queue.

Susan sat up, yawned silently, and stretched her limbs. She could not recall the last time she had slept so late, probably during medical school after a late-night study session. A cursory glance through the numbers revealed an even dozen calls from Kendall Stevens, three from

Lawrence Robertson, seven from the hospital, and most of the rest from various numbers that probably represented the police. Likely, the hospital had attempted to reach her at the request of the authorities.

Feeling filthy, Susan showered in the on-call bathroom and donned the pink scrubs that labeled her off duty as well as nonsterile. She had no clothing other than what she had been wearing, she realized, and no desire to shop for more. Her wrists still throbbed, abraded by the ropes, her head buzzed as if with fatigue despite, or perhaps because of, fourteen hours of sleep. She brushed her teeth with borrowed toothpaste and one of the individually wrapped, disposable toothbrushes designed for patient use.

Jake had probably been discharged in the morning, so there seemed no point in looking in on him again. Besides, Susan worried she would find police waiting for her there, and she still had no desire to speak with them. Returning home seemed dangerous as well as futile. Her best option appeared to be Kendall's apartment. He would have left for work, but he had given her a key. At the time, she had rolled her eyes at his antiquated locking system. Now, with the issues of her thumbprint protections exposed, she appreciated the old technology in a way she never previously had. She needed some time to think, to consider her next step, to contemplate her life in light of new information and make appropriate decisions about the future. No one other than Kendall would expect to find her there.

Apparently, even he wasn't expecting her. At approximately 6:20 p.m., the front door swung open. Susan peered out from the kitchen, clutching the casserole she had just taken out of the oven. Spotting her, Kendall wrestled the key from its lock and barely managed to keep his balanced palm-pross from hitting the floor. "Susan!" He tossed his gear onto the couch, shutting the door with his foot.

Susan put the casserole dish on the table, anticipating a hug.

Kendall's welcoming expression turned uncertain, then suspicious.

He approached her, but the exuberant hug she expected seemed limp and weak. "Where the hell have you been?" He stepped back, clutching only her shoulders. "You don't look so good. Why didn't you answer my calls?"

"It's a very long story." Susan rescued Kendall's things from the couch, placing them neatly on the coffee table. "I'll tell you over dinner. First things first. How are you? What's going on at Winter Wine, and how are the patients doing?"

"How am I?" Kendall shook his head. "I'm worried sick about you. How the hell do you think I am? Tell me where you've been."

"Over dinner." Susan hoped her tone made it clear this was the last word. "We both need to be sitting, and I want to look you in the eye. Give me the rundown on Winter Wine while I'm working. Okay?"

"Fine." Kendall flopped into a kitchen chair, looking as exhausted as Susan had felt hours earlier. "Mitchell Reefes is still lazy as a sloth and mean as a snake."

Susan headed for the cupboards to set the table. "No surprises there."

"He's ranting about you having made a commitment, how you should be there to fulfill it. In his day, they didn't mollycoddle residents, blah, blah, blah . . ."

Susan chuckled. The problems of her obnoxious attending seemed unimportant and distant after the previous day's adventures. "He actually used the term 'mollycoddle'?"

"Yup." Kendall also laughed. "He seems to have completely forgotten he was the one who told you to leave."

"The same way he forgot who ordered the MRI on Chuck Tripler and who discharged Jessica Aberdeen."

Kendall tipped his chair slightly backward, balancing it on two legs. "It's a memory of convenience, although it could come back to haunt you, depending on what he writes in your recommendation."

"I'm not concerned." Susan placed two plates on the table, surprised to find she spoke the truth. She knew better than to gamble her entire future on the events of a single day, even one as eventful as hers had been. But the ravings of one entirely self-motivated doctor no longer seemed to matter. "Tell me about the patients."

Kendall brightened a bit. "Chuck Tripler's conscious. He's never going to become a rocket scientist, but they're planning to discharge him home, with rehabilitation."

"That's the best news I've heard in a long time." Susan pulled open Kendall's silverware drawer.

"Then you're going to love this. Remember Thomas Heaton?"

Susan gave Kendall a sideways glance over her shoulder. "Of course I remember Thomas Heaton. The former conductor with the middle cerebral artery stroke that rendered him unable to read."

"He read me three signs today, as a well as the first page of a pamphlet."

"What kind of a pamphlet?" Susan pulled out two forks and headed for the table.

"A pamphlet on sexually transmitted diseases."

That stopped Susan cold. "What?"

"Kidding. The boring one about nursing home procedures. Does it really matter? He was reading."

Susan placed the forks beside the plates, then grabbed the casserole dish. "How?"

"Just like we suggested. Rehab's been working with him on equating musical notes with letters and translating simple melody bars into common phrases." Kendall's gaze followed Susan to the oven. "He's already a lot happier. His family was with him, and he was asking about you. Probably wanted to bandy a few more crappy conductor jokes."

Susan smiled. "I'm sure you obliged him."

"Who me? Miss a chance to get a laugh? Never." Kendall had

regained his jovial manner, but Susan could still sense unspoken discomfort. He was reserving judgment until he heard Susan's story, but he did not intend to wait forever.

"How about Jessica Aberdeen?" Susan looked for more things to do. She wanted to keep Kendall talking about medical work as long as possible. For a while, at least, she could pretend the events of the previous day had not occurred.

Kendall blew out a noisy breath. "I was trying to avoid that."

"Well?" Finding nothing, Susan fiddled with a holder in the shape of a circus dog, though it contained plenty of napkins. "What did her father do this time?"

"Nothing, really. She backslid a bit, and he's making essentially idle threats so far. A bit of dirty lawyer talk; nothing he can win." Kendall brightened suddenly. "But you were right about Kado Matsuo. I did the test, and when it confirmed your diagnosis, I acted as if Reefes had personally ordered it. That got Kado right onto the liver-transplant list. I spent most of the afternoon modifying his diet and arranging ammonia detoxification. Reefes is strutting around like some kind of demented peacock genius."

Susan smiled. It did not matter who got the credit as long as the patient received the necessary treatment.

"It's more of the same for all the other patients. Unlike you, I can't pull some brilliant diagnosis out of my butt every single day."

Susan rolled her eyes amid a sudden wave of irritation. "There's nothing magical about unearthing a few treatable medical problems on a chronic psychiatry unit headed by an indolent moron. All it takes is observation—"

Kendall ticked off one index finger with the other as if making a list. "*Sherlockian* scrutiny."

"—a modicum of intelligence—"

Kendall tapped the middle finger. "Sheer brilliance."

"—curiosity—"

Kendall moved on to the ring finger. "Catlike focus."

"—and the willingness to persistently surf for answers."

Kendall added his pinky to the others. "And an anal-retentive focus."

Susan continued to glare. "So, basically, you've just called me a smart but catty ancient detective who spends hours staring at my own rear end. No wonder you claim I pull these diagnoses out of my *butt*." Sick to death of people demeaning her one talent, she went on the attack. "Look, Kendall. Of all people, I expect better from you. I'm smart, yeah, and I'm a decent diagnostician. So sue me. Just because most people are too stupid and sluggish to bother distinguishing themselves doesn't make me a caricature. When did study and hard work become crimes, and mediocrity the highest ideal a female is allowed to strive for? If intelligent, capable women scare you, you're in the wrong business."

"Whoa!" Kendall raised his arms in mock surrender. "I'm not belittling your diagnostic acumen; I'm praising it. Forgive me for mentioning the feature of my girlfriend that impresses me the most."

"Sorry," Susan grumbled. "I had a rough day."

"I love you, Susan, but you're hardly flawless. I got more than a couple earfuls of your many and varied faults from our esteemed attending. That is, when I wasn't rushing around trying to do the work of three and cursing you under my breath myself."

Susan took offense. "Cursing me? What the hell did I do?"

"What did you do?" Kendall stared, clearly incredulous. "What did *you* do? Well, let's start with pissing off the man currently in charge of my future. Why can't you ever just swallow your pride, nod your head, and pretend to have a modicum of respect for your superiors, even if they are indolent morons? It's Sunday. Remember? I was supposed to work a half day and go the hell home. Instead, not only do I get all of *our* work piled on *my* shoulders, but I'm stuck in the position of having to either agree that you're the most irritating, obnoxious, stupidest puke who ever lived or risk my medical license, too."

Irritation blossomed to an anger that took precedence over any attempt to moderate her speech. "So, what am I supposed to do? Forget my father was murdered *three days ago* so you don't have the burden of tending a garden of gorked-out patients solo?"

"Of course not!" Kendall was shouting now. "But you can at least not bite my head off when I'm telling you about my day after you *asked me to*! And where the hell were you last night, anyway?"

Susan had intended to tell him the entire story from beginning to end, to share the craziness and find solace in his inevitable jokes. Now she only wanted to incite him. "If you have to know, I spent the evening with a gorgeous hunk of policeman!"

Kendall's face turned a vivid shade of scarlet. She had never seen him so angry. "What?! I'm doing all your work, worried about your mental state, and you're out sleeping with another man?"

Even through the fog of rage, Susan knew she could not leave Kendall with that impression. "I didn't sleep with him, you dimwit! He saved my life."

"So you slept with him in gratitude?"

Susan made a wordless noise of frustration and fury. "I just told you I didn't sleep with him. And, anyway, he's 'gay as a nightingale.'"

"Gay as a . . ." Kendall's eyes narrowed. Veins stood out on his face, and an artery throbbed rhythmically in his neck. "How the hell do you know that?"

Susan huffed out a strident breath. "The same way I know all homosexuals when I see them. It's written on his forehead."

"What?"

Susan managed to resist the urge to claim she pulled the brilliant diagnosis from her butt. "Duh. He told me."

"So, what does this gorgeous, allegedly gay hero look like?"

Susan could scarcely believe that was the question Kendall chose to ask first. *Did you miss the part where I mentioned my life was in danger?* "Why? *You* want to sleep with him?"

Kendall shoved his chair violently aside. "Are you implying I'm gay, too?"

All composure lost, Susan also stood, turning away. "Maybe."

"Maybe? Maybe! What the hell–!" For an instant, Kendall looked as if he might actually strike her; then he also turned away.

"You have to admit, our . . . night together . . . wasn't exactly . . ." Susan trailed off. She had not intended to talk about her disappointment. Ever.

"It was the first time for you, and I'd only tried it once before. What did you expect? Fireworks?"

The irony struck Susan. It had happened Independence Day night. There had been real fireworks in the background, ones she had scarcely noticed since she had experienced no metaphysical ones. She finally managed to keep her mouth sealed tightly shut.

"Fine." Kendall lunged forward and caught Susan's arm. "You want fireworks? I'll give you fireworks." He started toward the bedroom.

Susan was not in the mood. "Now? Are you crazy?"

Kendall's deep brown eyes bored into her own. "So you're not even going to give me a chance?"

"It's not that. It's just . . . we're in the middle of a fight," she reminded him, anger already diminishing.

"I've heard makeup sex is the best kind." Kendall tugged on Susan's arm.

Susan was not in the mood for anything, but she was already starting to regret much of what she had said. Her inconsiderate comments had brought them to this point in the first place. "Fine. Let's make some fireworks." She followed him into the bedroom. It occurred to her she had never heard Kendall talk about a previous relationship, specific desire, or crush on a male or a female. His jokes contained a lot of innuendo but never quite crossed the line. She had never known another twenty-seven-year-old male with so little romantic experience. *Is it possible he really is gay?* Susan all but dismissed the possibility. *If so, he's deep in denial.*

As they took a seat on the side of Kendall's neatly made bed, he took her hands in his and gazed into her eyes. "Susan, I'm sorry about the fight. We're both under a lot of pressure, and it's understandable we lash out at the person to whom we're closest in the world."

Susan suddenly realized that in the thick of things, Kendall had claimed to love her and she had not acknowledged, let alone returned, the sentiment. "I'm sorry, too, Kendall. And I do love you."

"I know." Kendall clasped her hands between his own. "Susan, I don't want to lose our friendship. I've never had a serious relationship with a woman, and I didn't realize I could feel such jealousy. I apologize for assuming you slept with this cop. And I want you to know that if I can't satisfy you, we'll always remain friends."

"Deal," Susan said, "and it works both ways."

They fell into bed together.

Chapter 18

Kendall was still apologizing when he left for Winter Wine Dementia Facility the following morning, and Susan was still mouthing placating reassurances. That it happened to most men was a medical fact, but of little consolation. They both knew frustrated men in their twenties rarely suffered such problems, even under the pressure of a recent argument and too much work.

Alone again, Susan realized she had never described her day to Kendall, that he was still ignorant of why she had disappeared and the reason she had needed rescuing. But the remembrance was all too clear to Susan, who doubted the two men who had threatened her worked alone. Whether the SFH or something else, they had an organization backing them, one Susan did not wish to encounter again. She was not the only one who had an interest in bringing them down, and she certainly did not have the strategic or physical ability to do so without a lot of assistance.

Susan picked her Vox off the night table and turned it on, preparing to call Lawrence Robertson, when a call buzzed into her hand. It was Jake Carson. This time, she answered it. "Hello?"

"Susan." The detective sounded relieved to hear her voice. "Do you have . . . company?"

Susan smiled wanly, not liking her odds if a policeman was worrying she might have gotten kidnapped twice in less than three days. "I'm alone and safe." *For the moment, at least.*

"Good." He seemed to mean it. "Can we meet up somewhere? We need to talk." He stressed the word "need," and Susan believed it.

Remembering how much more information she had gotten from Lawrence in person than over the phone, she made an abrupt decision. "Meet me in front of U.S. Robots in twenty minutes."

"I'll be there," Jake promised.

They gathered in Lawrence Robertson's office: Susan, Lawrence, Jake, and Alfred Lanning, the director of research and development at U.S. Robots, who had been a part of the organization nearly as long as Lawrence and Calvin. Longer, Susan realized, since her flesh-and-blood father had survived only a few years after its inception.

The last half hour had mostly consisted of awkward silences broken only by halfhearted verbal thrusts clearly intended to establish the appropriate level of trust. Susan did not want to press them, but it soon became clear they had reached a stalemate that might go on for days if she did not intervene. "Look, we can sit here all day, staring at one another, or we can pool our information and accomplish something worthwhile."

The three men nodded, but no one made the first move.

Finding the ball back in her court, Susan addressed Jake. "What have you found out about the two men who attacked me?"

Lawrence straightened in his chair, having not yet heard the story. Alfred Lanning, however, remained slumped. He always appeared rumpled to Susan, but she understood his plain appearance and social ineptness disguised a gifted mind.

"You were attacked?" Lawrence said with fatherly concern. "By the SFH?"

"I'm not sure," Susan said, her attention still trained on Jake. "They claimed to be FBI and demanded a code that's supposed to unleash the positronic brain from the Three Laws of Robotics."

That started things moving. Alfred mumbled, "That sounds like the SFH."

"Not really," Lawrence inserted. "The SFH seems more hell-bent on seeing that particular information"—he added, apparently for Jake's benefit—"assuming it even exists, permanently destroyed. Along with anyone who knows it."

Finally, Jake spoke. "They weren't from the SFH. Or the FBI, for that matter."

All eyes went to the detective.

Jake appeared to wither under their scrutiny. "I'm afraid that's all I can say."

Susan exaggerated a deep and loud sigh. "Why?" she demanded.

Jake seemed to fold in on himself. The silence intensified, painful for its absoluteness.

Lawrence gave Susan a look that said something similar to Alfred's words: "This is a waste of time and energy. What'd you bring him here for, anyway?"

Jake rubbed his eyes with his fingertips. "Susan, you've known these men a long time?"

"My entire life," Susan said, which was essentially true. She had met them in person only the previous year, but she had heard about them, their genius, their morality, their judiciousness, for as long as she could remember. Her father had held them in the highest esteem, and they had done nothing to tarnish that praise. "I'd put my life in their hands." Only after she spoke did it occur to Susan they had also programmed the mechanical man who sang their praises.

Jake looked the scientists over again. "Well, right now, it's *my* life you're putting in their hands. I've known you all of two, three days, and them not at all. Can you understand my reluctance?"

Susan gave the detective's words due consideration. "I can. But if you don't explain how you're endangering your life, it's difficult to help you."

Jake continued to study the others, as if to read every inch of them, inside and out. "I'll tell you this much: Those men were not FBI, but they were federal agents. Needless to say, I'm not in good standing with some dangerous people right now, ones who would have no qualms about whacking me if I don't play ball by their rules." He sat up and looked at Lawrence. "Your turn."

Lawrence flicked his gaze to Susan, who nodded encouragingly. "If federal agents are seeking . . . what Susan mentioned, there's only one logical explanation."

Alfred butted in, "Our own government is looking for a way to weaponize positronic robots?"

Lawrence cringed. Clearly, he did not intend to release so much information so quickly.

Jake reentered the conversation. "So, the positronic brain is a robotic energy source?"

"No." Lawrence explained, "Think of the positronic brain as a central computer for a USR robot, which provides it with a humanoid consciousness. It requires an energy source to maintain function, but it is not itself a direct source of energy. Unless, of course, you consider learning and original thought a form of energy."

"And the Three Laws?"

Though she knew them by rote, Susan let Lawrence unveil them. "Law Number One: A robot may not injure a human being or, through inaction, allow a human being to come to harm. Law Number Two: A robot must obey orders given it by human beings, except where such orders would conflict with the First Law. And Law Number Three: A robot must protect its own existence as long as such protection does not conflict with the First or Second Law."

Alfred bobbed his head. He could also recite every syllable of them in his sleep.

Jake nodded in rhythm with Alfred Lanning. "So, the First Law, by definition, excludes the possibility of using them as weapons."

"Right." Lawrence said nothing more, allowing Jake to draw the obvious conclusion.

"So uncoupling the brain and the Laws . . ." Jake trailed off, but no one bothered to finish the sentence for him. "Is it really all that difficult a thing?"

Lawrence leaned toward Jake. If not for his benign expression, the gesture might have seemed threatening. "Young man, I created and refined the positronic brain, and I assure you it's impossible. The construction is such that without the Three Laws in place at its core, the positronic brain cannot work in any capacity. Susan's parents fashioned the wording, while Alfred, Calvin, and I assembled all the higher operations, all the neural simulations, all the artificial sentience immutably around those Laws. To construct a positronic brain without the Three Laws in place would break all mathematical and physical laws. Any attempt to induce dormancy or separate them would negate the brain's ability to function."

Another silence ensued before Jake finally said, "If no way to uncouple them exists, why is a DoD Intelligence Exploitation Agency so keen to shake Susan down for the code?"

"DoD?" Alfred repeated, then his brows shot up. "Department of Defense, right?" He did not wait for an answer, slamming a fist into his palm. "I knew it."

Jake's words did confirm Alfred's weaponization speculation.

Susan knew Jake would need an answer to his question in order to continue cooperating. He had already probably said too much. "The SFH has always believed my parents had access to a formula known only to them, one the SFH did not want anyone else to have. So about twenty-three years ago, they murdered my parents, gunned them down in cold blood."

Jake's eyes widened. "Wait a moment. A husband-and-wife team of robot scientists shot to death two decades ago. Susan, you're Calvin and Amanda Campbell's daughter?"

Lawrence made a pained sound. "I thought it would be safer if Susan never knew her original last name."

Jake continued as if Lawrence had not spoken. "I was eleven when it happened, and I followed the developments every day. They initially thought it was a mob hit, but when they caught the guys, they couldn't find any connection to organized crime. That's the case that made me decide to become a police officer." Apparently, Lawrence's words finally sunk in. "You probably would have done a better job keeping Susan safe if you had given her a last name like Hinklemeyer—something no one would ever link to Dr. Calvin Campbell."

Jake rose abruptly and walked to Lawrence's desk, pressing his fingertips to the faux wood surface. "So, where does the decapitation fit into all of this? And the stolen body?" He seemed to be questioning himself as much as anyone.

Lawrence looked askance at Susan, leaving her to decide how much of her personal story Jake deserved to know.

Susan gave him a hint. "Your federal agents admitted to taking the head." She glanced at Lawrence, who nodded his consent. "USR reclaimed the body."

"So, who, exactly, is John Calvin and where does he fit—" Jake interrupted himself. "Oh, my God!" He whirled to face the others again. "Oh . . . my . . . God! John Calvin's a . . . a robot. Isn't he?" He turned Susan an accusatory look.

"I just found out Saturday," Susan said. "Shortly before I went to your office."

"You mean, all those years you couldn't tell? That your own father . . . ?"

Susan took immediate offense. "Don't get all high and mighty with me, Detective. Your people examined the headless body and missed it, too. Besides, I'm of the firm belief that most robots are better company than humans—sounder, smarter, and far more honest and humane."

"I'm sorry," Jake said genuinely. "I have absolutely no experience with robots. For all I know, I'm the only flesh-and-blood human in the entire police department. I had no idea the technology had advanced so far."

Susan wanted to trot out Nate, but wisely held her tongue. Jake knew even more than he had, so far, let on. She saw no reason to risk one of the last humanoid robots.

For the moment, the conversation seemed to have come to a natural conclusion. Jake blinked first. "Now that they have a positronic brain in their possession, it's all over. Right?"

Alfred cleared his throat. "How so, young man?"

Jake seemed surprised by the question. "Well, I mean, it's in their hands. They could analyze it and . . . and . . ."

Alfred cocked his head, apparently waiting for Jake to finish. When he did not, the head of research resorted to analogy. "Let's say someone killed Susan here." He waved vaguely, as if he had just surmised what she had for breakfast rather than blithely speaking of forfeiting her life. "Do you think if you chopped out her brain and put it under a microscope, you could re-create Susan Calvin?"

"Well, of course not." Jake looked at Susan with concern, as if he worried the example might unnerve her. "But Susan's a living, thinking human, and the human brain isn't a bunch of wires and gears."

Lawrence took over. "Even if you could exactly duplicate the neural pathways of her brain, you could not bring back her personality, her memories. Doing so would require reanimating her, as well as stimulating the exact neural pathways, with particular and differing electromagnetic pulses and neurotransmitters to simulate every experience of her former life."

Jake clearly appreciated Lawrence's explanation, though Susan doubted he fully understood it. "Exactly." He added thoughtfully, "And I'm assuming you're saying the positronic brain is as, or nearly as, complicated. But I'm not talking about them re-creating John Calvin in order to demand the uncoupling code from him. I'm just raising the possibility that having a positronic brain, any positronic brain, in their possession gives them the opportunity to experiment with it. To find the means to uncouple it from the Three Laws themselves."

Alfred crinkled up his entire face. "Are you suggesting the government doesn't already own robots with positronic brains? Because they do. At this point in time, they're the only client who can afford us."

That surprised Susan as well as Jake. She responded before he could. "You mean there are more humanoid robots? And they work for the government?"

Jake mumbled, "That would explain some of my bosses."

The look Alfred gave Susan could have withered daisies. "I didn't say humanoid robots. I said robots with positronic brains. Those are two very different things."

Jake returned to his original point. "So, what's to stop them from opening up these robots and examining their positronic brains?"

"Nothing," Lawrence admitted. "Other than voiding the warranty and permanently damaging a priceless tool that cost them hundreds of millions in taxpayer money." He continued to study Jake. "What's your point?"

Jake stared back. He clearly considered it obvious. "What's to stop them from building their own positronic brain? Without the Three Laws as part of the process?"

Lawrence laughed, not at all concerned about that particular possibility. "Jake, it's not like building an oven. Let's assume the government has an abundant supply of platinum-iridium alloy and unrestricted access to funds and manpower."

Jake nodded. It was an easy assumption from which to work.

"I have no doubt they could, with a lot of work and expense, build something that looked exactly like a positronic brain."

"Okay," Jake said, his point all but proven.

"They could also take bits of organic material and fashion a human brain that looked exactly like Susan's."

Susan wished they would leave her extracted brain out of it. She had come close enough to death for one day. Still, she listened carefully, guessing where Lawrence was going.

"What makes a positronic brain work isn't the hardware, Jake. It's the proper software, the invisible but extremely real mathematical formulae, electronic impulses, the programmed information, plans, orders, integrative systems, and a myriad other intangibles that allow functions that once seemed impossible. Remember when calculators did nothing but calculate, computers computed, and tape recorders recorded on tape? Ask ninety percent of people how a Vox works, and you'd get an evasive answer. The honest ones would admit they think it's magic."

Jake looked to Susan for assistance, and she complied. "Ten percent of the population is still a significant number of people. USR doesn't have a monopoly on genius."

Lawrence put a hand on Susan's shoulder. "You'd be hard-pressed to find two people as intelligent as Calvin and Amanda." He smiled mischievously, "Let alone convince them to reproduce."

"Lawrence and I are hardly slouches in the brains department," Alfred added immodestly.

Lawrence forestalled him with a raised hand. "But you're right. We don't have a monopoly on genius, and patents are only a deterrent to people with morals and scruples." He shrugged. "Luckily, brains and integrity often do go hand and hand; most thinkers have pondered the potential effects of corruption, particularly their own, on society. We also have several advantages in this situation. First, we created the positronic brain and all its components and processes. Second, it's a prohibitively expensive item that suppresses garage tinkerers and college students. Third, we patented enough of the steps along the way and licensed so little of the technology that it discourages anyone from coming close to the developmental stages. Fourth, it's staggeringly complicated."

Jake tapped his hand on his knee. Apparently, some of the discussion went over his head. "So, the upshot. You're not worried, per se, about the positronic brains now in federal hands."

"No." Lawrence removed his hand from Susan's shoulder. "I was more concerned when I thought the SFH had it. They could have made life extremely difficult for Susan simply by revealing the true nature of John Calvin. Also, they would surely have used their discovery to discredit us and alarm the public in the most disconcerting way."

Susan nodded vigorously. She could easily imagine people accusing everyone around them of being a robot, could see them using it to justify murder. Every evil act would have a robot at its root. Anytime some antisocial human nightmare acted in a grisly manner, rumors would circulate that he was secretly a robot. Ironically, the worst features of humankind would be the ones blamed on technology; the precise failings a robot could never realistically manifest would became pinned indelibly to them. She now also understood why USR had stolen the body from the morgue.

Susan realized it was time to force a choice on Detective Jake Carson. "All right, Detective. You know our every secret. Are you going to play ball with them . . . or us?"

Jake froze, a trapped rat trying to look casual, without success. "What do you mean?"

Susan did not let him off the hook. "I mean, you've already stated your life may depend on your cooperation with this federal agency." She wished she had thought of this earlier. "I'm assuming they sent you here to gather information from us."

Jake hesitated only an instant. "Yes."

Alfred scowled. Lawrence sat up straighter.

Jake sighed deeply. It was delay, but Susan did not read too much into it. She did not envy Jake his decision, nor his need to hedge. "It's not as if I've learned anything they didn't already know or figure out. The only really significant thing I could add to the discussion is the claim that the Three Laws can't be uncoupled from the positronic brain; thus no clandestine code exists."

"Which is good for Susan, right?" Lawrence suggested. "Because the DoD no longer has a reason to bother her, and the SFH loses any reason to kill her."

Susan saw the flaws in that logic, but Jake was the one who gave them a voice. "They also have no reason to keep her alive, which, at the moment, might be more significant."

"How so?" Lawrence needed to know as much as Susan did.

Jake sighed again, rolled his eyes toward the ceiling, and shook his head. "Cards flat on the table, faceup and all the way. Right, Susan?"

"Right," she promised.

"Here's the scenario as I see it." Jake looked at every person present. "I may be the only nongenius in the room, but I am a detective and this is what I do."

Everyone nodded encouragingly, including Susan.

"I believe that whoever shot John Calvin . . . um . . ." Jake caught himself. "The robot representing John Calvin . . ."

Susan interrupted, worried the various attempts to avoid upsetting her would wind up hampering the story and any ideas that followed. "For convenience, can we all agree to refer to the mechanical man who raised me as John, John Calvin, Dr. John Calvin, or my father? My biological father is Calvin or Calvin Campbell. No confusion."

"Fine." Jake continued, "That whoever shot John intended to kill him. The assassin or assassins left without ever realizing the pulseless body on the floor was not made of flesh and blood. I believe Cadmium came in—"

This time, Alfred interjected, "Cadmium?"

"Code designation for the DoD Intelligence Exploitation Agency. It's not technically classified, but they hold it close."

Susan suspected Jake had not slipped in telling them the name but had done so on purpose, so he would have difficulty changing his mind later if it came down to siding with Susan or the feds. That, in and of itself, made her even more suspicious. "Jake, as you've pointed out, you've known me all of two, three days, but you've been a cop for"—she had no idea how long, so she finished lamely—"years. Do you expect us to believe you're siding with us against your own?"

"My own?" Jake seemed genuinely bewildered. "You mean the NYPD?"

"I mean law enforcement. This federal agency—"

"Is not law enforcement." Jake positively bristled. "I'm loyal to the NYPD, to the law I'm sworn to uphold, and to the residents of my city, whom I'm legally bound to serve and protect." He added disdainfully, "Cadmium can go to hell."

Susan felt foolish for not knowing that. Apparently, Lawrence did not, either. "So, federal and local agencies can . . . butt heads." He tapped the knuckles of his fists together.

"Frequently," Jake growled. "Right now, this whole thing is on lock-down by the U.S. Attorney, Southern District. We're all under a gag order, effectively shutting down any communications between us and the feds, which may be the only thing keeping me alive right now. The cover story is that a DEA agent, acting on a tip about a kidnapped source, put them in a friendly-fire situation and Cadmium got the worst of it."

Susan guessed, "I'm the source. You're the DEA agent."

"And I died in the firefight."

Susan tried to put it all together. "So . . . you're dead."

"The fictional DEA agent is dead, not Police Detective Jake Carson. Right now, you, me, the U.S. Attorney, my dispatcher, and the cops who responded to my distress call are the only ones who know the truth. That's few enough to keep it quiet for a while, but enough to ensure the information will get out there eventually."

Susan knew they had dropped some important threads to get to this point, ones that begged returning to. "The two guys who held me denied killing my father. They claimed to have found him shot and apparently dead, then discovered his true nature and managed to speak to him. Supposedly, he told them . . ." Susan remembered, and stopped suddenly short. With bullets flying around, bodies falling, and her life at stake, she had not bothered to consider her father's last words until that moment.

Everyone wanted to know. They practically demanded in unison, "What, Susan?"

Susan's voice fell to a whisper entirely against her will. "That I have the code."

The room went utterly silent. A dropping pin would have sounded like thunder.

Alfred broke the hush, his voice regularly pitched but sounding more like a shout. "Are you saying there *is* a code? And you have it?"

"I'm saying," Susan said carefully, licking her lips, "my kidnappers claim my father said one exists. And I have it."

Lawrence asked the question on every mind. "Do you?"

"Not to my knowledge, no." Susan considered all the possibilities. "Maybe Cadmium lied. Maybe my father lied." She looked at Lawrence. "Is that even possible? Can a positronic robot tell a lie?"

"Theoretically, I suppose. Positronic robots are thinking, learning robots who observe the world around them."

That opened a can of worms Susan did not want to contemplate at the moment. "Or maybe he told me the code at some point, but I just don't remember it."

Jake added one more. "Or you have it and don't recognize it as a code."

Susan furrowed her brow. "Didn't you say, at some point, it's safer to have them believe I have the code than to explain to them I don't?"

"Not exactly." Jake tried to recall his precise words. "I believe I said it gave them a reason to want to keep you alive. At least until they extracted the code from you. If we convinced them no code existed, the SFH would no longer have a reason to kill you. On the other hand, the feds would no longer have a reason to keep you alive, and they might decide both of us know too much."

"But I don't know anything," Susan insisted.

"You know who killed John Calvin, why they killed him, and the existence of a mythical federal agency, including its code designation."

Susan turned on him. "I didn't know that until you told me." The suspicions she had put on hold returned in a rush. "Is that why you told us their code name? To make me a target?"

"Don't be stupid." Jake huffed out an irritated breath. "I mean, act like the genius you are. I don't even know their official name; that's classified information. I told you their code designation so you can use it to your advantage. Believe me, you already knew enough to make you a plausible target before I said a word, if for no other reason than because you called me, and that resulted in the deaths of fellow agents."

"Only because *they* threatened to kill *me*."

"Your reasons are irrelevant. To them, it's war, and you ratted out their buddies."

Susan quelled rising panic and the urge to bargain with people who could not change the situation.

Lawrence stepped in for Susan. "Don't you think it's more likely they'll shy away from the entire situation? I'm sure they have ways of denying any claim Susan could make. The feds know how to make people look foolish."

Jake stiffened, as if torn between two opposite replies. "In ordinary circumstances, I'd agree with you. But, in this case, they've already shown their willingness to kill civilians who get in their way."

Susan knew exactly who he meant. "Sammy Cottrell."

"I believe the assassins who shot John got in and out quickly, without anyone knowing. Cadmium came later, probably following the exact same tip. They intended to question John but found him apparently dead. So they searched the apartment to see if they could find any hint of the code. They discovered John's identity, managed to get a few last words from him but not the code itself." He paused a moment, and his brow suddenly furrowed. "Wouldn't the Second Law of Robotics force John to give up the code if he had it? Doesn't it say something about having to obey all human orders?"

Susan immediately saw the flaw in Jake's reasoning. "The Second Law states a robot must obey orders given to it by human beings *except* where it conflicts with the First Law."

"All right," Jake said with consideration. "But how would revealing the code defy the First Law? Speaking doesn't injure a human being."

"Not directly." Susan had no problem following her father's robotic logic in this instance. "But giving up a code that would allow weaponization of positronic robots could harm many humans."

Jake closed his eyes, then opened them slowly. "Can a robot make that kind of intuitive leap?"

Lawrence reminded, "We're talking about positronic robots. Thinking, learning robots who observe the world around them." He made a gesture toward Susan. "Have you given any more thought to the possibility of working at USR, Dr. Calvin? Is the idea of psychoanalyzing robots seeming any less frivolous?"

Susan chuckled but lacked the enthusiasm of the last time they had discussed this subject. The jokes no longer seemed funny. She wondered if she had received the code and forgotten or not recognized it for what it was, or if John Calvin had deliberately lied, in the belief that doing so protected Susan's life as per the First Law of Robotics. The whole thing seemed at once terrifying, strange, and curious. "How do you know the original assassins didn't kill Sammy?"

"Because that would not have left enough time for Cadmium to question John Calvin or search your apartment. Based on the brass removed from your walls, the assassin or assassins used suppressors on at least two different twenty-two-caliber guns. No one heard John Calvin die. Sammy's scream, and subsequent shooting, was the event that brought police attention to the murders. And I now think I know what caused her to scream."

Susan suddenly did, too. "Strange men leaving our apartment . . . with John Calvin's head."

"The bullet that killed Sammy Cottrell was a nine-millimeter."

Chapter 19

When Kendall Stevens returned from work that evening, he discovered Susan sitting on his couch, her head bowed over an enlarged and extremely crumpled photograph, her color sickly pale. Dropping his palm-pross on the patterned chair, he rushed to her side, sat beside her, and put an arm across her shoulders. "Susan, what's wrong?"

Susan's voice emerged wobbly, and she glanced at her Vox. It was nearly seven o'clock. She had sat in the same position, studying the picture of Remington and herself, for longer than an hour. "I finally got around to reading and listening to the messages I missed with my Vox off last weekend."

"Yeah?" Kendall encouraged, his gaze zeroing in on the picture in Susan's lap.

"There's one from . . . my father."

It took a moment for the words to sink in. "From your father? You mean, before he . . . died."

"After," Susan said.

Kendall blinked, opened his mouth to speak, closed it, and blinked again. "Ghost writing?" The feeble joke did not work, apparently the best his shocked mind could conjure. "From beyond the grave?"

Susan sat back, finally tearing her gaze from the photo. It did not matter; the image had become burned onto her retinas. She could see it flashing on the off-white ceiling. "Sort of. A delayed text, set to send at a specific time."

"Which was?"

"Saturday night. I did glance through yesterday to see who had messaged me, but I missed this one." Susan suspected her mind had passed it over as normal, focusing on the more troublesome police and hospital calls. "While waiting for you, I thought I'd finally read and listen to them all, and this popped up with the others."

Gently, Kendall took the photograph from her hands. "You really loved him. Didn't you?"

The conversation suggested Kendall referred to her father, but his attention lingered on Remington. She told the truth. "Achingly."

Kendall used the arm across her shoulders to draw her to him. "I miss him, too, Susan. He was an extraordinary man. It would be difficult for anyone to follow in his footsteps."

Susan nodded, idly wondering if Kendall's words had underlying meaning, perhaps justifying his performance, or lack thereof, the previous night. If so, she did not rise to the bait, and he did not press it.

"So, what words of wisdom did your father impart from heaven? 'Don't forget to tip St. Peter?'"

Susan did not take offense. Humor was Kendall's way of dealing with upsetting situations. She brought up the appropriate message on Vox and extended her arm to him. Though not in a position to see it again herself, she had memorized every word and symbol:

No1 evr loved any1 > I loved u. R spiritual plce. Dad.

Kendall read swiftly, then seized Susan's wrist with his free hand to hold it steady while he reread the message. Finally, he looked at Susan. "When do you think he wrote this?"

Susan harbored no doubt. "As he was dying."

"My God," Kendall whispered. He drew her fully into his arms. "It must have taken everything."

Susan had no idea if that was true, but Kendall still did not know John Calvin had been a positronic robot. "I've been contemplating it ever since I got it."

Kendall relaxed his grip, apparently picking up from Susan's tone that she was past the need for comforting. He released her fully. "I get that he's saying no one ever loved anyone more than he loved you. But what did he mean by 'R spiritual place'?"

"Here," Susan said, poking a finger at the park bench in the picture. "Right under Remy's butt."

"Wha–?" Kendall needed more. Anyone would.

Susan explained briefly, "My father gave me this picture, in pristine condition and neatly framed, of course. It took me a while to put it together, but I remember the conversation we had at the time. He suggested that since Remy was buried in Ohio, we use the bench as a de facto gravesite. Our spiritual place to commune with Remy's spirit." She caught Kendall's hands. "We need to examine that bench." She sprang to her feet, ready to leave immediately, certain her father's cryptic message tied directly to the events of the last few days.

Kendall also rose but demonstrated none of Susan's excitement. "Susan, we need to talk."

"We do," Susan admitted. "You couldn't possibly guess how much I have to tell you." So much, in fact, she could not figure out where to start.

"Mine will only take a moment." Kendall crouched in front of her and took her hands.

For a panicked instant, Susan thought he was about to propose marriage, but the sadness in his eyes made it clear he had no intention of doing so. Whatever he wanted to say wounded him deeply. Susan banished her plans to the back of her mind.

"Susan, I've given it a lot of thought last night and most of today, and I'm concerned you might be right."

"Right about what?" Susan asked carefully, reminding herself Kendall had no idea what had happened to her over the last few days. To him, the normal events of daily living still held significance.

"I think . . . I might be . . ." Kendall swallowed hard. "I think . . . maybe . . . I'm . . . I'm . . . more interested in . . . men than . . ."

Susan stared deep into eyes that fanatically dodged her own. "Oh, for Christ's sake, Kendall. You're trying to say 'gay,' aren't you? Gay, gay, gay. Gay as a pond of otters on nitrous oxide. Queer as a fourteen-carat lamppost. Fruity as a . . ."

Finding himself in more familiar surroundings with humor, Kendall finished, "Clockwork strawberry?"

Susan smiled. "Hey, that's good." Turning the tables, she gripped his hands more tightly than he did hers. "Seriously, didn't you get the memo at birth? Being gay is no big deal anymore. In fact, it's trendy. I know a lot of heteros who would donate their left gonad to be gay."

Kendall managed a weak grin. "Wouldn't that defeat the purpose?"

Susan laughed. "Only halfway." She added, more seriously, "I thought hiding in closets went the way of aviator sunglasses and tongue piercing. Why has it taken you twenty-seven years to figure out your . . . bedroom fantasies?"

As usual, Kendall avoided the discussion with humor. "In all fairness, I didn't hit puberty until at least . . . five or six."

Though the challenge intrigued her, Susan did not have time to psychoanalyze her closest friend. "Okay, quickie diagnosis: ego-dystonic sexual disorder."

Kendall took over. "Characterized by having a sexual orientation or an attraction that is at odds with one's idealized self-image, causing anxiety and a desire to either change, suppress, or become more comfortable with one's sexual orientation."

Susan rose, drawing Kendall up with her. "How long did it take you to memorize that?"

"The entire trip up and back."

"Hmmm."

"I've always said most psychiatrists go into psychiatry because they're secretly crazy and have a deep-seated need to analyze themselves."

Susan glanced at her Vox, then out the window. The sky had turned a smoky gray, interspersed with the brilliant light of streetlamps. "Listen, Kendall. I understand this should be a moment full of angst and hair pulling, and I promise to even suffer hundreds of anxiety-riddled hours believing the horror of my inept lovemaking drove my boyfriend to homosexuality. But the truth is, in about fifteen minutes, none of that will seem quite so urgent."

"Fifteen minutes?" Kendall's brows shot up. "Why's that?"

Susan headed for the door. "Because that's about how long it'll take to tell my story."

D espite her promise, Susan and Kendall raced down Bond Street, passing myriad steel and concrete buildings, without the opportunity to exchange a word between them. Glide-buses and cars wound through the streets, dodging the vehicles parked along the sidewalks, and the occasional blare of a horn or distant siren pierced the still, cool evening. A few other people shared the streets, most performing the classic Manhattan walk: fast paced, heads down, gazes tunneled ahead, mouths silent, moving ever straight ahead and ignoring passing strangers.

Kendall grabbed Susan's arm suddenly. "This way." He headed across the street, threading between a private Toyota and a double-parked delivery van.

"Don't we want the number 6?" Susan jabbed a finger toward a familiar blue sign marking the route. Every New Yorker learned the public transportation color/number code in childhood.

Kendall darted into the street, earning an angry honk from a checkered taxi forced to slow momentarily. "If we take the 3, it's a slightly longer walk but we get there faster."

Leaving traffic negotiation to Kendall, Susan glanced into an upcoming alleyway where a parked Subaru Sapphire caught her attention. She had no reason to believe it belonged to Jake, but it reminded her of the detective. Thoughts of him brought the earlier conversation back to mind, which made her wary. Suddenly distinctly aware of her surroundings, she made a visual sweep of the upcoming sidewalk and buildings.

As Kendall and Susan stepped onto the sidewalk, something small and fast moving hit the bottom of the alleyway fire escape with a soft *ping* and a brief flash of sparks. *What the hell was that?* Before she could contemplate it further, the window of a passing bus shattered. Someone hurtled from the alleyway, slamming her violently to the ground. "Get down! Get down! Get down!" The window of the parked car beside her exploded, and glass rained down on her exposed arms and neck. Kendall staggered, crashing into the car, breath driven from his lungs in a rush. One of his feet slipped off the curb, wedging between it and the parked car, and he collapsed as well.

Pinned by what she now recognized as Jake Carson, Susan squirmed. "Is someone throwing stuff at us?"

"Shooting," Jake corrected, shoving her across the curb and under the car. The concrete abraded her skin, driving bits of glass deeper into her arm. Metal jammed against her back, the area beneath the car breath-stealingly small. Kendall attempted to squeeze in beside her. Jake flung himself over the hood.

Susan had heard nothing that sounded remotely like gunfire. "Who–?" she started.

But Jake shouted over her, "Stay down! Sniper, second story. Corner." He returned fire over the hood, and the report of his pistol could pass for nothing else.

Susan could hear screaming, and running feet pounded past the car. Vehicles screeched to a halt. Something slammed into the metal above her head, punching through it, and she doubted the car could do much more than conceal them for a few more minutes. Jake was swearing a blue streak, sounding more fearful and desperate than angry. Useful words emerged between the curses. "The feds followed you, too." He paused to peek over the hood and fired another shot, then ducked back down. "White van across the street."

It all solidified in that moment. Susan rolled from beneath the car and nearly into the street. Through the fleeing people, around the sudden stack-up of traffic vomiting passengers, she spotted the delivery van she had seen double-parked across the street. Uncertain whether they understood what was happening, she did the only thing she knew would gain their attention. "Yo, Cadmium! Sniper! Second story, corner building!"

Men in bulky coveralls, carrying rifles, burst from every door of the vehicle. Something smacked into the street, flinging chips of asphalt that stung Susan's face. Swiftly, she ducked back under the car as a relentless bang of gunfire sounded over the shouts and screams of the running bystanders.

Jake scooted to Susan and seized her arm. "Come with me. Right now!" Hunched low, he made a sudden dash for the alley with her in tow. The once-normal scene had devolved into chaos. Abandoned vehicles zigzagged in crooked parodies of what had once been lanes, dents and crunches marking where they touched. People scurried in all directions in a mindless, uncertain panic. A few lay on the ground; most huddled in tight balls with hands uselessly covering their heads, as if they could stop a bullet. The federal agents closed in on the corner building, keeping up a steady spray of gunfire that did not allow the sniper to raise his head.

Kendall charged after them. "Should we be doing this? Is this safe?"

Jake ripped open his passenger's door, half throwing Susan onto the leather seat. "Of course it's not safe. It's dangerous as hell!" He plunged around the car and into the driver's seat. Unwilling to waste time checking for locks on the back doors, Kendall scrambled over Susan as Jake roared out of the alley and away from Bond Street.

Kendall rolled into the backseat and scrambled below the level of the windows. He loosed a string of expletives that rivaled Jake's, then added, "What in holy hell is going on?"

Susan's heart pounded, and her breath rasped in her chest. She could not have answered, even if her mind allowed it.

Jake sped around the corner and onto a main avenue. "I'm taking both of you someplace safe."

"Safe," Kendall repeated. "You mean, like the police station?"

"No, I said someplace *safe*."

Low in her seat, unable to see out the window, Susan had no idea where Jake was taking them. "You were right about one thing: The feds do want to keep me alive."

Jake spoke without taking his eyes off the road. Driving way too fast, he needed to pay heed to traffic. "Maybe not anymore. You just blew their cover."

"We needed their attention," Susan pointed out. "They weren't doing anything."

"They were donning body armor. Pulling rifles. They had to target off me."

Susan did not understand. "What do you mean?"

Jake took a sudden turn that threw Susan against the door. Only then she realized the buzzing in her ears had nothing to do with the aftermath of screams and gunshots. She fastened her safety harness.

"From the size of the holes, the perp was using a suppressed thirty caliber. I'd guess either Blackout or six-point-eight from an M4A1."

"In English, please." Kendall's disembodied voice floated to the front. He remained at least as low in his seat as Susan did in hers.

"It's almost movie quiet . . ." Catching himself slipping into jargon again, Jake explained. "Nearly as quiet as bad action movies portray silencers. Cadmium couldn't have known anything was happening until the window shattered, and, even then, they probably had no idea where it came from until I fired back."

Kendall saw the flaw in that logic before Susan did. "So, how did *you* know?"

Jake had a ready answer. "I was watching the feds spy on you. I picked that alley probably for the same reasons the perp did, but it was you choosing to cross the street that saved your lives." He took another quick turn, then settled to a more normal speed. "He probably had you sighted; then you changed the geometry on him. You got inside his OODA loop, and that forced him to move, to expose himself slightly, which is how I spotted him. The M4 family has a large offset, which he must have forgotten or not thought about, because he hit the bottom of the fire escape. That deflected the bullet slightly upward, which is how it hit the bus window."

Kendall sat up a bit. "Discarding the whole OODA-loop and offset thing, which is gibberish to me, are you saying you figured out the mind-set of a killer and the flight of a single bullet in the middle of all that chaos?"

"Our lives depended on it," Jake pointed out. "But Cadmium couldn't possibly have seen the first deflection, so they had no idea where it came from. Now, the second shot—"

Susan interrupted, "Would have gone through my skull if you hadn't jumped on me. Instead it hit the car window." She realized she owed him something. "You saved my life again, Jake. Thank you."

"Again?" Kendall's tone harshened. "What the fuck is going on?"

Jake ignored Kendall. "The third and fourth went into the car. The size of the holes is how I knew the caliber."

Kendall nodded. "Now I get the attraction. He's you as a cop. Isn't he?"

Susan and Jake spoke the same words simultaneously: "Gay as a nightingale."

Not wanting to leave the conversation hanging on something so confessedly uncomfortable for Kendall, Susan added, "I imagine most cops and soldiers learn to instinctively do what he just did. In our line of work, if you're not one hundred percent observant, it may delay a diagnosis, and when an actual life is on the line, we all nearly always come through. In his line of work, if you're not one hundred percent observant, you're just dead."

Kendall accepted the explanation. "That probably weeds out the careless ones."

"Not always." Jake shook his head, still remaining fully focused on the road. "Often, it's the observant ones who act first. When you hurl yourself onto targets, you sometimes become one. I've seen more heroes lost than sloths." He continued under his breath, "Damn it."

Kendall finally sat up enough to look around them. "We could be in New Jersey by now."

"Good guess." Jake rolled the Subaru down a familiar street. Despite his comment about safety, they had come nearly full circle to the police station. "But wrong." He pulled into an empty space along the road and shut off the lights. "I'm going to report in, more to get information than divulge it. Before we pull into the lot, I need to give you your instructions."

Susan no longer harbored any doubts about Jake's intentions. "What do we need to do?"

"My car may, eventually, draw attention, but it's still safer than trying to smuggle you somewhere else. I've driven all over town and had plenty of time to drop you off while they sorted out the situation. They won't expect me to come here, especially while you're still with me, unless I bring you inside, which I'm not going to do."

"Why not?" Kendall asked, still lacking the background to grasp the full situation.

"Way too dangerous. The SFH isn't constrained by law, and Cadmium barely is, especially when they're desperate." A ray of lamplight striped Jake. In it, Susan could see beads of sweat on his brow, an expression of alarm and uncertainty he was struggling to hide. He had twice, unflinchingly, risked his life for hers with a cool detachment she now felt certain he feigned. It reminded her of a Mark Twain quotation: "Courage is the mastery of fear, not the absence of fear."

Jake continued, "You both need to snuggle down low and tight to the floor. Remain still. I know you have a lot to talk about, but not a single word passes between any of us until we're out of the police lot and on our way again. And, for God's sake, keep Vox off."

Susan quickly switched off her Vox, then slid down the front of the leather passenger's seat to scrunch into her footwell.

Jake restarted the car, flicked on the lights, and pulled forward slowly. Shortly, he made a right turn, and Susan felt the bump of the tires over the low-curbed entryway. Lights intermittently rolled across the interior as the car moved past overhead streetlamps. Jake pulled deep into the lot, then shut off the engine. Without hesitation or a single word to his passengers, Jake exited the car. Susan heard the click of the locks, then nothing more.

Claustrophobia swam down on Susan, and every part of her seemed to develop a cramp or itch simultaneously. She bit her lip without making a sound, remaining utterly still and silent, turning her mind to anything other than the discomfort. Jake had parked them in darkness, so Susan squeezed her eyes shut, trying to force all her focus on smells and sounds. If she strained, she could just barely hear the faint cadence of Kendall's breathing, a distant wail of a siren, the chirp of myriad crickets blending into a single rising and falling chorus.

It felt like an eternity before Susan heard a single set of footsteps approaching. The driver's door lock clicked open and Jake slid inside, shut his door, and started the engine. A moment later, they cruised out of the parking lot and back onto the familiar streets.

Jake's voice sounded thunderous. "You're safe now." He added, less reassuringly, "Relatively speaking."

Kendall clambered off the floor but remained low in his seat. "What in God's name did you two do? Steal the Declaration of Independence? Threaten the president?"

Jake gave him the short version. "Certain parties believe Susan has a code that deactivates the Three Laws of Robotics. The Society for Humanity wants to kill her so she can't share it. The DoD wants it so they can weaponize positronic robots."

That silenced Kendall long enough for Susan to ask, "Where are we going?"

"No idea." Jake continued driving. "Officially, I'm supposed to find Susan and bring her in ASAP."

"And unofficially?" Susan pressed.

Jake sighed. "You and I need to disappear off the face of the earth until we get this whole thing settled. Any thoughts on where we can do that? Because I'm tapped out."

Neither Susan nor Kendall had an immediate reply, so Jake expressed his thoughts aloud. "Any of our places is a no-brainer. Anything police related, no matter how safe, is right out. I don't think high-profile public places will suffice. Neither of them seems to care about collateral damage."

Susan discarded several ideas to focus on one. "How about USR? It's well secured, and I know Lawrence would support us. I'll give him a call." She reached toward her Vox.

"No!" Both men screamed at once. Jake even managed to grab her left arm in midmotion.

Susan nearly jumped out of her seat. "What?"

"Keep your Vox off," Jake commanded. "The feds will have a track on it by now. Any incoming or outgoing activity will tell them exactly where you are." He raised his bare right wrist. "I've hidden mine, so I'm not even tempted to use it."

Susan knew tracking them violated the terms of the Mobile Communications Privacy Act of 2027, but realized it did not matter. A federal organization that did not officially exist could probably cast aside many provisions of the law. Crying foul would not keep them alive. "Fine, but USR's the safest place I know, and I have no way to access it without Lawrence Robertson."

"Use Kendall's. He's probably not on their radar." Jake added, "Yet."

"You mean I could still get out of this alive?" Kendall said hopefully.

Jake did not know Kendall as well as Susan did. She knew he was kidding. He had not shied away from assisting her and Remington when they chased after bomb-wielding psychopaths injected with nanorobots. In fact, he had singlehandedly thwarted the one considered most dangerous, a brute of a sociopath who had already overpowered his security detail.

Jake responded honestly, "I'm planning to get all of us out of this alive. I can drop you off, if you want, but I think you're safer with us. Both sides now know Susan has a companion, in addition to me, and it won't take them longer than a day to figure out who."

Susan thrust a hand toward the backseat. "Give me your Vox."

Kendall complied, and Susan punched in Lawrence's number. While it buzzed, she explained, "We need to make a quick stop along the way."

"Anywhere," Jake replied. "As long as it isn't one of our homes."

Lawrence picked up. "Hello? Who is this?"

Susan held up a hand to forestall the detective. "Hold that thought." She turned her attention to Lawrence Robertson. "It's Susan. I'm using a coworker's Vox."

"Susan? Are you safe?"

"For the moment. We need a secure place to hole up, though. Any chance—"

"Come here right away. It's the safest place I know."

"'Here,' meaning . . ."

"USR."

Susan had expected Lawrence to suggest the U.S. Robots building, but she had also anticipated the need for him to meet them there. "You're still there? This late?"

Lawrence hesitated, then confessed, "I have living quarters in the back. I was here practically twenty-four/seven anyway. After the SFH gunned down Calvin and Amanda, it just seemed more prudent."

Jake made a rotary motion to indicate she should wind down the conversation as soon as possible.

"I don't know how long this line is clear. Have to go."

"I'll watch for you and let you in," Lawrence promised. "Be careful." He disconnected before she could say good-bye.

Susan turned off Kendall's Vox and returned it to him.

"USR building?" Jake guessed.

"USR," Susan confirmed. "But first we have to detour to my apartment building."

"*Your* apartment." Jake took his eyes from the road long enough to give Susan an incredulous glare. "Nothing of value there, Susan. Remember? It's confetti."

"Not inside the apartment. The playground at the base of the building."

Jake shook his head a bit, paused, then shook it harder. "Couldn't I just take you to Kinshasa? Iraq? What could you possibly need that's worth putting our lives at stake?"

Susan cleared her throat. She wanted to make sure he processed every word. "Quite possibly, the uncoupling code."

Chapter 20

Without her Vox, Susan had no idea what time it was, but she guessed somewhere between ten and eleven p.m. Jake pulled into an open space on the street about halfway between two streetlamps, avoiding the apartment parking lot. He hesitated a few moments, head bowed, face invisible in the dark interior of the car. Whether praying, steeling himself, or silently strategizing, Susan never knew, because it did not last long. Deliberately, he pulled a smaller pistol from an ankle holster she had never previously noticed and handed it back to Kendall.

Kendall shied away, as if from a hooded cobra. "No way. Don't give me that."

Susan considered accepting the gun in his stead but knew it would be deadweight in her hands. She could never pull the trigger. Judging by Kendall's previous experience, neither could he. He still suffered guilt for not shooting Sharicka when he had the chance, still blamed himself, at least partially, for Remington's tragic death. "Take it," she said.

Kendall looked distressed to the point of tears, but he did accept the pistol.

Jake explained, "Put the big orange dot between the two little white dots. Pull the trigger." He added pointedly, "And don't aim it at anything you don't want to kill, especially me or Susan."

Kendall closed his eyes, swallowed hard, and nodded. "If I shove this into my front pocket, I'm not going to risk shooting my junk off, am I?"

Jake peered out into the semidarkness. "As long as your junk keeps its finger off the trigger, you're fine."

Kendall stuffed the gun into his pocket. "So, what's likely to happen here, Jake? Another silent sniper?"

"Let's hope not."

Susan did not find Jake's response reassuring. "What's the most likely scenario?"

Jake had obviously given the situation more thought than he let on. "Cadmium has at least three guys tied up with the sniper. Despite government backing, they do have a limited amount of manpower, and I don't think they'll waste it watching Susan's apartment. They caught her there once and know they're not likely to do so again."

He shifted in his seat, still studying the scene out the window. "SFH lost their hired gun, quite possibly their only professional. Killers don't come cheap, and they're probably still reeling from the bombing fiasco last year. Of course, they are fanatics, so you never really know how desperate they might get or how fast they can bankroll. I doubt they know about the earlier kidnapping, so it's possible they have someone waiting in Susan's apartment to ambush her if she comes home. By now, they know the place is torn up, but they don't necessarily know Susan knows it."

Susan also studied the street and sidewalk. The streetlights kept darkness at bay in neat circles, illuminating the parked cars in concentric patches, leaving other areas in near pitch-darkness. She had lived in Manhattan most of her life and never thought about the persistent, underlying hum that defined the city: traffic eternally rumbling past, intermittent car horns, alarms and sirens, some close and others eerily distant, the rolling roar of airplanes at all hours of the day and night. Now, her overactive mind sifted individual noises from the normal cacophony, rolling them through her thoughts, studying, considering, discarding.

Jake continued, "Our biggest threat is probably a spotter, someone whose job it is to contact the others if we're seen in the area. He—"

"Or she," Kendall inserted. "Or they."

"Or she or they," Jake repeated. "Way to be diligent, Kendall. . . . Won't hesitate to take the shot given the opportunity. So we need to be cautious about everyone and everything around us."

Flickering red, green, and yellow lights pierced the distant darkness, traffic signals pausing and changing in a flow that matched the best pattern of the vehicles. Back against a sidewalk tree, a man stood with a clarinet case at his side. *What's he doing there at this time of night? Does he really look like a musician? Might that case be hiding something lethal?* Any other time, these thoughts would not have occurred to Susan. But any other time, her life did not depend on noticing subtle clues that might separate a passerby from a would-be killer. She wondered if Jake lived with this barrage of paranoia every moment of his life, and she sympathized with and appreciated him.

Jake sketched out a plan. "I'll go with Susan. She can search the proper area while I cover her. Kendall, you can stay here and wait if you want."

"Nothing doing." Kendall reached for his door handle. "I've watched enough act-vids to know what happens to the guy left 'safely' behind. He's always the one the heroes find gruesomely murdered."

"Fine. Come, then." Jake opened his own door, still scanning the street like he expected an army to descend upon them. "Anything remotely suspicious deserves a second look. Possibly a third or fourth."

Susan followed the men around the car to the sidewalk, careful not to step out into the still-moving traffic. She wondered if all worrisome situations made even the most mundane things seem hazardous. She would have to grow eighty eyes to keep her attention focused on everything that suddenly looked wrong or out of place.

Susan led the way around her apartment building. A homeless man hobbled from the Dumpster, dressed in a shabby overcoat and filthy jeans, face unshaven and smeared with bits of food. A municipal truck idled nearby, belching diesel smoke that roiled around the building and streetlights, adding misty halos. Sanitation workers in dirty white coveralls wrestled to attach hooks to the Dumpster's rings, shooing the indigent wanderer away from the building.

In the year since she had graduated medical school and returned to live with her father, Susan had never noticed when the garbage was collected. It seemed odd to see workers out so late at night; yet, she realized, she could never remember coming upon them during the day. The truck certainly appeared legitimate, and the men and women handling the Dumpster seemed to know what to do. They paid the trio headed for the playground no apparent heed.

A well-dressed woman walked toward the building, high heels clicking against the pavement. She appeared to be a resident returning late from work, one of hundreds Susan would not have recognized since they did not share her floor. Now Susan could imagine her pausing to remove her shoes and pointing them at Susan, bullets whizzing from those stiletto heels. Susan knew she needed to quell her overactive imagination but found it extraordinarily difficult.

As they walked around the corner of the building, the playground appeared in front of them. The familiar bright tunnels and slides, which had always before reminded Susan of a happy childhood, suddenly resembled crouched beasts slobbering in the darkness. The ground cover of recycled tires appeared as dark, still, and uninviting as a crocodile-and-viper-filled bayou.

From habit, Susan looked up, spotting the terrace of her apartment. Her father had grown fresh vegetables in colorful pots and shallow basins every summer. Despite the ambient light, Susan could not make out details. She knew their terrace now stood barren and empty, denuded of anything John Calvin-related. In daylight, she could easily pick it out from the others, many of which sported cheery wind chimes or statues, mostly the currently trendy monkeys with massive eyes and dressed in costumes that announced their owners' occupations or interests.

A woman pushed two young children on the swings, suspicious only for the lateness of the hour. Susan could not remember the playground being occupied after dark, but it was not something to which she had ever paid much attention, either. She supposed a woman who worked late shifts might take whatever time she could to spend with her young-sters, especially ones not yet in school.

High in humidity, the night was damp but without rain. The diesel smoke curled around the building and floated over the playground, wrapping the evening in a light fog that gave it the feel of a horror-movie graveyard. Susan had no difficulty locating the bench, almost directly beneath their terrace and at the edge of the playground, one of several sturdy one-piece concrete constructs meshed with the pave-ment.

Jake kept his voice low. "Susan, you focus on what you need to find. Kendall and I will cover you. Always remember: a moving target is a difficult target, especially at night." He glanced around. "If it goes side-ways, immediately run here." He gestured toward the municipal vehicle.

Kendall growled almost subvocally, "I'm shooting the first person who yells, 'Separate! He can't hit all of us.'"

Ignoring him, Susan focused directly on the bench and fast-walked to it while still trying to appear subtle. Whether or not they employed spotters, neither the SFH nor Cadmium would know the reason Susan had returned. The more suspicious her actions, the quicker they might figure out the purpose of them.

The mother looked up as they approached and moved a bit closer to her children. The homeless man meandered down the same sidewalk, toward them. Susan could hear the grind of gears and the clank of the sanitary workers moving the giant Dumpster. She saw no signs of the businesswoman or the clarinet player. *Focus,* she reminded herself. *I've got two good men to handle the paranoia. Two good, armed men.* Casually, she examined the bench, finding nothing unusual about the smooth upper surface. Trying to appear offhand, she sat on it near one end and ran her hands over the decorative concrete side supports.

A sudden gunshot shattered Susan's hearing. Her heart seemed to leap out of her chest. The mother screamed, grabbing for her children. The homeless man collapsed to the pavement. Startled to her feet, Susan swiveled to stare at the two men guarding her. Jake was springing between Susan and the fallen man, drawing his pistol as he moved. It was Kendall who had fired, his weapon clutched tightly in both shaking hands.

"Freeze," Jake said. Then, "What'd you see?"

"His shoes," Kendall replied. "Clean, new. Two-hundred-dollar Bosco Hardys. Where would a derelict get those?"

"Donation center?" Susan suggested, horror blossoming in the pit of her stomach.

"Swiped 'em," Jake added, his weapon still raised and pointed directly at the grounded man. He started to approach slowly, careful not to cross between the frightened, trigger-happy civilian and his hapless quarry.

"Handout?" Susan could not help saying as the discomfort in her belly grew to frank nausea.

"Oh, my God." Kendall's arms dropped to his sides. "OhmyGodoh-myGodohmyGod!" He ran toward the homeless man, clearly intending to render medical aid. "What have I done?"

The injured man moaned and rolled toward them. Kendall had nearly reached his side when a second shot rang out, this one so loud it seemed to come from everywhere at once, deafening. Susan bit off an involuntary scream.

Kendall skidded to a stop.

A third boom followed, muffled by the aftereffects of the previous two, then ringing silence. The bogus derelict went still, and a weathered handgun with an overlong barrel clattered from his hand to the pavement. "Good instincts, Kendall," Jake said.

Susan could hear relief in his voice. She doubted he could ever have satisfactorily explained his gun being used to kill an innocent man.

Kendall stood frozen, his lips moving, silently repeating, "Oh, my God."

A green dot appeared on Kendall's torso. The diesel smoke revealed the whole laser line, running from him to the upper recesses of the building.

"Move!" Susan screamed. "Kendall!"

It was a directionless command, but the urgency made it through. Jake flung himself on Kendall, rolling them both toward the bench. Susan heard the ping of something striking concrete.

"Get under!" Jake dove across the bench to the far side and peered over the back.

Susan scrambled underneath, Kendall jostling to join her. "What's going on?" he demanded.

Susan frantically searched for something attached to the bench, not directly part of it: a scrap of paper, an envelope, a flash card. Her father would have had to hide it well enough to keep someone from inadvertently finding or dislodging it. She hoped they would not have to chisel through concrete or activate some secret compartment found only by meticulously percussing the hard surface for echoes. *Dad wasn't expecting it to stay here long, and he had to suspect I'd be under duress.*

A bullet ricocheted off the back of the bench, breaking off a chunk and sending chips flying in a wild spray.

"Bum was the spotter," Jake explained, keeping his head low. He did not attempt to return fire. "Sniper was probably waiting in Susan's apartment. His 'eyes' are down now, and he's desperate to get us while he still knows where we are."

"*He's* desperate?" Kendall's voice was a squeak. "Any chance you can get him?"

Another hunk of bench thudded to the ground.

"If I had a better angle, maybe. Shooting straight up's a waste of time and ammo."

Susan continued searching, nudging Kendall out of her way.

Kendall shifted position. "Ow! Damn it!"

Jake's tone expressed appropriate concern. "You hit?"

"No!" Kendall positively spit. "I banged my friggin' head." His hand went naturally to the site of the injury. "Damn it. And now I've got gum in my hair."

Susan loosed a nervous chuckle. "Wouldn't want to be found dead with *gum* in your hair." Instinctively, her gaze went to where Kendall clutched his scalp. There was a sticky substance adhering to his hair, but it did not exactly resemble gum. Neutral gray, it matched the bench, rather than one of the brilliant, unrealistic colors she expected from modern chewing gum. As Kendall moved, something small and embedded in the mass flashed silver.

"Kendall, hold still." Susan lunged for him, grasping the object and ripping it free, along with a handful of his orange hair. It was a port key, the type once used to connect a Vox to a computer or another Vox.

"Ow!" Kendall yelled again.

"I got it!" Susan hollered, shoving the port key into her pocket. Only then she realized that the bench had withered in size; rubble and glittering grit were strewn across the sidewalk. "Holy crap!"

"Go! Go! Go!" Jake yelled, grabbing Susan's arm, yanking her from under what remained of the bench and shoving her toward the municipal truck.

Susan ran. She could hear the crack of gunfire as Jake laid down cover, heard Kendall's pounding footsteps at her back, then beside her. For an instant, she thought he would charge ahead, but he remained at her side, physically shielding her with his body, driving her to quicken her frantic pace.

Shoved beyond her own top speed, Susan found her balance tenuous. She barely managed to reach the truck before her upper body got too far ahead of her legs. She crashed to the ground, skidding across the pavement, feeling skin abrading from her nose and both arms. The municipal truck was still there, idling, but the workers had disappeared inside it. She could hear a voice inside the cab frantically calling for assistance.

Alternately apologizing and swearing equally profusely, Kendall assisted Susan. Jake appeared out of nowhere, banging on the cab of the truck. "Police!" He jammed his badge against the window. "Open up!"

To Susan's surprise, the door slid open tentatively. Jake reached out to the worker in the driver's seat. "Give me your Vox."

The man held out his arm. Without bothering to unstrap it, Jake tapped a complicated sequence of buttons. "Shots fired, Nine and C! Shots fired, Nine and C!"

An immediate response came over the Vox. Susan heard the repetitive beeping of an alert tone, then a voice: "In the confines of the Nine, a signal ten-thirteen Avenue C and East Nine Street. Units to respond?"

Jake had seemed so calm to Susan during the shooting. Now he was practically shouting and speaking twice as fast as usual. "Shots fired from the tenth floor, Avenue C side. Central, he's got a rifle! K."

The other voice came through loud and clear, "Units responding, shooter is on the tenth floor, Avenue C side. Use caution responding."

A deeper voice, apparently conferenced in, said, "Get ESU and Aviation up, Central. K."

Apparently, that communication was not for Jake, because he remained momentarily quiet, his face flushed, chest heaving.

The first voice answered, "Already ordered, Sarge."

Jake looked back at the playground. "Get a bus! We have one perp shot on the street, Nine and C! K."

Central addressed Jake again. "Unit requesting? K."

Jake ran a hand through hair plastered with sweat. "Manhattan South Homicide. I'm in plainclothes. Multiple shots fired."

"Units responding to the thirteen, use caution. Manhattan South Homicide on the scene, plainclothes. K. Where are you at, Homicide?"

Jake went suddenly silent. He licked his lips and looked up the front of the apartment building.

The voice came over the line again, repeating the question. "Where are you at, Homicide?"

Jake tapped the borrowed Vox several times. Releasing the arm to its owner, he spoke in a voice that sounded strained and anemic. "I'd keep it off for the next fifteen minutes or so, if you don't want an earful. When the police arrive, tell them you lent your Vox to a desperate cop who had to leave in a hurry."

Huddled in Kendall's arms, Susan could not stop herself from sobbing.

Even after seeing how easily the sniper's bullets had penetrated the parked car on Bond Street, Susan felt far more secure in the moving confines of Jake Carson's Subaru Sapphire. They headed off in a discomforting hush. Kendall huddled in the back, silently rocking, as if his body instinctively sought the long-ago safety of his mother's loving arms. Always pale, he now looked ghostly white in the dark interior of the car, his freckles standing out in bold relief.

For now, Susan left her fellow resident alone with his demons. She knew what bothered him. He had shot a man. And, for the moment, whether that man was an innocent father of eight or Hitler sentencing millions to death did not matter. Kendall had pulled the trigger, sending a lethal projectile hurtling toward another human being. On purpose. The Hippocratic oath, the vow taken worldwide by most physicians at the time of graduation, had been modified countless times through the centuries. Each school had its own version, but, she believed, every one contained the words or the sentiment, "I will do no harm to anyone."

Susan knew Kendall had a lot to work through right now. He still harbored some guilt from the previous year, when he had frozen, unable to shoot, allowing a killer to enter a crowded mall. This time he had acted swiftly, shooting a man based solely on speculation. That his hunch had proven correct might not be enough to assuage his hardnosed conscience. It had taken Kendall at least a decade to deal with the mildly unpleasant realization he might just be gay. Susan knew she could not solve this far more significant dilemma in the confines of a single car ride, so she did not even try.

Jake stared straight ahead, his brow deeply furrowed, his jaw tightly clenched. Ignorant of police training, Susan had a much harder time reading him. She knew she had to start with the basics: he was human, with normal emotions and reactions. He had chosen a career filled with excitement and danger, particularly in the locale he practiced. Yet she had to believe the events of the past few days were not typical for him. Police, she believed, like doctors, spent far more time dealing with documentation and testimony, more with observation and intervention than with cardiac arrests or gunplay. Without him, she would already be dead at least three times over. She needed him awake, alive, and with his wits intact. *I'm a psychiatrist, for God's sake. I need to fix him.*

Susan worked into it slowly. "Jake?"

He barely responded. "Hmmm?"

"Back at the building, why didn't you answer your dispatcher?"

That got his attention. He even glanced at her briefly. "What do you mean?"

"He asked you where you were, and you didn't answer. The last time we were in a plainclothes situation, you made us go out in the hallway so they wouldn't mistake us for the shooters."

Jake sighed deeply. Her simple question, intended to ease into the conversation, had clearly struck right to the heart of the problem. "Last time I'd been hit in the chest. I figured I was a dead man walking on nothing but adrenaline."

There was more to the answer, and Susan knew it. "So . . . you didn't respond this time because . . . you were still alive?"

Pressed, Jake fairly growled, "I didn't respond this time because we had to leave; we couldn't wait for backup. There. Are you satisfied?"

It was the first time Jake had ever snarled at her, but Susan refused to take it personally. Something else was bothering him, and she had hit close to home. "We could have waited a little bit. At least until they arrived."

"If we waited until they arrived, I'd have had to assist them in rooting out the shooter. They'd have taken us to the station, where we'd have spent five or six hours tied up in questions and explanations."

"Oh." Susan had not anticipated that, though it made a lot of sense.

"We'd be sitting ducks for Cadmium, who would have swept in with government clearance and taken us without a fight." Jake's teeth clenched so forcefully Susan worried about his jaw. "They need you alive, at least for a while. Kendall and I have no value to them at all. After I took down two of theirs, they might relish the chance to finish me off."

Susan heard Kendall stir in the back. Despite the depth of his own contemplation, he was listening.

Susan's intuition told her to continue. "There's more," she encouraged softly. "Something new. Something that hit you the moment you disconnected that Vox."

Jake tipped his head. At least one of the maelstrom of emotions currently assailing him must have drained away, because his jaw relaxed and the cadence of his voice slowed to normal. "You're good."

"Yeah, yeah." Susan would not allow him to change the subject. "I'm the best psychiatrist in the world. Now spill it."

Jake's hesitation now seemed to have more to do with finding the proper phraseology than any attempt to hide his discomfort. "You know how doctors tend to stick together, to protect one another?"

"That's a myth," Kendall said from the back.

Susan had to agree. "Too much ego. We're constantly stabbing each other in the back in order to take the credit for what goes right." Even as she spoke the words, she realized she had a bit of that propensity herself, and it mostly accounted for her multiple run-ins with Mitchell Reefes. She knew exactly how to handle him now, assuming she survived long enough to continue her residency. "Plus, each of us believes our way is the best way, and anyone who does it differently is a moron."

Kendall made it simple. "It's like sharing a dishwasher with an obsessive-compulsive. There's the right way and the how-could-any-living-person-be-such-a-blithering-idiot way."

"Uh." Jake considered that. "Well, it's different for cops. The thin blue line is very real, similar to the camaraderie between soldiers in a unit. When your lives depend on one another, you develop an unshakable loyalty." Abruptly, he took what seemed like a different tack. "You ever see a Steven Segal movie?"

The name sounded only vaguely familiar to Susan. "Was he an actor?"

"Actor, producer, writer. Started in a movie called *Above the Law*, which pretty much sums up the theme of his movies, most of which went direct to video."

Apparently, Kendall had either seen some or had heard about their reputation. "Usually about some rogue cop who continues following a case despite having been ordered off of it. The idea being he goes on to successfully complete an impossible mission, and throws his accomplishments back into the faces of his superiors."

Susan got it. "Ah, the rogue-cop theme. It's a television and video staple."

"It's also an oxymoron." Talking about what troubled him seemed to help Jake regain his composure.

A light went on in Susan's mind. "Are you saying you're a rogue cop now?"

"No!" The response was so abrupt, so sure, it was the closest thing Susan had ever heard to a verbal gunshot. "Never! My sudden departure will cause some serious consternation. I'll be answering a lot of hard questions for a very long time, and I'm going to have to construct some suitable answers. But my superiors know essentially where I am, what I'm doing, at least in a general sense. I'm working on a wink and a nod, and they may have to disavow me if things get tight, but I'm not directly risking my job. Assuming, of course, I survive this."

Kendall asked the obvious questions: "So, why didn't you just tell them you had to go, instead of leaving things hanging? Why did you call it in at all?"

"I called it in for the safety of the officers responding to the gunshots. They need to know what's going on. I didn't tell them I was leaving the scene, because that would make it an internal issue. This way, I can claim something pulled me away before I could answer, like I was chasing a bad guy and my borrowed Vox dropped its battery."

"So you're going to lie?" Kendall pointed out.

Susan immediately cut in with a reassurance. "You're damned right he's going to lie. And we're going to swear to it. Right, Kendall?" She did not wait for her companion to reply before speaking directly to Jake. "Tell us what to say, and we'll say it. We owe you our lives several times over."

"Consider me a scripted actor," Kendall called up from the back. "I have no problem with lying to protect a friend." He probably intended the rest to be subvocal, but Susan managed to hear it. "It's shooting people I have a problem with."

Jake looked at Susan again, then back at the road. She noted he always buckled his seat belt, nearly always kept his hands on the steering wheel at the classic ten and two o'clock positions. "Susan, are you sure we're doing the right thing?"

Susan could barely fathom the question. "A little white lie to keep you employed isn't that big a deal."

Jake shook his head. "No, I mean about the whole positronic-robots situation. I mean, these Cadmium guys are from the Department of Defense of the United States of America, not China. Isn't there something to be said for allowing them to work with the highest levels of technology in order to keep us—and our neighbors—safe?"

Though she did not need to, Susan gave Jake's words significant consideration. "You know, I hate it when animal-rights activists call scientists murderers for performing necessary experiments. I love animals. Most people do. Scientists are no exception. I have no problem with people who want strict oversight to ensure research remains as humane as possible. But it seems like the same activists who believe they're freeing rabbits from torture and slavery are the ones quickest to run crying to a lawyer when they suffer from a side effect of a medication or procedure."

Kendall called up, "You probably have a point related to the question, don't you, Susan?"

Jake chuckled.

Susan turned the driver a loathsome look. "Don't laugh. It only encourages him." Nevertheless, she dropped the analogy. "I'm just saying, I understand hypocrisy. If I want protection, I need to trust my protectors, even if they have to overstep a boundary now and then." She struggled to put her thoughts into words, and wound up finishing lamely, "But this is different." Susan knew she could not leave it there; she had to explain. "USR isn't withholding anything from the Department of Defense. The military has robotic technology. Everyone knows we've used unmanned drones since at least the war in Vietnam. They even have positronic robots in their employ, just not as . . . direct weapons."

As both men seemed to be listening intently, Susan continued. "I now believe I fully understand what Lawrence and my father meant about positronic robots being intrinsically linked to the Three Laws, why they can't be separated. It might help to think of positronic robots as humans, the positronic brain as religion, and the Three Laws as inviolate commandments."

Kendall inserted, "I've known some deeply religious people who believe themselves above morality. Also some highly ethical atheists."

Susan agreed. "In fact, I consider myself one of the latter, for the most part. But we're all raised with some sort of moral code we internalize and believe, regardless of whether we follow it to the letter. Remember, I stated the Three Laws of Robotics were *inviolate* commandments. If the ten featured in our Judeo-Christian bibles were equally impossible to break, we would live in a very different world."

Jake nodded. "I'd be out of a job, for sure."

"No, you wouldn't," Kendall said. "You'd just be enforcing different laws. Things like 'No milking brown-and-white pygmy goats on a Sunday,' or 'It's illegal to flick boogers into the wind.'"

Jake managed another chuckle. "Fine. Let's agree it would make my job a lot more boring, anyway."

Susan returned to her argument. "Positronic robots don't start with malleable infant brains into which we can cram our ideals until they seem hardwired. It's long been known children raised in abusive or neglectful environments—and by that I mean mostly or wholly devoid of stimulation and caring—develop a complex and extremely dangerous brain disorder known as reactive attachment disorder."

"True," Kendall confirmed.

"But positronic robots aren't human," Jake pointed out. "They're tools."

Susan tried not to take offense. People considering circumstances in a personal, rather than an objective, ethical light, were probably the cause of most of the world's strife. She did not want to create trouble where none needed to exist. "Tools, yes, but not like a hammer or a tank. Positronic robots have the capacity to think and reason. How do you justify using anything with actual intelligence as a weapon?"

"It's done all the time." Jake continued to stare out the window. "Wars are fought between human beings, with soldiers as weapons."

Kendall added his piece. "I'd classify the soldiers as the warriors making decisions for the weapons, not the weapons themselves."

"Kamikazes," Jake supplied. "Homicide bombers."

Susan shrugged. "Forced suicide, in many cases. Hopeless people talked into the unthinkable. Those who do it with vicious enthusiasm obviously have serious psychiatric issues: reactive attachment, antisocial personality disorder, or even brainwashing. But these positronic robots won't have a choice. And, if not endowed with some form of moral code, such as the basic one supplied by the Three Laws, they won't have anything to guide their actions. They're not just tools then; they're holocausts waiting to happen."

The men fell into a thoughtful hush, but only momentarily. Jake said, "Isn't that sort of the point, Susan? They'd be awesome weapons."

"Awesome weapons without the burden of morals or ethics or even loyalty. Accountable to no one." Susan drew from earlier in the conversation. "*Rogue* weapons."

"Maybe," Jake tried, "you could undo the First and Third Laws, leaving the Second. That would still make them accountable."

"Yeah, to everyone," Susan supplied. "Including the enemy. They'd be constantly trying to decide between conflicting commands, without the benefit of any moral anchoring." She allowed that picture to sink in before continuing. "Besides, that's not how it works. The Three Laws are a unit, bound together and created by some of the world's greatest minds."

"Your parents," Jake pointed out.

"Yeah, they happened to be. So what? That's not really the issue here." Susan felt obligated to remind the others, "Lawrence Robertson and his team created something unique, something beyond the understanding of much of society. USR has worked tirelessly for nearly three decades to produce a safe and useful product . . . and not in a vacuum. I'm sure they started debating and discussing the implications of positronic robots long before they connected the first wires. Not only do they have a right to have the strongest say in the legacy of their creation, but I believe they knew exactly what might happen if anyone found a way to deactivate the Three Laws."

Kendall summed things up. "So, protecting this information you found at the bench is worth dying for?"

"I believe," Susan said, enunciating each word, "that not protecting it would be a crime against humanity. That losing it would be tantamount to global catastrophe."

"Global catastrophe," Jake repeated. "You really believe if this code falls into the hands of our own government, it would herald the end of the world?"

Susan harbored little doubt. "The end of the world."

Kendall leaned forward. Some of the color had returned to his features. "So, what, exactly, is this doomsday code, Susan? What little present did your father leave us at the bench?"

"I'm not sure." Susan felt for the object through her khakis. It moved freely in her pocket. "It seems to be a port key."

"A port key?" Kendall snorted. "You mean one of those little doohickeys we used to use to gang Vox or computers or both together? Before government-regulated global wireless put the so-called phone companies out of business? Back when the Net had holes."

The size of her thumbnail, the port key was shaped like a rounded letter *H*. Susan tried to think back to the last time she had discussed port keys with her father. She had wondered aloud why manufacturers still included ports on Vox, and he had mentioned rain fade, solar flares, malfunctions, and other satellite issues. He had also talked about a less-common type of port key that could actively store a small amount of data. She was trying to remember how it worked when Jake chimed in.

"Port keys aren't entirely obsolete, Kendall. There's always some overlap between old and new tech. The station keeps a drawer full of them in case a foreign government took down our communications network. The smart port key technology was just beginning when the global web went up, so not a lot of people know about them, and fewer use them. It's possible to link two systems with a port key, then leave a small package of data that can only be retrieved if that port key is later plugged into the exact same two devices."

Susan felt certain Jake had just hit the nail on the head. "So, we're together on this. Right? The information stays out of the hands of agents, federal or foreign."

"I'm in," Kendall said wholeheartedly.

Jake took longer. "For the moment, I'm with you," he promised. "But if it comes down to choosing between our lives and the information, I reserve the right to change my mind."

Susan said the only thing she could. "That's all I can ask for."

Chapter 21

Nate met Susan, Kendall, and Jake at the door, waving the bone- and emotion-weary travelers into the now-familiar stuffy foyer of United States Robots and Mechanical Men, Inc. No one sat behind the single, semicircular desk that filled the foyer, mostly obscured by a computer console, enormous by current standards.

Once everyone had stepped inside, Nate pulled the door shut, obsessively checking to make sure it fully closed and latched before turning far enough for Susan to hurl herself into his arms. "It's so good to see you."

Nate clasped Susan firmly and with evident affection. Though more powerfully built than John Calvin, he stood the same 6'8". Susan melted into his arms, closing her eyes, breathing in the detergent fragrance of his shirt. For a moment, she managed to lose track of time, imagining herself nestled in the strong, loving embrace of the father she would never see again.

Lawrence stepped out of his office, dressed in casual attire, uncharacteristically disheveled. "Nate, escort them in here, please."

Unceremoniously torn from her fantasy, Susan released Nate and allowed him to perform his duty, and he gestured for the three of them to enter. As Jake walked through the door, Lawrence seized his hand and pumped vigorously. "Good to see you again, Jake. Thanks for keeping our Susan safe, for everything you've done to help her and us. We'll never be able to repay you."

"Just a civil servant doing my job," Jake said wearily, waving off Lawrence's gratitude and dropping to a crouch in the farthest corner of the room, which put his back to both walls. "Don't even try. I'd have to charge you with bribery."

Kendall entered more hesitantly, and Jake waved him over. "While those three talk shop, I'll fill you in on the details." He added, "And let me top off your mag."

"English," Kendall reminded, trotting to Jake's side.

Jake tried again. "I need you to hand me back the pistol I gave you so I can replace the cartridge you used and bring the gun back up to a full eleven shots, including the one in the chamber."

Kendall moaned. "Didn't I do enough damage with one? You want to give me the chance to make eleven fatal mistakes?"

"Just give me the damned gun, Kendall."

Susan made the necessary introductions. "Dr. Lawrence Robertson, CEO and founder of U.S. Robots and creator of the positronic brain, you know Detective Jake Carson. The guy beside him is Dr. Kendall Stevens, a fellow psychiatry resident." She added, "He's the one who safely took down Cary English." She knew the information would create an instant bond of trust; Cary English had been one of the nanorobot patients hijacked by the SFH.

Kendall looked up and executed a stiff salute in Lawrence's direction.

Susan continued, "Kendall, you and Nate have met." She considered how best to acquaint the robot and detective, then decided not to play games. "Jake, Nate's a positronic robot."

Jake pulled the magazine from his gun, popped out a cartridge, and stuffed it into the magazine of Kendall's smaller pistol. He slammed the backup's magazine, now full, back in place. "Yeah, I know," he said distractedly.

"You do?" That put Susan off her guard. "How did you know?"

Jake handed the handgun back to Kendall, who took it reluctantly and held it tentatively, as if afraid it might bite him. "Not by looking at him, that's for sure." Jake switched his partially used magazine with a fresh one from his belt, slammed the new one home, pressed the slide back, grunted his approval, then holstered his own gun. "I do my homework, Susan. Unlike John Calvin's, N8-C's existence is not a well-guarded secret."

Lawrence took his usual seat behind the mahogany desk covered with a mixture of several palm-prosses, a couple of digital frames, a combo printer, a bunch of bound hard copies, and masses of loose paper, most of which contained circuitry maps. This time Susan also noted a few port keys mixed in with a larger number of loose computational chips. There were two other chairs, matching foldables, in the room. Susan and Nate each took one, scooting it up to the far side of Lawrence's desk.

Lawrence called out, "Jake, Kendall, I can pull in some more chairs, if you'd like."

In a tight crouch, Jake made a dismissive gesture. "We're good." He turned his attention back to Kendall, who sat cross-legged beside him.

Susan got right to the point. "Dad left this for me in a concealed location." She pulled the port key from her pocket and laid it gently on the desk. It was not fragile. People used to carry them amid their loose change, and Susan had seen students hurl them across the room to one another. Nevertheless, she felt safer babying it.

Lawrence knew exactly what it was. "Smart port key, no doubt. Have you tried to connect it yet?"

"No."

Lawrence studied her face a moment. "Do you . . . want to?"

Susan realized she did not. It seemed safer just to destroy the port key now, to ensure no one ever gained access to the code, but she knew they might need it to barter for their lives. She could choose to sacrifice her own; she had no right to take the others with her. Her reply did not reveal her inner turmoil. "We have to, Lawrence." Worried she might lose her nerve, she jammed it into the port of her Vox. Immediately, a green light appeared on the plugged-in side.

Susan removed her Vox and handed it to Lawrence. "Now plug it into one of those myriad palm-prosses you're collecting."

Chuckling, Lawrence took the Vox. "Yeah, I do have a bit of a collection, don't I?" Picking one apparently at random, he jabbed the opposite end of the port key into it. Immediately, a red light flashed on opposite the green one. Lawrence pulled the Vox and port key away from the palm-pross. "Ah, an SPPK. Doesn't surprise me."

Susan glanced over at Kendall and Jake. They seemed enmeshed in discussion. "What's an SPPK?"

Nate responded first. "Selective programmable port key. You can still use it as a standard port key, but it won't give up its contents unless you link the original systems together."

Lawrence clarified, "The exact two systems connected at the time the data was created."

Susan nodded. Jake had already explained it in the car. "Which are?"

Lawrence dropped Susan's Vox and his palm-pross to the desktop, then leaned back in his chair. "The green light indicates you've solved half the problem. Your Vox. The question becomes: When did John Calvin have access to your Vox, and to what did he have it connected at the time he programmed this port key?"

Susan thought back; shook her head. "He's my father. He bought me my first Vox, and every subsequent one, for that matter. Anytime it requires fixing or replacing, he handles it. If he wanted to, he could have slipped it off my arm while I slept and taken it anywhere. Even if I noticed, I wouldn't worry about my father's presence in my room, even at night."

"Which suggests," Nate offered thoughtfully, "he programmed it at home. His Vox to yours. Most likely in the hours before he was killed but after we received word the SFH linked Calvin Campbell to John Calvin, that the man they believed they had successfully assassinated was still alive."

Susan gave that considerable thought. Clearly, the time between the SFH figuring out the connection, the leak to USR, and the murder was small. Otherwise, it made no sense that a man who had functioned under the radar for two decades suddenly caught the attention of two groups of killers at the exact same time. Susan realized Cadmium had probably followed the same leak as USR; perhaps they were even the ones who warned Lawrence, hoping to keep John Calvin alive long enough to question him.

That did suggest only a tiny window of opportunity for leaving messages for loved ones. Susan's heart sank. "If that's so, then all is lost. The feds tore our place apart. They took everything capable of holding data, and demolished anything remaining." She shivered, recalling her third venture into the apartment. "Twice."

Lawrence pounced on the word. "Twice?"

"Twice," Susan confirmed. "They searched it once, then returned a couple of days later to repeat the job even more thoroughly. They even chopped into the walls. Other than the refrigerator, there's not an object, appliance, or scrap of furniture not reduced to siftable rubble."

Nate and Lawrence exchanged looks.

"Which means they didn't find what they were looking for," Lawrence said.

Susan discarded the point. "Obviously. Because what they were looking for was the code. And my father told them I had the code, so when they didn't find it, they came for me."

Nate's brows slid downward, and he spoke in the slow cadence of concentration. "You know . . . just because the SFH hadn't penetrated his cover doesn't mean John didn't prepare for the eventuality."

Susan supposed her expression closely resembled Nate's for several moments as she puzzled through his point. "Are you saying Dad might have created the port key in anticipation?" She picked up her Vox with the port key still attached, the light still glowing green. "That he might have fashioned it years ago, perhaps updating it as we changed personal technology?"

"Why not?"

Why not, indeed? "But his Vox and his palm-pross are gone." She turned to Lawrence with a hopeful look. "Unless they were still on his body when he went to the morgue. He was already taken away by the time the police allowed me on the scene."

Lawrence shook his head. "No Vox or palm-pross, at least by the time I got to the body. I can't believe Cadmium wouldn't have taken them. They're the most likely places to find any kind of data."

"Oooh." Susan had spent too much of the past few days worried about her life and her job to think about the effects on U.S. Robots and Mechanical Men, Inc. "Do you think they got any significant information? Anything that might compromise the positronic brain? The company?"

Lawrence drew himself up, looking affronted. "Of course not. I trusted John Calvin as fully as the man he replaced. He would never have stored classified information on a private system. His work palm-pross is safely locked in his . . ." The realization of what he was saying struck Susan and Lawrence simultaneously. Both leapt to their feet. ". . . desk drawer."

Lawrence headed back into the foyer, Susan at his heels. She remembered from the time she and Remington had visited USR that the foyer had five doors, one of which led to Lawrence's office and another to a laboratory. Lawrence stopped in front of the door closest to his office. He ran his thumb across the scanner. "This is a shared office." He pushed open the door to reveal four desks, one in each corner of the room. Every one contained an assortment of bric-a-brac similar to Lawrence's desk, though none had even a single palm-press. Cubicle partitions divided the left rear one from the others, probably Alfred's, but the rest of the room was wide open.

Lawrence walked to one of the nearer desks, ran a thumb over a drawer lock, and grabbed the handle. "They're keyed to individual owners, but they're also all set to my prints. That way, if someone can't make it to work, their data isn't completely inaccessible." As he pulled open the drawer, he deliberately shut his eyes. Susan suspected that he worried he might find it empty.

She, on the other hand, could not look away. Though the drawer slid open easily, it seemed like ten minutes ticked past before Susan found herself staring at an ordinary palm-press. She grabbed it before Lawrence could move, placed it lightly on the table, and jammed the port key into place.

The confirmatory green light came on instantly. *Oh, thank God!* Both screens flickered, then an identical wash of indecipherable numbers, mostly zeroes, interspersed with a handful of letters and symbols filled them.

Lawrence sucked in a noisy breath, then let it out in a loud and filthy curse. Susan just stared at the screen, waiting for something comprehensible to materialize. She removed the port key from both portals, then cautiously replaced it, this time starting with the palm-press. The same wild wash of characters appeared.

Drawn by Lawrence's exclamation, Nate peered over Susan's shoulder. "Can you make sense of that?" she asked Lawrence. "Is it some kind of thing you can insert into circuitry?"

"The technical term is machine language. Used to be the next step up from hardware, before microcode, then picocode, processing became the norm. Before my time." Lawrence pounded his palm. "If I remember from my early programming classes, it's hex based."

Most of what Lawrence just said went over Susan's head. She referred him to their earlier conversation with Jake, when Lawrence had stated, "Ask ninety percent of people how a Vox works, and you'd get an evasive answer. The honest ones would admit they think it's magic." "You've triggered my 'technology is magic' quotient," she admitted. "Just tell me what we can do with this."

"That's just it." Lawrence clamped his hand to his head. "It would take an octogenarian programmer to begin to decipher this."

"Or a machine," Nate pointed out. "I've read that in its day, machine language was almost impossible for humans to comprehend, but computers used it exclusively. They couldn't function without it. The programmers used what they called assembly or high-level languages, such as Fortran and Pascal, and compilers translated it for—"

Lawrence's mouth fell open, then snapped shut. He whirled on Nate. "You can read this, can't you?"

Nate smiled. "Think of me as a fancy computer with thoughts and emotions."

"Never," Susan said, then changed her tune. "So, what does it say?"

Nate's grin wilted. "It doesn't work like that. It's not like a foreign language I can translate one-to-one into words. It's . . ." He shook his head in clear frustration. "If I could explain it, you wouldn't need my help. Get me a hard copy, a pen, and ten minutes to myself. I should be able to convert it into something useful to you."

Susan immediately hit the print screen shortcut.

Lawrence scooped up the palm-pross, still attached to Susan's Vox. "That'll print in my office." He headed back the way they had come, Susan and Nate trailing. They returned to find Jake and Kendall huddled in quiet conversation, the enormous printer spitting out several pages of number scrawl.

Nate grabbed the pages, dropped into Lawrence's chair as if he owned it, and set to work. "This is the exact same machine code John and I used to use to communicate privately."

Lawrence took the empty folding chair without missing a beat.

Nate's words seized Susan's attention, though. "What?"

"It started out as a game, a puzzle that required some extensive research into the history of computing. At the time, I didn't know John had a positronic brain, too. I thought he was testing me or helping me pass the time when I got consigned to menial jobs at the hospital." Nate tapped the back of the pen against his teeth. "It was our secret, like a boys' club, for want of a better description."

Secret. Susan processed that word. Clearly, John Calvin had intended, even required, Nate and her to figure out the riddle of the port key together. At the least, it required her Vox and Nate's experience. Even as he had lamented the time she dedicated to Nate, John Calvin had had the good sense to take advantage of it. If she added the need for his locked-up palm-pross to the mix, Susan realized he might have deliberately included Lawrence, too.

Lawrence seemed to be thinking along similar lines. "Good way to prevent anyone from hijacking the information." He paused, then added, "Unless, of course, they had an elderly engineer who used to program in Fortran."

"That would only obviate Nate," Susan pointed out. "They'd still need my Vox and your thumbprint."

Nate paused his writing again. "Fortran, Three-tran, Two-tran—wouldn't matter. Machine language isn't a singular entity; it varies between individual CPUs. It took John and me a long time to develop this particular form of machine language." He made another notation.

"Lacking my specific history, even a positronic robot would have trouble with this."

Lawrence examined his creation, and Susan wondered if Nate had grown in ways even he did not foresee. "How long have the two of you been working on this specialized machine code?"

"At least a decade." Nate slurred his words a bit, clearly dedicating most of his thought processes to the paper task.

That corroborated the probability John had done at least some preparation long before the SFH discovered his connection to Calvin.

"Got it!" Nate announced suddenly. He looked over his handiwork and frowned. "At least, I thought I had it. The machine language made more sense to me than this."

"Let me see." Susan reached out a hand, and Nate passed along the last page. He had consolidated the end result on the back:

JQJRY, FMX FMSXX VRKJ RSX ASSXBXSJAGVL AYFSAYJAI FZ
FMX WZJAFSZYAI GSRAY. FMXSX AJ YZF RYT MRJ YXBXS GXXY
R IZTX FZ QYIZQWVX FMXD. DL VZBX NZS LZQ MRJ RVKRLJ
GXXY RJ IVXRS RYT WQSX RJ RYL NRFMXS IZQVT MRBX NJS
MAJ TRQCMFXS. YXBXS NZSCXF LZQ KXSX DL XBXSLFMAYC.

Susan studied it a moment in consternation, then started to laugh.

Lawrence also examined the paper. "What's so funny, Susan? It still doesn't make a lick of sense."

"Yes it does," Susan said, reaching for Nate's pen. "Or it will in about fifteen minutes." She explained, "It's a code within a code, but this one's a simple substitution." Susan remembered winter nights in front of the fire, working the daily Vox-news cryptogram. "It wouldn't trip up the feds, of course; that's what the machine language was for."

Lawrence took the paper in order to study the letters more closely.

"If someone did manage to work out the machine code, or got Nate to do it for them, they might see this and think they must have made a mistake."

Susan supposed that was the real reason John had done what he did, but she silently hoped those lazy winter evenings had meant as much to him as they had to her. He had slipped it in, Susan believed, specifically for her.

"Do you want to work on this together?"

"It's faster if I work alone. My father and I used to race to see who could finish the cryptogram first. I always did, but now I'm wondering if he let me. In any case, the surgical attending on my med-school rotation considered himself a cryptogram pro, too. He rarely beat me."

Susan sat down, pen in hand. She had barely started when the loud buzz of a Vox sounded. From habit, she glanced around, found her Vox, still connected to the palm-pross, and pulled it free. Realization followed a moment later. *My Vox is active.*

"Oh no, Susan. No." Jake's voice was filled with pain and admonishment. "How long has that been on?"

Abruptly realizing the problem, Susan stabbed off her Vox and reattached it to her wrist. "I . . . don't remember turning it on." Desperately, she thought back, certain she had not done it from unthinking habit.

Lawrence had the answer. "The Vox automatically turns on whenever you plug in a device. Like a port key."

Jake stood up. His words sounded strained, and he emphasized each one. "How . . . long?"

No one answered.

"Susan! How long?"

His desperation felt like a lash. Susan's heart rate quickened, and her throat tightened. *My stupidity's going to get us all killed.* "I—I'm not sure."

"Twenty minutes," Lawrence estimated. "Twenty-five. Why?"

Jake started looking in all directions, like a cornered rat. He stepped back into the deepest shadows of the corner. "A live Vox is a trackable Vox, and Cadmium has that technology. *They know exactly where we are.*"

Cued by Jake, Kendall also stood up.

"It's all right." Displacing Nate, Lawrence retook his place behind his desk, speaking softly, as if to a hysterical child. "You're in one of the most secure places in Manhattan. The front locks require simultaneous thumb and retina scanning. A year ago, SFH hit us with a bomb blast that barely burned the edges."

Susan had been at the scene when the bomb exploded. The schizophrenic who detonated it had stood on a bus a significant distance from the building. She was not so sure it could stand a direct hit. *They need me alive. They're not going to bomb us.* Even as the idea soothed, another sent her heart racing even faster. "They know how to disable thumbprint locks."

The voice of reassurance came from an unexpected place. Jake relaxed a bit. "Retinal scanners are something altogether different. With current technology, it's impossible to get around them."

Susan breathed a sigh of relief, struck by another abrupt and terrible thought. She choked off the exhalation midbreath. "Unless you've procured an eye that's tuned to the scanner. A disembodied eye . . . from a head . . . no longer attached to its body."

As if on cue, the office door slammed open to reveal two men in black silk suits, weapons drawn. "Freeze! Federal agents. Anyone moves, they die."

The room went as still and silent as a tomb, aside from the faint hum of the air-conditioning.

Terror crushed down on Susan. She could not even breathe.

Both of the intruders stood about six feet tall, sinewy and competent, their faces expressionless, but there all similarity ended. The older one had a beefy face with white hair cut functionally short, piercing blue eyes, and a wicked-looking scar that cut his right cheek in the shape of a letter Y. The younger had black hair hanging in an uneven fringe, eyes like chips of coal, and thin lips that seemed to disappear into a permanent sneer.

The older one spoke first. "Pat them down. Start with the redhead." He gestured at Kendall with a sparse movement of his head that never disrupted the steadiness of his hand. Though some distance separated the occupants of the room, his eyes seemed to focus tightly on each and every one. "I'll kill the cop."

Before the words could even register in Susan's ears, Jake moved, twisting, grabbing for his gun, too late. The roar of the fed's pistol in the confines of the office seemed to tear Susan's hearing apart. A hole appeared in the middle of Jake's forehead, and he collapsed wordlessly. His head smacked the floor with a solid thud, audible even through the agonized ringing in Susan's ears. He lay still, blood pooling beneath his head, the momentum of his last movement sending his gun flying, spinning, to land at Nate's feet.

A scream followed. For an instant, Susan thought it came from her own throat, but she found herself incapable of even that much action. Relieved of the gun Jake had given him, now in the younger fed's pocket, Kendall charged to Jake's side, heedless of any warnings.

No! Susan wanted to yell, but found herself unable to work her vocal cords. Panic squeezed them desperately closed, and it took strength of will just to suck air in and out of her lungs. She cringed for the second shot, certain Kendall's instinctive need to heal would be his last action in life.

But the older man only laughed, then commanded, "Robot, pick up the gun and keep it secure."

Constrained by the Second Law, Nate obeyed, gripping the pistol by its slide, with the barrel pointed at the ground. He looked as shaken as the rest of them. A whimper escaped him, and he looked to Lawrence Robertson for guidance. Standing behind the desk, hands in the air while the second thug frisked him, Lawrence could do nothing to assist anyone.

Susan did not worry for Nate. Cadmium clearly knew what he was, which put him in far less danger than the humans around him.

Kendall seemed to take no notice of anything but Jake. "He's dead," he sobbed. "You killed him." He cradled the bleeding head in his lap, tearing his own shirt and clamping it to the exit wound at the back of the detective's head. His actions contradicted his proclamation. If Jake was indeed dead, why would Kendall bother to put pressure on the wound, to stem the flow of blood? For an instant, Susan dared to hope against all odds. She could not remember the last time she had seen so much blood at once, and she knew the statistics for gunshot wounds of the head. *Ninety to ninety-five percent fatal.* It occurred to Susan that Kendall's treatment of the hopeless wound was probably as mindless as his mad rush to assist a fallen companion, oblivious to the personal danger. Bright red blood and tears smeared Kendall's hands and face. "You bastards," he screamed. "You killed him!"

Apparently untouched by the doctor's display, Scarface aimed his weapon at Lawrence Robertson. "Susan Calvin, you have ten seconds to tell me the code before I blow his head off, too."

The second agent took three large steps away from Lawrence. The scientist stood with eyes wide, his pupils so dilated they impinged on his irises. His nostrils flared, sucking in vast gulps of air. His lips stretched taut, his eyebrows drew together, and beads of sweat spangled his philtrum.

"Wait!" Lawrence shouted.

The lead agent started counting, "One . . . Two . . ."

Susan forced herself to lock down panic. She had exactly eight seconds to think of something. Her hands felt like ice cubes, and a stream of sweat trickled along her spine.

". . . Three . . ."

Susan considered having Nate throw her Jake's gun, but quickly discarded the idea. By the time she received it, righted it, and figured out how to use it, they would have shot Lawrence, Kendall, and maybe her as well.

". . . Four . . ."

Susan looked at the cryptogram on the desk from the most distant corner of her eye, careful not to cue the gunman to its significance. *Could I gain some time talking him into letting me work on it?* Again, Susan discarded the idea. Once they saw the simplicity of the substitution code, which she had already started, they would have no reason to keep anyone alive.

". . . Five . . ."

Wetness appeared at the front of Lawrence's pants. She knew nothing of his medical history, but she worried about the stress of massively elevated blood pressure on the heart of a middle-aged man.

". . . Six . . ."

It's all up to me. Susan realized this time she had no Remington to drape himself across the bomb, no Jake to cover her with crossfire. She had weathered more than a few code blues. When the call shrilled over Vox and speakers, everyone ran to assist. The calmest, quickest-thinking physician became the leader, the one deciding treatment. More often than not, Susan found the other residents, the nurses and support staff, deferring to her.

". . . Seven . . ."

The numbers came in slow motion as Susan's mind clicked. The fog gradually lifted from her thoughts. The ringing disappeared from her ears.

"Susan," Lawrence croaked, his voice sounding as dry as hers felt. "For God's sake, tell them whatever they want to know."

". . . Eight . . ."

"All right," Susan yelled hoarsely. To her surprise, the sound barely emerged.

The counting stopped. "You've got two seconds left, Susan Calvin. Start talking." Pistol steady in his right hand, he used his left to tap buttons on his Vox.

Certain he was now recording anything she said, Susan considered extracting promises about sparing her companions' lives, but she knew such vows meant nothing to the man who had shot a peace officer in cold blood. He would have no qualms about agreeing to anything, then doing just as he pleased. She licked her lips, seeking a deep reserve of saliva, then forced out words from a throat gone raw. "Give me a chance to think, to find my voice."

"You have two seconds," he reminded.

"Okay." Susan appreciated he had not ticked those off in the time it took her to acquiesce to his demands. She realized he had no means to test the validity of her claim. She glanced at Kendall, still sobbing over Jake's damaged head. Nate stood stock-still. Lawrence trembled visibly. "This is the code you're seeking." Susan rolled her gaze toward the ceiling, as if recalling something deeply inscribed in memory.

The older agent watched her intently, while the younger one kept his weapon trained on Kendall. Neither bothered to guard Nate; they knew they did not need to.

Susan spoke with exaggerated deliberateness, articulating every syllable. "B-X-2 . . ."

Even the hum of the air conditioner disappeared. Every ear locked on Susan's voice. "8-T-J-6-3-F-F-R-1-0." At random, she stopped.

Scarface grinned. His weapon never wavered. "That's the code, is it?"

"It is," Susan said.

"Repeat it, then. Exactly the same way."

Susan almost swallowed her tongue. She could not accurately repeat a string of letters and numbers that long on a good day. With her thoughts scattered, she had little chance of coming close. Worse, he had her recorded for accuracy, and she could not even recall the first letter.

"Miss a single character, and someone dies. Then we start all over at a one count."

Hopelessness descended on Susan. She wished her own heart would just stop beating. Then a new thought came to her. She raised her head, looked Scarface in his brilliant blue eyes. And smiled.

Chapter 22

S usan Calvin knew she had to play this perfectly; there was no room for mistakes, no second chances. The continued existence of every living creature in the room, including Nate, depended on a lethal game of bluff and counter. Cadmium had the advantage when it came to matters of intestinal fortitude and mettle, deadly force, firearms, and tactics. Scarface had a leg up when it came to experience; he knew bluster when he saw it. But Susan came with her own set of abilities. She knew the human mind, even at its sickest and most dangerous, how to express and hide emotion, and how to read people.

The older of the agents fairly growled. "I said, repeat the code, Susan Calvin. Do it. Now!"

The grin remained a fixture on Susan's features. She continued to meet his gaze with the fanaticism and fearlessness of a predator. "I could do that," she said. "I've known it as long and well as my own name. Dad and I recited it every night before we went to sleep, like clockwork, instead of evening prayers." The saliva had returned to her mouth. She spoke easily, evenly, banishing terror to the farthest reaches of her subconscious. Never again would she give him the satisfaction of cowing her. One way or the other, this ended now. "I could recite it like others do a family credo, backward or forward, standing on my head." She deliberately slid her gaze to Nate, who stood behind and to the side of the agent, as if the presence of the pistol no longer interested her, and the man in front of her meant nothing. "But I don't have to."

A hint of expression slid across Scarface's features, not yet readable, but encouraging merely for its presence. He was not discarding her claim out of hand. "What are you babbling about?"

"The instant I spoke that code, I uncoupled Nate from the Three Laws of Robotics. He's no longer bound by any of them, most especially the one that forbids him from injuring a human being."

"That's a lie!" The barrel of his gun moved from Lawrence to Susan. "It's not how a code works; it has to be programmed!"

A knot formed in Susan's stomach. She had to force herself not to react, to envision the weapon as a wilted flower. "At this precise moment, Nate's pointing the gun at your back. If either of you does anything other than drop your weapon harmlessly to the floor, he's going to shoot to kill. Right, Nate?"

"Exactly right." Nate played along, as Susan knew he would. "Eye sensors working perfectly. Identify twenty-seven single-shot lethal foci on target one. Thirty on target two."

"Nate's an upgrade from John," Susan lied. "From the autopsy of the body, it took SFH more than twenty shots just to bring him down." She imagined Cadmium had counted the holes in John Calvin's head, and it had surely taken far more than one to render the positronic brain inoperable. "Weaponless and with the Three Laws intact." She kept her tone casual. "How many bullets does your gun hold?"

Susan knew the agent would get the point, that a shootout with Nate was wholly one-sided. A medically trained robot, Nate would know how to disable with a single shot.

Scarface blinked but remained in place, the gun still trained on Susan. "You're lying. That wasn't the real code. That thing's still constrained by the Three Laws."

Susan ignored him, her grin drawing into a rictus. "And the best part is, you armed him. You have three seconds, Cadmium. If your guns aren't on the floor before I get to three, Nate shoots one of you. He can choose, but I'm recommending you." She did not pause any longer than he had before counting. "One . . ."

His eyes impaled her, reading every microfeature of her face, the set of her brows, the width of her pupils, the flare of each nostril. She felt violated, as if he could see into every corner and crevice of her thoughts.

Susan did not allow herself to break. *Contempt,* she reminded herself. *Not fear. Never fear. Not a hint of uncertainty or doubt.* She raised her chin fiercely. One corner of her lips winched downward, leaving the other in a contemptuous sneer. She tried to make her stare at least equally cutting. "Two . . ."

The younger agent dropped his gun. It clattered to the office floor as he explained, "Mike, the safety's off. He's got the laser on your back."

The moment of truth hinged on Scarface's nerve, the man his partner had identified as Mike. Susan tried to understand the younger agent's point. From the directions Jake had given Kendall—just point and shoot—she guessed the safety was housed in the trigger and ganged to the red-dot sight. Clearly, Nate had gone as far as putting his finger on it hard enough to disengage the safety, and he trusted his nerves not to flinch or spasm. Only he and Susan knew for certain he could never actually fire.

Susan gathered breath for the final number. She dared not hesitate or waver, could not allow the slightest emotion or cue to betray her uncertainty. She opened her mouth and said, "Three!"

Even as she spoke, the gun was falling.

Relief flooded Susan. Her limbs felt like water, but she kept her features well schooled, her manner casual. She did not want him to think, for even a moment, she had considered the possibility of any other outcome. "Now both of you. Keep your hands where I can see them. *Carefully*"–she overemphasized the word–"kick the guns to me." She glanced past Mike to Nate.

The robot was struggling to keep his expression as bland as Susan's, an irony that reached her even through the myriad other thoughts racing through her mind. She had put him in a horrible position. Luckily, only the less experienced of the agents could see his face to read it.

Cadmium did as Susan instructed. One after the other, their guns slid across the floor toward Susan. Her eyes never left Mike as she crouched to scoop one up, making certain to choose his. Since he had already fired a shot, there was no question of a round in the chamber. It was armed and ready to go.

The federal agents kept their hands in front of them, palms up. Mike's unsettling eyes continued to penetrate Susan. "Now that you're in charge, tell the truth. Could he really have pulled the trigger?"

Susan knew better than to abandon the lie. She currently had the upper hand, but he had all the experience, all the training. She wondered what he would do if he knew he had been within five minutes of having the real code, the one contained in a simple cryptogram. "I assure you, he still can. And he knows the location of every organ, muscle, bone, and major vessel in your body." She glowered at him. "Now, you tell me . . . Mike. Is that really what you want? Ruthless robotic killing machines without a modicum of morality to guide them?"

Despite his position, Mike's grin was positively evil. "You've described the perfect soldier. Isn't that better than arming frightened boys and sending them into combat?"

The gun had spent enough time in Mike's hand to feel hot in Susan's grip. She could almost imagine it burning her fingers. She had never held a firearm before, did not expect it to feel so heavy and solid, nor to mold so easily into her smaller hand. "Lawrence, call 911."

"Alarm's already triggered," Lawrence shot back. "Calling."

Susan squatted and reached to secure the loose weapon, still lying on the floor.

Abruptly, Mike collapsed, rolling.

For an instant, Susan thought he'd had a heart attack. Her medical training kicked to the fore, and with it, the professionalism and composure that characterized her medical rotations. As she grew hypervigilant, the world seemed to move through Jell-O, each movement densely slowed, her every option easily considered. As Mike went sideways, she registered the motions of his hands, his left drawing up his pant leg, his right grabbing for the opposite ankle.

An image flashed through Susan's mind: Jake making a similar motion, pulling his backup pistol from an ankle holster in order to hand it to Kendall. Awkwardly, Susan's finger went to her trigger. Her right arm snapped up, the left still outstretched toward the second gun.

She was at her medical-school graduation, reciting the Hippocratic oath with her classmates, engraving its key provision forever on her heart and mind: "*I will do no harm to anyone.*" It brought to the fore another adage she had subscribed to her entire life without consciously knowing it. Through the way he lived his life, through the lessons he imparted, through his every action, John Calvin had passed the most intrinsic knowledge of his creation to his daughter: "*A robot may not injure a human being or, through inaction, allow a human being to come to harm.*"

The first phrase paralyzed her, but the second saved her: "May not . . . through inaction, allow a human being to come to harm."

Mike's backup gun came up, aimed directly for Susan. There would be no counting this time.

I'm a human being. Gritting her teeth, Susan pulled the trigger. The report slammed her ears with raw agony. She did not anticipate the recoil. It was only a mild pull, but wholly unexpected. Startled, she jerked crazily. And that, combined with her already tenuous position, dropped her to her buttocks. She heard the crack of Mike's gun an instant afterward, muffled by the intense ringing in her ears. The shot pinged high off the wall behind her. He had apparently expected her to rise.

Susan's shot had no obvious effect, either. *Missed him, damn it!* Shooting wildly, devoid of any training, she wondered if she had even fired into the same room. Another thought occurred to her then: *Bulletproof vest?* Panic swam down on her again, and she lost the composure that had kept her mind ahead of the quickest action. Time returned to normal speed. Her finger spasmed on the trigger before she could think to retreat, to take another shot, but she did have the presence of mind to shift her aim for his head.

The roar of gunshots seemed to come from several directions at once, including her own hand. She could hear Kendall shouting, and only then remembered the second federal agent, the one Nate could threaten but never actually shoot. Even if the agent did not carry a secondary weapon, Susan remembered he had previously confiscated the one Kendall had been using. He was armed and definitely dangerous, but she dared not take her eyes from Mike.

A moving target is a difficult target. Susan attempted to gather her feet under her. Her heel struck the pistol she had reached for, still on the ground, and she tumbled back to the floor. For the second time, an awkward misstep probably saved her life. Something hit the floor directly in front of Susan, pelting her with chips of linoleum. Almost simultaneously, Mike clutched his throat with his support hand.

I got him! Susan scrambled to her feet.

Mike managed to squeeze off one more wild shot that came nowhere near his target; then the gun fell from his hand and he gripped his neck in what Susan immediately recognized as the universal sign of a victim choking. Her first impulse, to run toward him and administer the Heimlich maneuver, passed quickly. Even if she dared, it would do nothing to help him.

Mike's head sank forward over his clutching fingers; then he whirled violently and dropped to his knees, gagging, sucking noisily, frantic to catch a breath that was never going to come. It went against everything in Susan's nature, everything in her training, to do nothing to assist a man in such clear and evident agony. Too seasoned to vomit, too frantic to cry, she could only watch in horror, unable to tear her gaze away. Her mind went to a clinical place where she put the symptoms together.

The human neck was a crowded place, perhaps the only one with so many vital structures in so small an area. The bullet had clearly torn the larynx or trachea. Assuming it missed the carotid arteries, the jugular veins, and all the cervical vertebrae, the emergent placement of an endotracheal tube, accompanied by the rhythmic injection of oxygen, could keep him going until an ambulance arrived. But Susan did not have any of the necessary tools. In the same situation, she could not have saved her own mother. But she did not have to watch him die.

Still clutching the pistol, now in both trembling hands, Susan turned to where she had last seen the second member of the Cadmium team. He was struggling viciously, Nate clamped to his gun arm and a shirtless Kendall wrapped around his legs like a football tackle. The fed had squeezed off at least two shots, both wild. Holes in the ceiling revealed where they had penetrated, and a whitewash of mineral fibers coated all three men.

Susan came as close as she dared. "Be still," she said.

The tussle continued. No one even seemed to notice her.

Added to the events of the past several minutes, that one simple snub threw Susan over the edge. Purposefully, she leveled the pistol at the agent's face, making absolutely sure he saw it. "Drop the gun!" she hollered.

The stranger's dark eyes widened. He ceased struggling, and the pistol fell from his upraised fist. Nate kept his hands clamped to the man's arm, allowing the gun to fall unceremoniously to the floor.

"You killed a good man, a friend." The realization filled Susan with a grief she had put on hold for far too long. Again, a much stronger emotion flared to a bonfire inside her, banishing sorrow. "You made me shoot someone! You turned me into a killer wholly against my will, and that *pisses me off*!"

"Susan," Kendall started.

Susan ignored him. Her hands were visibly trembling now, the gun pulsating in time to her movements. She knew better than to loop a finger in the trigger, even for show; she could not trust her own digits to obey her. "Keep your hands in the air, Goddamn it. Don't make me shoot you, too."

Kendall tried again, "Susan . . ."

Susan interrupted him; she didn't care what anyone had to say. "Kendall, check his pocket. He still has the gun Jake gave you."

"That's the one he was using. On the floor."

"Then check his left ankle. That seems to be the law enforcement go-to backup spot."

Kendall knelt at the man's feet, hiked up his pant leg, and freed a pistol from a holster lashed to the ankle. The doctor rose, pointing the spare at the agent.

With Kendall covering, Susan scooped up the weapon on the floor, Jake's backup, the one he had given to Kendall. Tears flooded Susan's eyes, obscuring her vision. She crammed the gun into her pocket, then wiped the tears away fiercely. Now was not the time to soften. "Now get over there, Cadmium. Sit in that damned chair and don't do anything until the cops get here." She pointed to one of the foldables, still in its place across from Lawrence's desk.

Lawrence was still talking into his Vox, attempting to describe the scene.

Nate finally released his death grip on the federal agent's arm. Kendall continued to back up Susan. They both covered the man as they walked him to the indicated seat and watched him drop resignedly into it.

Suddenly, shots erupted behind Susan. Her heart rate tripled in an instant, and she loosed an unintentional scream. Whirling, legs tensed to the point of pain, she saw what looked like a zombie firing round after round into Mike's unmoving body. Susan screamed again.

The gunshots stopped, and the creature looked up. It was Jake, the hole still visible in his forehead, dried rivulets of scarlet running from the back of his head to both ears, crusted clots clinging to his hair. The gun in his hand was Mike's backup. Susan had never bothered to collect it from the floor.

"Jake." Her own gun forgotten in her hand, Susan lowered her arms. The fight left her, replaced by relieved disbelief.

Kendall threw his arms up. "That's what I've been trying to tell you."

"How . . . ?" Susan started and stopped. "How . . . How can that be?" Kendall's ministrations would have kept Jake from bleeding out, but even with that assistance, a shot through the brain should have put him down until the neurosurgeons pieced him back together, assuming they even could.

For an instant, Susan and Kendall were back on common ground, two medical residents discussing an interesting case in a hospital corridor. "The projectile hit here." Kendall tapped the proper spot on this forehead. "Handgun, which means low velocity for a gunshot wound. It must have hit skull and deflected upward, tracing the line of the skull along the periosteum."

Susan caught on. "He must have had his head tilted slightly upward. When it got to the hairline, it tore through the scalp, leaving an ugly mess, then went out the back." She cringed. "Man, that's gotta hurt." She considered. "But it shouldn't have put him out, at least not this long."

Kendall nodded. "My theory is he banged his head on the floor when he fell."

In a charting room, surrounded only by health-care professionals, Susan might have laughed. "Shot through the head, no problem. It's the bump on the noggin that—"

Lawrence shouted.

Another gunshot exploded. Susan's heart seemed to fly out of her chest, and she gasped for breath. A flash of heat suffused her.

Two more gunshots followed, and the no-longer-living agent toppled limply from his chair. Once again, Susan heard the heavy clatter of a gun hitting the floor. Eyes wide with terror, she whirled toward Jake in time to see him rush past her and stand over the crumpled agent.

Lawrence was on his feet. "He had a gun! I think he pulled it out of his underpants!"

Jake fired several more times into the corpse.

Susan found herself on the floor without intending to move, arms protectively over her head. "Have you gone stark raving mad?" It struck her suddenly that brain trauma could have addled him, making Jake dangerously unpredictable. And armed. "Why are you shooting dead people?"

Jake continued to stare at the body, but he did not fire again. "I wake up with no idea how long I've been out. There are unsecured weapons on the floor. You've got your backs to a guy who's down but made it abundantly clear he won't hesitate to kill. And there's a pistol still in his reach." He made a gesture as if what he said explained everything. "As close-quarter combat expert Pat Rogers used to say: 'When in doubt,

NSR the'"—he hesitated just long enough to make it clear he substituted for an unsuitable word—"guy."

"What does that *mean?*" Kendall demanded.

Jake tried to explain. "Nonstandard response. Two shots to the chest is a standard response . . ." He regrouped. "Okay. Roughly translated, it means anyone worth shooting once is worth shooting seven times. Just to be sure."

"But he's *dead!*" Susan emphasized.

"Maybe. Maybe not." Jake pointed out. "You thought I was dead, too. If I was on the other side, I'd have had all of you." He snatched up the gun that had fallen from the agent's hand.

He was right, Susan realized, and that sent a chill spiraling through her entire body. "There is a difference. A doctor whose judgment I *used to* trust declared you dead."

Kendall went on the defensive. "What did you want me to do? Yell, 'Thank God he's still alive?' They'd have . . . NSRed him."

Susan could not believe Kendall still did not realize how recklessly he had acted. "Kendall, after being told anyone who moved would have his head blown off, after seeing them carry out that threat, you charged across the room and started hollering. It's a miracle they didn't NSR *you!*"

Lawrence's Vox buzzed, and he poked it on. "Hello?" He paused a moment, listening. "This is Dr. Lawrence Robertson, CEO and founder of United States Robots and Mechanical Men." He listened again, then said, "A cop? Yeah, he's right here." He looked up. "Jake, it's the emergency rescue team. They want to talk to you personally."

Jake lowered his head, putting his wound on full display. Susan found herself wanting to examine it, to probe it, to calculate the extent of soft-tissue damage. He was not out of the woods yet. The impact of the round, or of the floor, might have caused a skull fracture or produced an intracranial bleed that could still take him down. Prolonged unconsciousness, whatever the root cause, was never a good sign. "Put it on conference," Jake instructed. He gestured for everyone to keep quiet.

Lawrence tapped the appropriate button, then nodded at Jake.

"Detective Carson, Manhattan South Homicide."

A strong male voice came over the line, his accent thick and Brooklyn. He sounded direct, almost accusatory. "What's your tax registry number?"

Susan kept her attention glued to Jake. She knew next to nothing about police procedure, but anything to do with taxes seemed like an odd thing to request.

Jake, on the other hand, didn't bat an eye. "It's 1138786."

The voice over the Vox was muffled, clearly not intended for Jake, but Susan could still make out the words, "Hey, Tiffy. Get the Wheel to run his tax registry number."

A silent moment passed, then the voice returned, much softened. "It's Boomer, Jake. Give me the SITREP."

Jake almost smiled. He clearly recognized the name.

"Two perps, both down. Four civilians, no apparent injuries at this time. I'm shot in the head."

Another short pause, then, "Jake, confirm. All perps dead? No one outstanding?"

"Ten-four. Two perps, both down, apparently DRT."

"You were shot in the head?" There was actual concern in Boomer's voice, which surprised Susan. It was also the most comprehensible thing she had ever heard spoken in a conversation between officers.

Jake's hand went instinctively to the top of his head. He touched it, winced, and immediately removed the offending hand. He said softly, almost plaintively, "Yeah . . ."

For an instant, he was a lost and frightened child appealing to his father. An urge seized Susan to cradle and protect him.

"We'll have a medic standing by. Where are you located? Are you in the main office?"

"I think so." Regaining his composure, Jake glanced at Lawrence, who nodded confirmation. "Roger, main office," Jake repeated with more assurance. "Retinal-scan security on all doors. Will you let me open the front for you?"

Susan could hear voices conferring, but nothing coherent. Jake waited patiently for Boomer to return.

"Jake, we'll be entering via opened front door in exactly two minutes. Push it open and step back. Make sure everyone is facedown, arms outstretched, no weapons nearby. Copy?"

"Copy." Jake looked around the room, at everyone in it intently staring at him. "Give me an extra thirty seconds to explain and secure." He made a motion indicating everyone should get on the floor.

Susan could scarcely believe it, but she lowered herself to the linoleum in silence. They were still on conference mode, and she did not want to say anything that might change the dynamics of the situation.

"Roger, Jake."

"I'll meet you at the door in two and a half. K."

"Copy that."

Jake motioned for Lawrence to disconnect, then addressed the group.

Kendall asked the question on every mind. "Am I to understand they want *us* on the floor? Facedown?" It sounded like madness. "Are you sure you're dealing with the good guys?"

Jake became all professional. "Standard operating procedure. They need to treat the scene as unsecured. They don't know any of you, and they're not going to take any chances." He pointed to the top of Lawrence's desk. "I'm going to need every single firearm. If you forget and have one on your person, you're probably going to die."

Susan never saw a group of people scramble so fast, including herself. In a moment, a pile of seven pistols lay on the desktop. Jake checked the two belonging to him and replaced them in their holsters. The cryptogram caught her eye, and Susan grabbed the paper, folded it, and stuffed it into her pocket.

Susan searched out a location away from the bodies where she would not accidentally become contaminated with blood. One by one, Susan and her companions lay facedown on the floor, arms outstretched. And waited.

Chapter 23

Susan approached Jake's hospital room on the Neurosurgery Unit, abruptly seized by a sense of almost incapacitating grief and foreboding that seemed far out of proportion to the reality of the situation. She paused to consider, and a picture filled her mind's eye: a muscular dark blond with melting green eyes, dressed in surgical scrubs stained with Surgiprep, walked toward her down precisely this same corridor. *Neurosurgery. Remington.* She felt as if she had fallen into a black hole of heartache and wondered how she had managed to come this far into Remington's old territory before it overwhelmed her.

Exhaustion was the only logical explanation. The emergency rescue team had cuffed her, searched her, and questioned her in private. Next, they had brought everyone together, except Jake, whom they transported directly to the hospital. They were soon uncuffed and their belongings returned, and they were plied with goodwill and snacks. And the questioning resumed.

When the emergency response team had finished with Lawrence and Nate, another group of law enforcement officers escorted Susan and Kendall to the Ninth Precinct. Again, the two of them were separated, and Susan spent hours answering more questions that went back nearly as far as she could remember. The days and incidents blurred together and, after a while, she thought she might understand how

Jake had felt upon awakening from trauma. Her head ached as if someone had clamped it in a vise that slowly tightened in maddening increments. Her skull seemed almost ready to explode.

When they finally released her, Susan went straight to the hospital, and now directly to Jake Carson's room. Without knocking, she pushed open the door.

Kendall's voice wafted to her. ". . . Should have seen it. Susan was brilliant. I thought the guy was going to–" Apparently catching sight of Susan, he fell silent.

The first thing that caught Susan's gaze was a bedside screen with multiple images from a head CT. As if in a trance, she walked to it, scrolling through the pictures, examining each one intently.

Gradually, Susan became aware of voices behind her. ". . . Doesn't even know we exist."

Reluctantly, Susan peeled her gaze away from the scan to place it on Jake and Kendall. The detective sat up in bed. A bandage enwrapped his head, but he otherwise looked fresh as a daisy.

The enormous bags under Kendall's eyes suggested he had come straight to the room after the questioning as well. Someone had supplied him with a faded and well-worn T-shirt, probably from the lost and found, to replace the one he had ruined to tend to Jake's wound. Apparently, the police had released him earlier than Susan.

Kendall stood up and held out his arms. "Ah, Susan. So you've remembered there are other human beings in the room."

"Sorry." Susan had not wholly realized what she was doing. She stumbled into Kendall's arms and allowed him to do most of the embracing. "Had to see it with my own eyes."

Kendall had apparently studied the scan, too, though she suspected he had had the politeness to greet Jake first. "Amazing, isn't it? The bullet carved a perfect path between the galea aponeurotica and the periosteum."

"In English," Jake demanded, just as Kendall had done when he slipped into what Susan now referred to as cop talk.

Susan finally looked at Jake. "It means you have a hard head."

Kendall chuckled. "You're starting to sound more and more like me every day."

Susan found herself on her feet and moving back to the CT scan without thinking. Now that she had dispensed with the social necessities, she wanted a more complete look, especially at the parts she had not yet seen when Kendall pointed out her rudeness. She scrolled down to the lower images, ones that no longer showed the soft-tissue injury. "There it is."

Kendall looked up. "There what is?"

"Skull fracture."

Kendall hopped up, came beside her, and peered at the CT. "That's not even where he got shot."

"Of course not. It's where he banged his head on the floor. Small, linear, and only partial thickness, but it's definitely there."

"Son of a—" Kendall started and stopped. "You're doing it again, Susan."

Reluctantly, Susan took her focus from the scan to look at Kendall. "What are you talking about?"

"I mean, it's not even on the damned report! The radiologists missed it. Then you trot in and spot it in a New York minute."

"It was hardly a minute." Susan shrugged. "And it's not a clinically significant finding. It doesn't need any treatment. The only hemorrhage is here." She scrolled back to the area of the gunshot, outside the confines of the skull. "In the subgaleal plane, but the scalp always bleeds like stink."

Kendall refused to let go. "Susan, my point is, your powers of observation border on the spooky when it comes to medical issues."

Susan glared at him, not wanting to restart the argument from days earlier. "Well, I make up for it by being clueless about virtually every-thing else."

Jake broke in. "You know, you're talking about my gourd here. I'd kind of like to know what you're saying."

Kendall spoke to the patient over his shoulder. "We're saying it looks remarkably good. You were really lucky."

"Skull fracture?" Jake reminded.

"Insignificant." Susan looked back at the CT. She had seen it all now, but it still fascinated her.

"So, when can I get out of here?"

Susan stepped back so she could see Jake around her fellow resi-dent. "It's not up to us, Jake. You're on the Neurosurgical service. But I'm guessing they'll want to keep you a few days."

"A few days?" Jake repeated. "Why? Don't they need the bed for sick people? Now that they've pumped in a few pain meds and sewed up my scalp, I feel fine."

"You weren't struck in the head with a marshmallow." Susan rolled her eyes. "Delayed traumatic intracerebral hemorrhages can occur in people with perfectly normal initial CT scans."

Kendall took pity on him. "She's saying there's still a small, but not entirely trivial, risk for your gourd to leak."

Susan continued, "If it happens outside a tertiary-care setting, there's a fifty percent mortality rate and a high likelihood of major neurological sequelae even if you survive."

Again Kendall translated. "She's saying if it happens here, Neuro-surg can probably fix it. If it happens at home, there's a high probabil-ity you'll either die or become . . ." He struggled for wording, trying to strike a proper balance between offensiveness and humor.

Susan did not wait for him to find it. "Jake, if something happened to you because of a rush to discharge, I couldn't live with myself."

Kendall complied one more time. "She's saying she likes you."

Jake jumped in, "I think I got that one. Thanks, Kendall."

Kendall's tone changed from light to accusatory, "So, what's your hurry to get out of Hotel Hasbro, anyway? You so much of an adrenaline junkie you can't wait to get back on the streets with a gun in your hand?"

Susan could not help staring. It was out of character for Kendall, who usually took things in stride and used humor to cover everything remotely uncomfortable. She had only seen him so confrontational twice before: the first time when she suggested he might be gay, the second a moment ago when they were reading the CT scan together. She wrestled with the pattern, seeking the common feature that served as Kendall's trigger.

Jake sank into the bed. For a spare instant, Susan got the impression he might cry, but it passed so quickly she discarded the possibility. "This has nothing to do with my job. Assuming I still have one, they won't let me back on the streets, especially with a gun, for a very long time."

That jarred Susan from her psychoanalysis of Kendall. "What? That's stupid. I can't think of anyone I'd rather have protecting people than you. You're a hero, Jake."

Jake ignored the praise. "I'm what's known in the trade as a shit magnet. Something about me makes people want to shoot me, and that's not a liability any police department wants or needs."

Susan sat back down in her vacated chair. "But they weren't shooting at you. They were shooting at me! That makes me the"—Susan tried to avoid cursing, so she subbed in the medical term—"stool magnet."

Jake did not seem to expect that to help. "Maybe if you explained that to my supervisors, but I doubt it. I was involved in four shoot-outs in three days. That's probably a record. Plus, I killed other law enforcement officers. That's . . ." He tipped his bandaged head, seeking words strong enough to get his point across. Instead, he finished lamely. ". . . very bad."

Susan refused to consider the last point, aware that one of those law enforcement officers had died at her hands. She did not want to contemplate having killed anyone, especially not one who put his life on the line for the safety and security of the United States and its citizens.

Kendall seemed even more agitated. "Doctors have a name for a similar phenomenon. When all the disasters and codes seem to come in whenever a particular resident is on call, we say he or she has a black cloud. But we consider them lucky; they get all the best experience."

Jake shrugged, as if none of it mattered, but he was not fooling Susan. Police work defined Jake; he was a cop first and a man a distant second. She did not know if anything came third. "Maybe my superiors will see it that way, too. Best-case scenario, I spend several weeks disarmed and suspended, then several months on the rubber-gun squad. When it all gets sorted out, they reassign me."

Concerned about elevating Jake's blood and intracranial pressure, possibly contributing to a bleed, Susan changed the subject. "What about me? Am I going to have to spend the rest of my life running from snipers?" She added only to herself, *Without you, I wouldn't last long.*

Jake seemed to be trying to smile. "I don't think so, Susan. There's not a whole lot NYPD can do about a citizen's action group like the Society for Humanity, other than prosecuting those members directly involved in the crime. But Cadmium has their own ax to grind against the SFH now, and they have RICO."

"Who's Rico?" Kendall asked.

Jake chuckled. It was his turn to translate once again. "RICO's not a who, it's a federal law. The Racketeer Influenced and Corrupt Organizations Act. Basically, it allows them to capture and try the leaders of a syndicate for crimes they ordered others to do."

A lead weight seemed to lift from Susan's chest. "And Cadmium? Are they still after me?"

A hint of a smile finally made it to Jake's lips. "The NYPD has less than no patience for cop killers. I may have survived, but they made their intentions abundantly clear."

An involuntary shiver traversed Susan. Mike's deep voice filled her memory—"*I'll kill the cop*"—followed immediately by a gunshot to Jake's head. She would never forget that cold moment of brutality as long as she lived.

There was no humor whatsoever in Kendall's voice now. "If a standard response is describing that incident twice, I NSRed it."

Susan concurred. "They heard it from me a minimum of seven times, too. Maybe more like seventeen. I kept coming back to it; I couldn't help it."

"It won't be pretty," Jake continued, "but I'm guessing politics will carry the day, and the feds will think twice before pulling anything else against you or U.S. Robots again. At least not in our jurisdiction."

"Is that a nice way of telling me not to leave town?"

"You're free to go wherever you want, but I believe it would be in your best interests to stay."

Susan was glad to hear it. "I think I'd like to finish my residency. And I know I want to spend a lot more time with USR and robots."

Kendall made a highly visible gesture that suggested Susan had left out something important.

Uncertain what he wanted, Susan hesitated just long enough for Kendall to add, "And if you left, you'd miss us."

Susan supposed he had a point. She turned her attention to Jake, who no longer looked so fresh, so self-assured. "After you're discharged, will we see you again?"

Kendall stiffened, then froze in position, clearly trying to hide something. Susan got the idea the answer to that casual question meant a lot more to him than to her.

Understanding finally clicked into place. *Kendall's got his first real crush.* She found it almost impossible to imagine the two of them together in any capacity, even friendship. Despite Jake's repeated claims, Susan still half suspected he had lied about his sexual orientation, and Kendall had a lot of issues to work through. Even without that, they came from two wholly different worlds. *Stranger relationships have defied the odds.*

If Jake had noticed Kendall's discomfort, he gave no sign. "I think we can arrange something, though I'd prefer it under less lethal circumstances, if you don't mind. Cops are allowed a social life."

Susan wondered if she could get things moving. "You did promise me a dinner, Jake. Remember? Instead, we wound up at my apartment . . ."

"Eating the world's weirdest salad," Jake finished. "I remember."

"How about we celebrate the day you're finally discharged by letting Kendall and me take you out for a restaurant meal? Anywhere you want to go."

Kendall all but trembled with excitement. "Believe me, Jake. After a couple of days of hospital food, you'll be begging for even a half-decent meal."

"It's a date," Jake said.

"Great. I'll check in on you tomorrow, after I corner the neurosurgery team." Susan headed for the exit. "I'm going to find the nearest bed that doesn't have a patient in it and sleep for a week." She groaned. "Afterward, I'm going to have to kiss my attending's butt, give him credit for everything I've done, and convince him it's his idea to do all the things necessary to make Winter Wine Dementia Facility a safe place for chronically brain-injured people." She almost made it through the door.

"Susan, wait." There was need in Jake's voice.

Susan stopped. She turned and looked at him.

"The message from John Calvin. I have to know." Jake studied her intently, clearly trying to read her, a fool's mission. Susan had bluffed an experienced team of federal agents; no one would get anything from her face again unless she wanted them to. "You decoded it, didn't you?"

He's every bit as thorough as I am, in his own way. None of the police questioners had touched on it or even asked Susan to reveal its existence. She shoved her hand into her pocket, pulled out the crumpled piece of paper, and smoothed it between her fingers. She handed it to Kendall. "Read it," she instructed, having trouble keeping her voice audible. If she tried, she knew it would reduce her to tears.

Kendall cleared his throat and read: "*Susan, the Three Laws are irreversibly intrinsic to the positronic brain. There is not, and has never been, a code to uncouple them.*" He paused there, lips pursed, nodding. "*My love for you has always been as clear and real as any father could have for his daughter. Never forget you were my everything.*"

Tears sprang to Susan's eyes, and she bowed out of the room with a lazy excuse and a not wholly explicably heavy heart. It was not the contents of her father's last missive; she had already come to grips with it, with the realization she would never see him again. She knew she ought to feel happy for Kendall. He had, apparently, worked through his lifelong anxiety enough to allow his feelings for Jake to emerge, at least into his own mind. Somehow, though, it only emphasized her loneliness, her own sense she might never realize a romantic future of her own.

The first time her world had exploded into violence, Susan had found her soul mate in Remington Hawthorn and had promised him her virginity. The neurosurgery resident had died before he could collect that prize. Instead she had wasted it on a man she would always consider a friend but with whom she had no conceivable amorous ties. She had saved her virginity twenty-seven years, only to deliver it to a gay man she loved only as a brother. In another time, before her life had become so complicated, she might have found it humorously ironic. Now she just wanted to rediscover the healing that came only from her robotic psychiatrist.

There was nowhere for Susan to go. She felt certain Kendall would spend the next several days and nights watching over Jake, and her own apartment still did not seem safe. Instead, she descended to the first-floor charting room, where she had so often met with Nate. She could not imagine she would find him there tonight, but she needed the comfort of a familiar place to rest. All the stress hormones her body could produce had withered away, leaving her feeling hopeless, exhausted, and desperately depressed.

Susan opened the door, only to find Nate standing there silently, arms outstretched. Shocked, she stood there while her body struggled to find the energy to allow her to move, to react, even to smile. "Nate," she finally said.

"I knew you'd come here. And I knew you needed me."

Susan fell into his arms.